# The Mahdi

"Since the death of Muhammad in 632 A.D., every Muslim has believed that eventually another great new prophet will appear. He is referred to as the Mahdi, and he will command the loyalty of every Muslim.

"A retired British intelligence agent convinces the American CIA director that, with the use of the space shuttle and some laser technology, they could create a miracle and convince the Muslim world that the Mahdi had arrived. From then on the Western powers, controlling the Mahdi, would have no more problems with turbulence in the Middle East.

"The plan seem to be going ahead very nicely when the Russians move in. Quinnell weaves a very complex plot and arrives at very surprising if cynical conclusions. A very different book with enough novelty almost on every page to keep anyone reading."

*Boston Herald American*

**Another Fawcett Crest Book
by A. J. Quinnell**

**MAN  ON  FIRE**

# The Mahdi

## A.J. Quinnell

FAWCETT CREST • NEW YORK

Library of Congress Catalog Card Number: 81-14095

ISBN 0-449-20168-6

This edition published by arrangement with
William Morrow & Company, Inc.

Manufactured in the United States of America

First Ballantine Books Edition: June 1983

For all believers of Islam

*that the simplicity and totality of their
faith not blind them to the dangers*

These stories may be far from history, where one usually reads that such and such a King sent such and such a General to such and such a war, and that on such and such a day they made war or peace, and that this one defeated that one, or that one this one, and then proceeded somewhere.

But I write what is worthy to be recorded.

—AL-BUKHARI, *Ta'rikh*
(Ninth century)

# Book
# *one*

# one

IT WAS A PILGRIMAGE. A journey to satisfy a soul.

He turned off the main Kuala Lumpur–Penang road onto a dirt track and into deep jungle. "Go to the Klang River," he had been told, "and then turn left. You'll know it when you see it." He felt he should have sent a message —perhaps in a cleft stick carried by a loinclothed runner —but the station man had laughed and shaken his head. "He will know you are coming. Take a tuxedo. He always dresses for dinner."

In the headlights the track appeared to grow progressively narrower as it wound through tall, forbidding trees. Occasionally a small animal would flit across in the dim, bouncing light, and doubts began to play across his mind. Had he taken the right turning? What was he doing here anyway, in the thick of the Malayan jungle? In truth he should have caught the afternoon plane to Tokyo and, after a night's layover, been on his way to Washington, home, and Julia.

But he was in a mental magnetic field—drawn to meet, and pay his respects to, the doyen of his profession. Nevertheless the doubts continued to build, until suddenly and dramatically he turned a corner and in the headlights stood two white Doric columns and between them huge black wrought-iron gates. He braked gently to a halt. He should have sent a message—the gates were firmly closed. He sat still in the car for several moments, trying to make up his mind, then he was about to get out for a closer inspection when the gates slowly began to open inward and he discerned the small sarong-clad man behind. He eased the car forward, and the man bowed from the waist and gracefully gestured him on.

Now the jungle took on formality. The trees and shrubs had been culled to a less cluttered pattern. The track improved to a road and swung in toward the wide river, and then he braked again, for in front of him stood the structure. Not a house, not a villa or even a palace, but a curious blend of all three. Soft floodlights threw more Doric columns into shadowed relief. It stood perched on the very edge of a wide, sluggish river. A white Christmas cake—a gross intrusion amid the surrounding jungle but with a strange, arrogant elegance. Now curiosity coursed through him, and he moved the car forward again down the drive and up to the wide flight of steps that led to massive teak doors. They opened as he climbed out of the car, and another sarong-clad Malay appeared. He showed no surprise as he came down the steps—just a gentle smile.

"I'm Hawke, Morton Hawke; maybe I should have sent a message."

The Malay bowed and asked, "Have you luggage, Tuan?"

Hawke nodded and started to mumble something about not wishing to disturb, but the Malay moved past him and pulled out a small suitcase and then with another smile he started up the steps. Hawke shrugged and followed.

Later he stood under the old-fashioned shower head, letting streams of hot water wash away the dust of the journey and trying to bring himself back to reality. The Malay had shown him to a vast upstairs guest room complete with a bar and a brimming bucket of ice. While Hawke had surveyed the room and the moonlit view over the river, the Malay had laid the suitcase on the four-poster bed, moved to the bar, poured three fingers of Canadian Club into a tall glass and added two lumps of ice and a splash of soda. He passed it to the astonished American and said, "Dinner will be at nine on the front terrace, Tuan. Now I unpack for you and press your tuxedo. I return in half an hour." So Hawke sipped his drink and took his shower and wondered how the doyen knew not only that he was coming but what he drank.

"Information is power." Pritchard wiped his lips with a snow-white napkin and surveyed his guest benevolently across the table. "And, my dear Hawke, I am dedicated to power and so are you—or you wouldn't be in your profession."

Hawke swallowed the last mouthful of chicken and nodded agreement. He had said little during the meal, first because he was hungry and it was delicious, and second because he had been content to let Pritchard hold the stage. The old man had obviously enjoyed himself, reminiscing with a blend of irony and cynicism.

The two men made an elegant, if incongruous, tableau, sitting in isolation on the wide terrace, the blackness of their tuxedos contrasting with the white of the Irish linen tablecloth and the sparkle of the moonlight on crystal glasses. Pritchard was an old man, his short hair silver-gray, his face brown and lined by the sun and age. He had deep-set black eyes under almost white, bushy eyebrows, but the dominant feature of his appearance was his nose— large and hooked, and giving him a birdlike air. He had a long, thin neck, jutting from an old-fashioned wing collar, and his wide-lapelled tuxedo hung from a stooped and angular body. Hawke decided that he resembled a bird, a scavenger maybe—a vulture. A vulture grown finicky about the nature of its pickings. It was curious that Hawke should visualize him so, for he himself had an appearance that mirrored his name. He was aggressively middle-aged, his energy and manner constantly proclaiming disdain for the passage of years. His features were sharp, with narrow, piercing eyes and jet-black hair clipped unfashionably short. If Pritchard was a scavenger, Hawke was a predator, with a strong sinewy frame and long arms and fingers.

He laid down his fork and a servant materialized from the shadows and cleared away the plates. A silence developed, but a strange silence, enveloped in the background noise of a tropic night. The chatter of crickets, the hooting of night birds, the sudden intrusion of a nervous call from one animal to another of its species. Pritchard gestured and a girl approached, pushing a small trolley. Hawke's breath drew in at the sight of her. She stood no higher than five feet and was dressed only in a sarong, tied at the waist. She had dark skin, gleaming copperlike in the subdued light, and small, high, perfectly formed breasts. But it was her face that transfixed Hawke. A face that lodged itself in the core of his brain and in the months to come would float out into his vision. A very young face of exquisite proportion and without a single angle—only curves, one blending into the other. Eyes slanted but wide. Eyes with a hint of humor above full, curved lips. Her blue-black hair hung straight down to her waist.

"You'll take a Cognac—and a cigar?"

With a massive effort Hawke switched his attention back to Pritchard and nodded. The girl struck a match and brought it to the wick of a small oil lamp, then she took three large balloon glasses and warmed them over the flame, her fingers moving with practiced grace. She picked up a dark, unmarked, but very old bottle and poured amber measures into all three. Two of the glasses she placed in front of the men. The third was left on the trolley. Hawke's eyes followed every movement as she opened a mahogany box and extracted a large Carlos y Carlos cigar and, holding it to her ear, rolled it between her palms. Satisfied, she took a small silver guillotine and snipped the end and then held it over the flame, turning it and warming it rhythmically between her slender fingers. Hawke raised his eyes to her face, found her watching him, a hint of mischief in those almond eyes, and suddenly, vividly, her actions, her fingers slowly rolling the cigar, took on the deepest eroticism. He prided himself in always controlling his reactions to any situation, but at this moment he could only gawk like a boy as she lowered her head to the cigar, gently closed her lips over one end and rotated the other end in the flames. The aroma of the Havana tobacco drifted across the table. Her hair swung down, framing her face, and Hawke drew a shuddering breath. Finally, she picked up the third glass, dipped the end of the cigar into the Cognac, and, with her first smile, held it out to the American. He was paralyzed. He tried to lift a hand but it would not move. Her smile deepened a trace and she raised her arm, bringing the cigar to his lips, lodging it between them and then gently brushing her fingers down his cheek. Her perfume dominated even the aroma of the smoke.

"You enjoy music, I understand."

The words penetrated and Hawke focused back on Pritchard. The old man was watching him in evident amusement.

The girl was now preparing another cigar and Hawke tried to lock her out of his vision and mind.

"Yes . . . er, yes, I do . . . some."

Pritchard smiled. "Beethoven, I believe, is your favorite."

He gestured again and a few moments later Hawke's senses were once more undermined. From across the wide, dark river came rolling the opening bars of Beethoven's Fifth Symphony. The sound, the sheer volume and richness, was awesome. All the insects, the birds and mammals of the jungle were instantly mute—unable to compete, or simply inspired to silence by the majesty of the music.

Hawke shook his head in disbelief and looked the question. Pritchard took his cigar from the girl and waved it expansively at the river.

"I have eight one-hundred-amp speakers in the jungle over there, custom-built by Lansing."

He smiled. "I like a little after-dinner entertainment."

The music helped. After twenty minutes or so Hawke had himself back under tight control. In spite of the fact that the girl now sat alongside Pritchard with an arm around his waist and her head resting against his shoulder, he was able to look at her with a measure of equanimity. He decided that she was a mixture of Malay and Chinese and that she was in her midteens, although experience had taught him the difficulty of measuring the ages of Asian women. Even when she stood to refill his glass he kept his composure, keeping his eyes half closed to the music, merely nodding in acknowledgment. He was mildly irritated with himself for he had been determined to present to Pritchard a poker-faced exterior.

Pritchard. He evoked, in Hawke, contradictory emotions. As a modern, highly trained intelligence expert, the American should have viewed the old man as nothing more than a picturesque anachronism. An antique to be admired with dusty devotion. But in spite of his age and the pseudo-colonial setting, Pritchard had a curious immediacy.

To bring his feet to the ground and his mind to reality, Hawke reviewed his own position. As Director of Operations of the CIA he could be considered the supreme working spy of the free world, a pinnacle he had reached after thirty years of single-minded devotion. That and an innate gift for survival—both in the naked field of covert operations and in the overdressed corridors of Company politics. And yet he had survived without becoming a sycophant to authority. He had maintained a precarious hold on mental independence—a streak of the maverick in a well-built corral.

It was the maverick in him that had brought him to see Pritchard. It was the end of a satisfying trip. The new conservatism in Washington had ordained that the muzzle had to be taken off the clamped mouth of the CIA. No more was the Agency a pariah. Suddenly and gratifyingly Congress and the White House had seen the light. You cannot fight a forest fire with a Dixie cup of warm water. Watchdog committees were abruptly dissolved, constricting congressional bills were repealed, and vast additional funds were voted. To cap it all, the Director CIA was even reinstated on the guest lists of the more discerning Washington hostesses.

But for Hawke it had meant a period of intensive activity. While the Director went to parties, Hawke went to Asia to visit every station: to generate once again the sleeping giant; to activate long-filed projects; to motivate tired and disillusioned agents; and to quantify the overconfident opposition.

Malaysia was his last stop, and it was at dinner, two nights before at the Merlin Hotel, that the local station man had mentioned Pritchard and inquired whether Hawke had ever met him.

Hawke had not, but he knew much about him, as did every senior intelligence officer of every major power. Quite simply Pritchard was a legend, but, more fascinating still, he was an enigma.

He was English, or so it was thought, and he had first surfaced in the thirties in the Middle East, working for an obscure department of the British War Office. As the European powers jockeyed and cajoled for influence on that volatile chessboard, Pritchard popped up and down. Always up when a major piece was moved—or removed. Always down at the moment of checkmate.

At the outbreak of war he had disappeared. It was rumored that he had fallen out of favor with the British authorities in Cairo, even that he had committed the then cardinal sin of marrying an Arab woman, who had borne

him a son. It simply wasn't done. One could go native—
but not that native. So he fell from grace and favor and
his shadow no longer darkened the portals of Shepheard's
Hotel or the British Club. But in 1944 the Turkish government was one day presented with a list of every German agent in its country. The scale of the penetration
helped sway that vacillating government not to join the
Axis. Pritchard, it seemed, had not been inactive. After
the war he moved farther east and there the enigma began.
As the much-vaunted British intelligence service began to
come apart at the seams, Pritchard came under increasing
suspicion. Apparently he had been at the wrong college
in Oxford, had been lectured by the wrong tutors and had
some dubious left-of-center friends. It is possible that
had he shown the slightest homosexual tendencies, or even
displayed a greater degree of intellect, he would have been
quietly dropped by a panicking MI6. Instead, he was made
resident agent in Saigon and he promptly started working
for the French on the side. Hawke remembered reading in
a file a comment allegedly made by Pritchard at the time:
"After all, the French are not exactly the Russians—and
the value of the pound is not what it was."

Subsequently he moved to the then Dutch East Indies
and stayed there until the rebels won the war of independence and Indonesia came into being. It had been thought
that the Dutch might have been using his services as well
as the British, but there were two events that tended to
disprove this. First, the rebels won, and second, the newly
installed President Sukarno gave him a small but profit-
able rubber estate in southern Sumatra.

But still the British kept him on, presumably knowing
something about which everyone else was ignorant.

He moved around a lot after that. A spell in Japan and
then the Philippines, followed by several years in Taiwan,
all ostensibly for MI6. No one knew what had become of
his Arab wife and child, for he led the life of a fastidious
bachelor.

It was in Taiwan that the CIA first had an inkling that he might also be on the payroll of the KGB. That organization was very active in Taiwan, trying vainly to embarrass China, and Hawke had seen several reports indicating that Pritchard was in contact with known KGB agents. It was then that the CIA put great pressure on MI6, and then that the enigma deepened. At first the British were not even disposed to discuss the matter, but as the pressure was intensified at the highest levels, they relented and a senior MI6 bureaucrat arrived at Langley with a large briefcase full of files. Hawke was one of three CIA officials allowed to peruse those files, while the pinstriped Englishman sat watching them—much as a store detective would watch a hippy in the jewelry department.

They contained details of reports that Pritchard had made over the years. Reports to bend the imagination. Pritchard had been working not only as a double for the French, Dutch, Japanese, Russian, and sundry other governments, but also as a triple for various organizations opposed to those governments. The one thing the reports could not prove was that he was ultimately loyal to the British.

Hawke had asked two questions: Why did the British tolerate such massive duplicity? And how had Pritchard lived so long? The Englishman had shrugged an elegant shoulder and answered that every report Pritchard filed had turned out to be accurate, and useful; and as for living so long, perhaps the reports he filed to other governments proved the same.

In short, Pritchard was that rarest of species: the master spy, employed on an international level, and protected by his knowledge and the indiscriminate nature of his loyalties.

Hawke had surprised himself by recommending to the then Director that far from curtailing Pritchard's activities, the CIA would be well advised to add themselves to his mailing list. His advice had been followed, and over the years a number of senior CIA officials generated an affection for Pritchard and an admiration for his always imaginative information. But Hawke had never met him, for shortly after those events he had been promoted to head the South American Directorate and had spent six years attempting to keep unpopular dictatorships in power. When he had finally returned to Washington as Director of Operations and a massive rearguard action against liberals in his own country, Pritchard had already retired to the jungles of Malaysia—the doyen of his profession and a very wealthy old man.

The string section moved the symphony into its last movement, and Hawke's mind switched to Washington and his forthcoming report to the Director that his trip had proved that the Company's effectiveness in southeast Asia could be rapidly strengthened. Only two station heads would have to be recalled to desk jobs, and he had good replacements in mind. Within a year he expected to have a nucleus of active cells in Vietnam, Laos, and Cambodia. A satisfying prospect. Next he would concentrate on the Middle East. A large segment of the Company's budget was taken up with that area and the results of such expenditure were disappointing.

He turned his thoughts to various stratagems until the symphony wound up in majestic chords. The jungle fell silent and then gradually resumed its nocturnal noises.

"My thanks," Hawke said. "It has been a very pleasant and interesting dinner."

Pritchard inclined his head. "I have enjoyed it. An old man in retirement always appreciates company. You'll have a nightcap?"

Without waiting for an answer he patted the girl, and she stood and poured more Cognac into the glasses. Pritchard spoke a word to her in Malay. She smiled and picked up the third glass and moved back to him and sipped from it and gazed impassively at Hawke across the rim.

"How was your trip?"

Once again the American had to force his attention back to Pritchard.

"Fine. We have a bit of catching up to do. You can understand that."

Pritchard nodded. "Of course; but now the pendulum is swinging for you—and rapidly." His eyes narrowed in thought. "It won't be too difficult. Of course you'll have to replace Braden in Jakarta." He smiled. "And Raborn, unfortunately, has succumbed to the demon drink, so he'll have to go. Pity. He was a good man in his day."

Hawke did not return the smile. He felt a needle of irritation and asked, "How long are you retired now?"

Pritchard shrugged. "Oh, five years. But one keeps in touch. Now and again people come out here to see an old curiosity—just as you did."

Hawke's irritation dissipated. "From all walks of life, no doubt?"

The old man's smile deepened. "Yes, indeed. Just last week I had the pleasure of Koslov's company for dinner. Incidentally, if you ever entertain him, he's very partial to Chopin."

Now Hawke had to smile. Uri Koslov was the head of all KGB operations in southeast Asia.

"So even in retirement you keep your options open?"

Pritchard's face appeared to turn serious but there was a hint of an impish twinkle in his eyes. "Mr. Hawke, I will tell you a secret. You can keep a secret, can't you?" Yes, there was a definite twinkle in those dark eyes. "Good," he went on. "I never actually worked for the Russians. You could say that occasionally I took a little retainer, but that's akin to having a lawyer and never using him."

"Never?"

Pritchard shook his head. "Perhaps they already knew everything I could possibly tell them."

Now Hawke decided to edge in his own needle.

"But a spy never truly retires."

The old man smiled at the pinprick.

"Koslov came only for the food—and Chopin. He had probably heard of my sound system."

As Hawke digested that, Pritchard gently pulled the girl onto his lap and absently caressed her left breast. Then he saw the American's eyes on him and said, diffidently, "Unfortunately, at my age, a caress is all I have left. What about the Middle East?"

The abrupt change of subject again jolted Hawke's senses. He was to remember later how, during the entire evening, the doyen had constantly kept him off-balance. For a moment he wondered if the old spy was telepathic.

"What about it?"

"Well, now that you've finished your inspection trip out here, it must be much on your mind."

Hawke nodded. "It's on everybody's mind; that area must have caused more sleepless nights in Washington than the city's entire corps of call girls."

Pritchard raised an eyebrow in mock astonishment and remarked, "From what I know of Washington that's quite an achievement. So, what are you going to do about it?" A smile. "The Middle East, I mean."

Hawke stood and carried his glass to the edge of the terrace and stood looking out over the river. He had moved partly to take his eyes off the contradiction of Pritchard's bony old fingers and the girl's young breast, and partly to collect his thoughts. It was possible that this visit even had an unconscious motive. A need to bounce a few cerebral balls off the thick wall of Pritchard's experience. He knew that during the coming months most of his working hours would be taken up with trying to maintain his country's position in the Middle East. A position made almost desperate by years of mismanagement, clumsy policies, and lack of willpower. He turned back to the table.

"Obviously we'll be sharply raising the level of our activity—throughout the area."

Pritchard took his hand from the girl's breast and gestured graphically.

"So, instead of having a couple of thousand dedicated agents running around achieving nothing, you'll have four or five thousand doing the same thing."

Hawke felt the needle again.

"That would still make us sparse on the ground compared with the Russians."

"True," Pritchard agreed. "But then the Russians have been getting some results lately—at least in their basic policy of destabilization."

The needle was definitely going deeper, and Hawke's voice took on a defensive tone.

"They've had a relatively clear field. We've been hamstrung for four long years. All that's changed now. The KGB, and the rest, will find out soon enough that the Company's back in business."

Pritchard smiled cynically. "We're all delighted, my dear chap, but I repeat that sheer effort, however commendable, is not going to be enough."

"Obviously not. No doubt you have a simple solution to the greatest problem we all face?"

"I might have a suggestion." Pritchard gestured at the empty chair. "Why not sit down and hear it?" He smiled with great charm. "It would be a pity if you had come only for the food and Beethoven."

Hawke hesitated for a moment and then walked back to the table. The girl moved from Pritchard's lap, poured more Cognac, resettled herself, and gazed at Hawke enigmatically.

"Religion."

Again Hawke had to call his brain to order. "What about it?"

Pritchard leaned forward and said very seriously, "Religion, Mr. Hawke, is the simple solution to your very fundamental problem."

"Ah, I see, you mean we should all pray that the problem goes away."

For the first time a trace of irritation crossed Pritchard's face.

"You are an intelligent man, Hawke, I know that. I also know that you now command great respect among your worthy colleagues—and within the new Administration. You asked for a suggestion and I am about to offer it. Please do me the courtesy of listening seriously to an old man, but one who is not yet in his dotage."

Hawke was suitably abashed. He didn't say anything but simply nodded in understanding and in acceptance of the mild rebuke.

"Religion is the key," Pritchard went on. "Islam in all its forms and variations." His eyes had half closed in concentration, his voice dipped lower, and Hawke leaned forward to pick up the words.

"Most analysts wrongly believe that the schisms of Islam work in the interests of the great powers, that they serve to divide the world's Islamic states and that this is a good thing. They point to the war between Iran and Iraq. The tension between Egypt and Libya, between Jordan and Syria, and so on."

He shook his head. "But the analysts are wrong. They fail to understand that Islam is not like other religions. Not like Christianity, or Judaism, or Buddhism. It differs in one fundamental—it is a religion that demands total obedience from its believers. Obedience not just to religious principles, but obedience to rules that govern every waking and sleeping hour of the faithful. It is an aggressive, young, and expanding religion, the only major religion in the world that could be so described. The very word Islam means submission."

Hawke had to interrupt. "I understand that very well and I can't think of anything more frightening than a united Islam. Its power would be immense."

Pritchard held up a hand. "Let me continue. Certainly its power would be immense. But that power could be controlled."

"By whom?" Hawke asked incredulously.

"By you—by the West. Don't smile at me. You asked for a simple solution and I'm giving it to you."

Hawke kept his smile and asked casually, "You mean we first arrange to unite the Islamic religion? That would be infinitely more difficult than uniting, say, Catholics and Protestants. Then we take it over?"

"Exactly."

"How?"

"By subverting it."

Once again sarcasm crept into Hawke's voice. "So we unite Islam, take it over by subversion, and thus effectively control the one billion Muslims in the world's forty-five Islamic states." He felt rising impatience. Maybe the old man was, after all, in his dotage. "Well, it's a splendid idea, Mr. Pritchard, and certainly simple. The one little remaining question is: How do we do it?"

Pritchard ignored the sarcasm. He took a sip of Cognac and answered:

"A miracle."

Hawke burst out laughing. "A miracle? That's just about what it would take."

Again Pritchard held up his hand and stilled the American's laughter.

"Are you telling me that a country which developed nuclear weapons, a country which put a man on the moon"—a faint smile—". . . a country which built Disneyland, couldn't produce a full-blown, Lloyd's-registered, copper-bottomed A-one miracle?"

Hawke tried to keep a straight face. "Let's say we could; what would be the purpose?"

Pritchard sat back in his chair, once more caressed the girl's breast and said:

"The miracle would authenticate, beyond doubt, the arrival of the new Mahdi." He looked directly into Hawke's eyes. "And I will tell you all about the Mahdi."

# two

HAWKE TOOK ANOTHER SHOWER. He needed it for several reasons. First, the night was hot and humid; second, he had drunk too much; but above all, his brain was in disarray. He kept his head directly under the stream of water, slowly turning down the hot tap until finally the water was cold. It helped. Then he stepped out, wrapped himself in a large towel, walked into the bedroom, poured himself a tumbler of ice water, and once again stood looking out over the dark river.

Hours had passed since Pritchard had dropped the single word "religion" into the conversation. Hours during which Hawke had said very little, occasionally interjecting with a query, but all the time becoming increasingly intrigued and astonished by the old man's knowledge and soaring imagination.

Pritchard had thought it right through. It would, he pointed out complacently, be the intelligence coup to end all coups. Hawke had agreed.

"It would be like having the Pope on your payroll," he had commented.

"Better," insisted Pritchard. "The Mahdi would wield total power. Every head of an Islamic state would have to bow to his authority, or be overthrown by a popular uprising."

He had gone on to explain the mystical background that made every Muslim believe and pray for the coming of a new prophet. How, ever since the death of Muhammad, there had been dozens of false alarms.

The British, in their imperialist heyday, had fought and killed two such pretenders. Recently the ruling family of Saudi Arabia had executed a young zealot and most of his followers for daring to believe that he was so blessed.

Hawke had felt his interest growing and remarked that even the Ayatollah Khomeini was thought by some to be the new Mahdi. Pritchard had nodded and smiled and quoted another Ayatollah who had said that indeed one day the new Mahdi would arrive, but not on an Air France jumbo jet!

Pritchard then sketched out the present state of Islam, its youth and vigor. Fifty years ago there had been only four Islamic states. Now there were forty-five. By the end of the century over half the population of black Africa would be Muslim. By the same date Russia would have over sixty million Muslims in its southern and eastern regions. Not even Communism could slow its growth, or its control over much of the world's natural resources, and especially oil. Eighty percent of the world's oil reserves lay beneath Islamic states.

Pritchard had stressed that the danger to the West lay in the uncontrolled State of Islam. "It's worse than a bull in a china shop" had been his analogy. A great, hulking, unruly child bursting out all over. The long-awaited arrival of the Mahdi would change all that. He would bring order out of chaos. Pritchard had smiled and said: "He might even decide that the present price of oil be construed as profiteering, and the Koran is very hard on profiteers. Yes, it's Sura nine: 'On the day they shall be heated in the fire of Jahannam and therewith their foreheads and their sides and their backs shall be branded: This is the thing you have treasured up for yourselves;

therefore taste you now what you were treasuring.' Very
apt, don't you think? Perhaps the fires of Jahannam will
be fueled by Arabian light crude!"

Hawke was now completely attentive. Although he was
not a man given to great flights of imagination, his work
had conditioned him to accept that very little was impossible when it came to fooling all the people for a very long
time. But then the practical side of his character pushed
itself forward.

"Exactly how?" he wanted to know. Okay, a "miracle"
maybe could be arranged, and maybe it would establish
the new Mahdi. But what about the details? How to select
him? How to build him up? And, above all, how to control him? Had Pritchard thought all that out?

Pritchard had worked out all aspects of the plan, from
the planting of early rumors throughout the Muslim world
to the selection of the individual based on his history and
his common appeal. The main problem, he pointed out,
would be to exercise total control over the Mahdi once he
was proclaimed. This was something which Hawke and
his experts would have to work out. Surely it was not beyond the capabilities of an organization such as the CIA
to be able to select an individual and then control him in
even the most delicate operation. He went on to describe
the general effects if the Mahdi was indeed proclaimed,
how it would be possible, stage by careful stage, to influence policy in every Islamic state, even to cause the over-
throw of governments unfavorable to the West. There was
a massive resurgence of Islamic fundamentalism and even
totalitarian governments such as Syria, Libya, and Saudi
Arabia were already fighting a rearguard action against
extremists such as the Muslim Brotherhood, whose sole
aim was a return to rigid Islamic law in all aspects of life.
Iran had been the first and most significant example.
Pritchard pointed out that with a controlled Mahdi in position, even Iran would have to toe the line. Hawke listened in rapt silence. Only once did his years of training

surface, and Pritchard saw him glance uneasily at the girl, sitting mute and now sleepy on the Englishman's lap. Pritchard had smiled and told Hawke not to worry. Assured him that she spoke only Malay, and besides, she was not a Muslim. "She's a virgin," he explained, and smiled again, "and that's a mystical religion unto itself."

Hawke sipped his ice water and released his mind to wander over the possibilities. Pritchard had sketched out the framework of the operation. Hawke could imagine him sitting here in his retreat by the river and, night after night, plotting a devious and convoluted attack against the world's most vibrant and aggressive religion. It was a question of playing on weakness, singling out the aspects of Islam that were most vulnerable to modern technology. As Pritchard explained it, Islam was a religion which discouraged innovative thought, and hence science. It had reached a stage similar in its development to the Spanish Inquisition. The fundamentalists were frightened of every deviation from the norm. And so Islam looked inward and backward for theological purity, shunning innovation.

This aspect, combined with its mystical fervor and the belief in the coming of the new prophet, the Mahdi, was at the core of Pritchard's strategy.

Hawke had seen the pitfalls.

"What if the plan is exposed?" he had asked. The reaction in the Middle East would be devastating. Every Islamic state would turn off its oil faster than a whore shuts off her charms after withdrawal. Pritchard had smiled and cocked his head and examined his guest critically. Then he had asked, What was the first lesson every intelligence agent ever learned? While Hawke's mind had gone back twenty years to his training days, Pritchard himself had impatiently supplied the answer.

"Always let some other agency spearhead your actions. In the event that things go wrong, pass the blame on—and vanish into the smoke."

Hawke had nodded in agreement, and asked who in this

case could be the spearhead. At that point Pritchard's smile turned sardonic. "There are two candidates," he said. "The Israelis or the British."

He had considered the question very carefully and had finally plumped for the British. He rolled out his reasons in logical sequence. First, Mossad, the Israeli intelligence service, was too shrewd, indeed too cynical, to allow itself to be so used. In the event that the operation was a success it could well alter the rules at the end and keep all the benefit to itself. The British, on the other hand, were the ideal spearhead. They believed they had special knowledge of Arabia. They had romantic illusions about their role in the history of the Middle East. They could and did talk endlessly of Burton and Lawrence. It was curious, Pritchard had noted, that a country with the dampest, dullest climate imaginable should have such an empathy for the deserts of Arabia. Also, in the event that they were exposed, the Islamic states could do little against Britain. They had, after all, their North Sea oil, which was good for at least twenty years. Also, the Americans could pull the strings.

Hawke had demurred. Like most American intelligence officers he had a deep suspicion of his British counterparts. Sure, they had successes during, and shortly after, the war, but now they were in a sorry state. They were more riddled with moles, he had pointed out, than the lawns of Windsor Great Park. He had ticked them off on his fingers: "Philby, Burgess, Maclean, Vassall, Blunt; and only God and the KGB know how many more—as yet undiscovered."

But Pritchard had disagreed, believing that MI6 in particular, the overseas arm of British intelligence, was now relatively clean, had purged itself during the seventies, and would be eager to re-establish itself in the world's intelligence community by pulling off a spectacular coup. Its position had also been strengthened of late by the assertive politics of Britain's Prime Minister. Pritchard had commented that the "Iron Lady" would support any scheme that would add to Britain's security—no matter how risky.

Hawke had not been convinced, but anyway it was academic. The plan, though beautifully imaginative, was just more than he could sell to his Director, let alone the President.

He also wondered at the direction and scope of Pritchard's loyalties. His mind went back over everything he knew about the man, and ultimately he concluded that whatever loyalties Pritchard had were entirely contained within himself and to the art of his profession. The very fact that upon retirement he had isolated himself away from any establishment and created a small environment with himself at the center showed that Pritchard wanted no link with his antecedents. Whatever emotions he may have engendered in his life had now been crystallized to cynicism and the exercise of his introverted intellect.

Pritchard had sipped his Cognac and let the silence develop, a silence that left Hawke still thinking and imagining. He started to put together a hypothetical presentation that he might make to the Director. Started mentally to parry the obvious and immediate objections. Even thought of the consequences, to his own career, of success—or failure. Pritchard had kept his counsel, and his silence, merely gazing out over the river, and absently caressing the somnolent girl.

Finally Hawke had come back to reality—and the moment; had pushed back his chair and risen and thanked his host for a memorable dinner. Even then Pritchard had said nothing, simply nodding. Hawke said good-night and moved toward the lattice doors. He had passed into the shadows before the old man's voice stopped him.

"If you take my suggestion further," he had said, "there is one man, and only one man, in MI-Six who could do it."

Hawke moved slightly back toward the table into the light. It was a significant motion. A desire to make fantasy less unreal.

"Gemmel," said Pritchard. "Peter Gemmel. He's the Deputy Head of Operations at MI-Six—an Arabist. Do you know him?"

Hawke had shaken his head.

"Perhaps that's as well," Pritchard continued. "He's one of the new breed—the untainted ones." A silent smile. "He didn't even go to Oxford or Cambridge; but he has a brain and he's tough. You might like him."

"And his father?" Hawke asked. "Was his father an Arabist?"

Pritchard burst out laughing, a thin, reedy laughter of appreciation. His guest had finally shown wit and perception. The girl's eyes opened and she giggled, unaware but in sympathy.

The old man's laughter stilled and he shook his head slowly. "Even you, Mr. Hawke, would not visit a son's sins onto his father." He smiled. "But if it makes you feel easier, I believe that Gemmel's father was a coal miner. As I said, he's one of the new breed."

Hawke had nodded and turned away into the shadows and through the latticed door.

Now he drained his glass, poured more water, added ice cubes, and preened himself slightly. His parting remark about Gemmel's father had been a riposte to show Pritchard that he was not ignorant, either of the Arab world or of British intelligence. Pritchard had mentioned Philby. Kim Philby, perhaps the most embarrassing traitor in the history of British intelligence. A mole for the KGB who had virtually destroyed the postwar fabric of MI6. By coincidence, Philby's father—St. John Philby—had been a famous scholar and authority on Arabic and Islamic culture. But, he mused, the old man was right—you cannot blame a dead father for his son's sins.

He turned at the merest sound and watched the door slowly open. The girl stood there in the dim light. She moved forward and he saw that she was carrying a tiny silver tray. On it was a small, tightly rolled white towel.

Hawke remained motionless as she placed the tray on the table, shook out the towel, and gently wiped his face. The towel was damp and icy cold and she gently probed with it into his eye sockets and ears, then brought it down onto his bare chest. Then, with a gentle smile, she dropped it onto the tray and moved to the bed. She turned back the starched sheet, loosened her sarong, and let it flutter to her feet. She was a misty, gold, motionless mirage and, again, Hawke's brain passed into fantasy. He put down the glass and moved toward the mirage.

It was months later, a lifetime later, that Hawke remembered that the old man had lied to him: she had not been a virgin.

# three

JULIA HAWKE WAS A WOMAN OF FLEETING AND EXTRAVagant whims, which, combined with an overabundance of energy, made her a difficult woman to live with. But to her credit, she was constantly aware of her flaws, and although unable to correct them, tried hard to compensate in other ways. She paced up and down the elegant living room of the elegant house in a Washington suburb, glancing frequently at her watch. She had already phoned the airport and knew that her husband's plane had landed half an hour before. He would have been whisked through formalities and into a waiting Agency limousine and should be arriving at any minute. She never, ever went to the airport to meet him or to see him off, because she always became overemotional and she had realized early on that this embarrassed him, for he was an intensely private man, uncomfortable at a show of affection even in front of close friends.

She was waiting with rising trepidation, because she knew Morton was going to become very mad the moment he walked into the house. The root of the problem went back to her father, who was a very wealthy property de-

veloper in Houston. She had been an only child and her
father had doted on her, refusing her nothing. Consequently, by the time she had arrived in college, she was
a very spoiled young lady. She was also blond, tall, beautiful, and vivacious, and Morton Hawke, a third-year student in political science, had pursued her relentlessly for
eight months before she had accepted his proposal of marriage. It had been a good marriage. She bore him a son
after two years and another a year later and they had
grown up into intelligent, personable, but individualistic
young men.

There was one flaw in the marriage and that was her
father, who didn't see the result of the union as gaining a
son, but merely as retaining a daughter with an appendage.
Morton Hawke came from a humble background. His
grandfather had been a sheet-metal worker in a Detroit
auto factory and his father had gone to the same factory
and risen to become a production line supervisor. There
had always been enough money, but never enough to
spare, and Morton had grown accustomed to being frugal.
He had gone to college on a football scholarship, but after
his first year had found academic life more stimulating,
and he had concentrated almost exclusively on his studies
until he had met Julia. He was also a man of high and
somewhat rigid principles, and after Julia had accepted
his proposal, he had explained that after the marriage he
alone would support her and they would have to live accordingly. Very much in love and totally naïve about the
limitations of money, Julia had happily accepted the situation. Her father had not. He liked Morton Hawke im-
mensely, and although Morton was from an undistin-
guished background, her father approved of the match.

The trouble started with his wedding present, a small
but beautifully furnished house in one of Houston's better suburbs. When a thrilled Julia had told Morton of the
gift, he had grated his teeth and gone off to a stormy
showdown with her father. The tough old Texan had fi-

nally given in to what he thought would be a temporary situation, and Morton and Julia had moved into a tiny apartment on the fourth floor of a walk-up building in one of Houston's less salubrious districts. Morton had decorated it himself and fitted out the small kitchen. He liked working with his hands and found it relaxing to paint walls and work with wood and see the results of his own efforts. Julia thought the apartment was cute. She set to learning how to cook and to operate the old washing machine and to iron Morton's shirts. Even when the limitations of space and the society of their neighbors depressed her on occasion, the novelty of marriage and the love they felt for each other sustained her. Her optimism told her that in a year Morton would graduate and be offered a high-paying job and that she would be able to live again in style. She also believed that in the course of time Morton would relax his principles and would allow a measure of subsidy from her father.

But her father's indulgence had no patience. After three months Morton came home one evening to find several of the neighbors' young children admiring a brand-new, bright green MG sports car—a gift for his little girl. There had been tears when Morton sent the car back, but he was adamant and had continued to be so through the years. He had been recruited direct from college by the CIA, but trainee recruits in the Agency were not highly paid. For the next half-dozen years, while the young couple moved around the country and raised a family, they continued to live modestly. Julia's father never let up in his efforts to change the situation. He had been astonished when Morton had refused a high-paying job in his own company, although having a spy for a son-in-law did give him a certain cachet among his friends at his exclusive club. So this problem never ceased, even when Morton began to climb the promotion ladder and his income increased accordingly. As far as Julia's father was concerned, even if he became Director of the Agency, his salary would never be

enough to buy the good things that his little girl deserved.
Julia's mother, on the other hand, understood and approved of Morton's attitude and did her best to calm her
husband's rages when even expensive gifts for the grand-
children were returned. "A fifty-dollar maximum," Morton had stipulated, and Julia's father had answered in
astonished indignation, "Fifty bucks wouldn't buy a night
out in Lubbock, Texas!"

This principle of Morton's continued to be one of the
two clouds in the otherwise blue sky of Julia's life, and
even that cloud grew smaller as Morton began to reach
the top in his profession and was able to buy her more
expensive clothes and, occasionally, a piece of jewelry.
The other cloud was his "do it yourself" syndrome. He
loved to fix everything around the house and every year
or two decorated the place himself. The trouble was that
in this respect he had only the optimism of the dedicated
amateur, and while this might have sufficed for a tiny
nuptial apartment, it was not enough for a four-bedroom
house in Washington, D.C. Julia's friends used to make
joking comments about it, suggesting, for example, that
Morton should give up being a spy and go into interior
decorating.

So Julia had finally rebelled. When Morton had gone
off on his extended inspection trip to southeast Asia, she
had called in one of Washington's top designers and had
the house done over from top to bottom, from curtains to
carpets, chandeliers in the dining room, new tiles in the
bathrooms, and an entirely new kitchen. Halfway through,
among the chaos, second thoughts had overcome her, especially when the designer's cost estimate had proved to
be wildly optimistic. Her elder son, home from college, had
walked into the house, shaken his head, and said, "Mom,
the old man's going to blow every fuse he's got." It was
said with a grin, but Julia knew the truth of it, especially
when the bill was presented and especially as Morton had
told her, with a light in his eye, that the first thing he was

going to do on getting home was to start in to decorating the house.

She heard the sound of the car pulling up on the gravel drive and walked nervously to the front door and opened it. The Agency driver was opening the rear door and Morton climbed out, carrying his briefcase. He gave her a wave and a smile and spoke a few words to the driver and then bounded up the steps, hugged her, and gave her a warm kiss. She had decided not to say anything at all and just let him see for himself. They walked in, with an arm about each other's waist.

"How was your trip, darling?"

"Fine, but I'm really glad to be home."

"Are you very tired?"

He gave her waist a squeeze. "Yes, very. But with the time change I probably won't sleep"—he winked at her— "unless you make me even more tired."

They walked through the lobby and through the wide doors into the living room. Light was gleaming on the two new crystal chandeliers.

"I'll fix you a drink, dear," she said quickly, and crossed to the bar and poured a glass of his usual Canadian Club, with a dash of soda. He had followed her to the bar and she handed him the drink. He took a deep gulp.

"How've you been?" he asked. "Keeping busy?"

"Er, yes, doing one or two things." She couldn't understand. He had walked across the new, deep-pile carpet, past the new velvet-covered furniture, and stood at his favorite bar, which she had covered in a natural wood veneer; and although she knew him for an acutely observant man, he hadn't appeared to have noticed anything, but then he did notice her troubled, puzzled look.

"Is anything wrong? Are the boys all right?"

"Yes, they're fine," she answered tentatively. "You must be very tired, Morton. Don't you notice anything?"

He studied her face closely and then, with rising impatience, she said, "The room, look at the room."

Slowly his eyes swept around, and then, silently, he took another large gulp of his whisky. He nodded very slowly.

"I thought you might be too busy," she said hurriedly. "After all, you did say you might have to go on soon to the Middle East." She watched him anxiously and then laughed in relief as she saw the start of a slow smile.

"You don't mind?" she asked. "You really don't mind?"

"Damned right, I mind," he said, shaking his head in wonder. "But what the hell can I do about it?" Then a thought struck him. "How much?"

She took his glass and poured another three fingers of Canadian Club.

"How much?"

She passed it back without bothering to add the soda.

"Well, it was a complete redecoration, even upstairs and the bathrooms . . . and the kitchen."

"How much?"

"Twenty-three thousand," she said in a very quiet voice.

He drew a deep breath, but before he could say anything, the door opened and his two sons came in and greeted him warily but affectionately, and demanded to know all about his trip, or at least those parts of it that he could talk about.

Later, after dinner, which Julia had prepared lovingly in the new kitchen, they went up to the bedroom, and before he had a chance to discuss the matter any further, she had helped him out of his clothes and pulled him onto the bed. For the next hour she made sure he had other things on his mind.

But her strategy was unnecessary, for since leaving Malaysia, Morton Hawke had been totally preoccupied. His efforts to banish all thoughts of the dinner with Pritchard had been unsuccessful. On the long flight from Tokyo he had watched two movies and between them had become involved in a deep conversation with a passenger who sat next to him; a retired admiral with very firm views about defense, which coincided closely with Morton's own. But every few minutes mental pictures had crept back into his head: the Christmas cake of a house, the wide, dark river, the enveloping sounds of Beethoven, and the cynical snowy-haired old man with his vivid imagination. Pritchard's scheme had bounced back and forth in Hawke's mind like a tennis ball in a long rally. Several times he had discarded it as being wildly ridiculous, but each time the incredible possibilities had punched the ball back over the net. He had long decided that Pritchard's motivation was simply pride and professional satisfaction; an attempt to instigate a final intelligence coup that would crown a lifetime of achievement. Inexorably Hawke had begun, almost by a process of osmosis, to absorb the old man's motivation for himself. Yet the thought of even presenting such a scheme to his pragmatic Director was daunting.

He was due to report to the Director on the following afternoon, after his secretary had typed the handwritten report in his briefcase. He had decided that he would let the tennis rally in his head continue for a few more days before deciding what to do.

His thoughts turned again to the almond-eyed girl and he felt a needle of guilt. He was not by nature promiscuous but he was a virile man and easily stirred by feminine beauty. But he also had a loyal nature and it was this loyalty which created a feeling of guilt, and, in part, this had muted his response to the redecoration of the house. He loved his wife, in spite of the fact that she exasperated him constantly, and his few past infidelities had always bothered him more than they should have. So, as he lay in bed with her head on his shoulder and, in spite of Julia's ministrations, wide awake, he was in a troubled mood.

Curled up beside him, Julia was both content and puzzled. She had been relieved that he had not erupted on first entering the house, but now she could sense his preoccupation and she wondered at it. During dinner he had not talked much of his trip, only saying that on the whole it had been very successful, and passing on regards from

several people she had met over the years. She decided
that something else was bothering him and thought fleetingly of another woman, but then discarded the idea. After
twenty-two years of marriage she decided that she knew
her husband. She could accept an occasional peccadillo as
long as she was not confronted with it. She knew that with
his reserve and his principles, he would never allow that
confrontation to happen, so in this case she preferred the
serenity of ignorance. But something was definitely on his
mind. Perhaps he would discuss it with her later. She
drifted into relaxed sleep.

It was three in the morning when she awoke. The bedside light had been switched on and Morton sat on the
edge of the bed with his back toward her. There were two
phones on the bedside table; one was a normal house
phone, the other was green and bulky and connected him
directly with the Agency. It was into that phone that he
was talking. She listened as he gave instructions that as
soon as the Director entered his office in the morning, he
was to be told that Morton Hawke would like an urgent
meeting in private and that the Director should clear all
other appointments until lunch. He also ordered that the
file of one James Vernon Pritchard be placed on the Director's desk prior to his arrival. He hung up and swung
his legs back into the bed.

"Haven't you slept?" she asked.

"No. I'm wide awake. I'm still mentally operating thir-
teen hours ahead of Washington time."

"Can I get you something? Will you take a sleeping
pill?"

He shook his head firmly. "No, Julia, I need to be very
clear-headed in the morning."

"Is it trouble?"

He smiled grimly. "No, it isn't trouble. Let's just say
that I volleyed a ball and I hope it didn't go out of court."

She had heard such enigmatic phrases many times before during her married life, so she merely pounded her

pillow into a more comfortable shape and went back to sleep.

The Director listened for forty minutes without a change of expression or making a single interruption. As soon as the monologue ended he opened a file in front of him and for a further twenty minutes studied it in silence, then he raised his eyes and said to Morton Hawke:

"I was appointed to head up the Agency six months ago. In that time I've heard of some wild, harebrained schemes, but nothing that comes even close to this. Frankly, Mort, if anyone else had brought it to me I would either have laughed or sent them to an Agency psychiatrist."

Hawke was irritated, not because of the mention of harebrained schemes or psychiatrists, but because he had once told the Director that he hated being called Mort. The Director either had forgotten or was now using his position to show that he would call anyone by any damned name he wanted to. Hawke's maverick streak came out.

"Well, Dan," he said, "I'm sure that in six months you've become aware that running an intelligence agency is a little different from running a bank."

Daniel Brand had been a president of one of the country's largest banks and a longtime supporter of the new President. His reward for that support had been the plum job of Director of the CIA. He looked at his immediate subordinate steadily for several seconds and then he smiled.

"The first thing I learned around here, Mort, was that you are one mean-minded son of a bitch." His smile broadened. "That's probably why I like you and probably why I've listened to you about this wild scheme."

"It's not as wild as it sounds. My first reaction was the same as yours, but for the past seventy-two hours I've been giving it a great deal of thought."

"And are you going to tell me, with an edge to your

voice, that after twenty years' experience in this business, you think it's feasible?"

"I'm not sure," Hawke answered. "It's still too early, but I think it's worth going down the road awhile."

Brand looked down at the file again and then tapped it with a finger. "The details of the man are in here," he said, "a so-called master spy, sitting out in the jungle, surrounded by servants and giant loudspeakers, probably drinking too many gins and having hallucinations. But because you're here and you're obviously serious, I take it that you have a different view. Or are you just being sentimental about a revered member of your profession?"

"I'm not a sentimental man and Pritchard was not having hallucinations, and incidentally he drinks very good Cognac, not gin."

"And where do his loyalties lie? What's his motive—I mean his personal motive?"

Hawke shrugged expressively. "Those are two very difficult questions to answer, and they've occupied my mind constantly. I believe his loyalties are only to himself. His life's work has tended to show that. As to his motive, it could be pride. He's come up with an astonishing idea. He's the sort of man who likes to see his ideas put into practice."

Brand looked skeptical. "A sort of crowning glory to his career?"

"Exactly. Frankly, Dan, you can't get an accurate picture of the man from his file. You have to know him, talk with him. He doesn't see things the way we do. It's as though he was an academic, perhaps a mathematician, taking pleasure from a complicated formula."

"I accept that," Brand said, "and believe me, I'm not opposed to pure thought in this business. The question is, If he has no loyalties, except to himself, why did he give the idea to us? Why not to the British, or even the Russians? You mentioned that Uri Koslov had been to see him recently."

"Yes," agreed Hawke, "and I asked him exactly that question. His answer was that the Russians would blunder about and be too obvious; besides, the event would probably have to take place in Saudi Arabia, and our connections there are infinitely better than theirs. As far as the British are concerned, they simply don't have the money."

"But he suggested that we use them as the spearhead, the fall guys, if things go wrong. It's a bit strange coming from an Englishman."

Again Hawke shook his head. "It's not strange at all. As I said, his loyalties are only to himself. He's worked for the British when it suited him, just as he worked for anyone else when it suited him, and his idea makes good sense. If we get caught with our pants down, the repercussions would be horrendous."

"And do you think the British would go for it? And if they do, would it be safe? Aren't they riddled with moles?"

Hawke now sensed that the Director was becoming positive. He was, after all, looking into the mechanics of the idea. Hawke's voice took on a note of rare enthusiasm. "Yes, I think the British would go for it. At this time the politics are right in that country, and as to the present state of MI-Six, we're fairly confident. They've had a big cleanup in the last ten years. Most of the Soviet penetration was in the counter-intelligence service, MI-Five, and they won't be in any way involved. Pritchard mentioned a man called Gemmel. He's a Deputy Director of Operations at MI-Six. I called for his file first thing this morning and he looks like a good man. He's also an Arabist and he's not Establishment."

Abruptly the Director stood up and started pacing back and forth across the spacious office.

"Let's balance the risks against results. If the risks can be minimized by having the British stick their necks out, then there's almost no balance at all, because the benefits would be totally incredible. You saw that last intelligence digest on energy that we sent to the President? The Saudis are totally against our stockpiling oil. Our coal conversion program is wildly optimistic and so is the shale extraction program. The Arabs have got us by the nuts, and it's going to get a lot worse before it gets better. They don't want us to have any military bases in the Gulf and the stark truth is that if anything goes wrong in Saudi Arabia itself and the oil flow is cut off, this country is going to have an industrial depression that'll make the Great Depression look like an economic boom." He stopped pacing and turned to face Hawke. "So, wild as this idea appears, it does hold out a chance that if it succeeds, we can pull all the strings in that area."

Hawke didn't say anything. He knew by now that Brand was ready to go at least a little way down the road.

Brand started pacing again. "It's a question of selling it to the President and, after that, keeping Congress right out of the picture." It was now as though Brand was talking to himself. "First I'll have to get Cline on our side. I could probably talk the President into it, but he listens to Cline as much as he listens to me, maybe more, and if Cline's against it he'll talk him out of it."

He was referring to Gary Cline, National Security Adviser to the President and a man renowned for his cynicism, perception, and bloody-mindedness. Brand went on to talk of Congress.

"It'd be almost impossible to get formal approval from the intelligence watchdog committees. There would have to be an unofficial approach, probably to Sam Doole. Although the clamps are coming off, there are several members of his committee who would scream to the rooftops if they knew that the CIA was involved in trying to subvert a whole religion."

At this point Hawke finally interrupted. "At least we would have the Moral Majority on our side."

Brand grinned at him. "That's for sure. They'd probably go along with dropping nukes on every Islamic state on earth, but still it's Congress we have to worry about and, first, Cline."

"Do I give you a written report on it?" Hawke asked.

"Hell, no," Brand replied, shaking his head vigorously. "I want nothing in writing, nothing at all. We'll go down that road very carefully and very slowly and if we get the green light at this end, you'll go over to London and talk to MI-Six, but nobody, nobody at all, is to hear even a whisper of this idea. He looked at his watch. "I'll set up a meeting with Cline first and get his reaction. After that we'll see how far we can go."

Hawke stood up and started for the door. As he was about to go out he asked, "And what about my trip to the Middle East? I'm due to leave in a couple of weeks."

Brand stood in the center of his office, rocking back and forth on his heels. "By this time tomorrow I'll have Cline's reaction, and then we'll see."

Hawke turned to leave but Brand added something. "By the way, it was good thinking and I'm glad you didn't delay in bringing it to me. Well done, Morton."

Hawke was smiling as he walked down the corridor to his office.

# four

THE WIND CAME FROM THE NORTH, DOWN ACROSS THE
Pyrénées, gathering speed as it crossed the coast and into
the Mediterranean. By the time it reached the island of
Majorca it was gusting to fifty knots, and it made Xavier
Sansó very unhappy.

He sat in the crowded bar of Palma's Club de Mar,
drinking Soberano brandy and surveying the remnants of
his crew.

Xavier had several passions in life: his manifold business empire, his wife and children, his extensive wine cellar, various girl friends; but above all he loved yacht
racing.

Outside on one of the club moorings his racing sloop,
*Sirah IV*, tugged impatiently at its warps. She was the
pride of his life, forty-six feet of sleek speed, a German
Frers design built in Barcelona under his own critical eye.
Yacht racing is a sport for fanatics—rich fanatics—and
Xavier liked to win. Tomorrow was the start of the Pepe
Tomas Trophy, a race around the islands of Tagomago
and Cabrera and back to Palma. Normally a strong, gusty
wind would have pleased Xavier, for *Sirah IV* was one of
the biggest and strongest yachts in the fleet, but on this

night Xavier had crew problems. He liked to race with a crew of twelve, at least half of them big, strong young men who might not have much between the ears but who could pull ropes and change sails in any conditions. He himself did not expend too much energy for he weighed in at three hundred pounds. He was, he liked to remark, "both skipper and ballast."

But he had crew problems. Two of his big, strong young men had fallen out and fought and done each other enough damage to spend a few days ashore. Another had slipped off for the race without telling his eight-months-pregnant wife, but just an hour ago her belly had preceded her through the bar doors and she had hauled him off home.

So Xavier was reduced to nine men—actually eight men and a girl. A winsome, sad-eyed girl, but one who was good on winches. Xavier liked to have at least one girl in his crew, someone to look at during a flat calm; but looking at her now only compounded his problem. He needed strong men on the foredeck if he was to have any chance of winning the season's most important race.

He gazed morosely around the packed and cheerful bar, but among the crowd were only racing men already committed to other boats, or hangers-on who wouldn't know a cleat from a topping lift. He decided that unless the wind dropped to a force one or two by morning he didn't have a hope. He sighed and signaled the waiter to bring another Soberano. A hangover would not help, but it couldn't hurt much either.

The waiter had just put the glass in front of him when he noticed the stranger enter the bar from the dining room. A man dressed elegantly in a dark blue suit. He moved easily through the jostling crowd until he stood across the table.

"Señor Sansó?"

Xavier nodded.

"I was talking to the waiter downstairs. He told me you were short of crew for the race tomorrow."

The voice was very quiet, the accent clipped and English, but even through the hubbub of the noisy room every word carried clearly. Xavier nodded again and the Englishman said:

"I'm here on holiday and a little bored." A pause. "If you need more crew . . . ?"

Xavier heaved his bulk forward. The rest of his crew watched with interest. The sad-eyed girl picked up her glass and surveyed the stranger quizzically.

"It's not a pleasure cruise," Xavier said bluntly. "I race to win and the forecast is force five to six."

The stranger shrugged and said nothing.

"Experience?" Xavier asked.

"Not extensive," said the Englishman. "I've done the Sydney–Hobart twice, the South China Sea Race once, and the odd regatta here and there."

The man did not seem disturbed by the frank scrutiny of the eight men and the sad-eyed girl. He stood easily, his eyes never leaving Xavier's face.

"How old are you?" The question came sharply from a young, brawny man sitting beside the girl.

"Forty-four."

"Shit!" The young man rolled his eyes and turned to Xavier. "We need foredeck men who can stand up all day and night and change sails and get wet and tired and still use muscle—not a passenger!"

"Jaime!" the girl admonished, but Jaime ignored her and emphasized again to Xavier, "We need muscle!"

Xavier started to say something but then looked up at the standing man—and the words stopped. The stranger was looking at Jaime. A curious look, not menacing or angry or hurt. An impassive look but with a hint of condescension.

"You think you're stronger than me?" The voice was very flat, very quiet, and very clear.

Jaime sat back in his chair and gave the stranger a critical survey. He saw a man slightly under six feet, a lightly built body, almost slender in the well-cut suit. Dark short hair above a chiseled, tanned face. The eyes were narrow and gray. A straight mouth above a cleft chin.

Jaime's eyes moved to the man's hand, held loosely at his sides, and he smiled, for the hands were also slender, with long fingers and neatly clipped nails.

"Yes, I do." Jaime said it insolently.

"Prove it."

Jaime sat up straighter, for now the flat voice held a menacing note. He glanced at Xavier, who just shrugged, but from the expression on his face he was beginning to enjoy himself.

Jaime grinned and gestured at the table in front of him and laid his right elbow on it.

"Here in Majorca," he said, "we like to arm-wrestle." He looked down at his massive forearm and huge hand and his grin widened and he looked up with a query in his eyes.

The crewman opposite Jaime stood up and with a parody of gallantry offered the stranger his chair. A murmur swept around the bar and the crowd moved in closer to watch. The stranger took the proffered chair and laid his elbow on the table. The two hands were joined and there was a brief movement of fingers as they groped for position.

"Right," said Jaime with the grin still on his lips, then his mouth tightened as he applied pressure. The expression on the stranger's face never altered, only his eyes narrowed further as they gazed straight at Jaime's face.

For a full minute nothing happened.

The two hands and arms were sculptured in stillness. Then, very slowly, the cords in Jaime's neck started to bulge as he built up to full pressure. Still not a movement of the arms.

"Are you ready?"

The stranger's voice was calm and without effort and slowly Jaime's face came up and he looked into the gray eyes and his face showed puzzlement and Xavier began a rumbling laugh. And then the slim fingers began to tighten and Jaime's face twisted in pain and his hand quivered and there came an audible crunch, followed by a sharp crack as the back of Jaime's hand hit the table and Xavier threw back his huge head and laughed at the ceiling. And then there was a silence throughout the bar and the sad-eyed girl was smiling.

Slowly Jaime drew his hand toward him, the fingers curled up as though atrophied. His other hand moved forward and touched them and he winced and turned to Xavier.

"You're going to need him," he said through clenched teeth. "I think the *coño* broke my hand!"

More laughter rumbled out from Xavier's vast bulk. "What's your name?" he asked.

"Gemmel," came the reply. "Peter Gemmel."

*Sirah IV* swept around the northern tip of Cabrera at dawn. Like the red, rising sun, the abating wind came out of the east.

"Spinnaker," grunted Xavier from behind the wheel, and the foredeck crew, cocooned in oilskins, groped for handholds and dragged their exhausted bodies down the wet deck. It had been a terrible night: the wind at force seven for ten hours after rounding Tagomago, a night cold for the season, and a vicious, uneven wave pattern. In the dogwatch another of Xavier's strong young men had become a casualty, slipping on the bucking deck and breaking his arm against a stanchion. Xavier had never considered abandoning the race. The sad-eyed girl had taken the injured man below, and using sail battens as splints, had bound up the arm and helped him into a lee-side bunk.

"The weather side!" Xavier had growled, peering down the hatch. "This is a bloody race. If he can't keep his feet the weight of his body can be of some use!"

So the young man had lain, moaning with every pounding of the green hull, as they hammered north on a broad reach and then turned for home at dawn. The remnants of the crew had become cold, wet zombies as Xavier called the sail changes in answer to the wind. For the past two hours it had been decreasing and Xavier craved to drive his boat to the limit and so more canvas went up exactly as each limit was reached.

But Xavier was not just an expert at gauging the wind. He knew men and their limits, and as he watched them wrestling with the spinnaker he knew that this had to be the last sail change and he prayed that the wind would hold and drive them into Palma Bay and the finish line.

Only the Englishman had any reserves left, and in the ritual of the foredeck the rest of the crew now unconsciously deferred to him and took his quiet orders in silence.

The bound spinnaker snaked up to the masthead, the girl knelt over the winch and spun the handle, the pole swung out, and in a rippling crack the multicolored sail ballooned out. *Sirah IV* surged for home.

The girl worked the winches, trimming the huge sail, watched only by Xavier and Gemmel. The rest of the crew sat slumped, heads between knees. Xavier reached forward and put one of his huge hands on Gemmel's shoulder and squeezed briefly—a rare gesture of thanks. The girl looked up and for the first time saw Gemmel smile. It was quiet now that they ran before the wind and the pounding had ceased. Even the moaning from below had stopped. Xavier turned and looked astern. Only the island. No sails. He grinned at the girl and said, "If I win this race with half a crew, I'll stay drunk for a week!"

The girl smiled back. "So what's new?"

Gemmel looked up at her voice. He had noted her accent earlier.

"You're Dutch?" he asked, and she nodded and said, "Xavier was right. It hasn't been a pleasure cruise. Why do we do it?"

Xavier supplied the answer. "It's like the man who always wears shoes two sizes too small." He waited for

Gemmel's look of query and went on, "The only pleasure he gets in life is when he takes them off at night!"

Gemmel smiled and asked, "You have no other pleasures?"

Xavier roared with laughter. "Plenty, my friend, plenty!" He patted his vast stomach. "Good food, good wine, and good women! But I'm the skipper; I don't have to wear tight shoes."

"And you?" the girl asked Gemmel. "Do you have other pleasures?"

"A few, yes."

"What do you do, back in England? Do you work?"

He nodded. "I do research for a rather boring government department."

"Is that why you like sailing?" the girl asked. "To counterbalance boredom?"

"Perhaps." Gemmel's answer was abrupt, almost curt, as though to resist further questions, but the girl was curious.

"And that's all you do, work and sail? Do you have a boat?"

Gemmel shook his head. "No. And I don't sail enough. Our climate doesn't encourage it most of the year." He hesitated and then said, "I like the ballet; it's sort of a hobby."

Xavier looked astonished. "You dance? You!"

Gemmel smiled again and shook his head. "No, I watch and listen. I find it relaxing and stimulating."

The girl had been working the winch again, keeping the spinnaker filled, but now she turned back and asked, "Have you seen any Spanish ballet?"

Gemmel shook his head and said, "But I will. I learned that Antonio and his troupe are at the Auditorium from Wednesday. I've arranged to get a ticket." A pause. "Are you going?"

The girl shook her head. "I hadn't planned to." A pause. "But I'd like to."

Gemmel glanced at Xavier, who in turn glanced at his watch and looked astern again.

"If that bastard yacht *Todahesa* doesn't round Cabrera within two minutes we'll win on handicap as well as taking line honors." He grinned at Gemmel. "So I'll be drunk for a week, so take the girl to the ballet. Christ. I'll even buy the tickets!"

The club steward watched *Sirah IV* tie up and saw the injured man helped off and to the ambulance that had been summoned by radio. He noted the weariness of the small crew as they went through the motions of clearing the deck. Far out to sea he could just make out the colored spinnaker of *Todahesa*. He picked up the cablegram and said to the bartender, "You'd better get another case of Soberano up. In about ten minutes Xavier Sansó is going to want to swim in it."

Then he went down to the mooring. The crew had started to come off, tossing their gear onto the concrete. He picked out the Englishman and handed him the cablegram.

"Mr. Gemmel, this arrived at your hotel last night; they sent it over this morning."

Gemmel opened the envelope and read the slip of paper. The girl watched him. Then he looked up at the steward and asked, "When is the next flight to London?"

"At one forty-five, sir."

Gemmel turned to the girl. "I'm sorry," he said. "I have to be on that flight."

The girl's winsome mouth turned down at the corners. "It's trouble?" she asked.

Gemmel shook his head. "It's just my boss. I'm needed back in London—urgently."

She nodded very slowly. "To do research?"

"Something like that," he answered quietly.

He said his good-byes to the crew and Xavier.

"Come and sail with us anytime," Xavier said. "Anytime!" And he slapped him on the back and headed for the bar.

So the steward called a taxi and Gemmel left, watched by the sad eyes of the girl.

It was a discreet lunch in one of Washington's most discreet restaurants, one of the few restaurants in the world regularly checked by experts for listening devices.

The maître d' had been known to boast that the cockroaches in the kitchen had a higher security clearance than the fleas in the White House carpets. The three men sat at a secluded corner table. They wore sober business suits with sober neckties but they drank large, ice-cold martinis.

"Very unofficial, of course," said one of the men.

"Of course," acknowledged the man opposite.

The third man sipped his martini and nodded in agreement.

"I mean this is simply to examine procedures," continued the first man. He was elderly and precise in his speech and after every sip of his drink he dabbed his lips fastidiously with his napkin.

"Examine away," said the man opposite. He was of a similar age, but very different in appearance, a large, florid man who perspired slightly in the heated room. He wiped his face with a dark blue handkerchief and took a gulp of martini.

The third man was younger, with a monk's bald pate and fringe. Quick intelligent eyes peered out from beneath pale eyebrows. His hands moved restlessly, rearranging cutlery in front of him, rolling an ever-present cigarette between his fingers, and brushing ash from his vest. He was a man who obviously liked to talk a lot and so always paid a sort of compliment when he listened. He listened now.

"It's very unofficial."

"For God's sake, Dan," said the florid man, "if it were official you'd either be at the House or I'd be out at

Langley. You want to go by the back stairs so you soft-soap me with a good lunch. Get on with it—I'm partial to fine food."

The fastidious man smiled and said, "Sam, times have changed. The last Director couldn't even have waved at you across the street without having a House subcommittee calling for televised hearings."

The florid man laughed easily. "You're not a politician," he said. "You have to understand motivation. A leader of the French Revolution once said, 'I have to find out where my people are going so I can lead them.' Well, in the case of the United States Senate we learned that lesson a long time ago. The people voted. They threw out the nice guys and put in the bastards." He grinned disarmingly. "That's because they want us to be bastards, so that's what we're going to be. Now, let's examine your procedures."

Across the restaurant sat two elderly ladies. Very gratified women. They existed on the outer fringes of Washington society and often ate in this restaurant in the hope that they might spot a personality "in" with the Administration so they could later drop a name at one of their fringe parties. Their vigil had been amply rewarded, for the three men were Daniel Brand, Sam Doole, and Gary Cline, respectively the Director of the Central Intelligence Agency, chairman of the Senate Subcommittee on Combined Intelligence, and National Security Adviser to the President. The two ladies wallowed in proximity.

"You're not going to like it," the Director said.

"Try me," answered the Senator.

"We want carte blanche."

"I'll need one hell of a lot of convincing."

The Director shrugged and looked at Cline, seeking support. He got it.

"I was convinced," Cline said to the Senator. His voice took on a reverential tone. "And I convinced the President that not only should the Director have a free hand but it would be circumspect for the President himself not to know details."

The Senator looked his astonishment.

"Believe me," went on Cline. "The President's comment was 'I don't want another goddamned U2 incident.' I pointed out that the only embarrassment Ike suffered was having to admit that he knew about it. The President liked that. He believes in delegating authority."

The Senator was impressed, and it showed. "Well," he said, "if you want to keep my committee off your back I'll need to know a good deal."

Brand and Cline glanced at each other knowingly; it was going to be a simple trade-off. As long as Doole was given the personal power of inside information he would keep the rest of his committee quietly in the dark.

"Well, it's like this . . ." began Brand, and the three men leaned in toward each other.

The two ladies were into their third coffees. They were not going to move until the lunch party across the room had broken up. It was obvious that an important discussion was taking place. Every time a waiter approached the table the conversation stopped—an impatient pause until he had departed. The Director did most of the talking in a low monotone. Only once did the ladies overhear a semblance of a word from the group. That was when the Senator leaned back in his chair and said something that sounded like "Shee-it!" Obviously they had misheard.

Eventually the lunch ended and the three men moved toward the entrance, escorted by the obsequious maître d'. As they passed their table both ladies smiled avidly and bobbed their heads. Only Sam Doole, with a politician's instinct, acknowledged them with a courteous nod, and so rounded off their perfect lunch.

Outside, the three men stood under the striped awning and watched three black limousines pull up to the curb.

"Do you think the Limeys will buy it?" asked Doole.

The Director smiled. "Since we'll be paying for it,

there's a good chance—and I think the idea will appeal to their devious minds. Perryman once told me that they prefer cerebral activity as opposed to the blood-and-guts stuff we tend to get into. I think it was a mild insult."

"Who's Perryman?"

The Director smiled again. "He's the current head of MI-Six; the British like to keep those things secret. Anyway, we'll soon know. Hawke is flying over tonight to see him."

Three uniformed chauffeurs now stood holding open three rear doors, and Doole moved toward his car. Cline's voice stopped him.

"You're one of only four now, Senator."

"Four what?"

"Four people who know any details at all of the operation. We three and Hawke."

Doole was obviously pleased by this cachet of exclusivity. He nodded solemnly and said to Brand, "The need to know, eh? Don't worry; I'll keep it tighter than a witch's crotch, Dan. Thanks for lunch. You'll keep me up-to-date?"

Brand nodded and Doole entered his limousine. Brand and Cline watched it drive away.

"You've taken precautions?" Cline asked.

"Of course," replied Brand. "We've bugged the phones at his home, his office, his girl friend's apartment, the cathouse he visits on Friday nights, and the three bars he drinks in."

Cline smiled and said, "It must be pleasant having the fetters off at last."

"Believe it," Brand answered fervently. "Believe it!"

Cline turned to his car, saying over his shoulder, "Let me know when Hawke reports in. The President will want to know that our allies are with us."

He got into the limousine, and before the chauffeur could close the door he added, "And that's the last thing he'll want to know until it's over."

# five

A GROUP OF SMALL BOYS PLAYED AMONG THE HALF-CON-
structed shell of a gasoline station on the outskirts of
Medina, chasing each other through unfinished openings
of doors and windows. Within an hour workers would arrive and drive them away, but now it was barely an hour
after sunup and all the world over children like to play on
construction sites. They were playing a form of tag. One
boy had to chase the others and touch one of them, so
passing on the role. The youngest was called Bahira, which
means monk, but his energy and impishness belied his
name. He was just eight years old and had only recently
been allowed out to play with his elder brothers and their
friends. He was crouched behind a mound of concrete
blocks, listening intently, for his eldest brother was "it"
and he didn't want to be tagged by one of his own brothers
—it somehow wasn't right. As he listened he looked down
the dirt road toward the town and the trees and shrubs
that gave color to this oasis community. Behind him the
road passed out into brown desert. His attention was
caught by the figure of a man walking out of the town. He
walked in a curious manner, slow but purposeful, as
though setting out on a long journey. Bahira couldn't

51

imagine where he was going, for the road went to Mecca,
almost two hundred miles away, and young as he was, the
boy knew there was nothing but desert in between. As the
figure drew closer, Bahira's attention solidified. He saw a
man of about forty years, of average height, wearing traditional robes and leather sandals. He carried only a goatskin gourd, slung over one shoulder. He was sturdily built
and had a fair complexion, with large black eyes, a hooked
nose, and a wide, heavy-lipped mouth. His air of detachment and his steady, plodding pace now drew the boy's
total attention, and it was only his brother dislodging a
piece of loose concrete with a clatter that alerted him. He
darted away from the pile of blocks with a shriek, looking
back over his shoulder. His brother was in close pursuit
and gaining, and then Bahira's foot came onto a loose
stone, his ankle twisted under him, and he fell, skidding
onto the road and at the man's feet with a cry of anguish.

At first, and immediately, came tears, for his ankle was
badly sprained and he had grazed his knee on the packed
sand of the road, but as his brothers and the other boys
crowded around, the man knelt and put an arm under his
shoulders and lifted him to a sitting position, and in a deep
but quiet voice steadied him. The contact was at once
comforting, and even as the man's fingers probed gently
at his ankle, Bahira held back his tears.

"You will learn," said the man, "that the sheep who
turns to look behind him ends up in the belly of the desert
dog." He smiled down at the boy. "Or at best twists an
ankle and cannot run for a few days."

The other boys crowded close as the man took the
gourd from his shoulder, pulled out the stopper, and
splashed cool water over the graze on the boy's knee.

"Your mother will need to clean that properly. What
is your name and where do you live?"

The eldest brother answered for him. "He is my brother,
Bahira, and we live over there." He pointed with his chin
to a small, modest house on the very outskirts of the town.

The man put the stopper back into the gourd and lifted the boy easily in his arms and, with the others trailing behind, carried him solemnly home.

"His name is Abu Qadir," Bahira's father said, in answer to his young son's question as he watched the man resume his journey. The boy's ankle had been strapped and the graze cleaned, and the man had topped up his gourd from the well and wished the boy farewell.

"But where do you go?" Bahira had asked.

The man had smiled and said, "I go to hear the silence and see myself." And he resumed his journey.

"Where does he go?" Bahira repeated the question, this time to his father.

"He goes to the caves at Al Hafar."

"Are they far?"

"They are two days' journey on foot."

The boy looked after the receding figure and said, "But he carries no food."

"No," agreed his father, "and he will stay there for three or four days and then he will walk back."

"Without food?"

"Without food—only with water."

"But why?"

The father sighed. "Because that's what he wishes to do." It could be hard to answer an eight-year-old's questions, especially about such a man, for Abu Qadir was in a way a mystic and a mystery. Most people in Medina knew him or of him and treated him with good-natured tolerance. It was said he had been born in Medina of good Hashemite stock and that his father had been a merchant in a small way. When Abu Qadir was still a young boy the family had moved first to Riyadh and then farther on to Cairo and elsewhere. He had returned to Medina eight years ago, saying that his parents and younger brother had died in an earthquake in Algeria. His only living relative in Medina was an old and sickly aunt, who could barely remember the boy who had left so many years before. She lived in a small, dilapidated house and existed on the charity of the Mosque. Abu Qadir had moved in with her, repaired the house, and cared for her until she had died five years later. He was a man of few words and those words were usually couched in sayings from—or related to—the Koran, for he was a religious man. Some believed that he was simple in the head and he only spoke that way because he had learned the Koran like a parrot and knew of nothing else. But the Imam scolded such talkers and pointed out that to know the Koran was to find favor with Allah and to follow its teachings was to guarantee a passage to Paradise on the day.

Abu Qadir was a man who appeared to need little. He hired out his labor on a casual basis, either as a herder of animals or as a carpenter. Possessions counted for nothing with him and he was trusted by those families of Medina that either owned substantial herds of livestock, or needed a man who worked well with his hands. So he worked when he wished and had much free time, and he spent it either at the caves of Al Hafar or at the Mosque. He would often go to the tomb of Muhammad—not to pray but to sit in quiet contemplation. The guards who protected that most holy place knew him well and never had to restrain him, like so many others, from approaching too close. Yet many thought him simple and feeble-brained, but he was tolerated.

A week later Bahira waited by the roadside in the early evening and watched him approach from the distance; the same purposeful, plodding walk. As he drew close, the boy saw that his face was gray with fatigue and the goatskin gourd was slack and empty. Bahira jumped up and walked beside him. Abu Qadir glanced down at the boy's foot.

"Your ankle is well?" he asked.

"Yes," said Bahira. "How were the caves?"

"As always," replied the man. "As always."

It was a sunny but cool day in London, and both Hawke and Gemmel wore topcoats as they strolled in Hyde Park.

They sauntered down to the edge of the Serpentine and watched the people rowing about in shirt sleeves and pretending it was summer.

"It's extraordinary," Hawke said.

"What is?"

"The way you people work." It was said without rudeness, only a mild astonishment.

"In what way?"

Hawke smiled to take the edge off what was coming. "Well . . . it's kind of amateurish."

Gemmel returned the smile and continued walking down the path. The American hurried to catch up.

"Don't take me wrong."

"Oh, I don't," said Gemmel. "It must seem that way, but surely you've worked with our Department before?"

Hawke shook his head. "Never directly, never at such a high level."

They came to a bench and Gemmel gestured and they sat down, facing the lake. After a brief silence Gemmel said, "I've never worked with you people before either, so tell me how we differ."

"It's a matter of approach. Assume that our roles were reversed and you came to Washington with a proposal similar to the one I brought here." He glanced at Gemmel and received a nod to go on.

"Well, the first thing we'd do is appoint an action group to study the plan in every aspect. It would contain experts capable of a broad spectrum of inputs, and wide lateral feedbacks."

He saw the start of Gemmel's smile and held up his hand.

"Okay, forget the jargon, but the result would be that

my Director would be given several in-depth points of view, several differing position papers from which to make a decision."

"And the result?" Gemmel asked.

"The result," said Hawke emphatically, "would be that he would have a better-than-fifty-percent chance of reaching the right decision."

Gemmel nodded slowly and said, "I agree."

"You do?"

"Certainly."

Hawke was disconcerted. His face showed it.

"You think I'm being disloyal?" Gemmel asked, but before the American could reply, said, "Wait, don't answer. First tell me how we treated your proposal."

Hawke spread his hands and laughed shortly. "Perryman was most polite. He gave me a glass of his very best sherry and listened patiently, then he invited me home for dinner."

"Poor you. Did he serve lentil soup?"

"Exactly!"

Gemmel patted his shoulder. "Don't worry. He does that to all Americans. He once had dinner at Ten Downing Street when President Johnson was here. Lentil soup was on the menu and Johnson loved it. Ever since, Perryman has assumed that all Americans love it. Go on."

Hawke laughed again. "Don't get me wrong. He was very pleasant. It was a very hospitable evening."

"But?" asked Gemmel.

"But that's all. The whole night he never talked about the operation. Never mentioned it!"

"That would have been rude," admonished Gemmel. "A gentleman never mixes business with pleasure. Even with lentil soup!"

"Okay," agreed Hawke, "but I need some reaction. I have to report back. When he saw me out he told me you would be around to have a 'chat,' and that he'd give the matter some thought."

"I see," said Gemmel. "And that's amateurish?"

"We'd do it differently."

Abruptly Gemmel stood up. "Shall we head back?" he asked, and Hawke shrugged and rose and they walked again.

"How long," Gemmel asked, "would it take your Director to receive all the inputs, the lateral feedbacks and differing position papers?"

"A week—ten days at the most."

"All right," said Gemmel. "I'm going to be indiscreet in order to set your mind at rest. Your first meeting with Perryman was at three P.M. Wednesday. By five o'clock that evening six men were in conference. Myself, an expert from the Foreign Office, a representative of the Prime Minister, a certain professor from the School of Oriental and African Studies in London, our Deputy Head of Operations, Middle East." He stopped and smiled disarmingly. "And our expert on the inner workings of the CIA."

Hawke was speechless, and Gemmel took his arm and continued up the path.

"That meeting," he continued, "lasted until eleven P.M., when a recommendation was telephoned to Perryman at his home; I believe you had just left. At eight the next morning another meeting was convened at which Perryman himself presided. I cannot, and would not, tell you who were present. At eleven A.M. Perryman was at Ten Downing Street, making a recommendation to the Prime Minister. I believe the Foreign Secretary and the Minister of Energy were present. I cannot tell you what the recommendation was, or the PM's decision. I can tell you that I am here so that you can get a firsthand impression of the man you will be working with in the event that we cooperate."

Now Hawke stopped their progress. "I didn't realize," he said apologetically. "I mean, there was no sign."

"Well, we do work differently," Gemmel answered. And with a glance at his watch, he propelled the American on up the path.

"I'm to drop you off at Petworth House to see Perryman

at four o'clock. You'll get your decision then." He smiled disarmingly. "Exactly forty-nine hours after you first made your proposal." His voice took on a hardness. "Amateurish, Mr. Hawke?"

Again Hawke stopped and the Englishman turned a couple of paces ahead.

"Okay," Hawke said. "So I take my foot out of my mouth, but why so casual to me, why not give me a schedule?"

"It's very simple," Gemmel answered. "You treat us with suspicion—perhaps with good reason. We have had our problems, but, believe me, that's past. However, your outfit looks way down on us. There was no chance Perryman could react until every aspect of your proposal had been examined and until the Prime Minister had given approval to his course of action—especially as, if things go wrong, we'll be left holding the proverbial bag."

Hawke nodded in understanding. "I like it," he said. "And if we get the go-ahead, I think I might enjoy working with you."

Gemmel smiled. "Good. Just as long as you don't call me Pete; not even my worst enemy calls me that."

"What's so bad about Pete?" Hawke asked as they walked on.

"It's an old and famous pornographic poem allegedly written by Rupert Brooke. It's about two characters from below the Rio Grande who meet up with a legendary lady called Eskimo Nell."

"So?" asked Hawke.

"So, there are forty-two stanzas and the two characters are always referred to as 'Dead-Eye Dick with his mighty prick' and 'Pete with his gun in his hand.'"

"So?"

"So, I'd rather be Dick!"

Hawke threw back his head and roared with laughter. "All right, Peter, and in return don't ever call me Mort and we'll get on just fine."

* * *

Gary Cline took the call at the White House tennis court, where he'd been playing the President's press secretary in a vain attempt to contain his waistline. He panted slightly as he listened to the Director CIA.

"Good," he remarked, when the Director had finished. "I'll inform the President. What was Hawke's general impression?"

"In fact he was very impressed," the Director said. "He told me that they even know how to reach a decision, and that they have a sense of humor."

"If things go wrong they're going to need it," Cline said, and hung up.

Perryman and Gemmel dined at a discreet London club. Perryman was an elderly man dressed in the traditional pinstripes of a senior civil servant. They sat at a corner table and talked of trivialities until the coffee arrived. Then Perryman remarked:

"I must say Hawke was most cooperative."

"Really?" Gemmel rejoined politely.

"Yes. And most flattering about you. Said you were the kind of man his own outfit could use." Perryman smiled slyly. "I take it he meant a compliment."

Gemmel said seriously, "I don't think Hawke should be underestimated. He's got a good record and a long one—and he's tough."

"Quite so."

Perryman signaled the waiter and ordered two Cognacs.

"In any event," he said, "they're going to provide the total budget, and whatever the result, we'll be able to siphon off enough to keep us in business for ten years."

"But they're not fools," Gemmel said. "Far from it."

"I agree," Perryman answered. "But they are free with their money."

They broke off as the waiter brought the Cognacs. Then Gemmel asked, "That's all? That's the sum total of our aims?"

"Certainly not." Perryman sipped his Cognac appreciatively and continued, "You'll need a good team. Who do you want?"

Gemmel considered carefully, then said, "I'd like Alan Boyd as my immediate assistant. He's practical and speaks good Arabic."

Perryman raised an eyebrow. "That's all?"

Gemmel shrugged. "Oh, I'll need the usual legmen and communications service, and I may have to call on certain experts now and again—but they only need to know what they have to. Boyd will have to be fully in the picture."

"As you wish," Perryman said. "You have a free hand. Incidentally, I'd like you to go over to the Defense Ministry and see a man called Clements. Eric Clements."

"And?"

"Well, he's some kind of boffin specializing in advanced weapon and guidance systems."

"So?"

Perryman waved his glass in an expansive gesture. "So, if the Americans have to come up with some spectacular great miracle, it's possible that you might guide them into using some of their new stuff."

"So?"

"Don't be obtuse, Peter, it doesn't suit you. In the process of them using it, we could learn something. So talk to Clements; he could have some ideas."

"All right," Gemmel agreed, "but I don't want any interference from that direction. Incidentally, I'm going to need Cheetham—and with full clearance."

Perryman's face turned grave. "You think it will come to that?"

"Yes, I do, and on more than one occasion. An operation like this is going to get unpleasant."

Perryman sighed. "Very well. He'll be under your control."

A brief silence developed and then Perryman said, "I want you to use Beecher." He held up his hand to stave off the immediate protest. "In a very minor way, of course, and without access to any details."

Gemmel sat back in his chair and thought deeply. "So, at last you'll use him?"

"Indeed I will, and this operation is perfect for it."

Abruptly Perryman changed the subject. "How was your curtailed holiday?"

"Cold, tiring, and wet!"

Perryman leaned forward with a smile. "Tell me. It seems I called you home just in time."

As the porter helped them on with their coats, Perryman remarked that Hawke had been quite effusive about the efficiency of the Department.

"I told him you had formed an action group," Gemmel said.

"What's that?"

"Something that gives you inputs and feedbacks and allows you to make a well-balanced recommendation to the Prime Minister."

Perryman smiled and took his tightly furled umbrella from the porter. "At this stage," he said, "if that good lady had the least idea of what was hatching, she'd have my guts for a suspender belt!"

Gemmel smiled and said, "Sir, as head of MI-Six, you should at least have been let into that little secret." Perryman raised his eyebrows and Gemmel added, "She's worn pantyhose for the last seven years."

The two men went out into the rain.

"Okay, now we get serious."

The two men opposite the desk stopped chattering and looked respectfully at Hawke.

Fifteen minutes earlier they had been given broad details of the operation, now code-named "Mirage." They had at first been stunned, and then surprisingly amused; neither of them was a religious man. Hawke had been careful to avoid that. So he had let them chatter for a few minutes, watching both in turn and assessing their reactions.

On his left sat Leo Falk. He was a member of the Agency's Office of Strategic Research. His specialty was the Middle East and he held a doctorate in Semitic studies from Cornell University.

He was a man in his early sixties with close-cropped blond hair, a ruddy complexion, and clear blue eyes behind rimless spectacles. He was the only one among the group who had wartime experience with the old OSS. Among the younger and less reverential agents Falk was known as "The Cloak" and Hawke as "The Dagger."

On Hawke's right sat Silas Meade, his personal assistant and, at thirty-five, the youngest of the group. He had a round, studious face topped by lank black hair. He chain-smoked Kent cigarettes during most of his waking hours.

"Right," Hawke said. "I want you to clear your desks, hand over everything to your deputies."

"My deputy's sick," Falk remarked.

Hawke scowled. "For Christ's sake, Leo, make whatever arrangements you have to, but by oh-eight hundred hours, Thursday, you are both full-time on Operation Mirage. Those are the Director's orders."

Falk leaned forward and said, "I'm slightly confused, Morton. Sure it's a major operation, one of the most important—no, I'll say it: the most important in the Agency's history. But if the British are going to be virtually running it, why does it need two of the most senior people around here to be tied up for what could be many months?"

Hawke picked up a pencil from the table and twirled it between his fingers. He surveyed both men in turn and then said quietly, but very emphatically:

"Because I don't intend to let the British fuck this one up. It's too important. I'm going to monitor them every step of the way. Every single step! We're supplying the money and all the technical backup and this operation is not going to get fouled up."

"Or it's your ass!" Falk commented with a grin.

Hawke returned the grin but it had an edge to it. "It's

all our asses, Leo. If this one goes wrong we'll be studying the Help Wanted column in every paper in the land."

"Incidentally," Falk said, "I know this man, Gemmel."

"You do?"

"Sure; and he knows his stuff. He was on the NATO liaison group that advised on the Camp David accord. Most of them were a waste of time, but Gemmel provided some useful inputs. He knows the Middle East." He smiled at the memory. "He forecast that the moment the Agreement was signed, the Israelis would start building settlement camps on the West Bank at a speed to rival the six days it took God to create the universe—and that they wouldn't rest on the seventh day!"

Hawke nodded in agreement. "I liked him. He's different from the usual pansy type you find in MI-Six. He also indicated that they're getting more efficient. Using modern methods and systems—it's not too soon, I can tell you!" He pulled his chair up close to the desk. "Now listen. We don't have much time and there's a lot to do."

For the next hour he briefed them while Meade took notes. He told them that in ten days they would be meeting the British team. Lisbon, Portugal, had been chosen as the venue. It was thought not wise to have either the British in America or the Americans in Britain. Within that ten days the teams would work out detailed proposals for implementing the operation. These would include the type of man who would be created the Mahdi. How to locate and recruit him and, above all, how to control him—that was the main problem. Then there was the "miracle" itself. What kind of miracle? How could it be created? And where, and when, should it take place for maximum effect?

A further aspect was the headquarters of the team itself. This should be somewhere in the Middle East. Finally, Hawke went through procedures and communication matters. The team was to be isolated from the rest of the Company forthwith. Absolute secrecy was to be maintained. If any outside expert assistance was required, and it would be, all such contacts must be compartmentalized and airtight.

Hawke knew his tradecraft; and while Meade bent his head over his notebook, Falk listened attentively. Finally Hawke sat back and asked, "Comments?"

Falk spoke first, musingly. "Control," he said. "Control of the man himself. We create virtually a god on earth. Once in position, how do we control him? How do we hold the reins?"

"That's the crux," agreed Hawke. "It must be simple and foolproof. Above all, it must be us in control—and not the British."

"Ten days is not a long time," mused Falk. "Not to crack that nut."

"But that's your area," said Hawke. "You're in this team to provide exactly that answer. Be sure that the British will have their own ideas." He turned to Meade. "Silas, what's your impression?"

"I was thinking of the miracle," Meade answered. "It's got to be one goddam spectacular event, and very public." He shook his head. "What kind of happening can we come up with?"

Falk snorted in mirth. "Don't worry, Silas. If this country can elect a movie actor to the office of President, we can sure as hell produce another miracle!"

Meade capped his pen and murmured, "Amen!"

In the Coliseum in London the Royal Ballet was performing *Giselle* to a packed and enraptured audience. Enraptured—with the exception of Peter Gemmel in the tenth row of the stalls. In spite of the soaring music and the grace and technical brilliance of the dancers, his mind was elsewhere.

Ten days, he was thinking; and we'd better be well prepared.

That afternoon he too had briefed Alan Boyd. His mind roved over the meeting. Like Hawke, he had made sure that Boyd had no deep religious principles. In fact, he was an atheist. After incredulity came a mild form of hilarity. The idea was so preposterous that he could not at first take it seriously. But Boyd had a good knowledge of Islam and slowly his mirth had stilled as the implications and possibilities sank in.

"Christ!" he had said reverently. "What a coup that would be!"

He had immediately looked at the practical aspects. He pointed out the cynicism of the Americans in using MI6 as a spearhead. They would have very little risk but would reap all the benefits.

"We'd be the fall guys," he said. "That's what they call it: the fall guys."

Gemmel had shaken his head and said, "Not exactly. There are certain possibilities. We could do quite well from it. There might be areas where we could benefit."

Again, as Hawke had, he went on to outline the way they would work, and again he stressed that the key factors were control of the would-be Mahdi and the need for total plausibility of the miracle. At the Lisbon meeting in ten days both sides would present their proposals, and from those would come the final scheme.

"The game plan," Boyd had remarked.

Gemmel looked blank.

"It's what they call it: the game plan; it's taken from American football. They plan every move of every game. It's like chess."

"Well, we'd better be on the ball," Gemmel had rejoined. "I've been trying to convince Hawke that MI-Six is a hive of activity and efficiency, so in ten days we'd better have a good game plan."

The first act was building to a climax, with the entire company onstage and Giselle dancing her melancholy and beautiful solo, but still Gemmel could not focus his mind or his senses on the scene in front of him. He thought instead about Boyd, with whom he would be working closely in the coming months. He found it easy to identify with him, for like himself Boyd came from a humble background. He was in his early forties, a large, robust man who had first won a scholarship to Manchester Grammar School and then a state scholarship to that city's university. He was an athlete as well as a scholar and had played both cricket and rugby for the university. He had a genial sense of humor and was much addicted to the "real ale" version of draft beer. He concealed a sharp and incisive brain behind his bluff exterior, and Gemmel much appreciated his practicality. His last major job had been in the Gulf sheikdom of Oman, where he had played a significant role in the victory over the rebels supported by South Yemen. Gemmel had selected him as his assistant in the knowledge that esoteric and fantastic as the project might be, Alan Boyd would keep his feet firmly anchored to the ground.

Gemmel came back to reality as the curtain closed on the first act. He was mildly irritated with himself for not having drawn much enjoyment from the dancing. As he made his way to the bar he determined to clear his mind and let it relax with the rest of the ballet.

Once in the crowded bar, he was forced to concentrate on matters other than his work, for he was quickly drawn into a discussion by several people who were members of the London Ballet Circle. Gemmel himself was a committee member of this group of amateur balletomanes who spent much of their leisure and patronage in promoting ballet in Britain.

The point at issue was the appalling conditions backstage at the Coliseum. The dressing rooms for the stars were hardly bigger than cupboards and the lesser dancers had to put up with facilities that would have shamed a maximum security prison. The London Ballet Circle had started a fund-raising scheme to make improvements, but some committee members were in favor of using the bulk of the money to subsidize a tour of the Royal Ballet to South America. Gemmel was buttonholed by Sir Patrick

Fane, chairman of the committee. Fane had been watching out for him, and pressed a gin and tonic into his hand.

"Peter, old chap," he said earnestly, pulling him to one side. "Wet your whistle and listen."

Gemmel sipped the gin and listened as Fane solicited his vote at the next committee meeting. He reflected that Fane was the sort of man who probably enjoyed committee meetings more than the ballet itself. But still he had a point. In a few months the Maly Ballet Company of Leningrad would be performing at the Coliseum. Putting on the full-length *La Bayadère*, no less, with a company of over fifty. How in God's name could they be put in the cattle stalls backstage?

Gemmel nodded in acquiescence. How indeed! He didn't remark, as he would have liked to, that Russian ballet dancers were accustomed to a measure of hardship —and if they complained they soon ceased to dance.

He was saved by the chimes heralding the second act and dragged himself away, promising to give the matter his deepest consideration.

"But by the way," he said to Fane, putting his empty glass on the bar, "I usually drink Scotch."

Sir Patrick looked after Gemmel's receding back, totally convinced that he'd just lost a vote.

# six

HAJI MASTAN COULD HAVE SOLD USED CARS ANYWHERE IN the world. It wasn't that he looked like a used-car salesman. On the contrary, he resembled a benign, bovine animal—a contented, brown-eyed cow. He had a fat, humorous face above a plump body. It was only a close examination of those brown eyes that revealed the agile brain behind. He spoke slowly and always courteously, with much gentle gesturing of his arms and plump fingers, and he had a knack of always getting his own way.

Haji Mastan didn't sell used cars, but he sold used, retreaded tires in the Red Sea city of Jeddah. As the vast Saudi oil revenues fueled the march of progress, so progress became identified with the status symbol of the car—big, expensive, luxury cars. A whole industry grew up around this new method of transportation. It was said that Haji Mastan's father and forefathers had once traded in camels but no one knew for sure, for Haji was by birth an Iraqi and had come to Jeddah fifteen years before, after making the pilgrimage to Mecca and hence changing his name to Haji, or "one who has made the pilgrimage." It was said that his family had fallen out with the Baath rulers of Iraq and had splintered into various countries of the Middle East. His father had been wise and sent his four sons to different locations, all with enough capital to start a moderate-sized business. One of them, the father had reasoned, might make a success and so support the rest of the family, and future generations.

On his arrival in Jeddah, Haji had quickly found his niche. He had invested his capital in the equipment necessary to retread tires, bought premises in the Al Kandarah section of the city, hired a couple of workers, and sent them to Cairo to be trained. His brother, who had been sent to Egypt and had invested his capital in a restaurant, had overseen the training and ensured that the two men returned to Jeddah and their indenture. So, with these two men to do the work, and Haji to get the business, the small company had flourished in a mild way. At first it had been difficult, for most Saudis, when they bought a car, never considered that the tires would wear out, and when they did they bought new ones—or a new car. But inevitably the new cars became old, and a used-car market developed, and so the slightly less affluent sector of the society became a market. This market quickly discovered that tires wore out rapidly on the rough desert roads and that new tires were expensive. So Haji's business flourished, and finally blossomed when he secured the contract to retread the tires of all the vehicles of one section of the vast Aramco oil company, that Saudi-U.S. conglomerate which extracts the oil from the desert kingdom.

This had meant expansion, so more machinery was acquired and more men hired.

Haji Mastan was known as a deeply religious man, and he praised Allah for his blessings and modestly remarked to his friends that his own business acumen had little to do with his success, for was not all in the hands of Allah?

This made an impression on his friends, for they had long noted Haji's devotion to the five pillars of Islam: he constantly affirmed the faith; he paid a *zakāt* or alms tax, of 20 percent of his income, and he frequently paid more; he prayed five times a day with fervor; he observed Ramadan, the month of fasting, and—as Haji Mastan loved his food—to abstain from sunup to sunset was a genuine sacrifice. Finally, he always made the annual pilgrimage to Mecca, the Haj. This was no great imposition, for Mecca lay only thirty miles to the east and Haji could travel there in the comfort of his air-conditioned Mercedes.

So Haji Mastan was the epitome of the successful Arabic businessman who was able to include commerce within the dictates of the Koran. He lived modestly but comfortably with his wife and two daughters and contemplated an unruffled future.

Hawke was deeply embarrassed, and a touch resentful. Okay, Pritchard had come up with an ingenious idea and Hawke had sold it to the Director and the Director had sold it to the National Security Adviser, who had sold it to the President. But Pritchard had left out one vital element. How to control the Mahdi? On this point Pritchard had been vague. "There must be ways," he had said airily. "A man can always be controlled, one way or another."

At the time Hawke had nodded sagely—it had sounded eminently reasonable. But now, after ten days of intensive mental effort, none of his team—nor the experts they had consulted—had come up with a single foolproof plan.

So Hawke paced the floor of his suite in Lisbon's Ritz Hotel and let his embarrassment make warfare on his irritation. In fifteen minutes he was due to take his team into a meeting with the British and he still had no workable solution. The British would be politely disdainful at best.

Falk sat on an easy chair, watching Hawke as he paced. Meade sat on the sofa, a pile of files by his side, a notebook on his knee, a cigarette in the fingers of one hand, and a poised pencil in the other.

"You've got half a dozen options," Falk said belligerently.

"Options!" Hawke rounded on him angrily. "I've got half a dozen crackpot schemes from hiring out-of-work actors to bribing an Imam!" He flung his arms at the ceiling in exasperation. "I've heard about mind-bending drugs, coercion, blackmail, and simple patriotism. Does no one understand that we're planning to create a Prophet? A man who will dominate the lives of a billion people? Once he's there, once he's acclaimed, what's to stop him showing us two fingers? We have to rely on drugs or blackmail? How in hell do you blackmail a Prophet?"

Falk leaned forward and said, "Morton—believe me, force, bribery, blackmail, coercion, what you will, is the only way. I've run a thousand agents in my time; I know!"

Hawke stopped in midstride and glared at him. "You ever run a Prophet, Leo? Hmm? Tell me! You ever controlled God's Messenger on Earth?"

Falk shrugged. "He's still a man, Morton. We'll put him there, and whatever the believers think, he'll still be just a man."

Hawke sighed in irritation, but Falk pressed on.

"What do you have, Morton, when you have two little green balls in your fist?"

Hawke rolled his eyes at Meade and said, "Tell me, Leo, what do I have?"

"The undivided attention of a leprechaun." Falk burst into raucous laughter. Nobody else laughed and slowly he got himself under control.

"Force; power; coercion—it's the only way."

He looked at Meade for support but Meade merely shrugged and said, "I'd like to think we can be more subtle."

"I agree," Hawke said emphatically, "but so far we haven't come up with anything very profound."

"Ten days is not a long time," Falk said defensively. "Anyway, the British may have some ideas. How are you going to handle it?"

"Carefully. I'm going to let them give their suggestions first and then, if they have any great and subtle ideas, I can be condescendingly generous." He glanced at his watch. "Let's go!"

As Falk stood up he said, "At least we've got a spectrum of ideas for the miracle."

"Sure," Hawke grunted sarcastically. "Everything from
parting the Red Sea to giving Yassir Arafat a pink halo!
Let's go!"

The Ritz Hotel in Lisbon is one of the world's great
hostelries, and its smaller conference room reflected the
taste and comfort of a less hectic era. A long, polished
table filled the center of the room and was attended by
Louis XIV chairs. Tapestries depicting voyaging scenes
adorned the walls, and a deep, rich carpet sank graciously
underfoot. A small bar had been set up in one corner, and
Gemmel and Boyd were standing beside it, talking pleasantries and sipping drinks. Two men were moving around
the room. They carried several small instruments. Some
clicked and some hummed. The door opened and Hawke
entered, followed by Falk and Meade. The two men at the
bar turned. There was a silence, not so much pregnant as
that which precedes a doctor's slap on the bottom of a
newborn baby.

Both Gemmel and Hawke looked at the two instrument-
laden men.

"She's clean, sir," one of them said to Gemmel.

"A-OK, Morton," the other said to Hawke.

Another brief silence, and then Hawke strode forward
with a smile and an outstretched hand.

"Good to see you, Peter," he said as they shook hands.

There followed the introductions and hands were criss-
crossed and shaken and more ice clunked into more
glasses.

Gemmel smiled at Falk and said, "Good to see you
again. I'm glad you're in on this."

"Likewise," responded Falk, and said to the inquiring
Boyd, "Whisky and soda, thanks."

Gemmel handed Hawke a Canadian Club with a splash
of soda and two ice cubes. The others milled around, getting themselves drinks.

Finally Hawke turned to the two men who stood at the door. "Thanks, I guess we can start now. You'll keep monitoring outside?" Both men nodded and left the room, and the five men drifted toward the table.

It's curious the way people approach a conference table. First they look for name cards, and then, in their absence, they look at each other with tentative smiles, for the seating arrangements at a conference table can be more socially crucial than at a White House or Buckingham Palace dinner. More peace conferences have been delayed or canceled because of this prestigious aspect than any other reason. But on this occasion Hawke was affably diplomatic and firm.

"Peter," he said, "why don't you and Alan sit on that side, Leo and I will sit on this side, and Silas"—he slapped Meade on the shoulder—"can sit at the end and make whatever notes are necessary." He winked at Gemmel. "And keep the glasses refilled."

The five men settled down, and there came an expectant hush as all eyes turned to Hawke. He cleared his throat, leaned forward and spoke slowly and confidently.

"First, to recap briefly: the purpose of this meeting is to formulate a detailed plan for the selection and subsequent acclaim of a new Prophet—the Mahdi—for the Islamic religion; the methods of implementation, that is, the 'miracle'; and the ongoing control of the Mahdi, and through him the Pan-Islamic movement."

His eyes swept the table and the other men nodded solemnly.

"Finally," he went on, "to agree—subject to higher approval—on the general objectives of such an intelligence operation, which we have code-named Mirage." He now looked directly at Gemmel. "Peter," he said, "I would first like to tell you how pleased I am"—he indicated Meade and Falk—"and I speak for my associates, that you will be handling the operation on the ground floor."

Meade and Falk murmured noises of agreement and Hawke continued, "We want you to know that we have no intention of interfering in the day-to-day running of the field aspect. Naturally, in that our Agency is promoting and financing the plan, we need to have a close watching brief."

Gemmel inclined his head in understanding and all the others nodded in sympathetic agreement.

"Good," said Hawke, his voice warming to his theme. "Now, after deep and expert consideration, it is obvious to us that the key element is the selection and, above all, ongoing control of the man himself—the Mahdi." He smiled at Gemmel disarmingly, glanced at Meade and Falk, leaned forward and said, "Peter, obviously we have several very credible proposals. However, since you boys are going to be up front, why don't you let us have your thoughts first?"

Gemmel nodded slowly. "Thank you, Morton," he said. "We think we have a simple but effective plan." He paused and looked in turn at the three Americans. "The only slight problem," he continued, "is that I fear it's going to be rather expensive, and it's going to need not one, but two miracles."

The maître d' of the Ritz Hotel restaurant liked Americans. It wasn't that they tipped well—some did, and some didn't—but that they didn't complain. Not that there could be much to complain about in one of Europe's finest restaurants, but still some people did. The French and Italians in particular. He decided that Americans were so starved for good service in their own country that they were reduced to mute awe when confronted with the service he was trained to provide. The three Americans at the corner table puzzled him. The reservation had been made by the concierge in the name of a Mr. Beckett. Ten minutes before the party arrived, a furtive-looking man had come in, asked for Mr. Beckett's table, and then walked around it several times. He carried a large briefcase from which a wire snaked up to an earplug. Then, with a nod at the maître d', he had departed. When

Mr. Beckett arrived with his guests, the maître d' had felt constrained to mention the incident, but the American had merely smiled and pressed a bank note into his hand. The maître d' had shrugged. After twenty years in the job, nothing surprised him.

"It's gonna cost a bomb," Falk said, through a mouthful of smoked trout.

"But it's beautiful," Meade responded. "Beautiful!"

They both looked at Hawke, who was deep in thought, his plate of chef's salad untouched. Abruptly he looked up at them.

"It all hangs on the Mahdi's 'disciple,' " he said. "He's got to be our man." He slowly pounded the table for emphasis. "All our man, always our man, and only our man."

Falk agreed enthusiastically. "When Gemmel unfolded it," he said, "it was like a bell ringing as soon as he got to the disciple—a great, loud, clanging bell!"

"You're sure about this guy?" Hawke asked sharply. "You've got no doubts?"

Falk shook his head impatiently. "None, Morton. He's perfect. We planted him years ago, fertilized him, piled compost on top, and poured in water ever since. I tell you, he's perfect. Tailor-made; but it's going to cost a bomb."

Hawke nodded. "Somewhere in excess of two hundred million, I guess, but, Leo, that's about fifty minutes of oil supply for the entire United States. It could be worth it." He shook his head in wonder. "I tell you, they sure came up with one lulu of an idea."

A silence descended as all their thoughts turned back to the meeting.

Gemmel's statement that two miracles would be required had produced a total silence, finally broken by Hawke, who had remarked, "Now we need two Prophets?"

Gemmel had smiled and shaken his head, and gone on to explain that the only way they could see to control the man in question was to make him believe that he was, in fact, the Mahdi, and concurrently convince him—nay, instruct him—to turn to a designated person as a confidant and adviser. Such a person would be under control. Gemmel had paused for reaction, but receiving none, had gone on to explain that the first miracle would be private and personal to the chosen Mahdi. In effect, something like an apparition of the angel Gabriel, much as had happened to Muhammad. Gemmel had taken expert advice on whether such an apparition could be arranged and had been assured that, subject to virtually unlimited funds, it could be arranged, even in Technicolor. The second miracle, the one to authenticate the Mahdi in the entire Islamic world, would need to be somewhat more spectacular.

Again Gemmel paused, and this time Falk interjected, "The disciple of course would be prepared and waiting for the Mahdi?"

"Of course," Gemmel had answered. "And he would be our man—lock, stock, and barrel."

Falk pursed his lips in thought and then with a gesture indicated that Gemmel should continue. Gemmel did so, but first with a mild apology to Falk that what he was about to say would be very obvious to such an eminent Arabist. Nevertheless, the briefing was necessary so that the others could appreciate the fine points of his proposal. Falk inclined his head graciously and Gemmel continued.

He took them through a brief history of Islam from Muhammad to the present day. He explained the schisms that had split the religion ever since the death of the Fourth Caliph. He described the astonishing spread of Islam, first by conquest in the early centuries, and then by missionaries in more recent times.

There was, he pointed out, one abiding link among all the factions of Islam: Mecca and its Grand Mosque remained the focal point of the religion, and it was the duty of every Muslim, of whatever nationality or faction, be he Sunni, or Shi'a or Sufi or Ismaili, to make the pilgrimage —the Haj—to Mecca. Thus, every year over two million Muslims from over seventy nations poured into Mecca for the most fervent mass religious rites known to mankind.

"So it must be during the five days of the Haj," Gemmel had said, "that the miracle occurs, witnessed by all the pilgrims, who will then scatter over the globe and carry the word of the Mahdi."

Once again he paused and again there was a silence—a long silence, while each man exercised his own fantasies.

It had been Hawke who finally broke the spell.

"And the miracle itself," he said. "You have firm ideas about that?"

"We do," replied Gemmel. "But perhaps you'd like to put yours forward first?"

Hawke shook his head. "No, no, carry on, Peter. So far your ideas show a lot of promise."

Now Gemmel moved on to details. He asked them to envisage the scene. On the afternoon of the penultimate day of the Haj the multitude moves out of Mecca and into the valley of Minā. From noon to just before sundown the pilgrims face the small rocky hill of Arafat and pray and read the Koran and listen to sermons. Some of them also make sacrifices: lambs or goats, sometimes even a camel. Subconsciously Gemmel's voice had become more hushed at this point. The others leaned forward to catch every word. At that time, he told them, their man, surrounded by his followers and preceded by rumors, would move to the middle of the valley—the middle of the multitude—and place a dead lamb on the ground. His followers would clear a large circle around it, and the would-be Mahdi would cry out in a loud voice, calling on Allah to acknowledge his sacrifice.

Gemmel's voice had dropped even lower, his tone becoming reverential. The others leaned in farther toward him, their faces mirroring the imagination in their minds.

"Then," Gemmel had said, "from a blue, cloudless sky comes a vivid green ray of light, clearly seen by all two million pilgrims—seen as far away as Jeddah. The green ray strikes the lamb and it disintegrates in smoke."

He leaned back in his chair, his voice became matter-of-fact, and he said to his rapt audience:

"And the Mahdi is proclaimed!"

Falk had been the first to recover. "A laser beam!" he exclaimed, with a grin. "From a high-flying aircraft."

"From a satellite," Gemmel had answered, "from up in space."

Hawke began to pick at his food. "You think the miracle is feasible?" he asked Meade.

"Which one?"

"The big one—the laser beam."

Meade shrugged. "I don't know a hell of a lot about lasers, but Gemmel seemed confident and I guess he's taken expert advice."

Falk wiped his mouth with a napkin and said, "I remember reading a report from the Department of Defense, Research Department. They've made great strides in recent years. As long ago as nineteen seventy-three the Air Force shot down a winged drone with a prototype laser weapon and the Army and Navy have had similar successes."

"That's right," Meade interjected. "I saw that report, it was by Richard Airey. In nineteen seventy-eight the Navy knocked down a TOW antitank missile—only ten inches in diameter and it travels at a thousand miles an hour."

Hawke laid down his fork. "So it's likely to be feasible," he said, "but it's going to have to be one damn great piece of machinery and getting it up into space is going to be one damn great problem."

"We'll have to use the space shuttle," Falk said, "and NASA and the Pentagon ain't gonna like that one little bit. They've got that program booked up for years."

Hawke smiled grimly. "So we'll bring the required pressure to bear. Silas, I want you to handle that. You may have to use Gary Cline to twist a few arms. And within twenty-four hours of our getting back to Washington I want the top laser man from the DoD Research Department in my office with his bag of tricks and all the answers."

Meade nodded and scribbled in his notebook. Hawke

turned to Falk. "Leo, you proceed at the other end. Activate our mole in Jeddah and get him to start stirring things up. When the Mahdi comes out of the desert he's got to have a ready-made following. But first thing you do is have our man nominally transferred to the British. Liaise with Boyd. He'll be running him—at least he thinks he will—but I want the Agency to keep the very tightest grip on his short and curlies!"

Falk grinned. "Don't worry, Morton, the disciple we can control—and he's cleaner than the inside of a bottle of Listerine."

"Good." Hawke pushed away his plate. "I don't want any hiccups on this one." His eyes came to rest on Meade's bent head. "What do you say, Silas?"

Meade looked up and said, "Amen, Morton. Amen!"

Gemmel and Boyd talked in Gemmel's room. Boyd sat in the single chair while Gemmel sat on the bed.

"I think it went rather well," Boyd said.

Gemmel smiled in agreement. "They certainly liked the idea of control through a disciple, but that's because they've got a man in place and have had him quiet as a mouse for fifteen years."

"Rather clever, that," commented Boyd. "I didn't think the Americans went in for that sort of thing—I mean, the very long-range planning."

Gemmel grinned and said, "Neither did I. They generally like quick results."

"So now we take him over."

Gemmel nodded slowly. "Yes, in case he gets caught with his pants down. But that will be pure cosmetics. Hawke will keep a tight hold on him, and if the operation works we'll suddenly find that the disciple gets decidedly anti-British." He shrugged and glanced at his watch. "In ten minutes," he continued, "I have a final meeting with Hawke in his suite." He stood up and asked, "Where's Beecher?"

"He was in the bar last time I saw him."

Gemmel winced and said, "Go down, please, Alan, and make sure he's reasonably sober."

"I could fit my room into here three times," Gemmel said, looking around the lounge of the suite.

Hawke stood at the bar, fixing drinks. "I'll have a word with Perryman," he said, carrying the drinks over and settling himself into an easy chair. "Suggest that he ups your per diem."

Gemmel shook his head and smiled. "Perryman would have a mild heart attack at the idea of my paying a hundred pounds a night for accommodation."

There was a brief silence as the two men surveyed each other across the coffee table.

"I'm going to come clean," Hawke said abruptly, and Gemmel raised an eyebrow.

"I wouldn't admit it in front of the others," Hawke went on, "but the fact is, Peter, we hadn't come up with any particularly bright ideas either for controlling the Mahdi or for the miracle. Frankly, if your side hadn't had a brainstorm the project would be stymied right now."

Gemmel was obviously impressed by Hawke's frankness but he couldn't resist having a small dig. "You mean your 'Action Group' let you down?"

Hawke smiled wryly. "I guess so. It's lucky that yours didn't."

Gemmel shook his head. "The fact is, Morton, that both ideas came from Perryman. Despite appearances he's a very canny old boy."

"So it would seem," Hawke said quietly. "I can tell you one thing: I'm a lot more confident now than I was twelve hours ago. Maybe we can pull this crazy thing off." He took a deep breath and said, "Okay, shall we get down to details?"

They went on to discuss the future steps. It was agreed that they would meet again in a week, this time in Paris so as to avoid being seen together too often in the same city. Actually Hawke would have preferred Brussels or

Bonn. He didn't much like Paris, but Gemmel was curiously insistent. In the meantime Hawke would check out the feasibility of using a laser in space to effect the miracle, and if it was possible, whether it could be ready in seven months, which was when the next Haj to Mecca took place. If not, they would have to wait a further year.

Concurrently, Gemmel would set in motion the search for the candidate. He would have to be an Arab with perfect antecedents so that he would be acceptable to all factions of the Islamic faith. The first miracle and the conversion would have to take place at least three months prior to the Haj, so as to provide enough time for the candidate to build up a following. He would not, of course, openly declare himself as the Mahdi until the big miracle, otherwise the king of Saudi Arabia would likely cut off his head, just as he had cut off the heads of previous claimants.

They also agreed that MI6 would initiate a campaign of disinformation throughout the Islamic world. Rumors would be started of the coming of the Mahdi, rumors which they would build to a crescendo until the miracle in the valley of Minā confirmed them. Finally they decided that both their teams would set up a base camp in Amman, Jordan, as the operation gathered pace.

They had almost finished when a discreet tap came on the door. Both men looked at each other. Hawke shrugged, got up, went over, and opened it. A short, nervous, elderly man stood outside, holding a buff-colored envelope.

"I understand that Mr. Gemmel is here."

"Ah, Beecher," Gemmel called, "come in."

Hawke stood aside and Beecher crossed the room and handed the envelope to Gemmel.

"This just arrived from London, sir," he said. "I don't know if it's urgent. Mr. Boyd told me you were here."

"All right, Beecher, thanks," Gemmel said. "Did you confirm my reservations to Cairo?"

"Yes, sir, the flight is at ten o'clock. I've ordered a car for eight-thirty."

Gemmel had opened the envelope and read the brief message inside. He looked up and said, "Fine, Beecher, thank you."

Beecher turned, nodded at Hawke, and left the room.

"Who was that?" Hawke asked as he sat down.

"That's Beecher."

"He's part of your team?"

Gemmel shook his head. "No, he's just a messenger boy. He knows nothing at all of substance about the operation."

Hawke looked slightly relieved. "I hope you don't mind my asking," he said, "but is he a lush?"

"A lush?"

"Yes, you know, someone who likes the bottle. It's just that the smell of Scotch just about knocked me over."

Gemmel smiled. "Yes, I think he probably is. He seems to spend most of his time in the bar. Frankly, I haven't used him before and when we get back to London I'll slide him off onto some other department. Actually, he's only got a couple of years till retirement. Perryman's a bit soft like that—hates to fire anyone."

"I can understand that," Hawke said, "but a lush in this business can be a real liability. I had to fire one a couple of weeks ago—a good man in his time. It was painful."

Gemmel nodded in understanding and dropped the envelope onto the table.

"Was it important?" asked Hawke.

Gemmel smiled. "Yes, very. The Béjart ballet is performing in Paris next week. That was a note from my secretary, advising that she's managed to get me a ticket!"

"You son of a bitch!" Hawke said, but he was smiling.

## seven

THE EVENING PRAYERS FINISHED AND THE FAITHFUL ROSE
and rolled up their prayer mats. Some stayed to gossip
while others moved off home or drank coffee at the street-
side stalls that surrounded the Mosque.

The Imam dealt with a few people who had minor problems and then walked over to join Haji Mastan, who sat
in the shade of the high wall. Before the prayers Haji
had mentioned that he would like to talk, that he needed
advice. The Imam was pleased, for Haji Mastan was a
pillar of the community and a benefactor of the Mosque,
and in seeking the Imam's advice he was paying a compliment.

The Imam settled down and the two men talked idly
for a while about mundane matters. Finally they lapsed
into silence. The Imam waited patiently but curiously,
for he could see that Haji was deeply preoccupied, his
normally cheerful face was serious, and his fingers plucked
at the sleeves of his robe. Finally he said:

"I have had dreams."

The Imam's face showed his surprise, for he had been
expecting something of a practical nature. Perhaps the
instruction of one of Haji's children, or a problem in his

business. He knew that Haji had recently returned from a trip to Cairo.

"Dreams?" he asked blankly.

"Yes, dreams, always of a similar kind."

"What kind of dreams?"

Haji drew a deep breath. "Dreams of a man," he said. "Of a man who walks in the desert—a holy man."

"Do you know him?"

Haji shook his head. "But I see him clearly and he is always the same."

The Imam tried to gather his thoughts, tried to find words which would bring the conversation to a practical level.

"How do you know he is holy?"

"I just know."

"Describe him to me."

For a long while Haji sat silently, his face a mask of indecision. Then he looked the Imam in the eyes and said, "Describe to me Muhammad, may God bless him and save him."

The Imam sat back as though slapped in the face.

"Muhammad the Prophet?"

Haji nodded numbly.

"Muhammad the Prophet?" repeated the Imam. "You see him in your dreams?"

"I see a man," said Haji. "I see a man. Will you describe him to me?"

The Imam drew a deep breath. "You are a learned man, Haji Mastan, and you know how he looked."

"Describe to me the Messenger of God!"

With almost anyone else the Imam would have impatiently dismissed the matter, but Haji Mastan was not a man to dismiss lightly. Slowly the Imam intoned:

"He was sturdily built with a hooked nose and large black eyes. His mouth was large and when he laughed, which was seldom, though he often smiled, one could see the whole inside of his mouth. In complexion he was fair.

When he turned he did so with his whole body." The Imam stopped and said, "But you know all this."

"Yes," sighed Haji.

"And in your dreams you see such a man. You cannot know his face; no one can know his face!"

Haji shook his head. "I only know the face of the man I see in my dreams and now after many nights of dreams I know him well."

"And what does he do?"

"He walks in the desert."

"And to where does he walk?"

For a long time Haji didn't answer. He sat still as a rock, his face set and without expression.

"To where does he walk?" repeated the Imam.

"He walks here—to me."

The Imam sat back and clasped his knees. He found it very difficult to voice his next question, but finally it came.

"And what, and if, he comes—this man of your dreams?"

Again a silence, and when Haji finally spoke his voice was so low that the Imam could hardly catch the words.

"If he comes he will call me. And I will go."

Now the Imam sharpened his tone. "Haji Mastan. From dreams you decide so much? From dreams you already imagine something in the future? Are you well? Do you perhaps pine for something, that your mind forgoes you?"

"For six months," Haji said, "for six months I have had these dreams."

The Imam shrugged, by now made uncomfortable by the conversation. "So what advice do you seek?"

"Do I talk of it?" Haji asked. "To my family, my friends?"

The Imam shook his head vehemently. "You do not!" he said. "You know well where such talk can lead. You say nothing!"

Haji didn't respond and the Imam pressed his point.

"Dreams are dreams," he said. "You are a respected man and sensible. If you talk of such things people will laugh at you, will say that Haji Mastan has lost his mind."

"Do you laugh at me?"

"No, I do not."

Haji rose and gathered his cloak about him. "Then I will follow your advice," he said, looking down at the Imam. "I will not talk about it." He turned and left the Mosque.

He did follow the Imam's advice and he did not talk of it, but he knew the Imam well, knew him for a garrulous old man.

So the Imam talked and, in the talking, embroidered and invested the dreams. He talked in the Mosque, and in the bazaar, and in the coffee shops. And no one laughed, for Haji Mastan was a serious and respected man.

Gemmel entered the suite of the George V Hotel in Paris at 8 P.M. By nine-thirty Morton Hawke was in a towering rage. A rage that reverberated across the Atlantic and first bounced off the Director of the CIA, thence to the President's National Security Adviser, and finally came to a vibrating halt about the ears of the Secretary of Defense.

The meeting started out pleasantly enough. From their greeting it was obvious that Gemmel and Hawke were genuinely pleased to see each other. Hawke had Leo Falk and Silas Meade with him and a fourth man. He was in his early forties and had the calm detachment of someone totally confident of his particular expertise. Hawke introduced him quite formally.

"Peter, this is Elliot Wisner, who heads up the Directed Energy Technology Office of the Undersecretary of Defense for Research and Engineering."

Gemmel swallowed that and shook the man's hand,

took a drink from Meade, and the four of them sat down around a table.

"How was your trip?" Hawke asked.

"Good," answered Gemmel. "You could say that the ball's rolling."

"Well, that's fine," responded Hawke, "but frankly, Peter, we have problems at the other end."

Gemmel sipped his drink and remained silent.

"The fact is," Hawke went on, "we had assumed that when you presented your proposal for the big miracle you had fully researched the technicalities."

"I had." Gemmel's voice was flat and direct.

"It appears not."

Again Gemmel failed to respond, and Hawke eyed him closely for a few moments. A definite feeling of tension was building up. Hawke hunched himself forward in his chair.

"Elliot here," he said, with a wave of his arm, "is considered our foremost expert on the state of the art of laser technology. He has been closely identified with all aspects of our government's development programs in the use of lasers."

He leaned back in his chair and said with a hint of condescension, "So may we take it as read that Elliot can be considered as one of the world's foremost experts on laser technology?"

"We can," Gemmel answered.

Now Wisner leaned forward. "Thank you," he said in a high, nasal voice. "Mr. Gemmel, Morton asked me to make this trip so you could hear at first hand why the incident you have proposed is physically impossible." He gestured expansively. "Let me say, however, how much I admire the breadth of imagination—the vision—which prompted your suggestion."

He paused, but Gemmel remained impassive.

"How much do you know about lasers?" Wisner asked.

"I had a layman's knowledge," Gemmel replied, "but

obviously I've taken the trouble to acquaint myself with some details."

Wisner smiled. "I'm sure you will agree that a little learning can be a dangerous thing."

Gemmel sighed audibly. "Mr. Wisner, why don't you tell me why our proposal is physically impossible?"

Wisner was disconcerted. He glanced at Hawke and received a nod of encouragement. "Let's start at the beginning," he began.

For the next fifteen minutes he deftly gave a thumbnail sketch of the development of laser technology. He kept it simple, first describing a laser as a machine that projects a beam of light of a particular color. Even of a color at the extreme end of the spectrum which is invisible to the human eye. He explained that a pulsed laser can vaporize metal because a laser can be concentrated onto a minute spot as small as one millionth of a meter at a power of ten thousand million watts in the pulse. He paused for Gemmel's reaction and, receiving none, continued his dissertation. He pointed out that a laser beam travels, naturally, at the speed of light: one hundred and eighty-six million miles per second. So, in effect, it takes six millionths of a second for laser light to travel one mile, during which time a supersonic airplane traveling at twice the speed of sound will have moved little more than one eighth of an inch.

Wisner was a man who reveled in statistics and they rolled off his tongue. He talked about the development of the laser. How Einstein had put forward the theory of lasers nearly fifty years before the first prototype was actually built. How during the sixties the technology had accelerated to the point where today the United States had developed high-energy gas lasers of immense power. At this point he glanced at Hawke and said, "I don't think I'm talking out of turn, Morton, if I reveal that we already have a five-megawatt laser. Something almost undreamed-of ten years ago."

"Just get on with it, Elliot," Hawke said testily. "If you talk out of turn I'll redirect you."

Wisner smiled and switched back to Gemmel, who throughout had remained attentive but impassive.

"Your basic premise," said Wisner, "is quite feasible. Certainly we can put a laser in space. It is no secret that both we and the Russians are working on satellite-borne systems that can both destroy other satellites and also destroy intercontinental ballistic missiles as they leave the earth's atmosphere en route to their targets."

"I was aware of that," Gemmel said.

Wisner carried on, unperturbed. "However, those systems can only work in space itself. They cannot work in the earth's atmosphere. Do you understand why?"

"I'm sure you'll tell me."

Wisner ignored the edge of sarcasm. He was beginning to enjoy himself. "Let me explain it in the context of your plan," he said. "We put a high-energy $CO_2$ gas laser into space. Difficult but possible, using the space shuttle. It would, incidentally, weigh in the region of twenty tons. At a predetermined time the laser would send a green beam to a point on earth." He smiled at Gemmel. "I assume green because that's the color of Islam?"

Gemmel nodded and Wisner turned to Hawke.

"It's interesting and coincidental," he said, "that green is, or would be, the most convenient color. It is least absorbed in the earth's atmosphere. We use it for communications from satellite to ground. Also from satellite to submarine, for it passes through water most easily."

"Okay," grunted Hawke, "why not get on to the crux of the problem?"

Wisner turned back to Gemmel. "The problem is, Mr. Gemmel, that you require this green beam to strike a small object, and I must tell you that from space this is impossible."

"Why?"

"Because of diversion and jitter. Also you will remember from schooldays, Mr. Gemmel, that when light passes through materials of differing density it is bent or refracted."

Now Gemmel leaned forward, his eyes boring into Wisner. "I remember my schooldays," he said, "and I also know that advanced guidance systems can correct for refraction."

"True," Wisner agreed, "but they cannot correct for the influence of cloud and atmospheric pollution—ozone pollution, for example—which causes jitter and diversion of the beam. For example, when a laser was first used to measure accurately the distance of the moon from earth, the beam had spread to a diameter of two miles by the time it reached the moon's surface. This was caused by the beam having to travel through the earth's atmosphere." He paused for effect. "Hence, Mr. Gemmel, if we fire a laser from space to the earth's surface, the beam will spread to a diameter of up to five hundred yards on impact—rather too much for your purposes, I imagine."

Wisner sat back with a satisfied air, and there was a brief silence. Hawke shrugged at Gemmel and spread his arms resignedly. But the Englishman was looking hard at Wisner.

"I suppose," he said, "that's why the laser as a weapon is considered unsuitable to be used from space into atmospheric conditions?"

"Precisely," answered Wisner. "It is, of course, a marvelous dream. But for the effect of jitter and diversion we could have lasers in space which could knock out everything from aircraft carriers to tanks. As it is, we are limited to short-range possibilities within the earth's atmosphere. In space, of course, anything is possible."

Gemmel pursed his lips, deep in thought. The others waited for his reaction.

"So you see no possibilities?" he asked finally.

Wisner shook his head sadly. "I'm afraid not. Unless we mount the device in a high-flying aircraft. Up to fifty thousand feet the diversion effect would be minimal, especially in a cloudless sky, and in the clear air of a desert atmosphere." His tone became optimistic. "Perhaps it could be so arranged that the aircraft was between the sun and the observers at the moment of firing—thus becoming invisible."

Both Gemmel and Hawke were shaking their heads.

"Radar," said Hawke. "Either Saudi radar or the Russians. They'd certainly pick it up."

Another silence, and then Gemmel asked Wisner, "Then there's no solution to this divergence and jitter problem?"

Wisner smiled condescendingly. "Mr. Gemmel, you can't argue with the basic laws of physics." He spread his hands. "Even intelligence agents must accept that."

"It was a good idea, Peter," Leo Falk said gently, "but I guess it's back to the drawing board."

Gemmel hardly seemed to hear him, he was so deep in thought. Then abruptly he looked up and said to Hawke, "Morton, I'm sorry, but I have to talk to you—in private."

"In private?"

"Yes."

There was a sudden air of tension mixed with embarrassment. Hawke glanced at Falk and then shrugged.

"Okay, Peter; so we go in the bedroom."

The other three watched with some resentment as Gemmel and Hawke went into the other room and the door closed behind them. Wisner stood up and poured himself another drink.

"I guess no one likes to have a good idea shot down," he said.

Hawke sat on the bed. Gemmel stood with his back to the door.

"I thought this project had top priority," he said.

"It does."

"Bullshit!"

Hawke took a deep breath. Controlled himself. "Ease

up, Peter," he said. "I knew you'd be disappointed. That's why I brought Wisner with me—so you'd get it from the horse's mouth."

"I got it from the horse's arsehole!"

Hawke shook his head as if to clear it. Then he erupted. "To hell with you! What are you getting at?"

Gemmel watched him steadily. "Either you're lying, or he's lying, or you're both lying."

"About what?"

Gemmel didn't answer immediately. His eyes never left Hawke's face, narrowed eyes weighing up the American. Then:

"If Operation Mirage had top priority, then you can override any other government agency?"

"Damn right!" Hawke answered emphatically.

Another silence while Gemmel chose his words.

"I need to know. How high does your authority go?"

"The top—the very top."

Gemmel smiled grimly. "Then you're getting what I think you call the bum's rush."

"You better start explaining," Hawke said grimly.

Gemmel walked over to the window and stood looking out.

"Wisner talked about diversion and jitter," he said over his shoulder. "I can tell you that more than a year ago the DoD High Energy Laser Program overcame that problem. They conducted a test in Nevada on June twelfth. The test showed that divergence had been controlled to a coefficient of point zero zero three percent." He turned to face Hawke. "Which means, in effect, that a green laser beam fired from a satellite in space would arrive on the earth's surface with a radius of just under five meters—perfect for our purposes."

Hawke's mouth had literally dropped open.

"And incidentally," Gemmel added quietly, "Elliot Wisner directed that particular test."

Hawke came to his feet. "And how in hell do you know all that?" he asked tightly.

Gemmel smiled mirthlessly. "I think I told you in Hyde Park that you people look way down on us. Well, occasionally we manage to gather some intelligence. We don't know how you did it. As Wisner said, it's against the laws of physics, and certainly the problem still exists, but for practical purposes it's now controlled. Wisner knows that. I'm prepared to believe that you don't."

Hawke's mouth tightened. "Not only do I not know it, but I don't believe it." He stood up. "I told you our project has top priority. You think Wisner would come over here and talk a load of crap in front of me?"

Gemmel turned the knife. "It appears," he said, "that there are secrets that you and, indeed, your Director are not privy to."

Hawke took the bait. "I went to the DoD with top clearance," he snarled. "Maybe you don't understand what that means."

Gemmel merely shrugged.

"Okay, smart-ass," Hawke said, "we'll soon find out. You're going to stay here with Falk and Wisner while I go to the Embassy. I'll have the answers damn quick. Then you and I will talk about the laws of physics!"

He stormed out into the lounge, and the three men looked up in consternation at his furious face.

"You!" he pointed at Meade. "Come with me. Leo, you stay here with Wisner and Gemmel. I won't be long."

In fact, he was forty minutes. For the three men left in the suite it was a long forty minutes. Obviously Gemmel wasn't going to say anything significant, so they talked casually about how dirty Paris was these days, and how expensive it had become. Gemmel was relaxed, Falk was bursting with curiosity, and Wisner appeared to be a little tense. The silences had become embarrassingly protracted by the time the door opened and Hawke entered. He was in tight control of himself, but in the manner of the lever of a grenade being clamped down. In his left hand he held a slip of flimsy pink paper. He pointed his right forefinger at Wisner and said very quietly:

"Meade is waiting for you downstairs in an Embassy car. He will drive you to the airport to connect with Pan Am's night flight to Washington. At nine o'clock tomorrow morning you will report to the Pentagon—to the Secretary of the Joint Chiefs."

He held out the slip of paper and Wisner took it, read it, and nodded slowly.

"Morton, you know how it is," he said.

"Sure, Elliot," Hawke said tightly. "Now let me tell you how it is. Within five months you are going to design and oversee the manufacture of a laser. And, Elliot, if it's not ready and working on time, and delivered to the Kennedy Space Center all neatly packaged with pink ribbon, I'm going to turn your ass into hamburger and feed it to you with a toothpick!"

So Wisner left, and Hawke poured himself four fingers of Canadian Club and a fingernail of soda and slowly calmed down and filled in Falk and tried to explain to Gemmel about interservice and interagency rivalries.

"The fucking Pentagon!" he said. "When they heard the Company was going to co-opt some of their space shuttle time they went into hysterics. Jesus, you'd think we were the fucking KGB!"

He downed his drink and poured another and suddenly threw back his head and laughed. "Cline got the Chairman of the Joint Chiefs out of a dinner party," he said. "I hope the bastard got indigestion!"

He came back and sat down and said to Gemmel, "The Embassy's got one hell of a communications setup. While I was waiting for answers the guy in charge was explaining it to me. You know what they're using these days for the ultra-secret stuff?"

Gemmel shook his head and Hawke grinned.

"They bounce lasers off satellites!"

At about the same time that Elliot Wisner was taking

off from Charles de Gaulle Airport, Brian Beecher was walking down the Thames Embankment in London. He stopped frequently to gaze out over the dark river, and the lights of the moving river traffic. He was dressed in a dark overcoat a little too big for him, and he was a small, insignificant, lonely figure. Opposite the lawns of the Inns of Court he stopped yet again. A tug was moving down the river, towing three barges, loaded and low in the water. He could just make out their shapes in the light reflected from the buildings on the opposite bank. Behind him road traffic moved, one way toward the City and the other way toward the Houses of Parliament. But there were few pedestrians. He stood still, never looking around. There was a large trash can at his left, chained into a corner of the thick stone wall. After fifteen minutes there came the sound of the horn of a car passing. It hooted twice, and then twice more. Beecher reached into his overcoat pocket, took out a small brown envelope, dropped it behind the trash can, and moved on.

An hour later, another pedestrian moved down the Embankment. He too wore a dark overcoat, but he was a big man, and although he was alone, he did not have an aura of loneliness. However, he stopped frequently and surveyed the river, and he too eventually stopped by the same trash can. Again, after fifteen minutes, the same car passed behind him and played the same tune on it's horn. All was clear. He reached down behind the trash can and retrieved the envelope and continued on up the Embankment.

# Book
## two

# eight

It had snowed heavily during the night and a huge snowplow moved up the broad avenue, rearranging the wet mush into parallel lines on the edge of the sidewalk. Moscow is not a city with a traffic problem. In fact, anyone who owns a car has to be relatively important. Consequently that segment of society that could be inconvenienced by snow-filled roads is in a position of power. Consequently Moscow has one of the most efficient snow-clearing departments of any city in the world.

Vassili Gordik looked down from his eighth-story office window and watched the snowplow turn the corner, then he turned back to the room.

"So what is it?" he asked in his bass voice.

The six men and one woman grouped around the conference table looked at him in respect and silence.

It was a very large office and nicely furnished. Apart from the conference table, which dominated the center of the room, there was Gordik's own large leather-topped desk and in one corner a grouping of comfortable armchairs and a coffee table. A well-stocked bar with four barstools took up another corner. The furniture was all heavy and of a pseudo-antique design, but still gave off a solid and comfortable aura. The only jarring note came from the large televisionlike screen that covered half of the wall facing the desk.

"So what is it?" Gordik repeated, moving back toward the table.

The six men all looked anxious. The woman didn't. Obviously she was not required to provide any answers. She was in her early thirties, with an angular but attractive face, under black hair cut in a bobbed style. She wore an oatmeal tweed skirt and a pale blue cashmere sweater set, adorned by a single strand of large black pearls.

Gordik took his seat at the head of the table and sighed.

"There are gathered around this table the supposedly best brains of the KGB's Research and Analysis Directorate. For two days now you have all studied the information and yet you resemble a reject batch of stuffed dummies!"

From both sides of the table the men regarded him solemnly. The woman sat looking down at the small computer terminal on the table in front of her.

"Larissa," Gordik said, "perhaps you have an answer?"

His tone became sarcastic as his gaze swept the six men. "After all, you are not an expert; maybe your head is not filled with such knowledge and learning that your tongue is paralyzed."

She smiled and it softened the severe lines of her face. "The one obvious aspect," she said, "is that it's a major operation."

"Good! Good!" exclaimed Gordik. "Let's use that as a starting point." He turned to the man on his right. "Lev, I'm moving slowly up the intelligence ladder. As my assistant, surely you are less intelligent than the others gathered here today. Would you care to add to Larissa's observation?"

Lev Tudin also smiled. He had been Gordik's assistant for five years, and well knew his boss's bantering style. He also knew that the others around the table would never

volunteer an opinion. It was the way with a rigid bu-
reaucracy: never stick your neck out unless you absolutely
have to and especially not when Vassili Gordik was chair-
ing a meeting.

"It's a major operation concerning the Middle East," he
said.

Gordik sighed. "Brilliant! No, I mean it, Lev; don't be
discouraged." Abruptly his voice hardened. "Now, listen.
All of you. After forty-eight hours I've managed to elicit
the bare opinion that it's a major operation aimed at the
Middle East. I knew that forty-seven hours and fifty-nine
minutes ago!"

He pulled his chair up closer to the table.

"Now I'm going to recap," he said. "And then you are
going to offer at least a small segment of the fruits of your
gray cells." He steepled his fingers and gazed down the
table at the woman. "Larissa," he said, "put up the names
again."

The woman tapped at the keys and all the men turned
to look at the large screen on the wall. Five names appeared on it in two groups: Morton Hawke, Leo Falk,
and Silas Meade in one group; Peter Gemmel and Alan
Boyd in the other.

"Formidable," Gordik said. "You might even say the
cream of the cream. Now, what does that composition tell
us? First, that it's a major operation. Important enough
that Falk has been seconded from heading up one of the
CIA's most important departments. Gemmel, I need
hardly tell you, is Deputy Head of Operations, MI-Six.
Coincidentally, Falk and Gemmel are both Arabists."

He reached into his inside jacket pocket, extracted a
short, fat cigar, took a tiny silver guillotine from a fob
pocket, and snipped off the end. Tudin reached over and
flicked a lighter, and Gordik drew in the smoke contentedly.

"April fifteenth," he resumed. "They all meet up in Lisbon at the Ritz Hotel. Then Gemmel goes off to Cairo
for four days. He meets Hawke, Falk, and Meade three

days later in Paris. There was another American present; at this point we don't know his identity. That meeting took place at the George Cinq." Gordik smiled sardonically. "At least they have good taste in hotels. In the meantime Boyd has dropped out of sight."

He turned to the man on his left, a studious bespectacled type. "Now, Malin, how do you read it?"

Malin shuffled some papers on the table, adjusted his spectacles, and spoke in a nervous, high-pitched voice.

"First, I discount Israel. The Americans would not involve the British. Besides, they are convinced that the Israeli-Egyptian accord is the only solution." He glanced around the table for any sign of support, and receiving none, he plunged on. "I see three prime areas: first, the destabilization of Syria; second, a vengeful swipe at Iran; and third, an attack on the PLO—again an effort at destabilization."

He sat back in his chair, pulled out a white hankerchief, took off his glasses, and polished them vigorously.

"Not brilliant," said Gordik, "but not entirely stupid either. So, having started, let's continue."

One by one he elicited opinions from the other four experts. They were all similarly vague. A silence descended on the table, and Gordik puffed thoughtfully at his cigar. Finally Malin ventured to speak.

"We have limited information, Comrade Gordik," he said defensively. "Is it possible that our source can be more specific?"

Gordik shook his head. "Our source has been transferred to another department. We are lucky that briefly he had any contact with the operation."

"Is he under suspicion?" asked Malin.

Gordik snorted in derision. "I doubt it. He's having a long love affair with a particular brand of Scotch whisky!"

Malin became emboldened to ask, "So we have to rely on information from alcoholics?"

For a long moment Gordik eyed him, much as a tiger

might survey its dinner. Malin pulled back his neck down into his collar.

"Times change," Gordik finally said with a sigh. "We used to be able to ring up Petworth House and find out what the British Prime Minister was having for lunch, but they put down rat poison and our little alcoholic is the last of a long line." He smiled grimly. "But he may have come up with a drunken swansong." He stood up. "That's all, but try to keep your minds working, and do let me know if anything occurs to you."

He crossed over to the bar, and while the five men gathered their papers and filed out, he poured measures of Chivas Regal into three glasses. As the door closed, Tudin and Larissa moved to the bar and took their drinks.

"They weren't much help," Tudin commented.

"It's the system," Gordik answered with a grimace. "Whenever a department head wants to get rid of a bit of dead wood he shunts it off to the Research and Analysis Directorate. I didn't really expect anything—I was just going through the motions." He drained his glass and Larissa reached over and poured him another. She had worked for Gordik for three years now. Before that she had been a computer programmer in the KGB's main computer center. She had been required to write a program for the collation of all financial transactions within the organization. At that time Gordik had just come in from the field to reorganize the internal structure of the KGB. He was a hard worker who combined toughness with imagination. For two years he wielded a stiff broom and made several enemies, but he also impressed that section of the Politburo which oversaw the Soviet intelligence community, and he quietly built himself a solid power base. As a reward he was given the plum job of Director, Overseas Operations. His one regret was that he had been unable to do anything meaningful about the Research and Analysis Directorate.

Shortly after she had finished her program, Larissa had

been called to Gordik's office. He had first complimented her on the work and then gone on to question her for over an hour about her background and experience. A week later she was transferred to his department as his personal assistant.

It had taken about six months for her to fall in love with him. He was not an easy man to fall in love with. In the first place he kept his emotions tightly buttoned down and his private life very private. After that first meeting she had risked her security clearance and her position when she quietly ran a computer profile on him. She learned that he had been born in Riga forty-nine years before. Both his parents had been active in the Revolution and his father had risen to reasonable heights in the Agricultural Ministry. So Gordik had the benefit of an excellent education. Unlike many senior KGB officers he had not used the army as a stepping-stone, but had been recruited straight from university, where he had taken a degree in psychology. After training he spent seven years virtually as a Head Office administrator until finally he had maneuvered himself into Covert Operations and a field post in Mexico. From then on, his rise had been rapid, and he served in many parts of the world, ending up as Director of Covert Operations for first the Middle East and then southeast Asia, before being called to Moscow for his broom-wielding job.

She knew that he was married, with one son at university and another in the army. For the past five years his wife had spent most of her time at his official Black Sea dacha, and he hardly ever talked to her.

She looked at him now as he sat on a barstool, sipping his Scotch and thinking deeply, remote from Tudin or herself. He was a large man, not overweight but at first appearance seeming so, for he was broad across the shoulders and torso, and stood well over six feet. His size and strength were disguised somewhat for he always wore well-cut Italian suits. His face was also broad, with a strong mouth and jaw offset by wide, intelligent eyes. His hair was dark brown and, for a Russian official, surprisingly long. Since they had become lovers Larissa had trimmed it for him every two to three weeks. She had a gift for it, and it had become a ritual which always ended in lovemaking. In spite of his size he was a gentle and considerate lover. He had arranged for her to have a small but comfortable apartment close to the office, and during the early months he had brought back several gifts from his trips abroad. First a Sony micro-stereo set and half a suitcase of cassettes, evenly divided between classical music, which he liked, and modern jazz, which she preferred. Then a color television set and a video recorder, again with a good selection of films, and these they would exchange with friends who also traveled to the West. There followed clothes and small items of jewelry, for he was by nature a generous man. In the evenings she would prepare a simple but imaginative meal, and afterward they would listen to some music, alternating between her preferences and his. The television and video she kept in the bedroom and they would end up in bed, watching a movie or making love, or both.

She kept her life deftly compartmentalized between the office and home. At one, the perfect secretary and deferential assistant; at the other, an intimate companion. He had never yet told her that he loved her, but she knew he did. She was aware that she made him relax and she was content. Of course, their relationship was well known in the Department and Gordik made no secret of it. His nature, and his exalted position, made secrecy both distasteful and unnecessary.

But only Lev Tudin was able to judge the depths of feeling between them, for when the three were alone together Gordik allowed himself the ease of familiarity. Tudin was almost a younger version of Gordik. He too was a big, intelligent man who had joined the KGB straight from university. But he had less of Gordik's physical coordination, and although he had a sharp and intelligent mind, his body was somewhat clumsy. Gordik and Larissa used to tease him about it occasionally, a teasing which he took in good humor.

"I'm a chess player, not an athlete," he liked to point out.

He was a very good chess player, and the fact that Gordik was one of the few people he could not regularly and easily beat added a dimension to the respect he felt for his boss.

He looked up now and saw Gordik's eyes on him.

"I won't just wait," Gordik said emphatically. "I won't just watch and wait for something to happen!"

"You'll mount an operation?" Tudin asked.

Gordik smiled ruefully. "Yes, I will, but the only problem is, what kind of operation—and against whom?"

"There's no chance," Larissa interjected, "that our source can provide any more information?"

Gordik shook his head, stood up, and began to pace. "No, they've put him in charge of Pensions and Welfare; we know every MI-Six pensioner and we're not exactly interested in their welfare!"

He stopped pacing and looked at his two assistants sitting at the bar.

"In a way it's curious," he said. "After all, the British must know he's an alcoholic and yet they let him come close to something as big as this. Even though only briefly and only on the fringes."

"It could be a bureaucratic fumble," Tudin suggested. "It happens often enough, even here."

Gordik laughed shortly. "That's true, and obviously they quickly picked it up—or maybe the Americans did." He started pacing again. "Anyway, it's something to keep in mind. But right now we need to come up with something positive. I'm not going to be passive. Let's go over it again."

For the next half hour they went through the permutations. Occasionally Larissa would move to the computer terminal and put information onto the screen. Slowly they reached a consensus. The Americans were certainly

mounting and controlling an operation aimed at a Middle
East country or countries, and possibly the Russians' position in that country. The fact that they were using the
British as a spearhead must contain the vital clue. Obviously they would be reluctant to use the British for any
number of reasons, so therefore they were extremely nervous about being caught in a compromising position. The
British, on the other hand, were used to it. In a logical
sequence they eliminated country after country until they
were left with five prime possibilities: Libya and Syria,
because of the Russians' influence in those countries; and
the PLO and Lebanon, because of their connection with
a general Middle East peace settlement; finally—Saudi
Arabia. The Americans may have concluded that the ruling family were not going to hold the reins of power much
longer and the CIA may have decided to pre-empt a revolution and make sure that they themselves could control
any move toward a more democratic or popular government.

"After all," Tudin pointed out, "we must assume that
they have learned some lessons from the fall of the Shah
and what followed."

"And it would explain the British," Larissa commented.
"If the operation were exposed, they would take the blame
—and with their oil they have less to lose."

Gordik poured himself more Scotch and, glass in hand,
started pacing again.

"I agree," he said. "I like the logic of it, and such an
operation would account for the quality of the people involved. Anyway, it's certain that with their new freedom,
the CIA will be increasing their activities in the Middle
East. They're not going to sit around bleating about human rights and watching their influence there totally dis-
integrate. So, now we've managed to isolate several possibilities. It remains to decide on our response."

For the next hour they threw suggestions back and
forth, while the level of Scotch in the bottle dropped
steadily. Both Gordik and Tudin could be prodigious

drinkers, though outwardly they hardly seemed affected. Gordik claimed it helped to expand his imagination. Tudin claimed nothing; he just liked Scotch, especially Chivas Regal.

Gordik by nature was an attacker. While obviously he would increase surveillance on all the individuals concerned and put all KGB stations in the Middle East, the USA, and Britain on full alert, he was not content with that. No; Gordik would attack and learn more, and slowly the discussion turned to ways and means and, above all, a suitable target.

Once more Larissa threw the names up onto the screen, and each individual was discussed and analyzed, and one by one their known histories were displayed on the screen.

Finally Gordik said, "It's got to be one of the British. I see no chance at getting to any of the Americans. Apart from anything else, the CIA is infinitely more security-conscious than MI-Six—in spite of recent events."

"Boyd?" Tudin asked.

Gordik smiled and shook his head. "No, Lev, we aim at the top: Gemmel."

Both Larissa and Tudin showed their surprise. They both knew that Gordik had a definite respect, even admiration, for the Englishman.

"Yes, I know," Gordik said with another smile. "He's tough and unemotional, and very professional. He has a truly excellent record and on the surface he looks impenetrable." He paused for effect. "But neither of you is a psychologist, and although you know details of his life and his life-style, you fail to draw a conclusion about the man himself." He waved his hand at Larissa. "Put him up again."

She worked the keyboard and then they all looked up at the screen. First came a series of still photographs, some clear and some badly defined. Then a short segment of moving film, showing Gemmel coming out of a building, crossing the street, and getting into a car. The film was black and white and had obviously been shot from concealment and was of poor quality. But still Larissa thought him attractive and assured, and noticed his easy stride and athletic frame. Next came a photograph of a smiling young woman with the caption: "Judith Gemmel. Married to subject August 14, 1968. Died in childbirth together with premature son, 1971."

There followed a personal history of Gemmel, starting with details of his parents and his date of birth. It followed him through school and university, listing his academic and sporting achievements. It noted that he was an accomplished linguist, fluent in Arabic, Parsi, French, Spanish, and Russian, and with a working knowledge of six other languages.

Next came the date and manner of his recruitment by MI6 and his subsequent history with that organization. This became sequentially more sparse as various coded suffixes showing sources were eliminated from the screen. It was no coincidence that each period could be related to the uncovering of yet another KGB mole within the British intelligence community.

Then the computer gave details of Gemmel's private life: his hobbies and interests, the occasional name of a fleeting girl friend. Finally came the opinion of the KGB's Research and Analysis Directorate, which broadly confirmed Gordik's own view.

The screen went blank and Gordik said, "Very impressive, but now let's probe for a weakness." He spread his left hand and counted on his fingers.

"One: Gemmel is a tough, dedicated, unemotional professional. Two: since the death of his wife he has led a quiet, indeed reserved, social life. He has very, very few close friends. Three: his only hobbies are sailing and the ballet. Curious hobbies in a way—one very active and one very passive. You might say that the ballet is more curious than the other were it not for the simple fact that

Gemmel—Peter George Gemmel . . ."—Gordik smiled in anticipation—"is, deep down inside his cast-iron exterior, a romantic!"

Tudin and Larissa looked at each other and then Tudin burst out laughing. Gordik didn't react but watched Larissa carefully. She was silent for a long moment, and then as Tudin's laughter trailed off she started to nod her head slowly.

"You see, Lev," Godik said triumphantly, "a psychologist's analysis confirmed by a woman's intuition."

"You agree?" Tudin asked her.

"Yes, I see it now. Sailing is a romantic sport and ballet is the most romantic art form." She smiled at Gordik. "But, Vassili, that's not why I agree with you."

"No?"

"No, you're right; it's more intuition. I see it in his face, the way he moves."

Tudin smiled. "You find him attractive?"

"Yes, very. I can assure you that many women—most women—would find him attractive."

"Good!" Gordik said heartily.

Tudin began shaking his head—not negatively, but in a sort of daze. "A honey trap?" he asked the smiling Gordik. "You're going to try a honey trap on the Deputy Head of Operations of MI-Six?"

"Yes," Gordik answered firmly, "but a very special honey trap. One that would make a bear climb over the Urals from one side to the other with hardly a pause for breath!"

"That's why he never remarried," Larissa mused. She looked up at the two men. "Why he never took another woman. He's a romantic. He still loves his dead wife."

"You may be right, Larissa," Gordik responded. "But ten years is too long to pine over any woman. What do you think, Lev?"

"Far too long," Tudin agreed solemnly.

# nine

THE CROWD SURGED OUT OF THE PARIS OPERA HOUSE AND carried Gemmel and Hawke onto the sidewalk. They picked their moment and dodged the traffic and crossed to the other side of the street. Gemmel took Hawke's arm and guided him to a small bistro. They ducked in out of the cold, took off their topcoats, left them on hooks by the door, found a small corner table, and ordered coffee and Cognacs.

"I enjoyed it," Hawke said. "No, I really did. I did!"

"You fidgeted!"

"I always fidget!"

The waiter brought the drinks and Gemmel poured his Cognac into his coffee.

"I'll be honest," Hawke said earnestly. "In fact, if I hadn't liked it, I'd have left and gone to the Crazy Horse Saloon or something, believe me!"

Gemmel surveyed him closely, then he smiled. "Morton, I believe you. Don't protest too much."

Hawke returned the smile and visibly relaxed. "Okay, but I want you to believe me."

"I do. Were you surprised?"

Hawke thought about it for a moment and then nodded.

"I was. I mean, for the first fifteen minutes or so I wondered what the hell I was doing there. And then it sort of crept up on me."

"Good." Gemmel was obviously pleased. "I would have liked to introduce you to ballet in a less abrupt manner. Something classical; but the Béjart ballet is excitingly different and I didn't want you to be bored."

Hawke took a sip of his Cognac and then, as Gemmel had, poured it into his coffee. "I think I understand you a little better."

"You do?"

"Yes. For the past two hours you've been relaxed. It's the first time I've seen it."

In fact Hawke was quietly congratulating himself. He had sent Falk back to the States to watch over Wisner, and stayed on himself in Paris for a few extra days in an effort to get to know Gemmel better.

"I'll come to the ballet with you," he had said, and Gemmel had laughed.

"In the unlikely event that you get a ticket, you'd hate it!"

But Hawke had called the Ambassador and strings had been jerked and the best box in the theatre sequestered, and to Hawke's genuine astonishment he had enjoyed it.

"I spoke to Falk from the Embassy today," he said.

"How does it go?" asked Gemmel.

"I have to give Wisner credit. Once he got the word from on high he really moved. Falk says he's treating the whole thing as a personal challenge. He's already got his design team together and they moved to California yesterday. Air Force Plant Number Forty-two in Palmdale will build the laser. It appears there are no major construction problems. There is, however, the crucial factor of aiming the thing."

"I understand that," Gemmel said. "After all, it's got to hit a small lamb from a hell of a distance."

"Oh, it's quite feasible and you know it. The problem is that either we have to know the precise location of the target beforehand, or the target would have to contain a homing device that the laser could lock onto; that would mean a bigger lamb than you might be thinking of."

Gemmel smiled. "Morton, a lamb can be just so big, then it becomes a sheep! Let me think a moment."

Gemmel sat back in his chair, his mind moving ahead to the events that would take place in the Minā valley during the Haj. He pictured the vast multitude, perhaps more than two and a half million people.

Meanwhile, Hawke glanced around the crowded room. He wasn't concerned about security—listening devices or such. The bistro had been randomly selected at the last moment. He picked out his own two men from the Paris station. One sat in a corner, reading a newspaper. The other was near the door, trying to keep his eyes off an attractive brunette at the next table.

"It can't be done," Gemmel said, and Hawke switched his attention back. "I mean, deciding the exact location. There are going to be millions of people milling about. We could only define an area no smaller than an acre."

"That wouldn't do," Hawke said. "Which means we have to go for the homing device, and in that case Wisner suggests we incorporate a destruct mechanism which would burn up the lamb—or sheep. That makes the design of the laser easier; it wouldn't have to vaporize anything."

"How big would it be? I mean the homing device and mechanism?"

"We'll know in a week or ten days, so there's plenty of time, but Wisner thinks no bigger than a cigar box. It's incredible what chip technology has achieved."

"Then it won't be a problem. We just arrange for a largish lamb!"

Hawke glanced at his watch. "I'll stop off at the Embassy and call Falk. It'll be midafternoon in Los Angeles. Now, what about your end?"

Gemmel briefed him on the search for candidates for the Mahdi. They had set a deadline for the end of June for a final decision and for the end of July for the personal miracle. That would give them three months to cultivate a following.

In the meantime field agents were active in starting the program of disinformation. Gemmel explained that anytime now the rumors and talk of the coming of the Mahdi would start, from Indonesia in the east, to Morocco in the west, and particularly in the great Islamic crescent of the Middle East. The timing was perfect. This was the fourteenth-hundred year of Islam, and within Islamic lore and mythology there were many omens of the coming of the new Prophet who would purify the religion and heal the schisms.

After ordering more coffee and Cognacs they went on to discuss the recent handing over of the CIA's mole in Jeddah to Boyd's control.

"It went well," Hawke said. "As you know, he's already started the ball rolling."

"Yes," Gemmel replied. "Boyd thinks he's perfect."

Finally Gemmel made his pitch and Hawke smiled, for he had long been expecting it.

"I was thinking," Gemmel said casually, "that it might be a good idea if we had a liaison man at your end—you know, at the hardware end?"

Hawke also spoke casually. "You mean in California? With the laser?"

"Exactly; after all, as the moment gets closer, we're going to need instant communication."

Hawke grinned. "Forget it, Peter. Okay, so your guys found out that we've controlled the divergence problem. But that's all you're going to find out—not how."

"Oh, come on, Morton!"

Hawke kept his grin. "Falk told me something else today. Wisner is incorporating a destruct mechanism in the satellite that contains the laser. Within seconds of that green beam lighting up your lamb, there's going to be an explosion in space and all the little bits are going to be making an unending journey through the cosmos—on the direct orders of the Chairman of the Joint Chiefs!"

"That's understandable."

"Damn right it is. You look after your end, Peter, and we'll look after ours. Now, what about the next meeting?"

They decided that Madrid would be a good venue. They set a date six weeks hence, by which time Operation Mirage should be nicely rolling.

"I take it that Madrid has a good ballet company?" Hawke asked with a smile.

"Yes, it has." Gemmel laughed. "And I missed it the last time I was in Spain."

A group of small schoolgirls in white-and-blue uniforms stood in hushed awe near the door of the cavernous room. There were about thirty dancers going through their exercise and practice routines, but all of the girls were watching just one dancer, a young woman who was practicing alone at the wall bar. She wore black woolen leg warmers and a black leotard, which contrasted vividly with the white skin of her shoulders and arms. She had a narrow, pointed face, but so perfect in proportion as to appear only slender. Her jet black hair was pulled up into a ponytail, which swung gracefully as she practiced fouettés.

The girls were on an outing from the Leningrad State Ballet School, and each of them desired nothing less than to become, in time, a prima ballerina. So it was understandable that they largely ignored the other dancers and watched only the young woman in black, for she was Maya Kashva, prima ballerina of the Maly Ballet Company of Leningrad, and at twenty-four one of the youngest ballet stars of all Russia. Their instructor had told the girls that after the practice it might be possible for them to meet Miss Kashva, maybe even talk to her, and each of them felt a thrill of anticipation.

But they were disappointed, for a few minutes later an instructor entered the room, crossed to the young woman, and spoke to her.

"Maya, the director would like to see you in his office."

The ballerina's face showed surprise. "Now? During class? Why?"

"I've no idea. Obviously it's urgent."

With a faint look of irritation Maya moved to a chair, picked up a black sweater, and struggled into it as she walked with inborn and perfected grace across the vast room. The group of schoolgirls shuffled aside, and as she passed them, her face lost its irritation and she smiled, melting a dozen young hearts.

The director surveyed the anxious face across his desk.

"Believe me, Maya, I don't know. The Ministry of Culture rang, just half an hour ago. A plane is on its way from Moscow to pick you up. A special plane. You are to be at the airport in two hours."

"But why?"

The director sighed. "Truly, I don't know. If I did I would tell you. All they said was that you would stay in Moscow for about a week—so you will miss at least three performances."

"And the tour?" Maya asked desperately.

He smiled. "Relax, little one. I asked them about that. They said you will definitely be on the tour."

The exquisite face brightened a little.

"Come now," said the director, "it cannot be so serious. Maybe they want you for publicity or something—to take photographs perhaps."

"But they would have told you."

He nodded thoughtfully. "Yes, I suppose so. But one never knows. Obviously somebody very important wants to see you. They don't send special planes just for nothing."

It began in the Indonesian city of Macassar, on the island of Celebes. Within a week it had swept across the Sunda Strait to Java and the capital, Jakarta.

"The Chosen One will come. He will come at the time of the Haj."

Such rumors, such omens, are not uncommon. Not to Islam or to other religions based on the word of God being transmitted, or even translated, by mortals. Many people took no notice on this occasion, but a traveler moving between the islands would have heard the same rumor repeated—and always in the same vein—from Sumatra to Borneo, even to Bali. "The Chosen One will come at the Haj." The Islamic population of Indonesia totals over one hundred million, and the rumor quickly began to filter through.

In Pakistan it came out of the Punjab and within a week was being repeated and embellished on the shores of the Indian Ocean.

In Afghanistan it caused concern among the "occupying" Russian hierarchy. At the regular weekly meeting the political "adviser" brought up the subject. He did so tentatively, for his audience consisted of military men who dealt in facts, not rumors. But the General Commanding Soviet Troops did not react with disdain.

"That's the final straw," he said with a wince. "The rebels already consider that they're fighting a holy war, a jihad. The last thing we need is some prophet telling them to fight even harder!"

The military rulers in Turkey were similarly disquieted. Theirs was the first Islamic state, under Ataturk, to renounce the Koran as an instrument of government. The shock waves coming out of Iran were already rocking the foundations of the secular structure. Instructions went out that any such rumors were to be nipped in the bud. The military rulers never considered that such instructions could only have an opposite effect.

Iran itself provided the hottest bed. The majority of believers are Shi'ites, and it is a pillar of that sect that one day the son of the murdered Fourth Caliph will reappear as the savior of Islam. The timing was propitious.

Throughout the Islamic crescent the rumors started almost simultaneously, as they did south of the Sahara and among the fanatical Muslim sects of northern Nigeria.

"At the Haj" became synonymous with a password. Many of the faithful—as well as some of the curious who had not previously considered making the pilgrimage—were now determined to do so.

Particular concern was felt in the kingdom of Saudi Arabia and in Syria. The ruling family of Saudi Arabia considered themselves the guardians of the holy places in Mecca and Medina and had recently been massively embarrassed when a group of religious fundamentalists, led by a self-proclaimed Mahdi, had taken over the Grand Mosque in Mecca and held it for many days before being captured after great loss of life. It was to be expected that during the fourteen-hundredth anniversay of Islam there would be stepped-up activity by zealots; the palace guard and the religious police were already on the alert for the appearance of any new religious aberrations.

In Syria the government faced the problem of the Muslim Brotherhood, the Ikhwan, a secret society not only fundamentalist but dedicated to overthrowing the government by violence. The Brotherhood had slaughtered members of the army and the police, government officials, and even Russian advisers. The idea of their religious fervor being intensified by the appearance of a new Prophet didn't bear thinking about.

Had the Islamic states maintained a more intimate form of communication, it might have become apparent that the simultaneous start of the rumors was more than coincidence. But most observers put it down to the advent of the onset of the fourteen-hundredth anniversary of Islam.

Gordik was dumbfounded. After twenty-five years as an officer of the KGB he doubted that anything could really surprise him. But he was totally astounded.

He stood in his office looking down at Maya Kashva,

who sat perched on the edge of a chair, looking back with large, black, frightened eyes.

Larissa and Lev Tudin sat opposite her across the conference table. Their faces mirrored Gordik's astonishment.

He threw up his arms and exclaimed, "I don't believe it!"

"It's true," Maya said in a low voice.

"A virgin?" Gordik roared, and she nodded and cast her eyes down as though ashamed.

"I don't believe it!" Gordik repeated and looked at Tudin, who started laughing.

Then Maya began to weep and Larissa moved around the table to comfort her. She glared up at Gordik.

"Of course it's true."

"A virgin at twenty-four?"

"And why not?"

Gordik looked again at Tudin, who spread his arms in resignation.

"Some kind of swallow," he said, and stood up, moved to the bar, and raised an eyebrow at Gordik.

"Go ahead," Gordik said grimly. "And pour me one also—a big one!"

Gordik was in a quandary. The interview had started so well. He had felt a surge of confidence the moment the young ballerina had been shown into his office. Her beauty, her grace, her vulnerability had made an immediate impact. He could not imagine any normal man being able to turn away from such a creature. Especially when called upon to provide both protection and comfort.

He had gently explained to her what was required, and then, as she began to protest, had applied the necessary pressure. Reminded her that her late father had been a high official in the military branch of the KGB, that it was his position that had opened the doors for her first to be enrolled in the best state ballet school in Russia, and then to be accepted by the Maly Ballet Company at the unusually young age of sixteen.

Then he had seen the fire in her as she flared up and defended her talent, and her hard work. She pointed out coldly that there were thousands, tens of thousands of daughters of senior government officials who had the ambition to succeed in her profession.

"A dozen—no more," she had said disdainfully, "had the talent and the will to make it to the top."

Gordik had disarmingly agreed, but nevertheless her father's position had greatly helped. She owed a debt, both to her father and to her country.

Then she had become emotional. Her father would never have sanctioned such a thing. He would have been horrified. Again Gordik had agreed, but her father, regretfully, was dead, and it was left to others to ensure the security of the state, of Mother Russia. He regretted the necessity, but it was unavoidable. Besides, was it such a hardship? She was asked to defect in London while on the forthcoming tour. Not an event that was totally alien to Russian ballet dancers. She was to throw herself on the mercy of one man, a British official. Circumstances made it most probable that he would be very sympathetic. She was to gain his confidence and his affection and, thereafter, certain information. Having accomplished this task, she could then decide whether to stay in the West and pursue her career there, or redefect to the Soviet Union and be assured of a glorious professional future, and the unending gratitude of her government.

It had taken him two hours to break her down, alternately threatening and then cajoling. Finally she appeared to submit and asked in a small voice, "So I have to go to bed with this man? To sleep with him?"

Gordik had nodded. "I think that would prove necessary."

"And if he doesn't like me?" It was said with an ingenuous wistfulness, tinged with apprehension.

Gordik had studied her for a long moment and then glanced at Tudin. "What do you think, Lev? Is that a possibility?"

"Obviously," Lev had answered. "About as possible as Stalin being reincarnated as the British Queen's pet corgi!"

Gordik observed the young woman again and then said with satisfaction, "Even less possible, I imagine."

Maya had kept glancing at Larissa for feminine support, but Larissa's face was expressionless. Finally Maya had asked Gordik, "So I have to seduce this man?"

"Of course."

"Like a common prostitute?"

Larissa had interjected, "Miss Kashva, look at it that way if you wish. But it is no shame to prostitute yourself for your country. A country that has given you so much."

Another silence, and then Maya said quietly, almost speaking to herself, "But a prostitute has skills—must have skills—and experience. I have no such skills. I would not know even how to begin."

Gordik felt that they were making progress. "My dear Miss Kashva. Believe me, that will not be a problem. He is not an unattractive man." He glanced wryly at Larissa. "I am assured of that. You will simply have to treat him as you must surely have treated other men—other lovers."

And it was then that the prima ballerina had dropped her bombshell, saying, with embarrassed defiance, "But, Comrade Gordik, I have had no lovers."

"None?"

She shook her lovely head.

"None?" he repeated. "Are you telling me you're a virgin?"

She had nodded again and looked up at him with trepidation.

Tudin crossed the room and gave a glass of Scotch to Gordik, who took a deep gulp and sighed wearily.

Maya was drying her eyes with Larissa's handkerchief.

"Larissa," Gordik said, "take her out and give her some tea or something."

Larissa took the ballerina's arm and led her, still sobbing, to the door. As it closed behind them Gordik asked Tudin, "So, what do you think, Lev?"

"I think we send her to the Swallow School."

Gordik grimaced. "If I'd had my way I'd have closed that place years ago."

Tudin brought over the bottle and refilled his boss's glass. "On the other hand," he said, "they've had their successes and I can't imagine sending a totally inexperienced girl on such a mission. The least she needs to know is how to unzip his pants."

"You may be right," Gordik answered glumly. "But it's going to have to be a crash course. The Maly company leaves for the West in three weeks, and meantime she has to learn other types of tradecraft."

"What about control?" Tudin asked. "After all, she's young and impressionable. Patriotism alone won't be enough."

Gordik sighed. "I know it. Control will be through her mother. They are extremely close. The position will be made very clear. She does her best or her maternal attachments are ended forthwith."

Tudin knew his boss. He sipped his drink and looked at Gordik enigmatically. Gordik glanced at him and said irritably, "All right, all right! So I'll be bluffing. You know it and Larissa will guess it but our young ballerina will not! And she'll behave accordingly."

He thought for a moment and then said, "As well as the stick I'll offer her a carrot. If she behaves, and if she succeeds, and if she decides to stay in the West, I'll allow her mother to join her. What do you think?"

Tudin smiled but didn't answer.

Gordik snorted in irritation and said, "All right, I know what you're thinking. You're wondering how anyone as soft as me ever reached this far in our profession!"

Tudin's smile deepened to a grin. "Not exactly," he said. "I was hoping that Gemmel is as soft as you are!"

Gordik was about to respond when the door opened

and Larissa ushered in Maya. She was more composed, but still nervous.

"I think it might help," Larissa said firmly, "if Maya was able to get an impression of the subject."

She crossed to the computer terminal with an inquiring arch of a shapely eyebrow.

Gordik nodded and all three watched as first she considered carefully and then punched the keys. All their eyes turned to the giant screen. Larissa had selected the photograph with a woman's vision. It was a close-up of Gemmel's head and shoulders, slightly blurred by the enlargement. Half of his face was in soft shadow, and his eyes were narrowed as he looked away to his left.

"I know him," Maya said. All eyes turned to her, and although the office floor was thickly carpeted, a dropping pin would have reverberated in the silence.

Gordik was the first to recover. "What did you say?"

"I know him. His name is Gemmel—Peter Gemmel."

"How?"

Maya looked at him anxiously and he softened his tone. "How do you know him, Miss Kashva?"

"It was in Brussels," she answered hesitantly. "When we toured in the West three years ago. I was only a quarter dancer then, but I understudied Olga Lanov for her role in *Paquita*. She became ill and I danced the last performance. It was . . . it was a big chance for me and I danced it well. After the performance there was a reception and he was there. He was introduced to me as someone important in ballet circles in London. He spoke very good Russian."

"What did you talk about?" Tudin asked.

"Oh, just about ballet. He was very knowledgeable. He said it was a pity we weren't visiting London."

"Did you like him?" Larissa interjected quietly.

Maya lowered her eyes. "Yes, he was . . . he was sympathetic. And he told me how much he enjoyed my performance and that one day I would be a great dancer."

"What else?" Gordik asked, consumed with curiosity.

"That's all."

"That's all?"

"Yes. Comrade Savich came over and took me away."

"Who's Savich?"

Tudin interrupted. "Yarov Savich, tour control officer at the Ministry of Culture. One of ours."

Gordik nodded slowly. "I see."

"He told me to be careful," Maya continued. "He said that Gemmel was a Western spy. I didn't believe it."

"Did he indeed?" Gordik said ominously.

"Yes. I think he was jealous. All through the tour he'd sort of bothered me . . ." She looked up at Larissa. "You know what I mean?"

Larissa nodded in sympathy. Gordik gave a certain look to Tudin, who crossed to the table, took out a pen, and made a note.

"Did Gemmel like you?" Gordik asked. "After all, a woman always knows."

After a pause Maya answered shyly, "I think so."

"You only think so?"

She looked him firmly in the eye. "He liked me."

Gordik savored his fourth Scotch. He sat on a bar stool with his heels hooked over the bar rail. He had designed both the bar and stools himself. They were perfect for his height and the rail was of polished brass. He believed in the maxim that a good bar, a good stool, and a brass footrail added 50 percent to the enjoyment of a good Scotch.

"It's a beautiful coincidence," Tudin said from behind the bar.

"Beautiful, yes," Gordik replied, "and certainly a coincidence. After all, Gemmel travels a lot in his work. It's natural that being a balletomane, as they call it, he would go to a performance of a company as renowned as the Maly. It's also natural that being a committee member of the London Ballet Circle, he would be invited to the reception. It is also eminently natural that any red-blooded man, spy or not, would make every attempt to engage the exquisite Miss Kashva in conversation. Yes, it's beautiful."

The two women had left ten minutes before. Larissa was to accompany the ballerina to her hotel suite, stay with her the night, and in the morning take her to the Swallow School. She was also to stay with her there.

"You might learn something," Gordik had told her in a smiled aside. She was to report constantly on Maya's progress.

Gordik had taken the young woman through the spectrum of emotions, first sketching in the benefits and rewards of patriotism, then informing her that her mother would be his "guest" at his country dacha for the duration, and finally holding out the promise of reunion, even if the dancer elected to stay in the West. Maya had cried and implored and inevitably given way. It was not for nothing that her father had been a senior KGB officer. She well understood reality.

"You think she'll hold up?" Tudin asked.

"It's worth the risk," Gordik replied. "And she's tougher than she appears. I don't know a great deal about the ballet, but I do know that you don't get to be a prima ballerina at twenty-four just with talent alone—or an important father. You have to be tough and determined."

Tudin poured more Scotch into his glass. "I take it that Comrade Savich will not be accompanying the company on its tour to London?"

Gordik smiled grimly. "The only tour that lecherous, indiscreet idiot will accompany is a puppet show to Siberia."

# ten

PERRYMAN AND GEMMEL SAT ON A BENCH IN HYDE PARK, the same bench that Gemmel had occupied with Hawke several weeks before. They had enjoyed a good lunch at the Hyde Park Hotel, but in his customary fashion Perryman had declined to discuss business during a meal.

"We'll take a stroll after lunch," he had said, and patted his portly stomach. "It's good for the figure."

So they had walked to the lake and found an unoccupied bench and Gemmel briefed him on the progress of Operation Mirage. He explained that at the forthcoming meeting in Madrid the Americans would report on the progress of the laser satellite and the British on the search for the candidate.

"How many alternatives will you present?" Perryman asked.

"About a dozen, of which two or three will be serious contenders."

"And you're confident of the outcome?"

"Reasonably," Gemmel answered. "Fortunately Falk is well qualified to back us up for the right reasons."

"Let's hope so," Perryman said. "It's a pity Hawke

didn't go along with our having a man on the laser project."

Gemmel smiled. "We hardly expected it. Frankly I'd have been astonished if he had agreed. It cleared the air a bit though. He'd been waiting for it."

"How do you find him?"

Gemmel considered carefully and then said, "He's good. Better than he appears. He likes to affect a typical tough outgoing exterior, but, believe me, he's shrewd— and he's experienced. He's also a good man to work with. He doesn't come on with the usual Big Brother act."

"So you like him?"

Gemmel didn't hesitate. "Yes, I do. We get on well, and I suppose it's more than just mutual respect."

Perryman was a little surprised. In all the years he had known Gemmel and watched and encouraged his progress, he had never been aware of his forming any deep friendships, either inside or outside of his work. Since the death of his wife he had been even more withdrawn. It was curious that the big, predatory American should have opened up even slightly the shell-like exterior.

"And the project itself—how do you feel about that now?"

Again Gemmel thought deeply before replying. "At first," he said, "I treated it like an unconnected dream. A beautiful, imaginative idea which could have no substance. It was as though I'd stepped into Alice's Wonderland—a charming experience, but without basis."

"And now?"

"Well, once we started to introduce lasers and satellites and space shuttles, once we triggered off our fieldman and started opening files . . . well, the Wonderland began to take on a more mundane form."

Perryman sniffed. "I'd hardly call lasers and satellites, and so on, mundane."

"No, they're not," Gemmel agreed, "But in a way it's become just another operation. From being a dreamer I've had to become an administrator, so I tend to think more of paper work and fieldwork and forget the more esoteric aspects."

"And the moral issues?"

"They don't bother me at all. I'm an intelligence agent. I gave up being concerned with moral issues a long time ago."

Perryman slid him a look that was not without skepticism.

There followed a brief silence, then Gemmel asked, "Are you maintaining contact with Pritchard?"

"Oh, yes. He is anxious to follow the project as closely as possible."

Gemmel's curiosity was aroused. "What about his personal connection?" he asked. "And the ongoing control if we pull the thing off?"

Perryman hesitated for a moment, then decided to be at least a little forthcoming.

"His 'personal connection,' as you put it, is the entire basis of his motivation. His desire is to accomplish one last great intelligence coup, and the fact that the instrument of that accomplishment should be his own creation will give him enormous satisfaction. After all, he's been planning the operation for about twenty years."

Gemmel digested that and decided he would never understand Pritchard. Never learn how a man could strip himself of all family emotion for the sake of his profession. He didn't see himself in the same light. Even though, since the death of his wife, he had adopted a similar devotion to his work. Had she lived he could never have subordinated her to anything.

He changed the subject. "Have you briefed the PM?"

"I have," Perryman replied shortly. "Merely the barest details. I stressed that she might like to follow the President's example and retain a measure of blissful and virtuous innocence."

"May I know her reaction?"

Perryman savored his reply. "She authorized an immediate intensification of oil exploration in the North Sea!"

The Range Rover was painted a mottled, sandy brown, and it was bedded down behind a sandy brown hill. It had no number plates and no markings, only a tall, thin, whip aerial. The two men lay on a tarpaulin at the top of the low hill. One of them held a pair of powerful binoculars to his eyes. The other lay on his back, an arm shielding his eyes from the late-afternoon sun. A small canvas shade had been rigged—not to protect the men, but a variety of very expensive cameras and lenses. The men were hot, tired, and dirty, for they had been waiting in this desolate spot for three days. The Range Rover was air-conditioned but they had been forbidden to run the engine.

The man with the binoculars lowered them and wiped an arm across his eyes.

"Christ, it's bloody hot," he said fervently.

The man on his back replied with equal fervor, "George, if you say that just once more I'm going to kick you right in the goolies!"

George grunted and raised the binoculars again. Then he stiffened. "He's coming, Terry! He's coming!"

Terry rolled onto his stomach and peered over the brow of the hill. Then he reached out, selected a telephoto lens, and screwed it onto the body of a Nikon F3 camera.

Through the viewfinder he could clearly see the man rounding the side of the hill in front of him. He was dressed in traditional burnous and leather sandals, and he carried a goatskin gourd slung over one shoulder.

Terry glanced behind him at the lowering sun, picked out a filter, and clipped it onto the lens. Then the drive motor of the Nikon started, and moment by moment the moving man was frozen onto film. By the time he reached the gaping entrance to the cave, the first roll was exposed. As the cameraman quickly and expertly changed it, the Arab squatted on his heels and refreshed himself from the gourd. Again the Nikon's drive motor hummed and clicked. Terry wanted to get at least half a dozen rolls before the good light went and the man disappeared inside the cave. The watchers knew that cave better than anyone for they had spent an entire day carefully surveying and measuring its cavernous interior. They also knew that they would have to endure the sun for two or three more days, for that was how long Abu Qadir liked to meditate.

It was during the second evening that Terry suddenly realized what had been bothering him. He had taken all the photographs he needed and they were sitting in the back of the Range Rover, playing cards, when he looked up at George and said:

"There's something wrong with that fellow."

"Of course there is," George replied. "He's a nutter. Anyone who comes out to a place like this without food and sits around on his arse all day has to be a nutter."

Terry shook his head. "No, it's not that. He's supposed to be a very holy man. He comes out here to meditate and to commune with Allah or whatever, but, George, he never prays. You've seen all the other Arabs. Five times a day they unroll their mats, face toward Mecca, and prostrate themselves, but this bloke never does. And there's something else. I've got a feeling that he knows we're here."

"Don't be daft."

"No, seriously. For one thing he never looks up at the ridge. I must have taken five hundred photographs of him and I'll bet you that in not one of them he's facing directly toward the camera."

George took his eyes off the cards and looked at him curiously. "You really believe that?"

"Yes," Terry said emphatically. "Look, it's my job. I've taken photographs of hundreds of people for the firm. Always surreptitiously. I tell you, George, this fellow knows he's being watched."

"But he can't have seen us."

Terry shook his head. "No, he hasn't seen us. He just knows or senses we're here."

"Well," George said, "I don't care one way or the other. We've done our job. I just want to get out of here." He wrinkled his nose. "I don't know who smells worse, you or me. All I want is a hot bath and a cold beer!"

In Jeddah, Haji Mastan was again conferring with the Imam in the shade of the Mosque wall. As he talked, the Imam listened raptly, for in the past weeks there had been a continuous rumble of rumor and speculation. A far greater rumble than could possibly have been generated by the Imam himself. The regular travelers who arrived from the Sudan and Egypt and from the interior had told of the same rumors.

"The Chosen One will come at the time of the Haj."

"I will dispose of my business," Haji Mastan told the Imam.

"Such a great step you take?" the Imam asked breathlessly. "You are so sure?"

Haji looked deep into the Imam's eyes and said simply, "He will come, and he will call me and on that day I will have no ties to hold me back. No ties to prevent my following him and doing his bidding."

"You will sell your business?"

Haji shook his head. "I am done with buying and selling. I will give my business to my employees. They shall enjoy all the fruits of their labors. I have enough set aside for my needs and those of my family."

Now the Imam was truly impressed, for Haji Mastan had long been known as a man with an eye for a profit. True, he had never indulged in sharp practice or engaged in the sin of usury, but still, to give away his business indicated a profound change of heart.

"Do your dreams tell you when he will come, the Chosen One?"

Haji shook his head. "But inside of me I know it will be soon. And I will be ready."

The Imam edged forward and said quietly, "Heed my advice, Haji Mastan, and take care. The authorities are much concerned by the rumors. The religious police ask many questions. Even of you—and your dreams."

"I know it," Haji answered solemnly. "Already they have questioned me and my family. But they cannot punish a man for dreaming dreams."

"That is the truth," added the Imam. "But I beg of you to take care."

"Fear not," answered Haji. "When he comes he will answer all their questions."

The Swallow School was housed in a large dacha set in rolling woodlands some forty miles northeast of Moscow.

During the late fifties the KGB had succeeded in entrapping the French Ambassador to Moscow. He was a man very susceptible to feminine charms and they had used a beautiful young actress to lure him into a whole series of compromising positions. It had been a copybook operation and had been followed by many others, but usually involving the seduction of middle-aged secretaries working for Western governments.

Such operations became known as honey traps and the operatives—or seducers—as swallows. The strategy had become so widespread that in the late sixties the KGB had set up a special school to train swallows in both the psychological and physical aspects of seduction. The staff consisted of a director, a psychologist, and four instructors—two males and two females. There were never more than three or four pupils in residence at any given time, thus creating the ideal pupil–teacher ratio.

All this was explained to Maya by Larissa, as they drove through the wooded countryside in a large black limousine. They were separated from the driver by a glass screen. Maya was apprehensive, but she peppered Larissa with questions. How long would she stay? What exactly would she have to do? And to whom? On this aspect Larissa could tell her little, but her situation had been explained to the director by telephone and he would have a comprehensive program ready. She told the young dancer not to worry. They had much experience at the school and would surely handle everything with tact and understanding.

It was true that they had much experience, but as the director looked down from his upstairs window as the limousine pulled up to the front door, he felt a twinge of anxiety.

"One week," Gordik had told him on the phone, "and that girl had better be able to turn a monk into a mass of quivering anticipation."

The problem was that in all its years of experience the school had never actually handled a virgin. In truth, most of its pupils were vastly experienced, and their time at the school could best be described as postgraduate courses. He had held a meeting with the psychologist and the chief instructor, Georgi Bragin, and passed on Gordik's decription of the girl's total inexperience and extreme anxiety.

The psychologist explained that in such a case, the first criterion was to get her relaxed and completely at ease. The director told him of the time problem. Six days at the most. Or, put another way, five nights. He also pointed out acidly that Vassili Gordik had long been an enemy of the school, and failure in this case could have grave consequences for all of them. An argument started between Georgi Bragin and the psychologist. Bragin was for immediately breaking the girl in, sexually. In his experience anyone who was still a virgin at twenty-four needed some form of shock treatment. After that he might have a chance of teaching her something useful in the short time remaining. The psychologist demurred. It could cause a trauma and have a regressive effect. He pointed out that the physical aspect of seduction was no more important, and perhaps less so, than the mental aspect. He and Bragin glared at each other. They had been through this argument many times before.

It didn't solve the director's problem, although because

of the time element he tended to favor Bragin's course of action. As the two men argued he studied his chief instructor. He was in his early forties, a slim, dark man of medium height, with an aquiline face and deep-set, intense eyes. As he spoke he gestured frequently and eloquently. He had long, slender fingers—a pianist's hands.

His career had started with the seduction of a senior administrative assistant at NATO Headquarters, Brussels. He was then twenty-seven. She was a spinster of forty-six. For five years Bragin had her totally under his control until she had eventually been caught trying to photograph documents in the Deputy Commander-in-Chief's office.

His next assignment had been at the United Nations in New York. This time he had penetrated the Secretariat and a total of three secretaries, the most senior being the personal secretary of the UN Financial Director. For the next two years the KGB had access to all UN budgets and estimates long before even the UN Secretary General. The Russian delegation was able to apply pressure to its own financial benefit before other members knew what was going on. This assignment ended when the Financial Director's contract expired and he returned home to Holland. His secretary, who was not popular in the department, lost both her job and her lover.

Bragin went on to other, more minor successes as an embassy cultural attaché in various Third World countries. His targets were usually secretaries of other embassies who were bored with the limited social scenes. He had been called back to Moscow five years before and made an instructor at the Swallow School. Two years later he was promoted to chief instructor. He enjoyed his work and he thought the psychological aspects were overplayed. "Psychology ends below the neck," he liked to say. Freud would have found him a difficult subject.

The director ended the argument by stating that he would first interview the new pupil and then make a decision. In any event, there was no problem about allocating personnel. There were only two other current pupils, both men, and they were in the hands of the female instructors. No; his chief instructor would be able to give the new pupil his undivided attention.

He watched her now as she got out of the car and followed the other woman to the entrance. He noticed her lithe dancer's walk and also her apprehension as she looked nervously about her.

"I think you're wrong," Larissa told the director bluntly. It had taken him only ten minutes to decide on Bragin's course of action. The first impact of Maya Kashva's beauty and personality had convinced him that she would have no difficulty in making what he liked to call "the connection." There could be very few heterosexual men anywhere who would long resist her. The remaining problem, as he saw it in his somewhat confined view of life, was in giving her the expertise to follow up on the connection.

So he had summoned a maid to show the dancer to her room and explained his decision to Larissa, and she had objected.

"We have very little time," he protested. "Under normal circumstances we would keep her here for up to three months."

"Why do you think she's so inexperienced?" Larissa asked scornfully.

The director sighed. "Believe me, there could be a dozen reasons, ranging from homosexuality to frigidity. At the very least we shall eliminate those possibilities within twenty-four hours."

"By throwing her straight into bed with a man?"

The director became irritated and said sharply, "Please give us credit for a little intelligence!"

"You've had others like her, completely naïve and without any sexual experience?"

"Of course we have," he lied smoothly. "And, believe me, we have skillful instructors. Naturally such an important case will be handled by Comrade Bragin, our chief instructor. He will be both gentle and persuasive." He smiled archly. "It will be an experience that she will look back on with pleasure and, I might say, gratitude."

Larissa was skeptical, but then remembered her own embarrassing and painful initiation at the hands of a clumsy engineering student. She decided not to argue any further.

They met at lunch. Bragin sat alone at a table set for three. The other instructors and pupils sat at the opposite end of the room. They looked up curiously as Larissa and Maya entered the room and moved toward his table. Then they all looked at Bragin. He didn't exactly lick his lips, but no cat ever surveyed a bowl of fresh cream with greater anticipation. He rose from his chair and held out his hand to Maya.

"Bragin—but please call me Georgi; and you, of course, are the famous Maya Kashva. I am honored."

She shook his hand formally and he pulled out a chair for her and nodded to Larissa. They had been introduced earlier in the director's office.

Looking back on that lunch, Larissa found it difficult to find a flaw in Bragin's approach—or his strategy. Within a few minutes it became obvious that Maya was treating him much as she would treat any fan of hers. Correctly, but at a distance. He didn't try too hard, but instead turned his attention and charm on Larissa. She felt the force of it and of his personality. He was, she decided, a very powerful male animal. Her own reaction to him, had she not studied his file, would have been sympathetic and interested. A good man to have a blindingly vivid affair with, but no more. She realized that he paid attention to her in an attempt to arouse female combativeness in Maya. It failed. She picked at her food and listened listlessly to the conversation.

Bragin was quick to sense the direction of the wind and he dropped that particular strategy and moved smoothly into another gear. He suggested that he and Maya take a walk in the spacious grounds during the afternoon as it was a lovely spring day. Or would she prefer to play tennis? She shook her head. She didn't play tennis. Something else then? There was a heated swimming pool, or table tennis? Surely she enjoyed some sports? he asked teasingly.

"I dance," she said flatly, and Larissa couldn't help her snort of laughter.

Bragin gave her a glance of fleeting irritation, but he was undeterred. Maya Kashva may well be a talented and famous prima ballerina, but before the night was over, he, Georgi Bragin, would have her, soft and compliant, in his arms.

So after lunch the two of them went for a walk, while Larissa went for a swim and then to her room. She telephoned Gordik, who anxiously asked for news. It was too early, she told him, but her own belief was that their swallow would only fly with difficulty. She would report again in the morning. She hung up and concluded that she herself was in for a boring week. It had been decided that she would now stay out of Maya's way. The director had explained that Larissa's presence could only complicate matters. Everything was now up to Bragin. Larissa reluctantly had to agree.

Bragin's suite of rooms could best be described as sumptuous. A large, high-ceilinged lounge, with deep velvet easy chairs and a well-stocked bar. And an even larger bedroom with a giant four-poster bed, complete with canopy and drawn-back curtains.

Maya sat in the lounge on the edge of her seat, sipping a large balloon glass of French Cognac. It had followed two glasses of vodka before dinner and half a bottle of Burgundy during it. She was in control of herself, but only just.

Bragin sat opposite, slumped back in his chair and eyeing her with a mixture of frustration and irritation. They had walked for two hours in the afternoon—far more than he intended—and now his legs ached slightly. Several times he had tried to persuade her to sit down at some scenic spot and talk, or just admire the scenery, but she had shaken her head and resolutely pressed on with her long, lithe stride; and he had lost dignity as he hurried after her, puffing a little with the exertion.

During dinner she had hardly spoken. She knew, or appeared to know, little of the world, and his anecdotes and stories had bounced off her lovely but impassive face. He knew almost nothing of the ballet, so could not open her up in that direction. Finally he had resorted to plying her with drinks, and that too hurt his vanity. He had never needed such a device to lower a woman's defenses. But even that had failed, and as he looked at her now, sitting stiff and erect, he realized that he would have to fall back on nothing more than pure physical technique. He knew that he could not reach her mind, but he was confident that he, Georgi Bragin, could stimulate her body. He leaned forward and said flatly:

"Miss Kashva, listen to me."

Her eyes lifted, slightly puzzled.

"You clearly understand the position. I am chief instructor here. You are a pupil. Perhaps you don't wish to be here. I'm sure you don't. However, that's nothing to do with me." His voice hardened. "Now, I am getting slightly bored with the whole thing. I have tried to make it as pleasant as possible—but I have my job to do, and you are not helping, and there is little time. So now I am going to start instructing."

He paused for her reaction but her expression didn't alter.

He pointed at the bedroom and said coldly, "Go into the bedroom, take off your clothes—all of them—and lie on the bed. I will be there in ten miuutes."

She didn't hesitate. She put down her glass, stood up without looking at him, and walked into the bedroom, closing the door behind her.

Bragin swore under his breath, then went to the bar and poured himself another drink. Slowly he got himself under control, even laughed at himself a little. He would not fail. He drained his glass and moved across to the bedroom.

She had pulled the sheets right back and lay in the center of the bed like a white ivory statue. He walked over and stood looking down. He looked for a long time—a very long time. Often in his career he had been required to make love to unattractive women; some, very unattractive. But he had known in his life many beautiful women, and when on the occasions he'd had to visualize someone else, he had a large gallery to call upon. But as he looked down at Maya Kashva he knew that in the future his brain would conjure up only her form. There was no single edge of beauty, just a totality. He did not see perfect breasts or a slender waist or long, symmetrical limbs or small, delicate, arched feet or even the small, delicate, arched triangle at the apex of her thighs. Only the wholeness of the image as though his eyes had lost their power to concentrate on a single object.

He drew a slow, deep breath and said, "Look at me."

She turned her head on the pillow and watched as he undressed. He dropped his clothes one by one to the carpet, never taking his eyes from her eyes, willing her to react. To see in him what he had seen. He knew he had a fine athletic body. He had seen its effect on countless women, but on this one he could not judge. He saw her eyes drop to his middle, to his growing erection. Was there a hint even of curiosity?

He lay down beside her and ran his hands over her. Skin as soft as a kitten's belly, but ripples of taut muscles beneath the softness. It excited him further to feel the strength in her.

He probed for areas of sensitivity. He brushed her small nipples, breathed on them, and felt a thrill as they rose and peaked. He ran a hand down over the hub of her belly and slid his fingers through the black silk between her thighs. She shuddered involuntarily and he withdrew for a moment, confident of the ultimate result. Mentally he

had already discarded the possibilities that had worried
the director. This was no lesbian, and if she were frigid—
so Venus was frigid! Then he cast the director from his
mind. This was for him alone, to hell with everything and
everyone. For many minutes his hands and lips played
over her body. Instinct told him to move with the greatest
patience. He was getting two conflicting signals: one—
the slight but perceptible movements of her body—told
him yes; the other—an occasional jerkiness, almost a
cringing-away from his touch—told him no.

But his patience had a limit, forced onto him by his
own body and imagination. She was a virgin, untouched,
unsullied. He would be the first! He pulled her face toward him and probed her lips with his tongue. She tried
to pull away but he held her tight. Her lips opened slightly
but his tongue came up against closed teeth. His other
hand moved down to her thighs and again probed and
forced them apart and his fingers inched into her and he
gasped at her tightness and the hint of wetness. And then,
with a jerk, she rolled away and he was left panting, his
erection a pain.

He didn't care, didn't think. He gripped her shoulder
and pulled her back, tried to force his mouth onto her lips,
but she fought back, and again his instinct came through
and told him he had come close—so close.

But he didn't care. He would be the first—no matter
what. He pulled back his head and they looked at each
other. He saw a clenched mouth and eyes that screamed
No! She saw only lust.

So they fought. He was strong and so was she. He tried
to force his knee between her thighs. She twisted away as
he attempted to hold both her wrists in one hand. The
attempt failed and one wrist slipped and her nails raked
his face and he screamed as she broke clear.

She almost reached the door but he leapt from the bed
and got there first. Now there was rage as well as lust in
his eyes and he stalked her to a corner. She tried to dodge

away but he caught her wrist and spread his legs and swung her around to face him.

She pirouetted gracefully on the ball of one highly arched foot and the other came up with dancer's toes pointed and the strength and speed of ten thousand practice hours—and drove like a scalpel into his testicles.

# eleven

Just after midnight Larissa approached the door of her apartment. She heard the haunting tones of the second movement of Beethoven's Fifth Piano Concerto. It was a bad sign. Gordik always played that concerto when he was in a foul mood. He had once explained to her that when Beethoven had started to compose it he was having a passionate love affair with a Hohenzollern princess. The stirring first movement illustrated his joy over the liaison, but by the second movement she had left him for another man, and it reflected only a poignant agony. The determination of the third movement was the composer's affirmation that life goes on—and the hell with women anyway.

She held the key in one hand and her suitcase in the other, but she considered going back to the street and walking around the block a few times, at least until the third movement had started; but then, with a resigned shrug, she fitted the key into the lock and went in.

He was lying on the settee with his feet up and his eyes fixed on the ceiling. He turned his head to look at her briefly and then concentrated again on the music and the ceiling. She dropped her suitcase by the door and went

through to the kitchen and very slowly made herself a cup
of coffee. By the time she had filled the cup and carried
it to the kitchen door the third movement was drawing to
a close. Gordik was absently conducting with one hand.
At the final bar he dropped his chin onto his chest and
looked at her through narrowed eyes.

"Imagine," he said. "Imagine leaving a man who could
make such music!"

"Perhaps he had bad breath."

Gordik snorted and sat up. "A typical woman's reaction!"

She shook her head. "Believe me, Vassili, there's no
such thing. I found that out tonight."

He looked at her closely and noted her exhaustion. His
expression softened slightly—but only slightly.

"Ah, yes," he said, "I was thinking of offering Maya
Kashva to the Moscow Dynamos; maybe she can kick a
few goals."

Larissa didn't smile. She felt a rising irritation. It was
time for a few home truths. She walked to a window and
looked down at the dimly lit street. Over her shoulder
she said quietly, "You think because you understand me
that you understand all women. You are wrong. You only
understand me because I love you, and with that love I
expose everything."

She turned. He was watching her closely.

"With your ego," she went on, "and with your education and your experience, you also think you understand
most men. It's possible, but you don't understand them
all."

He sighed. "So I'm a bisexual chauvinist pig. Please
come to the point."

"I will. I will come to the point, but first tell me what
you have decided to do about Maya."

Gordik shrugged. "She's decided that herself. Gemmel's unlikely to pour out his heart while gripping his
crotch!"

"He won't have to," she said scornfully. "Now listen to

both my points. First, she is in love with Gemmel—at least in her imagination."

Gordik sat up straight and started to say something, but she held up her hand.

"Wait! Listen! She met him once. Three years ago— for no more than five minutes. Yet the moment she saw his photo—a blurred, ill-defined photo—she recognized and remembered him."

"So she has a good memory."

Larissa shook her head. "She doesn't. I've talked to her over the last couple of days. She can hardly remember the names of the people she danced with on that tour. She can remember very few names of Westerners whom she met. But his name and face she remembered instantly." Again she held up a hand as he tried to interrupt. "She told you he liked her. She was emphatic. That was wishful thinking. If you know women, Vassili, you know that they can always imagine a man liking them— if they want him to!"

Now he was watching her intently. "All right, go on."

"Secondly," she continued, "try to put yourself in his position. A Soviet ballet dancer defects while on tour. Nothing unusual. But this one—a very beautiful one— comes straight to his front door. Never mind that he's well known in ballet circles. His first reaction will be that of an intelligence agent: suspicion. And his first suspicion will be that she is a swallow, and we are setting up a honey trap. So he checks her out, and finds nothing, and maybe, just maybe, he is attracted, even falls for her. But always, Vassili, always he will have the doubt in the back of his mind. You would."

Vassili was nodding slowly and her voice rose in excitement.

"But then he makes love to her, and she doesn't kick him in the balls. No; she submits, and he discovers that she's a virgin! What will he think? Tell me, Vassili, what will he think?"

Gordik was smiling at her. "He will think of our tradecraft, which he knows all about. He will think of our thoroughness, which he understands well. He will think of our Swallow School, of which he is well aware. And, yes, Larissa, he will think, they would never, never sweeten a honey trap with a girl of total inexperience—a virgin!"

"Exactly!" she stated triumphantly, but then hesitated as she saw his thoughtful look.

"But there might be two problems," he said. "First, if you're right and she's truly in love with him—or falls in love with him—will she go through with it? Will our control over her mother be enough of a lever?"

"It's a risk," she admitted, "but I believe so. She is very, very close to her mother, particularly since her father died. And obviously you will first bring great pressure on her mother and be sure that she will transmit that pressure to her daughter."

"All right," Gordik conceded. "It's an acceptable risk, but now the second problem. How will he be sure she's a virgin? I mean, is she intact? I can't imagine what happens inside a ballet dancer—leaping about all the time like that, doing the splits and things."

Larissa smiled. "She's a prima ballerina, not a chorus girl! And, yes, she's intact. She told me so and we can check it easily enough."

Now Gordik stood up and started pacing the room, his mind racing ahead.

"All right, we'll try it. You've got three weeks to work with her. You and Lev. Drop everything else. Everything! She must be very well prepared in all aspects." He grinned at her. "All aspects except the physical."

Abruptly his face became serious as he remembered something. "Incidentally," he said, "we've identified the fourth American at the Paris meeting; one Elliot Wisner."

"And who is Elliot Wisner?" she asked, heading for the kitchen.

"He's the foremost expert in America on lasers."

She stopped at the kitchen door and turned. "Lasers?"

"Yes. In fact, the application of lasers to weapons systems."

"So what on earth . . . ?" she began.

"Exactly! What on earth can he have to do with an operation aimed at the Middle East?" He shook his head. "I don't know, but we have to find out. I do know that we are engaged in a desperate race with the West to develop the first viable laser weapon system, and at the last reckoning we were falling behind."

There was a thoughtful silence. Then he said, "If you're making more coffee, I'll have some."

As she filled the percolator the sounds of music floated in. It was the Oscar Peterson Trio. She smiled. He was pleased with her.

Had he been present, Gordik would have approved of the venue for the third meeting. It was the Hotel Villa Magna in Madrid, and while perhaps not having the reputation or the cachet of the Ritz in Lisbon, or the George V in Paris, it was eminently comfortable.

The meeting took place in the hotel conference room under the guise of a sales conference of one of Britain's better-known conglomerates. Both American and British teams were at full strength with the addition of Elliot Wisner on the American side. There was an air of camaraderie and anticipation as they took their seats. The British had distributed six large brown folders tied with green ribbon, and Wisner had set up a home-movie type of screen on one wall. He sat facing it at one end of the table with a slide projector in front of him. Meade was at the other end and Gemmel and Hawke were opposite each other with their lieutenants by their sides.

"Morton, we have to stop meeting like this," Gemmel said solemnly.

"Damn right!" Hawke grinned. "My wife's becoming suspicious. How's your suite?"

Gemmel bowed in appreciation. "Most palatial; are you

sure it won't appear in the accounts of Her Majesty's Treasury?"

Falk joined the conversation. "No way; we sneaked it in under 'towel service.' "

"Towel service?"

"Sure," Falk smiled disarmingly. "It's a euphemism for expenses incurred in providing female companionship for representatives of friendly countries—and, occasionally, unfriendly countries."

"A large slice of the Company's budget," Meade interjected drily.

Gemmel glanced at Boyd. "On our departure," he said severely, "I will count the towels personally." He smiled at Hawke. "Morton, we appreciate it."

When they had checked in that morning with their false identities, the manager had shown them up to a beautiful, two-bedroom suite instead of the single rooms they had booked. As Gemmel had started to correct the mistake, the manager informed him that it was on the instructions of Señor Beckett, which was Hawke's cover name. In the suite was a well-stocked bar and, propped against a bottle of Chivas Regal, a note which read: "Welcome to the New World!"

"No thanks are needed," Hawke said. "I only arranged it to stop myself feeling guilty." He glanced around the table and his voice became matter-of-fact.

"Gentlemen, shall we get down to business?"

They decided that Wisner would conduct his briefing first, and as Meade swiveled in his chair, Wisner reached forward to the slide projector with the air of a conjurer about to produce a rabbit. In spite of that, Gemmel had the feeling they were about to witness something impressive. He was not disappointed. A series of color photographs came up on the screen while Wisner quietly and precisely analyzed and explained them. The first showed an area of the earth's surface, an arid, uninhabited waste.

"The Minā valley," Wisner's voice intoned, "taken from an intelligence satellite seven days ago." He picked up a thin tube, pointed it at the screen, and pressed a button. A small, bright circle of light appeared on the screen and moved about as he indicated first the hill of Arafat and then the other salient features.

The next photograph was of the same valley, but this time it was dark and mottled.

"Late September last year. During the Haj. You are looking at an area of six square miles. An area which contains two point three million pilgrims, plus or minus two percent."

The projector clicked again, a foreshortened view of a score or so people grouped in a circle, surrounding a dark mound. One man was bending over the mound.

"Same day on the next orbit. The area depicted is one hundred and twenty square meters taken from an angle of eighty-two degrees."

The circle of light moved onto the dark mound.

"A camel has just been sacrificed."

"That's taken from a satellite?" Boyd asked incredulously.

"Correct."

The projector clicked. The first photograph again, but this time a small, black disk was superimposed near the center. The circle of light moved onto it.

"That has a radius of one hundred and fifty meters. We understand the problems involved due to crowd control, but for technical and topographical reasons we would prefer that the target be within that area."

Another click. Another photograph.

"The Grand Mosque in Mecca. The black object"—the circle of light moved—"is the Kaaba, which contains a meteorite, the most holy relic of the Islamic faith. Mr. Gemmel, this and the next half-dozen shots bear no relation to my end of the project. I selected them for your benefit. I have copies for you."

Gemmel turned and nodded his thanks.

"No nonbelievers are allowed in Mecca," Wisner went on in a complacent tone, "but I guess when they passed that law they weren't thinking of satellites."

"They weren't," Falk said sarcastically. "It was about one thousand three hundred years ago."

Wisner replied with a series of clicks, which produced more close-up photographs of Mecca and its surrounds. Then the show was over, but Wisner had more explaining to do.

Speaking directly to Gemmel, he first told him that the combined weight of the satellite and laser would be twenty-two thousand kilograms.

"That's excellent," Gemmel interjected.

"Yes, it is, Mr Gemmel! But why?"

"Because if it's launched due east from Cape Canaveral, as opposed to Vandenberg, the space shuttle can put it high enough for a geostatic orbit."

Wisner was obviously disappointed at having his thunder stolen. He slid Gemmel a narrow glance, and explained to the others that a geostatic orbit was one at which a satellite orbited at the same rate as the earth's rotation, thus remaining stationary over a given point on the earth's surface—in this case the Minā valley. Hence it would be easier to aim and hold the laser beam onto the target.

Finally Wisner advised that the homing and destruct device, to be placed inside the dead lamb, would measure approximately 25 centimeters by 15 by 8.

Again Boyd interjected, "That's all?"

"Yes, Mr. Boyd. It will be both sophisticated and simple. Sophisticated in its miniaturization. Simple in its function. It will contain a small but powerful incendiary device which has a photo-electric cell activated by the laser light. It will also emit a radio signal which the guidance system of the laser locks onto. In effect, the laser beam travels down the radio beam and zaps your lamb."

He sat down with a satisfied air.

Gemmel made appropriate noises of thanks and then asked, "Is the construction of the unit on schedule?"

"It is," Wisner replied emphatically. "We are planning an October-first launch."

"Don't worry," Hawke said, "the hardware will be in place. Now, what about your end?"

"It's all in the folders," Gemmel answered, and six pairs of hands began untying six green ribbons.

Inside the folders were eleven buff-colored files. Each had photographs clipped to the inside cover.

"These are the files of eleven possible candidates for the role of the Mahdi," Gemmel explained. "They are the result of an intensive search covering the Arab world. We have not considered non-Arab Islamic states because it is unlikely that any Arab would accept a non-Arabic Mahdi; but it does not work the other way."

Hawke glanced at Falk, who nodded his agreement.

"We believe that three of them are particularly suitable," Gemmel continued. "I will not indicate which three until you have studied the files. It will be interesting to see if you reach the same conclusions."

Hawke was leafing casually through the files. "The fact is, Leo here"—he indicated Falk with his thumb—"is the Islamic specialist on our team. We're going to have to follow his thinking."

Falk was also sifting through the files. "Peter, these are obviously brief details. I take it I can see in-depth reports if necessary."

"Of course, Leo. You can have everything we have." Gemmel looked at Hawke. "Morton, while you're reading the files we'll set up some drinks."

Gemmel and Boyd moved to the bar, mixed drinks for everyone, and passed them out. Then they left the Americans at the table and moved back to the bar. For half an hour there was silence, interrupted by only the shuffling of papers and the clink of ice against glass and the occasional splash of the soda siphon. Eventually Hawke piled his files together, glanced at Falk and Meade, and nodded to Gemmel, who led Boyd back to the table.

Falk had also put his files into a pile with the exception of three, which lay open at the photographs. As Gemmel sat down he looked at them and smiled.

"Did I hit the jackpot?" asked Falk.

"You did. And of the three, which do you favor?"

Falk pursed his lips and studied the photographs while Gemmel watched him closely. "I see it as a toss-up," Falk said finally, "between the shepherd from Medina and the Bedouin from Al-Jizah."

Again Gemmel smiled and said to Hawke, "It's pleasant to have one's own prognosis confirmed by such an eminent expert."

Hawke was obviously pleased by this accolade to one of his team. He gave Falk an approving look and said, "Fill us in on your reasoning, Leo, and why it parallels Peter's."

Falk put his elbows on the table and steepled his fingers. His voice assumed a lecturer's tone.

"The Mahdi must be acceptable to all the factions and nationalities that make up Islam. Therefore, his beliefs and his practice of them must be fundamental in the extreme. They cannot be open to interpretation. There is, in Islam, a collection of the recollections of what Muhammad said. This is called the Hadīth, or traditions. Obviously much of it is pure fabrication to suit the beliefs of one faction or another. Even so the Hadīth make up an important source of Islamic law. Then there is the total legal entity called the Sharia, which is drawn from the Koran, the Hadīth, and the traditions of the four right-guided Caliphs—that is, the first four. Again, the Sharia is open to interpretation by the different Muslim sects. So any Mahdi who based part of his belief on the Hadīth or the Sharia would have problems of interpretation."

He gestured at Gemmel. "So what Peter has done is to select candidates whose belief is centered solely on the

Koran, and, as you know, the Koran is considered by all
Muslims as being perfect and inviolate and certainly not
open to interpretations, even though some of the Suras
tend to contradict one another. The Koran is far more important to the Islamic faith than, say, the Bible is to Christianity or the Torah to Judaism."

He looked down at the photographs in front of him.

"Going further, both these gentlemen are Hashemite
Arabs. Again, in an effort to make the Mahdi acceptable
to all of Islam, Peter has narrowed down his search to
men who resemble Muhammad as closely as possible,
both in appearance and background. Muhammad was a
Hashemite of the Quraysh tribe, as are these two candidates. He was an orphan at six." He indicated the photographs. "They are both orphans. As a boy Muhammad
tended his uncle's camels—a task he recalled in adulthood
as a mark of divine favor. 'Allah sent no prophet who was
not a herdsman,' he told his followers." He pointed again
at one of the photographs. "He is a shepherd. In later
years Muhammad was a trader, handling the business of
a rich widow, Khadījah, whom he subsequently married."
He pointed at the other photograph. "The Bedouin is a
trader, although not very successful. Finally, both men
resemble Muhammad in external appearance. They are of
average height and stockily built. They have hooked noses
and black eyes and wide mouths and, for Arabs, they
have fair complexions."

He smiled across the table at Gemmel. "But there the
similarities end; for Muhammad, although supposedly illiterate, was highly intelligent, forceful, eloquent, and determined. These two men are apparently simple-minded."

He turned to Hawke. "That's basically it. I'll give you
a full report after Peter lets me have all the details."

Hawke looked at the two photographs and then asked
Gemmel, "Which of the two do you prefer?"

Gemmel shrugged. "Frankly, there's little between
them." He leaned forward and pointed at one of the photographs. "The only advantage this one presents is that

he often goes off alone to meditate. So it might be easier to arrange the personal and private miracle which convinces him that he's the Mahdi."

"It's a good point," Falk agreed. "Muhammad used to go off alone to meditate in the desert. It was there that the angel Gabriel appeared to him." He looked at Gemmel quizzically. "You are planning something similar?"

Gemmel nodded. "Very similar."

"By the way, Peter," Hawke said, "I'd like to be at that miracle."

"Is it wise?" Gemmel asked easily. "I thought you people wanted to keep a low profile."

Hawke grinned at him. "Maybe I'll have British papers! Anyway, I've never seen a miracle."

"As you wish." Gemmel appeared unconcerned. "All being well, that event will take place in three to four weeks."

Hawke leaned across Falk and pulled one file toward him. He studied the face in the close-up photograph for a long time. The others watched him. It was as if he were trying to look through the paper into the man's head.

"It's a good face," he said finally, and looked up at Gemmel. "An honest face."

He turned the page and read, " 'Abu Qadir—shepherd and carpenter.' "

# twelve

VASSILI GORDIK AND MAYA KASHVA WALKED IN GORKI Park. The sky was clear but it was very cold, and they were both dressed in heavy fur coats, fur-lined boots, and fur hats. Away to their left a score of skaters slid rhythmically across an open-air ice rink.

They had been walking for an hour. Maya's brief period of training was over. In four days the Maly Ballet Company would start its tour of western Europe and in a month it would arrive in London for its final performances. For the past hour Gordik had talked to her quietly and casually, asking questions and answering some of hers. He wanted to evaluate her mental state and readiness. He was reassured, for beneath a detached manner she had an incisive and absorbent mind. She had done well in the training, surprising her instructors.

"What if he's not there?" she asked. "In London, I mean."

"He will be," Gordik answered. "He's accepted an invitation to a reception at the hotel. Anyway, should he not be in London for any reason, you adopt the alternative strategy. Don't worry, Maya. Lev Tudin will be on hand and you will be kept informed."

154

A group of small boys ran past and the smallest of them slipped on a patch of ice, bounced on his bottom, and started to cry. Maya lifted him to his feet, and comforted him, then sent him on his way. She stood watching as he scampered after the other boys, then turned to Gordik.

"I'm just a gamble," she said. "You don't have very high hopes. You're sending me on the slim chance that I might learn something. Isn't it true?"

Gordik didn't hesitate. "Perfectly true. To be honest, I give you only a ten percent chance of finding out anything at all and only a fifty percent chance of getting to Gemmel in the first place. They'll give you a hard time, Maya. If you come through that, and if you get close to Gemmel, you will have already achieved a great deal."

She turned away from him and watched the skaters, her face immobile. He sensed the struggle inside her. When she spoke she didn't turn her head to look at him.

"Comrade Gordik, my father was very like you. He even looked a bit like you. He was an honest man to himself and to us, his family. But in his work, and because of his work, he had to lie a lot, even to us; but on those occasions I always knew he was lying—even when I was a child he could not hide it." She drew a deep breath, then asked very quietly, "You told me that if I do my best, no matter if I fail, you will still allow my mother to join me. Is that the truth?"

She turned and her small face was very white, framed in the dark fur. Her large, black, unblinking eyes watched him closely.

"It is true, Maya. You must understand that I don't have the power to protect her if you abandon your mission, but I do have the power, and the means, to send her to you if you succeed, or even if you fail in trying."

They looked at each other steadily in total silence. He was conscious that everything was suspended on this moment. Abruptly she walked forward and slipped her arm through his, and they started walking again.

"You are just like my father!"

He digested that enigmatic statement, but before he could clarify it she continued, "What if he falls in love with me but won't tell me anything?"

He smiled. "Maya, love is synonymous with trust. Of course he's not going to take you into Petworth House and open up his files for you! All we need is an indication, even a vague direction, so we can concentrate on a particular area. We know he's heading a critical project that could have grave implications for our country. That's all we know. Any other information, no matter how tiny, could be vital. You've been well briefed. You know exactly what to look for and listen for."

He stopped and looked down at her, studying her face, evaluating it, then he smiled again.

"We don't expect miracles, Maya. But I have faith in you. We are all sure that you will do your best."

They continued walking down the path, her diminutive figure dwarfed by his furred, bearlike form.


At the Stadthalle in Vienna the Blue Crystal rock band swung into its last number, and the audience roared its approval.

Toward the rear center of the giant concert hall Mick Williams sat at his sound console. He didn't look up at the stage, only at the flashing LEDs and at his fingers as they adjusted and balanced the controls and blended the individual outputs of the five instrumentalists through the giant stacks.

He was slim and curly-headed and in his early thirties, and he was very tired. This was the last number of the last concert of a six-week tour that had taken in thirty cities. He was tired of ever-changing hotel rooms and never-changing motorways on which the two giant trailers had trundled across Europe. Tonight he would supervise the loading of the twenty-two tons of sound and light equipment for the last time, and in the morning they would head back to London and home and a long rest. But first he would get drunk. Beautifully, totally drunk. He looked up at the stage, at the bass guitarist. "Speedy" King. They called him Speedy because outside of music and drinking he moved with the deliberation of a tranquilized dinosaur. Mick had a special rapport with Speedy, both in music and drinking. With a grin he leaned forward and edged up one of the faders, and the thumping, vibrant rhythm of the bass guitar took on an even deeper intensity. He looked again at the stage, and in spite of the distance could see Speedy's answering grin. Yes, tonight they'd go for it!

Seated two rows behind the sound desk and slightly to the left, Peter Gemmel watched and smiled at the interplay between the sound engineer and the guitarist. He was dressed in a black polo-necked shirt, a beige sport coat and slacks, and he looked out of place among the young and excited audience. But he had enjoyed the concert, surprising himself. His secretary had shaken her head in disbelief when he told her to make the booking. "It's not exactly *Swan Lake*, you know," she had said.

"I'm widening my horizons," he told her. "And book me first class to Vienna. If Perryman squeals, tell him Uncle Sam likes his surrogates to travel in comfort."

So he had enjoyed a good lunch on the flight, checked into a suite in the Sacher Hotel, and even enjoyed the concert. He had absorbed some of the excitement and exuberance, and his finely tuned ear had appreciated the subtleties and harmonies of the music. This had been heightened by watching Mick Williams juggling the total sound with both skill and obvious enjoyment.

The number ended and the audience erupted and Gemmel began to edge his way out to the exit.

Two hours later Mick Williams watched the road crew load the last flight case into the trailer, close the steel doors, and snap on the padlock. He heaved a satisfied sigh and was about to go for his jacket when a voice stopped him.

"Mr. Williams, can I have a word with you?"

He turned. It was the well-dressed stranger he had seen hanging about for the last half hour.

"What is it?"

"It will take a few minutes. There's a bar across the road. Perhaps we could have a drink?"

Mick shook his head. This fellow was obviously looking for an invite to the end-of-tour party. Probably trying to rediscover his lost youth, Mick thought, as he took in the man's clothing and his hairstyle. Thinks the place will be full of groupies, booze, and drugs.

"Forget it," he said shortly. "I'm tired and have no time."

"It's about a job, Mr. Williams."

"You can't have one." Mick started to move away. The man followed.

"You don't understand. I'm offering you a job. It's only for a couple of weeks and I know you're now free for at least a month. It pays well."

Mick became irritated. "Piss off, will you? Sure I'm free for a month, but I'm taking time out." He moved away again.

"The job pays fifteen thousand pounds."

Mick came to a halt and turned slowly.

"Fifteen big ones! For two weeks' work?"

The man nodded.

"Who are you?" Mick asked suspiciously. "And what's the bloody job? I'm only a sound engineer, pal!"

"I know exactly what you are," the man said. "The best sound engineer in Europe. As to what the job is and who I am, let's have that drink and I'll tell you."

He led the unprotesting Mick across the street and into the bar.

Gordik's country dacha was spacious and comfortable, as befitted a senior member of the apparatus. It was also very private, being situated in extensive forested grounds.

Maya had arrived an hour before, having driven from Moscow in Gordik's limousine. Now she sat at the kitchen table, watching her mother bustle around, preparing a meal. She was mentally exhausted, for during the past days she had undergone an intensive course in espionage tradecraft. She had also been prepared for the inevitable questioning which would follow her defection and her immediate contact with Gemmel. For many hours different teams of interrogators had thrown at her every question she was likely to be asked. At first she had made mistake after mistake, but as the days passed she found her responses becoming almost automatic.

"You must be word-perfect," Gordik had stressed. "If they catch you out on the smallest detail it's like the thinnest edge of a wedge and they'll hammer that wedge in until they crack you open. They'll most likely question you at a place called Mendley. It's a country house in the south of England. They might appear to be soft and easy, but, Maya, they're very clever and you must never let down your defenses."

They had finished with her in the afternoon and she had felt a strange satisfaction at the progress she had made. She had a drink in Gordik's office with him, Tudin, and Larissa, and they had congratulated her.

"You have a natural talent as an actress," Tudin had said. "You'll make a good agent. It's just a pity that we didn't recruit you a couple of years ago."

"That's a fact," Gordik agreed. Somewhat humorously, he said to Tudin, "Start looking around for other talented ballet dancers, you never know when we could use them." To Maya he said, "Tomorrow you go back to Leningrad to re-join the company, but tonight you go to my dacha. Your mother is already there and is looking forward to seeing you. I've explained everything to her."

"Everything?" Maya had asked in surprise.

"Yes," Gordik replied gently. "I considered it very carefully and decided to tell her everything. She is, after all, the widow of a senior intelligence officer and she understands such matters. She's also a very tough and patriotic lady. I think you'll find that she doesn't entirely disapprove of what you are doing."

Maya's mother had greeted her at the door of the dacha and hugged her warmly and fussed around her, but she hadn't as yet mentioned anything about her forthcoming trip. Maya watched her now as she tended steaming pots, and wondered what was going through her mind. They had always been close and particularly so since the death of her father, and they had always been able to talk to each other freely, but now it was as though a curtain had been drawn across their feelings, as if there were a third person in the room, who was inhibiting their conversation.

But later, after the meal was finished and they were sitting over coffee, the curtain was abruptly drawn aside. They had talked during the meal mostly about trivialities, and Maya had felt herself growing colder and colder and her emotions being compacted ever tighter, but then, suddenly, as her mother was looking down at her half-empty coffee cup, tears had suddenly formed in her eyes and coursed down her cheeks. Maya jumped up and ran around the table to her and took her in her arms and for ten minutes mother and daughter had wept together. Finally Maya had said haltingly, "I wish he hadn't told you —I mean everything that I have to do."

Her mother wiped her tears away with a napkin and shook her head vigorously. "No, Maya, it's better this way. I would have suspected the worst anyway."

"It's hateful, Mama, but I have no choice. I have to try my best."

Her mother stood up and fetched the coffeepot and refilled the cups. She had herself under control now. She was a tall, stately woman with graying hair and a still beautiful face. Gordik was right, for the face showed great strength of character, and now, in her eyes, was a rigid determination. She gestured at the seat across the table and Maya sat down obediently and listened without interruption while her mother talked.

She spoke of their lives, of their position within the system, of how both Maya's grandfathers had been activists in the Revolution, and Marxists to the core of their souls; how Maya's father had worked and striven to rise up in the hierarchy and what that had meant both to herself and her daughter. In essence, they belonged to the elite and for three generations had taken advantage of that. Their lives had been made inevitably more comfortable than the masses. They had been able to go for holidays to their own dacha on the Black Sea, to buy food and drink in special shops, and to have all the comforts of life in a country where most people had very few. She herself had joined the Communist Party at the age of nineteen, and although she had never pressed Maya to do so, she had been waiting expectantly for her to suggest it herself. It was a question, finally, of gratitude, of paying one's debts. Comrade Gordik had been explicit and frank. Maya was needed for an important task and all personal considerations had to be put aside. She had told Comrade Gordik that her family would do its duty as it had always done. Her voice trembled with emotion as she explained to Maya—as she had explained to Comrade Gordik—that it was unnecessary to apply pressure on Maya through herself. She understood the reasons for it and accepted them, but as far as she was concerned her daughter must act only in the interests of the Party and the country. She loved Maya and she felt great pain at the sacrifice she would have to make. That pain was no greater than her loyalty to a system that had given them everything.

Maya had never known her to speak so dramatically and she realized that it was the emotion and the sadness which had brought it out. She had always known her mother to have great strength, but she would never have believed that she could smother her affection for her daughter with loyalties which, to Maya, seemed bizarre. She began to argue, to point out that she owed the system nothing, that her talent was inborn and took no heed of politics or patriotism. Then her mother's anger erupted. She told her of the strings that had been pulled by her father to maneuver her into the best position to take advantage of her talent, of how he had even exerted clandestine pressure on the director of the Maly Ballet Company to ensure that not only would Maya be invited to join the company but that her ongoing career would be nurtured and promoted. Then she reduced Maya to dumbfounded shock and tears by telling her that on Maya's first tour to the West it had been arranged that Olga Lanov, whom she had understudied, should become sick before the last performance and so give Maya the opportunity to become a heroine. It was something she would never have told her, a secret she would have carried to her grave, but now, at this moment, Maya had to understand what was owed and who owed it.

Finally Maya was beyond tears. After the weeks of intense mental effort, all of this had become too much. She rose from the table and went up to her room, took off her clothes, and lay for several hours without sleep, her mind constantly turning over what her mother had said and what the implications were. At four in the morning she heard the bedsprings creaking in the next room. She crept out of bed and slipped on a robe and went to her mother's room and turned on the light. Her mother lay with her head against the pillow, her eyes open and red. They looked at each other for a long time, then Maya switched off the light, moved to the bed, and climbed in beside her mother. She laid her head against her breast and held her tight and, before sleeping, told her that she would do everything that was necessary.

It was all way beyond Hawke's understanding, but he arranged his features so as to look as intelligent as possible and watched closely as Elliot Wisner pointed out the various features on the model and talked of $CO_2$ containers, collimation lenses, high-voltage activators, and so on. The model was in a scale of 1 to 20 and Hawke tried to picture the size of the completed laser. It would be about as big as his bedroom, and that realization caused him to wonder at the scientific development which allowed it to be lifted thirty-six thousand kilometers into space and then to be positioned and aimed so accurately as to strike an object on earth inside a five-meter radius. He tried again to follow Wisner's lecture but he was now talking about the electromagnetic spectrum. Hawke gave up and glanced round the room.

They were in the "encapsuled security" area of the U.S. Air Force Plant Number 42 in Palmdale, California. Hawke was on an inspection tour to check on the progress of the laser construction, and on his home ground Wisner was having a field day. Apart from Hawke, Wisner, and Meade, who was looking frankly bored, there were two other men in the room, both wearing white coats and superior expressions, for they were scientists and knew what Wisner was talking about. Hawke felt he had to ask an intelligent question.

"What about the divergence control system?" he asked.

Wisner smiled at the two white-coated men and tapped a barrel-shaped bulge on the laser tube.

"That's contained in here. Frankly, Morton, you may have been able to follow my explanations up to now, but that unit and the principles behind it are far more difficult. However, I'll try if you like."

A look of consternation crossed Meade's face and Hawke smiled and said, "No, forget it, Elliot. Just as long as the damn thing works!"

"Oh, it will, Morton, it will."

Hawke glanced at his watch in an obvious gesture and Wisner said, "Well, that wraps it up in here. Now we go to see the telemetrics people."

They all stood and Hawke shook hands with the two scientists and mumbled something about "keeping up the good work" and "pressing on" and then he and Meade followed Wisner out.

There was a security desk outside the door and a uniformed guard checked their red identification tags and made a note on a clipboard. They entered a lift, descended two floors, and then walked along another corridor to another security check. After looking at his clipboard the guard gave them blue identification tags.

"Compartmentalized security," Wisner said airily as he ushered them through a door, and Hawke gave Meade a look which spoke volumes.

They entered a large white room. Computer consoles lined one wall and design tables another. Two men, also in white coats bearing blue tags, were working at the tables. Wisner introduced them as Gordon Rance and Vic Raborn. Then he gave another little lecture, about telemetrics and how the satellite containing the laser would be connected by computers, both on board and on the ground, which would talk to each other by radio signals. He waved a hand at Rance and said:

"Gordon here is one of NASA's top experts on telemetrics. He helped design all the systems for the *Apollo* moon landing missions. Have you got anything to add, Gordon?"

Rance shook his head. "I don't think so, Elliot, you've explained it very well."

Something buzzed in Hawke's head but he couldn't pin it down and Wisner was going on about how Rance and Raborn were also designing the homing device and destruct mechanism, and how that was mere child's play to them as the techniques involved were so simple. Anyway, their design job would be finished in about ten days and then they would be off back to Houston.

There was more handshaking and Hawke mumbled his little pep talk and they left.

It was an hour later and they were eating lunch in the canteen when the buzz in Hawke's head suddenly cleared. He put down his fork and asked Wisner sharply, "That guy back there—the telemetric guy. Where's he from?"

"Which one?"

"Rance. Where's he from?"

Wisner looked puzzled. "Rance? I told you, he's a NASA man, his home base is Houston—the Johnson Space Center."

Hawke shook his head. "No, I mean before. Where's he from originally? I mean, the guy's got a sort of British accent."

"Oh," Wisner nodded. "Well, he was British. He joined NASA back in nineteen sixty, after the British gave up on their Blue Streak missile project. A whole bunch of their scientists and technicians joined then, about a dozen or more."

Hawke slid Meade a look and then said coldly, "And you put him on this project?"

Wisner became irritated. "Look, Morton, he's been an American citizen for over fifteen years. Quite a few of their guys stayed on here and took out citizenship. He's got top clearance from you people. Check it out!"

"I will! Damn right I will!" He gave another look to Meade, who took out his pad and made a note.

"You have any more like him?" Hawke asked.

"No," answered Wisner. "But there are still three or four with NASA. Christ, Morton, get things into perspective. Those guys played a big part in helping us put Armstrong on the moon first. Hell, they even got citations from the President!"

Hawke leaned forward and said with intensity, "Elliot, listen to me. One of the reasons the British are going along with the project, and sticking their necks out for us, is that they would just love to discover how you people controlled the laser divergence problem. You forgetting that little farce in Paris, Elliot?"

Wisner started to protest, but Hawke held up a hand.

"And Gemmel already tried to get a liaison man over here to look over your shoulder and you can bet that they won't give up!"

Now Wisner made his voice heard, and he was angry.

"You're preaching to the converted! I worked on that breakthrough. Worked on it for years. You think I'd jeopardize that?" He waived his arm around the canteen. "You've seen our security setup here. I told you it's compartmentalized. Rance is cleared for the blue zone, and that's all. There's no way he can get anywhere near the laser, or the design rooms, or the crap-house used by the secretaries, so back off, Morton!"

"His work doesn't bring him into any contact?"

Wisner sighed. "I told you—he's pure telemetrics. He designs the signaling system which controls the satellite. That's all."

"And the homing device?"

"Sure, and that's going to be thirty-six thousand kilometers away from the goddam laser!"

Hawke sighed. "All right, Elliot, cool off. You say they'll be finished in a couple of weeks?"

"At the outside. And they'll have no more contact with the project. They don't even know what they're designing it for. They don't even know a laser's involved. I told you; we're compartmentalized."

Hawke was reassured and he made appropriate noises and ordered drinks. But still, as he and Meade drove out of the main gates, he told his assistant to double-check on every single member of Wisner's team.

The intercom on Gemmel's desk buzzed and his secretary's voice told him that Mr. Cheetham had arrived. He told her to send him in, and some tea. Then he opened a drawer and took out two files.

Cheetham was a short, fair man of indeterminate age. He affected a thin moustache and, like some of his countrymen, neglected to shave the fuzz from the top of his cheeks. This gave him a slightly comical air.

He sat across the desk from Gemmel, reading the files and looking at the photographs. Occasionally he reached forward and took a sip of his tea. After each sip he unconsciously wiped his lips with a white handkerchief.

When he closed the files and looked up, Gemmel asked, "Any questions, Ray?"

Cheetham shook his head. "No, Peter, they seem pretty complete."

"They have to look like very genuine accidents."

"Don't worry, they will. Thanks for the tea."

He stood up and headed for the door.

"They are not bad men, Ray," Gemmel called after him.

Cheetham turned. "That doesn't make it easier, you know."

Gemmel spread his hands. "Sorry, that was stupid. I hate the whole business."

Cheetham smiled without mirth. "At least, at the end, we get a pension."

He went out, closing the door quietly behind him.

# *thirteen*

IT WAS A TYPICAL RECEPTION OF THE TYPE GIVEN FOR touring ballet companies. The guest list was made up of a hard core of dedicated amateurs, who greeted each other with loud familiarity, and a large fringe of sycophants who were there for a little social mountaineering and the free drinks.

But Lev Tudin found it stimulating and interesting. He was on his first overseas assignment as the temporary tour control officer for the Maly company. Gordik had decided that Lev would be on hand when the swallow made her run.

The company had fulfilled engagements in Copenhagen, Bonn, Brussels, and Paris, and Tudin had vastly enjoyed himself. The only slight hiccup had come on the last night in Paris, when he had been awakened in the middle of the night to be informed that one of the young male dancers had disappeared and it was feared he might have defected, but they eventually found him in a gay bar in Montmartre and hauled him back into the fold. This was their first night in London, and on the morrow the company would start a week of performances at the Coliseum. Tudin thought it a strange name for a theatre. It evoked visions of the Roman elite watching Christians being torn to pieces by lions and tigers. His eyes swept the large room, taking in the company's various dancers. Not a lion among them, but he spotted one young quarter dancer who, a few nights ago in Brussels, had proved to be quite a tigress.

He could hardly see Maya Kashva because her diminutive figure was surrounded by a group of admirers. Her presence had caused a stir wherever the company had performed, for it was her first full tour as a prima ballerina and her reputation had preceded her out of Russia. So far she had received rave notices on the Continent, and although the London critics were noted for their acerbity, Tudin concluded that her dancing would melt even their hearts.

Among the group surrounding her he picked out his own people. Three in all. Two men and a woman. They had been carefully prepared for the forthcoming events, as had Maya herself. The only participant missing was the man himself. Tudin glanced at his watch and felt a twinge of anxiety. The London KGB station had confirmed that Gemmel was in the city as of that morning. He had been seen leaving his small mews house and entering Petworth House. But the reception had been under way for almost an hour and most of the guests had arrived long since.

Then Gemmel was coming through the door, and Tudin was blowing air through a gap in his front teeth, something he always did at moments of relief. He watched as Gemmel crossed the room toward the bar, stopping occasionally to greet acquaintances. Tudin glanced again at the group surrounding Maya and caught the eye of one of his men and nodded almost imperceptibly at Gemmel, who had now reached the bar. His man nodded back and Tudin leaned against the wall, sipped his drink, and carefully observed the unfolding scene.

It took fifteen minutes to bring Maya and Gemmel into casual contact. First, Tudin's operatives skillfully thinned out the group around Maya. The manager of the Coliseum was politely buttonholed by the director of the company and led away to discuss the next morning's rehearsals. Then the woman who wrote for the *Dancing Times* and *Guardian* was engaged in earnest conversation by the London *Tass* correspondent. Slowly, one by one, the group was broken up, finally leaving only Maya and two of Tudin's people. These three, talking together, moved toward the bar, where Gemmel stood chatting to Sir Patrick Fane, but watching the approaching dancer.

Even from across the room Tudin could hear Sir Patrick's high, nasal voice as he began the introductions.

"Peter, dear fellow, have you met Miss Kashva . . . ?"

But then Gemmel was saying something which Tudin couldn't hear and he was smiling and holding out his hand, and Maya was coolly shaking it. Moments later Sir Patrick was skillfully edged away, and Gemmel and Maya were left alone. They talked for ten minutes, and to Tudin's eye the small circle of carpet around them became a chessboard. The moment another guest stepped into that circle he or she was deftly intercepted by a Russian. It was like a ballet in itself and Tudin could see that Gemmel was completely unaware of it, his whole attention focused on Maya. Tudin watched her with fascination, as he had watched her at half a dozen similar receptions. He was beginning to understand how she had remained virtually untouched. She had an aloof, remote manner with men; her face showed little expression, whatever was being said to her. He knew that among the rest of the company she was known as "the iceberg." It was not a sign of disrespect, for on stage her dancing had a warmth and passion that clearly illustrated her depth of emotion. He thought that it might be the music that unlocked her feelings—the music and her physical interpretation of it. Perhaps all of her emotions went into her act, leaving nothing for personal relationships. During the past month he had seen dozens of attractive and personable men make extreme efforts to break down her reserves—and seen them all fail.

So he watched closely and, at first, decided that her

reaction to Gemmel was true to form, but then he saw the almost imperceptible differences, and his instinct told him that it was not an act.

She was quite small and usually liked to stand well back from people as she talked. Also she rarely looked for any length of time at a man's face, but would gaze away to one side while he talked to her.

But now with Gemmel, Tudin noted, she stood close to him, her shoulder almost touching his arm, and that although her face retained its normal detached expression, she was looking up at him, her gaze never wavering from his face. Anyone else observing the scene would have failed to notice, but Tudin could sense the intimacy of the moment. Then he saw Gemmel smile and reach into his inside jacket pocket and pass her something. She looked down and then tucked it into her evening bag and very formally they shook hands and she turned away and Gemmel moved to the bar. Tudin pushed himself off the wall, and without looking around, walked to the door.

She came into his room twenty minutes later, closing the door behind her and leaning against it. Tudin sat on the bed and looked at her through narrowed eyes.

"He's leaving tonight," she said quietly, sadly.

"For where?"

She shook her head. "He didn't say. Wouldn't say; just a business trip."

"Shit!" The expletive came out with great fervor, but then Tudin looked at her face again and she was grinning at him impishly.

"But he's coming back in four or five days and he expects to be at the last performance!"

"You little witch! Don't do that to me!"

He got up and crossed the small room to the dressing table and poured himself a large Scotch. She moved to the single chair and sat down.

"Would you like something?" he asked, gesturing at the bottle.

"I'd like Champagne!"

Tudin smiled, crossed to the phone, and ordered a bottle of Moët & Chandon, then sat down again on the bed.

"So tell me, little witch, tell me everything."

She crossed one slim leg over the other, savoring his impatience. "He invited me for dinner or, as he put it, 'supper,' after the last performance."

"So?"

"So I told him that might be very difficult, that I already had an engagement, which, however, I might be able to break—and could I telephone him?"

"And?"

She smiled a very satisfied smile. "And so he gave me a card with his home phone number and address."

She opened her evening bag, took out the card, and passed it to Tudin.

He read: "Peter Gemmel, 14 Burley Mews, Chelsea, SW3. Tel: 352 9911."

Tudin began blowing air through the gap in his front teeth. He looked up and grinned at the ballerina. "Perfect! Just perfect! What else did you talk about?"

"Oh, just ballet. He reminded me of our conversation in Brussels three years ago. Told me he had followed my career and how pleased he was that his prediction had come true."

Tudin was nodding in satisfaction. "Obviously he likes you. For a man in his position even to invite you for dinner, he must like you."

"Lev, don't be silly. He's a balletomane. They all invite me for dinner—and much else. Why should he be different?"

"He is different, Maya. But, tell me, how do you feel about him now?" His voice assumed a tone of mock severity. "Will you feel inclined to kick him in a tender part of his person?"

Very slowly she shook her head. "No, Lev. Peter Gem-

mel is not the kind of man that I would try to kick anywhere."

Tudin was surprised—not by what she had said, but by
the envy that stabbed through him. It was something that
had been building up inexorably. In fact, it had started
the moment he first set eyes on her in Gordik's office.
Tudin was a highly intelligent, politically motivated man,
and had never in his life truly fallen in love. In a way it
was his one uncertainty, for he saw himself as a clumsy,
gangling sort of person, and although he had an eye for
great beauty, he could never bring himself to believe that
any deep feelings he might have for an attractive woman
would be reciprocated. Throughout the tour he had felt
his feelings draw ever more deeply toward Maya, and
now, as she was about to start her mission, his emotions
were in a quandary. On the one hand, he was excited at
the possibilities of the mission; but on the other hand, the
thought of Maya giving herself to another man was painful in the extreme, especially after he had seen them together and had recognized the feelings in her that already
existed for Gemmel.

His face must have mirrored his thoughts, for suddenly
she asked, "Lev, why are you so sad?"

He shook his head. "I'm not sad, Maya, I was just
thinking."

Her smile was gentle and understanding. "No, I don't
think you were. I have some perception and I've watched
you the last month and I know what you're thinking."

He was about to say something, but she held up her
hand and said, "It's better not to say anything, Lev, but
I want you to know that your being on this tour and your
being here now has made it much easier. I just wish you
were staying on in London afterward. It would be a comfort knowing that you were nearby."

"I wish I could," he said, "but it's impossible. We have
to follow normal procedure and the British would be suspicious if I stayed on." He managed a smile. "But I'll be

thinking about you—we all will—and not just about your mission, or the success of it." He felt a rising embarrassment at the tone of his voice and forced himself to get the conversation back to a businesslike footing. "You haven't forgotten the code words and their implications?"

She smiled wanly. "No, Lev, they're all in my head, and especially 'fur boots.' I hope the weather doesn't get too hot or the conversation might sound ridiculous."

"Are you nervous?" he asked.

"No, I'm past being nervous. I've committed myself and I'll go through with it, no matter what."

There followed a silence, which was broken by a tap on the door. Lev stood up and opened it, revealing the waiter with the Champagne.

Morton Hawke was proud of his eyesight and he was determined to pick out the camp. He divided the valley, and the low hills beyond, into sectors and scrutinized them one by one. Three large trailers, Gemmel had told him, and two tents—in line of sight and within two miles. Hawke completed his survey. Nothing.

"Well?" Gemmel asked from behind him.

"Wait."

Hawke started again with the first sector. His eyes were beginning to ache with the concentration and the glare of the sun, but he was a determined man, and if there was a large camp housing a dozen men and a lot of equipment, he was damn well going to spot it.

But after another ten minutes he had seen nothing, and Gemmel's voice was becoming impatient.

"Well?"

Hawke turned and shook his head. "You're sure it's above the ground?"

Gemmel grinned and climbed into the driving seat of the Land Rover. "Let's go."

They bumped down the sandy slope and across the floor of the valley, with Hawke peering, gimlet-eyed, through

the windshield, but it wasn't until they had almost reached
the low hills on the far side that suddenly and dramatically
the camp appeared in front of him. Three huge trailers
forming a triangle, and in the middle, two tents. Everything was painted a mottled brown and the entire camp
was loosely covered in camouflage netting.

"My compliments to your camouflage expert," Hawke
said. "Apart from anyone walking into it accidentally, it's
damned secure."

Two men had lifted up a corner of the netting and the
Land Rover moved under it. Gemmel pointed out a small
dish scanner, revolving slowly atop one of the trailers.

"Doppler antipersonnel radar," he said. "It's manned
day and night, so no accident is going to happen."

Hawke nodded in approval. "I like it. I like it a lot."

They climbed out of the Land Rover as Alan Boyd
came down the steps of one of the trailers. After shaking
hands with Hawke he turned to Gemmel.

"He left Medina yesterday morning, so his ETA at the
cave is sixteen hundred hours today." He glanced at his
watch. "That's in just over three hours." He turned back
to the trailer and Gemmel and Hawke followed him into
the air-conditioned interior.

"This is our operations HQ and communications center," Boyd explained to Hawke. At one end of the trailer
was a bank of radio equipment and the Doppler radar
screen. An operator sat in front of it, watching the flickering light.

There were a table and chairs in the center and a water
cooler in a corner. Several large-scale maps lined one
wall. Gemmel was about to say something when Hawke
held up a hand for silence. They all listened intently, but
the only sound was a low hum.

"Whoever silenced your generating unit," Hawke said,
"did one hell of a job."

"Thanks." Gemmel pointed through a small window at
the two other trailers. "That's accommodation and mess-

ing and that one houses the sound and other equipment."

He turned and moved over to the wall maps. One showed detail of the area southeast of Medina. Gemmel pointed to a blue pinhead. "This is the cave." His finger traced a line and stopped at another pinhead. "We are here. One point seven kilometers away over these hills. The sound truck is connected to the cave by a multicore cable. It's lightly buried under the sand and enters the cave at the rear ceiling." He moved down a bit and pointed to a diagram of the cave. "Right here."

"And where are the speakers and everything?"

"I'll leave that for Williams to explain."

"Williams?"

"He's our sound expert—a top man, believe me." Gemmel turned to Boyd. "How's he holding up, by the way?"

Boyd grinned. "He's like a kid who's been let loose in a toy factory!"

"What's his normal work?" Hawke asked.

"He puts on rock concerts."

"Rock concerts?"

"Sure. When he saw that cave for the first time he said, 'What a fantastic gig I could stage in here!' "

Hawke was disconcerted. He turned to Gemmel. "Is he secure?"

"Don't worry," Gemmel reassured him. "He's signed the Official Secrets Act and after this we'll keep a close watch on him."

"But is he the right kind of man for a job like this?"

"Tell me, Morton," Gemmel asked, "have you been disappointed by what you've seen so far?"

"No," Hawke answered. "No, I haven't."

"And neither will you be by Mick Williams, or the setup he's put together."

Abu Qadir slept well that first night, at least until an hour before dawn. He had collected some brushwood and built a fire just inside the entrance to the cave, for the desert nights were cold. The only sounds in the night had been the occasional crack of rocks that moved and settled as the temperature rapidly dropped, but these did not disturb Abu Qadir's sleep, for they were the noises of the desert and he was used to them. But an hour before dawn, something did disturb his sleep. He awoke and lay very still, listening. He had heard a voice, or thought he had. A faraway voice, calling his name. He strained his ears for many minutes, but hearing nothing, he reached out and pushed more brushwood onto the embers, for now it was bitterly cold. Then he heard it again, but it was not like hearing it from outside or far away. It was as though the voice came from inside his head, reaching his ears from the center, and it was a voice both low and clear, a voice that echoed in his brain, twice:

"Abu Qadir! Abu Qadir!"

He slowly sat up and pulled his knees to his chest and clasped his arms around them. He had not moved when the sun rose, and he heard nothing more. He sat like that until long after dawn, then reached for his gourd and drank some water, then he went out into the desert and walked back and forth in front of the cave for many hours, only stopping occasionally to refresh himself from the gourd, and once to relieve himself. In the hour before sunset he collected more brushwood and built and lit the fire. He sat beside it and he didn't move. His eyes were fixed on the entrance to the cave, but they were glazed and he appeared not to notice the light grow dark. He did not sleep at all. Just sat as immobile as the rock around him. Again the voice came an hour before dawn, but this time it did not only call his name.

Mick Williams sat in a swivel chair that was mounted on casters. He wore faded, frayed jeans, an old T-shirt, and a pair of cowboy boots. His eyes moved constantly from the small red monitor screen mounted high on the wall to the array of equipment and LED readouts that formed a semicircle around him. Gemmel, Boyd, and Hawke stood at his back. Speakers were mounted in each top corner of the trailer. Hawke knew that they were J. B. Lansing monitors. He knew what all the equipment was because that afternoon Williams had lovingly explained for over two hours. He had shown him the multitrack tape machine which would carry the twelve parallel tracks of speech; the thirty-two-channel mixing console which operated the tape functions, leaving twenty channels for processing the special sound effects. These effects and the equipment that produced them were formidable.

During the afternoon Williams had demonstrated them by first taping Hawke's voice and then moving it through the sound spectrum, changing its entire character moment to moment, giving the voice disembodied movement and making Hawke twist and turn as the sound moved around the truck—at one moment seeming to come as an echo from miles away, at the next moment swirling around inside his own head. Williams had explained that in the cave it would be even better. The acoustics were fantastic. There were eight JBL studio monitors spaced out over the cathedral-like ceiling. The Arab would hear a voice like the shifting of the wind—a whisper in his ear, in his head, moving as he moved. A voice without source or direction. A voice that could belong to no mortal. A dozen ultra-sensitive microphones strung up around the cave would not only enable Williams to hear the Arab and select the appropriate tracks but he could even feed back any voice reactions via his racks of harmonizers, delay timers, equalizers, and modulators, thus increasing the disorientation of the Arab.

Also attached to the cave's ceiling were two closed-circuit, image-intensifying television cameras. The monitor now showed the vague red form of the sitting man. If he got up and moved around, Williams could move the sound with him—surround him with it, blending from one speaker to the next.

Finally there was a hologram projector, which produced, by the use of a laser, a three-dimensional image.

In this case it would be a vague, wraithlike form, suspended in the center of the dark cave.

As the lecture had ended, Hawke had felt a mounting optimism, but had also felt constrained to ask a question.

"There's no chance of any tape hiss or feedback?"

Willliams had given him a withering look. Gemmel had smiled and said, "Morton, the equipment's been tested and retested. Mick's put together one of the most sophisticated systems in existence."

Hawke had been convinced and had congratulated the sound engineer, who had merely shrugged and remarked that anything could be done with an open-ended budget.

"How much?" Hawke had asked Gemmel.

"With transportation and the whole team there won't be much change out of a million dollars."

Hawke had nodded soberly. Miracles didn't come cheap. But it was loose change compared with what was coming in a couple of months.

Now Hawke looked over Williams' shoulder at the TV monitor and the vague, sitting form of the man who was about to have a revelation. Out of the corner of his eye he saw Gemmel glance at his watch.

"Let's do it," he murmured softly, and Williams' hands reached forward and punched buttons, and one of the giant reels of tape began to revolve slowly, and strips of light-emitting diodes flickered, indicating various levels, and the voice came softly through the monitors:

"Abu Qadir! Abu Qadir!"

Four pairs of eyes watched the screen and saw Abu Qadir stiffen and sit up straight and then the voice went whispering on and Gemmel leaned close to Hawke and in a hushed voice translated the Arabic into English.

Hawke was mesmerized, his eyes never leaving the screen. Gemmel's voice assumed a rhythmic, hypnotic cadence as he conveyed the poetry of the Koranic language:

"Recite in the name of the Lord who created
Man from blood coagulated,

Recite! Thy Lord is wondrous kind
Who by the pen has taught mankind
Things they knew not—being blind."

Hawke had seen a translation of the tapes that had been sent to Falk a week before. He knew that the opening words were the same that the angel Gabriel had spoken to Muhammad in A.D. 610. The words that gave birth to a vast and vibrant religion that was to sweep across the world.

But now the words that Gemmel was whispering in his ear had not been spoken before. They told of the desolation of Islam, the corruption and deviation, of heretical thought and behavior. A twisting and abuse of God's Word as transmitted through his Prophet Muhammad. Now, through his messenger, Abu Qadir, the Word would be heard again, heard by believers and nonbelievers alike, until all believed and worshiped in the light of Muhammad's revelations.

At this Abu Qadir rose to his feet and slowly turned. On the monitor his features could not be discerned but suddenly his voice came through the truck's speakers, a quavering, moaning voice.

Gemmel stiffened. He knew by heart the twelve different options recorded on the multitrack machine and made his choice almost instantly.

"Track seven," he said flatly.

Williams' finger punched a button and then another. One channel was muted and another started.

In Hawke's ear Gemmel's voice was tense as he continued the translation:

"Did He not find thee an orphan, and give thee a name?
Did He not find thee in error and guide thee to the truth?
Now only wilt thou hear the Word,
For thou art blessed and wilt pass the Word on earth.
So that all may have the choice and on the day

Those who believe will enter Paradise.
Now thou wilt open thy mind and thine ears."

On the monitor the figure of Abu Qadir remained motionless. His head raised slightly. Gemmel called another number and Williams' fingers moved and cued another sound track. Over his shoulder he asked casually, "Hologram?"

"Wait," Gemmel said, and continued translating for Hawke. Now Abu Qadir was being instructed. He would go to Jeddah and there he would find "companions," *ashāb*, and he would find "exiles," *muhājirūn*, and "helpers," *ansār*. Above all he would find a man who would become for him just as Umar had been for Muhammad. This man would know him and would immediately follow him and in worldly ways he would advise him and assist him even as Umar had advised and assisted Muhammad.

For ten more minutes they watched the red, rigid figure of Abu Qadir as he stood immobile, listening to the voice. Williams could have been sitting at the sound console of a rock concert. He couldn't understand the words and hardly seemed to care, but he played on his instruments and the sound became a living thing, changing in pitch and tonality, moving through the speakers, whispering and rustling and filling the trailer and the cave, and then the voice stopped, and Gemmel's whispered translation tapered off with the words "Now thou wilt see, O Messenger."

His voice sharpened: "Hologram, Mick!"

Williams reached forward and punched a button and they all looked up at the screen.

"You won't see it," Gemmel said. "It won't come through on the screen."

"How does it look?" Hawke breathed.

"He will see only a vague form, but in his state and in his eyes that form will take on the image of the angel Gabriel."

"And what will he see?"

"What he wants to see. Look now!"

On the screen Abu Qadir moved. His head tilted and his arms slowly rose, palms upward, fingers outstretched, then abruptly he fell to his knees and then to his chest, arms still outstretched—the posture of total submission and obedience.

"End it!" Gemmel's voice cracked out and Williams tore his eyes from the screen and punched buttons and in the trailer there was a combined exhalation of breath. Then Hawke was pounding Gemmel on the back and then Mick Williams, who was grinning, and then Alan Boyd, who was rubbing a big hand over his sweating face.

"Turn it off. It's done!"

Williams fingered a button and the screen went blank, and there was a silence in the trailer as the others turned again to look at Gemmel.

He dropped his eyes and took a deep breath and said quietly, "All right, I know. It's an operation, and it succeeded. But that's a man in that cave. A simple, uneducated man." He shrugged his shoulders resignedly. "So we spend a million dollars and make him believe he's a messenger of God. So we think it's necessary—but let's not make heroes of ourselves."

There was an embarrassed silence and then Hawke said a bit caustically, "I thought you were an atheist?"

Gemmel smiled grimly. "I am. We're all that way, or we wouldn't be here." He looked hard at Hawke. "Morton, I'm not bothered in the least about the sacrilegious aspects of what happened. It's just that we've effectively warped a man's mind. Now, in a couple of months he's going to go out and in front of two and a half million people proclaim himself a prophet. He'll do it with total blind confidence because the angel Gabriel told him that on that day God will be with him." His voice hardened and he tapped Hawke on the chest with his forefinger. "And if you people don't make sure that God delivers on the day, some of those two and a half million people are going to tear the poor bastard to pieces."

"Don't worry." Hawke grinned. "God works in strange and, lately, scientific ways. He, or Elliot Wisner, will deliver. Now, what about a large Scotch?"

Gemmel shook his head. "Can't do it, Morton. You're in a fundamentalist Islamic state. The Koran bans all alcohol."

"You didn't bring any?"

"Certainly not." Gemmel gestured at the equipment. "It would be bad enough getting caught with this lot, but a case of Scotch would be adding insult to injury."

"Hell!" Hawke said fervently, and Alan Boyd smiled wryly.

"If we're wrong, and there is a God, that's exactly where we'll end up."

# Book
## three

# fourteen

In the London Coliseum the orchestra struck up the overture to *La Bayadère*; Maya Kashva, dressed in turban and tunic for the role of Lycra, peered through a gap in the curtains and watched Peter Gemmel take his seat in the tenth row of the stalls. He looked tired and drawn, much as he had sounded on the phone that afternoon. Tudin had told her that he had been seen entering his house and she had phoned an hour later. He had answered sleepily, but had come awake at the sound of her voice. She asked him how his trip had been and he told her: fine. Then she explained that she would be unable to have dinner with him. She had tried to arrange it, but such things could be difficult, especially as it would be the company's last night before returning to Russia and at such times certain people became nervous. So the whole company was expected to be at the end-of-tour party. She hoped he would understand. He had assured her that he did, and in any event, he was looking forward to watching her performance.

There had been a long pause, then he had asked, "Are you still there, Maya?"

"Yes," she had answered softly. "And, Peter, tonight you will be the only audience. I will dance for you."

And she hung up.

\* \* \*

As the ballet unfolded, Gemmel came to believe it. He well knew that a great dancer or singer was capable of projecting a performance to each member of an audience, but this was different. Maya Kashva was dancing only for him, and she danced with perfection blended with passion. The dividing line between technique and emotion became blurred and her intensity transmitted itself to the rest of the company and to the entire audience, but the sole recipient of her passion sat in the tenth row of the stalls and absorbed it and became one with her; moved with her; felt with her; and, finally, at the crescendo, was drained and exhausted. As the audience erupted and flung its combined adoration at the stage, he stood and pushed his way out, through the foyer, and onto the street and a wet, cold night, and walked the four miles to his small mews house, made himself strong coffee, poured a Cognac, and sank deep into an easy chair and tried to find himself.

There was barely space in the cramped dressing room, either for the flowers or the admirers. They flowed out down the narrow passage, a profusion of color and chatter.

Maya was tranquil but exhausted. She sat with her back to the mirror, slumped in a chair, hardly seeing or hearing the clamor. She relived the performance, movement by movement. Whatever was to happen, it would be forever etched in her mind and in her body. It was the rarest of occasions when events and circumstances combined to produce that final edge of an artist's soul. Maya Kashva knew that in the future she might dance as well, but never better, and she knew that one of the ingredients that produced that apex was the man she would now have to lie to, and perhaps destroy. But, no matter; over the past two hours she had given him a gift that was hers alone to give.

Lev Tudin stood at the door and watched her through the throng. He was experiencing a variety of emotions: tension at what was coming, emotion at what he had seen on the stage, emotion and a sadness, for he instinctively understood what had produced such a performance.

He saw her raise her eyes and look at him and nod, and he began to usher the people out. As he closed the door on the last of them, she swiveled her chair to the mirror and began wiping off her makeup. He remained by the door, watching her face in the mirror. Again he saw her look at him—a reflected glance.

"Maya," he said quietly. "I have seen you perform a dozen times over the past month. Tonight I saw you dance. I don't have the words to tell you how beautiful you were. I shall never forget it. I thank you."

She smiled at him in the mirror, a wan smile. "Perhaps it was the last time, Lev."

He shook his head. "I can't believe it. I won't believe it! Nothing could be so wrong."

She swiveled the chair again and looked at him directly, her face white with cleansing cream.

"All that is gone now," she sighed. "Soon I will be just a swallow looking for a nest."

He said it bluntly, painfully. "You danced for him."

"Yes, Lev. I danced for him. Maybe that's all I can do for him. Maybe that's all he wants of me."

He drew a deep breath. "We shall see. All the arrangements are made. You will slip out of the party at about midnight and then through a side entrance of the hotel. We have checked; there are always plenty of taxis on the Strand even at that hour. You will show the driver the card. It's a ten-minute journey, no more."

"No," she murmured. "It's a lifetime's journey."

Gemmel sat in a deep leather armchair in his small

sitting room. Books lined two walls from floor to ceiling. A Nakamichi stereo was mute in one corner. Other objects in the room also reflected the nature of the man. A small table, holding decanters of single-malt whisky, Polish grain vodka, Hennessy XO Cognac, La Ina sherry, and a set of Waterford crystal glasses.

Two Miró prints adorned a wall and on a side table stood a small Kendo sculpture of a rearing horse. But the room also had a casual, lived-in air. The myriad books were not so uniformly placed as to be mere decoration. Cushions were dumped haphazardly on the leather chairs and sofa and around the floor. A magazine rack held an untidy profusion of *Yachting* monthlies. The carpet was quite a good Persian, but one that in better days would have hung on a wall.

It was the room of a worldly, single man, not really wealthy but able to indulge certain whims, and one who was settling comfortably into his ways.

But at this moment Gemmel was unsettled. His brief sleep in the afternoon had not compensated for the long flight from Amman and the time change. That, and the emotional impact of the evening, combined to make him light-headed. He put a Schubert symphony on the turntable and poured himself another Cognac, but the drink remained untouched, and after five minutes, he turned off the music, his mind unable to cope.

He sat for over an hour, one moment almost asleep, the next wide awake as impressions filled his mind: a dark cave; green lights flickering on a mixing console; a girl, small and supple and lithe, dancing into his brain; the sun-baked sand of a desert valley; a girl dancing; the indistinct, framed image of a prostrated man; a girl dancing . . . and his doorbell ringing.

It was raining heavily, and although she stood under the small portico, her black hair was wet after a brief dash from the taxi. Gemmel watched as it did a three-point turn in the narrow mews and moved away; then he looked back at the girl, at her raincoated figure, wet hair, pale face, and large, frightened eyes.

Her lips moved as if to speak, but no sound emerged. The spatter of the rain amplified the silence, and then she put her hands to her face and convulsively started to sob and he reached out a hand and drew her in and closed the door on the cold, wet night.

The time difference made it five hours earlier in Langley, Virginia, and in his office Daniel Brand was reading the last page of Hawke's detailed report. The author sat across the desk, holding a thin cigar in his fingers and an expectant look on his face. Leo Falk sat beside him. He had also been reading the report but he was a faster reader than the Director and had already finished.

Brand finished reading, closed the file, tossed it onto his desk, leaned back in his chair, and surveyed Hawke through the cigar smoke.

"You surprise me, Morton."

"I do?"

"Yes." Brand indicated the report. "It's lyrical. I mean the way you wrote it."

"Lyrical?"

"Sure, like something out of the *Arabian Nights*."

Hawke leaned forward in his chair and said fervently, "It was, Dan, believe me, it was. You should've seen it!"

Brand sniffed, picked up the report again, selected a page, and read aloud.

" 'The operation was planned and carried out with the utmost precision. No detail, however minute, was overlooked, no contingency was unaccounted for. The satisfactory result was brought about by the highest level of professionalism.' " He tossed the report back onto the desk and glanced at Falk. "Morton, here, used to think the Limeys were a bunch of old women."

"A lot of them still are," Hawke said, "but this team is frontline and Gemmel, in particular, is one hell of an operator. You should've seen it."

Falk tapped the file on his knee. "But you said he was a little strange at the end of it."

Hawke considered for a moment and then said carefully, "He planned it and organized it—brilliantly. He's tough and highly intelligent and all his team hold him in the highest respect, almost reverence . . ."

"But?"

Hawke spread his hands. "I'm not sure. At the end there he was kind of affected—kind of emotional."

The Director indicated the report. "So, it seems, were you. I've read several of your reports. This is the first time I've detected even a shred of emotion."

Hawke's voice took on a defensive tone. "Well, sure, I have to admit it. I couldn't help being moved. I mean, watching a guy having a vision and all. The thing is, I kept it buttoned up, but I guess Gemmel showed it."

"You think he's having doubts?" Brand asked.

"No, I don't. I just think he's human and for the first time it showed."

Brand pondered deeply, rocking back and forth in his chair. Then he smiled again. "Maybe he's a mite more sensitive than you, Morton. Maybe a good man to play poker against."

Hawke shook his head. "That's what I thought, and after forty-eight hours in that damn desert I was down eight hundred bucks."

Brand roared with laughter and Hawke grinned and went on, "He's no chicken, Dan, and he expects us to deliver now. How's Wisner getting on? Did all his team check out all right?"

"Sure, Wisner's right on schedule and his team checked out—no wrinkles."

"Even the Limey, Rance?"

Brand's face turned serious. "Even the Limey. But that's by the by. Two days after he got back to Houston he took his cabin cruiser out alone in the Gulf for a day's fishing. It seems that while he was away some gas had leaked into the bilges. There must have been a short circuit or something. Five miles out, the cruiser and Rance blew up."

There was a long silence while Hawke gazed steadily at the Director. Very slowly Brand shook his head. "No, Morton, no! It was an accident. We wouldn't do that. I wouldn't sanction it. The guy checked out. He was A-OK."

"In that case," Hawke said, "I feel sorry for him and for my suspicions. It's just that Gemmel, in some ways, worries me. It's as though this operation is an annex to something else and I can't work it out. I like the guy and I respect his professionalism and we get on just fine, but I always have the feeling that he's holding back on something."

Brand leaned forward and rested his elbows on the desk. "You think the British are going to get cute?"

Falk interjected, "I don't see how they can. The candidate for the Mahdi was selected jointly on a random basis. The idea for controlling him through a 'disciple' was brilliant and that idea came from the British, but we control the disciple and so we control the Mahdi."

"It looks cast-iron," Hawke agreed, "but those guys can be trickier than a can of worms."

The Director considered for a few moments and then said to Hawke, "I think I'd like to meet this man, Gemmel. Can you ask him to come over here?"

"Sure," Hawke replied, a little surprised. "But we originally decided always to meet on neutral ground."

"Well, I'm too busy to leave the country right now," Brand said firmly, "and after all, it wouldn't be unusual for a senior officer in the intelligence organization of one of our allies to pay a visit to Washington." He tapped his fingers on the report. "I definitely want to meet him, Morton. See if you can fix it up."

Gemmel came into the sitting room, carrying a steaming mug of coffee. He put it on the table in front of Maya and sat down opposite. He had given her a towel, which she had wrapped around her wet hair like a turban, and it brought her performance as Lycra flooding back to him. She reached forward and picked up the mug in both hands and sipped the coffee, eyeing him apprehensively.

"You just walked out the door?" he asked.

She nodded. "I went to the toilet. I had left my coat there behind a cupboard. Earlier I had noted the way to the side entrance of the hotel. There were a lot of people about and I just slipped away."

Gemmel stood up and crossed to the drinks table. He poured two glasses of XO Cognac, carried one to her, and then sat down again. Maya poured the Cognac into her coffee and looked up to see the pained expression cross his face. Then he smiled at himself and took a sip from his glass and said:

"Maya, there are two things I must know immediately. First, why you defected, and second, why you came directly to me."

She answered the first easily: it was the same with almost every ballet dancer or writer who defected from the Eastern Bloc—artistic freedom. She talked of the rigid constraints of Soviet culture, the conformity of expression. She loved her country, but first and foremost she was an artist and she craved for artistic space, for the freedom to develop. She gave Nureyev and Baryshnikov as examples, how their talents had flowered and flourished in the West; Baryshnikov had even danced on Broadway with a cane and a straw hat!

Gemmel could clearly understand. At the remarkably young age of twenty-four she had already reached her creative limits in Russia. In the future she would have to dance only a limited repertoire approved by the system. It was no surprise to him that such a shining talent would seek broader fields.

To his second question she was hesitant. She had come to Gemmel for a variety of reasons, some practical, some whimsical. She spoke no English and he was fluent in Russian. She knew his address and that he lived alone.

He was interested in the ballet and could understand her motives. Simply, she had felt a bond of sympathy—a definite link. She knew she would be alone and she needed to be with someone who could talk to her and give her moral support.

"Were there any other reasons?" he asked, and she looked down at her half-empty cup of coffee. There was a silence while she obviously tried to reach a decision. Finally she took a deep breath, raised her head, and looked him straight in the eye.

"Yes. I knew that you were an important man in your government. In the apparatus here."

He looked at her very steadily and suddenly the conversation had taken on a different attitude. It had become an interview where a questioner keeps silent in the expectation that an answer might be developed. She shrugged and plunged on.

"I knew you were an intelligence agent." Now she looked at him defiantly.

His next question was one flat word. "How?"

She reminded him of their first meeting in Brussels three years earlier and told him how Savich, the control officer, had warned her off.

"And this time?" she asked. "Did anyone warn you off this time?"

She shook her head. "No."

He stood up. "Maya, I won't be long." He gestured at the drinks table. "Help yourself if you want more."

He left the room, and a few moments later she heard the tinkle of a phone being lifted. After ten minutes she crossed to the drinks table and poured herself more Cognac. This time she drank it straight.

It was more than half an hour before he returned. She watched him anxiously as he sat down. He spoke gently, but very seriously.

"Maya, listen to me carefully. Normally, if someone defects from the Eastern Bloc the procedure is straightforward. They apply to the Home Office for temporary asylum, which is almost always granted. Then they apply for permanent residence, either here or some other country of their choice. In your case, it's a little different."

"How?"

"Because you came straight to me." He smiled briefly. "That's not to say I'm an intelligence agent. It's just that circumstances make it different." He picked up his glass, drained it, and then crossed to the table and poured more. Over his shoulder he said:

"Maya, in a little while some people are going to come here. They will take you away to a house in the country and for a few days they will ask you questions."

He turned and saw her frightened eyes.

"It won't be bad, but you must tell them the truth—everything."

Her fright increased. She was twisting her glass in her fingers; her mouth began to quiver.

"It won't be bad," he repeated gently. "But it's necessary. Don't worry, Maya. They won't hurt you. It's very comfortable down there, really quite pleasant."

He watched as she brought herself under control.

"Will you be there?"

"No, that's not possible."

"Do I have to go?"

He sighed. "Yes, Maya. Even if you left here now and walked into a police station and asked for asylum you would still end up in that house in the country."

"Because I came straight to you?"

He nodded.

"Have I caused you a lot of trouble?"

"Not at all. I think I understand why you came to me. It's just that I have to be sure."

"They won't send me back?" The question was loaded with anxiety.

"Not if you tell them the truth."

She looked puzzled. "But what can I tell them? What will they want to know?" She turned her head at the sound of a car pulling up outside, doors slamming. Gemmel stood up and crossed to the door, saying, "They will want to know everything."

At first sight the two men appeared menacing, standing in the dim light under the portico, wearing dark, belted raincoats. But as they came into the light of the room and greeted Gemmel affably, Maya relaxed a little. One was in his early thirties, with a round, cheerful face and a ready smile. The other was small and quite elderly. When he took off his coat Maya saw that he was wearing an old cardigan which had a button missing. Gemmel introduced the young one as Mr. Bennett and the older one as Mr. Grey. As he poured them drinks, they talked to Maya about how terrible the weather was. They both spoke fluent Russian.

With everyone comfortably settled, Mr. Bennett took two pieces of paper from his jacket pocket and passed them to her, explaining that one was a request for temporary asylum, and the other was a statement confirming that she was going with them of her own free will. She saw that they were written in both English and Russian, and as she read the Russian, Mr. Grey said to Gemmel, in English:

"Big panic on already at the Russian Embassy, sir. Everyone rushing around, cars coming and going, we won't be the only ones who have a sleepless night."

"Be easy with her," Gemmel said. "She's frightened and she's highly strung."

"Yes, sir. I suppose all great artists are highly strung."

Gemmel smiled. "Some more then others. But she's very young."

Maya had finished reading and Bennett passed her a pen. She looked up at Gemmel. He gave her a nod, and she signed the papers.

They all stood up and Gemmel helped her on with her coat. Suddenly a thought struck her.

"What about clothes? I don't have anything."

"Don't you worry, miss," Mr. Grey said solicitously. "We have everything you need at Mendley, and afterward you'll be able to do some shopping."

She looked at Gemmel anxiously and he took her arm and led her to the door.

"You'll be all right, Maya, I promise you. I'll see you in a few days."

He stood at the door, watching, as the black car drove away. As it reached the corner of the mews he saw her white face peering back at him from the rear seat.

# fifteen

"JUST LIKE A HOMING PIGEON."

Perryman turned away from the window and the wet, gray view. From his seat in front of the large desk Gemmel spread his hands in a wordless gesture. They were in Perryman's office, and Perryman was in a cynical mood. He moved back to his desk, sat down, and gave Gemmel a quizzical look.

"But it's too obvious," Gemmel said. "Even for the KGB."

Perryman sat back in his chair, steepled his fingers, and gazed at the ceiling, which needed a coat of paint.

"Possibly," he said, "although on rare occasions they can be quite subtle. But why straight to you?"

Now Gemmel stood up and walked to the window. He found the view equally depressing and it darkened his mood still further.

"So what's come out so far?" he asked.

"Very little," Perryman answered. "Grey says her attitude is positive, but there are warning lights. First, her father was a high-up in the KGB; second, for a month before this tour she was absent from the company. She claims she had a torn ligament and was resting with her mother."

"It's possible," Gemmel interjected. "Prima ballerinas in Russia have a punishing schedule."

"So it's possible," conceded Perryman. "However, since her defection it's been impossible to verify her mother's whereabouts. Our people in Moscow have drawn a blank and she tried to phone her from Mendley but it appears the line has been disconnected."

"That's normal."

"Agreed, but it's not normal for defecting Russian ballet dancers to make a beeline for the Deputy Head of Operations of MI-Six."

Gemmel turned and sighed. "So that automatically makes her a swallow?"

Perryman reached forward and opened a file on his desk and studied the photograph clipped to the inside cover. "It automatically makes her a prime suspect. After all, she's very beautiful." He slid Gemmel a look.

"The majority of ballerinas are beautiful; it goes with the profession."

"Indeed," said Perryman enigmatically. "I favor the opera myself, and believe me, most prima donnas are as physically unattractive as their temperaments."

Gemmel sighed again. "There could still be other reasons."

"Tell me about them."

"Well, she knew me. She'd met me twice. She had no English and she knew I spoke Russian, and . . ." He paused and Perryman leaned forward, watching him closely.

"Go on, Peter."

"Well . . . well, there's an empathy between us."

"Really?"

"Yes."

Perryman said, almost to himself, "After two brief meetings lasting no more than ten minutes each and separated by three years, you detect an 'empathy'?"

Gemmel moved back to his seat and said thoughtfully, "It's not something one 'detects.' It's there or it isn't. The fact is, it exists, and thereby offers up an alternative explanation."

"But the timing, Peter. It's been two months; the timing is so logical."

"The concert tour was planned eighteen months ago."

Perryman conceded the point. "That's a fact, but the KGB can be very flexible. Would you like a sherry?"

Gemmel nodded and Perryman crossed to a drinks table in the corner.

"So what do we do about it?" Gemmel inquired of Perryman's back.

"We proceed accordingly." Perryman turned and brought the two glasses back to the desk.

"We didn't expect anything quite so obvious, but then we've often overestimated the KGB." He smiled ruefully. "Something they rarely do with us."

"So how do I proceed personally?" Gemmel asked softly, and there was a strained silence.

"Two months," Perryman said finally. "That's when the event is due to take place—and everything is on schedule?"

"It is," Gemmel answered. "The onus is now with the Americans. I'm due to fly to Washington tomorrow for a couple of days to work out final details for the joint HQ in Amman. It appears that the Director CIA wants to look me over. Boyd is monitoring the disciple in Jeddah. All other aspects are moving ahead well. Rumors are rife, and the media are starting to pick it up—with a little prompting. Come October there will be an air of great expectation."

"And the Americans are behaving themselves?"

"Up to a point. They've been rather obvious about keeping control of the disciple. Boyd ostensibly runs him, but they've got a whole field team in Jeddah, and they're not there for the sunshine."

"Neither for the drinks and entertainment," Perryman

said with a smile. "But that was to be expected. No; the point is that for the next month, you will be, in a way, marking time."

"So?"

"So, let's find out if Miss Kashva is indeed a swallow—an undertaking that can hardly be unpleasant."

"And if she isn't?"

"Then we shall have to look elsewhere, and you will be free to examine the parameters of empathy."

Gemmel gave him a hard look. "When will they be through with her?"

"Two or three days—by the time you get back from Washington. By the by, they all like her down there."

"Yes?"

"Indeed, Grey reports that she's charming, disarming, and intelligent. That her attitude under questioning is natural and straightforward."

"So?"

"So they all think she's a swallow—but a nice one."

The Imam saw it all and afterward talked of it widely and at length. The man came into the Mosque while the faithful were at prayer. The Imam spotted him out of the corner of his eye, and claimed to have recognized him, and that which was in him. He unrolled his prayer mat and then moved in a deliberate way to one of the faucets set in the wall of the Mosque, and washed his hands and his feet. At this time Haji Mastan had not seen him for he was prostrate in his prayers. The Imam watched the man as he moved back to his prayer mat. The resemblance was striking. He could only be he who had entered Haji Mastan's dreams.

The confirmation was dramatic. As the prayers ended and the faithful rose, Haji Mastan rolled up his mat and turned to move away, and then froze to the spot. Their glances had met even through the crowd, and then, as the Imam told it, a strange atmosphere descended, infecting all of the faithful. First one and then another looked at the two men, and the crowd stilled and then parted and very slowly Haji Mastan walked forward, and stood in front of the man and said:

"In the name of Allah, the All Merciful, thou hast come!"

The man reached out a hand and placed it on Haji Mastan's shoulder and looked deep into his eyes, and said:

"I came to seek thee out."

Then he dropped his hand and turned away to the entrance of the Mosque, and Haji Mastan followed him.

Hawke had an apron on, the kind with a bib front tied around the neck. It had a motif of the head of a jovial Longhorn, and if Hawke had grown horns, his face would have looked a little similar. He stood in the smoke behind the barbecue, turning the steaks with a fork and sipping from his long glass of Canadian Club. His two sons stood on each flank, also with drinks in their hands, and criticizing every move he made in a bantering way. Gemmel sat at a long trestle table with Julia, the girl friend of her elder son, and two other couples.

"He just loves to barbecue," Julia said. "It's one of the few times he really relaxes." She smiled ruefully. "The other times are when he's decorating the house."

Gemmel laughed. "Yes, he told me about that. What you should do is build a little guesthouse in the garden and let him tinker around with it to his heart's content."

"Now that's a great idea, Peter."

"Or why not build it himself?" the woman on Gemmel's right interjected. "That could keep him busy for years."

She was the wife of a two-star general who was serving at the Pentagon and they had rented the house next door. The other couple were younger, in their middle thirties. He was a partner in one of Washington's more prestigious law firms and apparently destined for a political future. His wife was attractive, vivacious, and, Gemmel decided, highly ambitious, but in spite of that he had found her easy to talk to and very charming. The general himself fitted the mold of what Gemmel assumed would be a senior Pentagon staff officer. His language was peppered with Newspeak—the product of the military/computer marriage.

In spite of being surrounded by strangers, Gemmel was feeling relaxed. His meeting with the Director CIA in the afternoon had gone off very well, or so Hawke had assured him afterward.

"You know what it's like, Peter," he had said as they drove back to Washington. "Now that the operation's gathering steam the Director wants to get his little pinky in the pie. He fights a constant battle at the White House against other advisers to the President, and if this thing comes off it's going to put Brand right on top, and he's one very ambitious son of a bitch."

Gemmel had been surprised at the ease with which Hawke talked about his superior because Hawke was a man who kept things very much to himself; but then Gemmel had realized the compliment he was being paid and also the friendship he was being shown. He knew that after the first miracle in the desert he had completely won Hawke's respect. With that respect had come the burgeoning of their friendship. This had been reinforced later when Hawke suggested that Gemmel might like to come home for a barbecue and meet his family and some friends.

Gemmel had accepted with some internal reservations. He was not very good at social chitchat and he was not sure how he'd fit into a typical American social scene.

His fears had been groundless. When they entered the house he was greeted warmly by Julia and the two sons. It was later, as Morton was preparing the barbecue and before the other guests had arrived, that Gemmel found himself alone with Julia in the kitchen, and with that frankness which characterizes many Americans, she told him simply how pleased she was that Morton had brought him home to meet her.

"It's very rare," she had said. "He almost never mixes his work with his home life." She smiled disarmingly. "I suppose that's natural, in the kind of business he's in, so it's a real pleasure to see you here."

Gemmel had mumbled something polite and she had cocked her head on one side and studied him for a moment.

"It's also rare," she said, "for him to make friends in his work. He keeps himself very aloof."

"Well, we have to work closely together," Gemmel had answered, slightly embarrassed, "so it helps if we get on."

She smiled. "You're so reserved. Do you know why he likes you?"

Gemmel could only shrug.

"You have similar backgrounds," she went on. "He told me that. He said you have come from quite a poor family and that you got where you are because of your own initiative, just as he did."

Gemmel smiled. "I think he's been reading my file."

"And no doubt you've read his. Did you know that I come from a very wealthy family?"

Gemmel nodded.

"And did you know that Morton never took a single cent from my father, even to this day, and would not allow me to, either, or the children?"

"I didn't know that, Julia, but it fits in with what I know of his character and why I like him."

They heard the sound of voices outside and she took him out to meet the other guests.

Hawke brought a tray of steaks over to the table and forked the biggest one onto Gemmel's plate. Gemmel looked down at it in astonishment.

"Am I expected to eat that? It's half a cow!"

"It's no problem," Hawke said with a grin. "As long as

you have plenty of lubrication." He gestured and one of his sons leaned over and poured wine into Gemmel's glass.

"Go easy." Gemmel laughed. "I've got an early-morning flight."

"The only way to travel," the general interjected, "is three parts cut. Whenever I make an outstation trip I like to get on the plane in that condition and get off even worse." He smiled broadly. "That's why I try to travel on civilian aircraft."

Hawke sat down and slapped the general on the back. "And it's why if we ever get our Rapid Deployment Force going it will take forty-eight hours even to find the guy in charge!"

The conversation moved on to the Middle East, but Gemmel noticed that the CIA was never mentioned. He listened with interest and noted that the three American men had very similar views on foreign policy. Views that fitted in neatly with the new Administration. In a nutshell, it was time to get tough. The Russians, or any other Communists, only respected an adversary who would stand up to them. They went on to heap praise on the British Prime Minister and described her as the only leader in Europe today with any balls. Gemmel was drawn into the conversation with a few deft questions from Hawke. As he talked and listened, the steak disappeared until his plate was clean.

"You see, it wasn't so much," Julia said. "Have some more."

Gemmel shook his head firmly. "I won't eat for a week, Julia, but it was really good." To Hawke he said, "Morton, you have hidden talents."

The two sons and the girl friend stood up and started clearing the table, and then the lawyer's wife said to Gemmel, "I understand you're an expert on the ballet. What about this dancer who just defected?"

Gemmel tried to keep his face expressionless, but Hawke noticed a slight reaction.

"Is she good?" Hawke asked. "Have you seen her dance?"

"Yes, I've seen her dance twice. She's among the top half-dozen ballerinas in the world."

"Will she stay in Britain?" Julia asked.

"I don't know," Gemmel said. "I understand she hasn't made up her mind."

The conversation turned to defecting Russian artists in general.

"It's a sure sign," the general's wife said, "that their system doesn't work. They're the elite of their country and better off than anyone else, and yet still they leave. You don't see any Western artists going the other way."

Gemmel said, "They probably come over for the steaks."

Everyone laughed and then the girl friend appeared with a huge apple pie and a bowl of cream, and to Gemmel's surprise he was able to eat a large slice.

Later they had coffee and liqueurs and the elder son announced he was taking his girl friend to a disco, and the younger son went up to his room to study. After a few more minutes the two other couples made their farewells and left, and Julia went into the kitchen, leaving Hawke and Gemmel alone on the patio with half a bottle of good Cognac. They drank and talked for another hour, mostly about Operation Mirage. Hawke had his excitement under tight control, but even so Gemmel sensed it. They discussed the setting-up of the field HQ in Amman and in particular the communications network that would allow them to follow events during the Haj from moment to moment.

Because of the friendship it had become a discussion between equals, and finally Gemmel decided to take advantage of that. Hawke had just poured two more measures of Cognac when Gemmel said, "It's obvious, Morton, that at the moment of culmination we're going to be pushed into the background—I mean MI-Six."

Hawke took a sip from his glass and gave him a level

stare. "Of course you're right. I guess you've always known that. I can tell you two things. First, that if the operation succeeds, the ongoing handling of control will rest with the President's Security Council. Second, that the Mahdi's influence will be used mainly against the Russians."

"If it's too obvious it could be dangerous," Gemmel remarked. "After all, the KGB is formidable and it will leave no stone unturned to counteract the situation."

"It's true," agreed Hawke, "and I would hope that we can be subtle and not push our advantage too hard or too fast." He shrugged resignedly. "But as I told you, it will be out of my hands. I can only promise that I'll do everything possible not to let them get too ambitious, and, incidentally, I'll work my damnedest to keep you and your people fully in the picture."

Gemmel knew that Hawke was being sincere and he saw vividly the dangers if the Americans became too aggressive with the advantage the Mahdi would give them. This made him think again of Pritchard in the Malayan jungle, and he marveled to himself at the man's ingenuity and subtlety.

A few minutes later Julia came back to the patio and Gemmel glanced at his watch and stood up. "You've left me with only six hours' sleep," he said.

Hawke stood up and moved to a phone, dialed a number, and spoke a few words. Then he said to Gemmel, "An Agency car will pick you up in a couple of minutes. You'll be back at your hotel in a quarter of an hour."

Julia went inside for Gemmel's coat and he finished the last of his Cognac and they walked to the front door.

"I've enjoyed myself, Julia," Gemmel said. "It was a great meal. Don't upset the cook, you can't afford to lose him."

She smiled and kissed him warmly on the cheek. "Be sure to come and see us again when you're in Washington. Even if Morton's away, you'll always be welcome." She smiled. "You never know, the food might be even better." She turned and went inside as a large black limousine pulled into the drive.

"So, the next time we meet will be Amman," Hawke said. "When do you plan to leave London?"

"It won't be for at least three weeks," Gemmel answered. "I've decided to take a couple of weeks off. I need a break."

Hawke looked a little surprised and Gemmel continued, "Everything's in motion, Morton, and until the Haj starts there's nothing much for me to do. Boyd is in control of Haji Mastan"—he smiled sardonically—"with a little help from your people; and the laser and the launch of it are all in your hands."

"Okay," Hawke said. "Have a good rest. When we get to Amman we're sure as hell going to be busy."

The Agency driver held the limousine door open and the two men shook hands and Hawke slapped Gemmel on the shoulder.

"It's been a pleasure having you here, Peter. See you in Amman!"

"Amman!" repeated Gemmel, with a grin. He climbed into the car and Hawke watched it drive away. He thought it fitted Gemmel's character perfectly that at such a time and with such mounting tension he had the sangfroid to take a couple of weeks' vacation.


It was the fourth day and Maya Kashva was still frightened. But not to the same intensity as the first day. As they had driven through the dark, wet countryside she had repeated to herself constantly that a great ballet dancer must also be a great actress. She also remembered the parting words of Vassili Gordik.

"There are only three things you must keep in mind: You could not dance during the last month in Russia because of a torn ligament; you defected because of your art; you went to Gemmel because you felt a bond of sympathy. In all other matters tell them the absolute truth. And don't be scared of getting angry."

She stood at the window of her room, looking down at the lovely garden. The sun had made a rare appearance, and the flowers and shrubs were in bloom. She smiled to herself at the memory of their reaction to her anger. It had come mainly through impatience, for they had been kind to her: Mr. Bennett and Mr. Grey, and the cook and housekeeper. Even the guards, whom Mr. Grey had called "extracurricular staff." But the questions had been endless, and as she tired, she had made small, and perhaps natural, mistakes. So on the Saturday before she left Russia her mother had cooked chicken, not beef—so what? And the flight had left Leningrad for Moscow at three-twenty and not two-twenty—so what?

But they had probed the mistakes and dropped in unrelated questions and she had become confused, and finally had burst into a temper and screamed at them. Mr. Grey had been imperturbable, merely sitting back and letting her tirade wash over him, but Mr. Bennett looked genuinely shocked, especially at some of her expletives. Well, she had thought, if you want to be an expert in the Russian language you have to take the bad with the good.

They had sent her up to her room and the housekeeper had brought her a pot of tea and smiled at her in conspiratorial sympathy, and Maya had decided that losing her temper had been a good idea.

Certainly in the morning things had been easier. Mr. Grey had taken her for a walk in the garden and explained that the house was of the Queen Anne period and had been the country seat of a minor noble family. Taxes and death duties had eventually forced them to sell to the government.

"We don't execute our aristocracy," he had told her with a gentle smile. "We just strangle them with taxes."

She had asked how long she would have to stay and he told her not to worry. It would soon be over. Then she had asked him about Gemmel, as she did constantly, and he repeated his stock answer: Mr. Gemmel was in touch but could not be involved.

He had asked her what she would do, once her permanent residence was granted. Already, every ballet company in Britain and many overseas were making frantic inquiries.

She had taken his arm then, as they walked alongside a small artificial lake.

"For at least a month I will do nothing. First I want to find out about your country, look at it and the people. Then I will decide."

Mr. Grey had smiled and asked, "Don't you get rusty? I mean, if you don't practice?"

She had laughed and let go of his arm and pirouetted down the gravel path in front of him, and he had stood still and watched her gravely and then she had stopped and said seriously, "Yes, Mr. Grey, I will get rusty, and creak and groan and be an old woman if you keep me here much longer!"

He had smiled again and hurried forward to catch up with her, and she had taken his arm again, and they walked on and she knew that he liked her.

She looked down at the garden and decided that later in the afternoon she would walk again, and if in the morning they asked her more questions, she would lose her temper again, and even in Moscow, Vassili Gordik would hear her screams. And then she saw a car coming up the drive. An old car, with lots of chrome and old-fashioned running boards and big headlamps. It pulled up to the door and Peter Gemmel got out and she was leaning out of the window and calling his name and waving, and he was looking up with a smile and waving back.

"You lost your temper?"

"Yes, so would you have."

"Was it so terrible?"

She didn't answer immediately. She needed to think about it. They were driving down a narrow country lane toward London. A few miles away a motorway could have sped them there quickly, but Gemmel had decided that she should see some of the countryside. She had immediately fallen in love with his car. It was a 1930 Lagonda, and she had decided that it suited his personality, and she had told him so.

"You mean it's old, but reasonably well preserved," he had suggested with a smile.

She had shaken her head seriously. "No, it has style, and it's solid. Not like modern cars, which look like streamlined plastic cans."

She had settled deep into the leather seat, and watched him out of the corner of her eye, oblivious to the scenery outside.

"Was it so terrible?" he repeated.

"Not really, but they asked a million questions. They thought I was a spy coming to undermine your government and turn you all into good Communists—or at least you."

He smiled. "Are you a good Communist?"

She made a face. "I'm a dancer, Peter. Please, no more questions."

They drove in silence for a few minutes, then she asked, "What happens now?"

He glanced at his watch. "We should be in London about an hour before the shops close, so you'll have time to buy some clothes and whatever else you need."

"But I have no money."

"Don't worry, Maya. The Ballet Circle has arranged to advance you a thousand pounds." He took his eyes off the road to look at her, and smiled at her surprised face. "It's what they are there for, and they're confident that once you start dancing again they'll soon get it back."

She digested that and then asked, "And after shopping? What then?"

"Well, you have a choice," he replied. "I've made a tentative reservation at a hotel, or if you don't wish to be alone, you can stay with a friend of mine. She's a dancer with the Royal Ballet. She has a large flat in Chelsea and she'll be delighted to put you up."

"She's your girl friend?" she asked quietly.

"Just a friend."

"I don't like the choice."

"Why not?"

"I'd rather stay with you. Is that not possible? Would you be embarrassed? Would I be a nuisance?"

He didn't answer. Just concentrated on the road.

"Or is it your work?" she asked sadly. "After all that, you don't trust me."

He shook his head. "No, Maya, it's not that. But you hardly know me. You're very young and my friend is your age. I'm sure you'll be more comfortable there. She will introduce you around, help you decide what you want to do."

He looked at her again, but her face was averted as she gazed out of the window at the passing countryside. They drove in silence for a few miles and then he heard a sound and glanced at her again, and then pulled onto the side of the road. He reached out and turned her face toward him and saw the tears coursing down her cheeks.

While he dumped the parcels on the bed in the spare room she moved around the small house like a cat inspecting a new domain. She ran a finger along a shelf, looking for dust. Prowled through the kitchen, opening and shutting cupboards and inspecting the oven, peeked briefly into his bedroom, noting the casual untidiness, looked approvingly at the surprisingly large bathroom with the sunken tub, and then joined him in the spare bedroom. He was taking sheets from a cupboard.

"A maid comes three times a week," he said, "but you have to make your own bed."

"Of course," she said lightly. "Don't forget, I come from a Socialist country which denounces such exploitation!"

Gemmel grinned. "Don't give me that nonsense. As a state artist you were pampered and cosseted! Can you cook?"

"Of course I can. I learned from my mother. She was very strict."

At the mention of her mother, the corners of her mouth turned down.

"You're worried about her?" he asked, and she nodded silently.

"It's quite usual," he said gently. "For a while you won't be able to get in touch. They'll make sure of that. We'll try to find out where she is," he added encouragingly, and Maya's face brightened a little.

"Do you want me to cook for you tonight?"

He smiled and shook his head. "No, tonight we'll go out for dinner, somewhere quiet, so you won't be recognized. Your picture's been in all the papers, and they're all looking for personal interest stories."

"I'll disguise myself," she said brightly. "I'll wear a blond wig and dark glasses."

"No, you won't." Gemmel grinned. "That would be like carrying a large sign. Anyway, it's not necessary."

It wasn't necessary. They went to a small, candlelit French restaurant around the corner from his house. Gemmel was obviously well known there and they were shown to an alcove table. It was an intimate setting, but for the first half-hour there was a slight strain between them. It was to be expected, for when two people who feel a bond are first alone together, they each naturally try to find out about the other's life—likes and dislikes, expectations and ambitions. But Gemmel, knowing what she had been through for the past three days, was wary of probing, and she was suddenly shy and nervous. But as the meal progressed, and after a couple of glasses of wine, she relaxed and began to enjoy herself. She talked of her early life as a dancer, and the years of training and practice. He was fascinated to learn of the selection and filtering system which allowed the State to channel the best talent from an early age to the best teachers. How once a dancer had been set on that path, everything else in her life became subordinated to her art. It surprised him a little that in spite of her restricted life-style, she had a good awareness of the world and events around her. She was avidly interested to learn about life in Britain, and the West in general, and he told her that he was due time off from the office and he would take two weeks' holiday, and show her around. In a couple of days she would have to attend a press conference. The media were clamoring for information, and would keep up the pressure until they received some. It would also make life easier for the home office, because the Russians were hurling protest notes like confetti, and hinting darkly about kidnap and coercion. A media expert from the Home Office would be around to give her a briefing and try to ease the ordeal.

As they started the dessert, he began to open up a little about himself. About his early life in a Yorkshire coal-mining community. Of his father, who spent thirty years on the mine face, and whose lifelong ambition was that his son should go to university and never see the bottom of a mine.

"And did you?" she asked.

"Yes. A year after I graduated he was killed in a pit collapse along with fifteen others. A month later I arranged to go down one of the deepest mines in Yorkshire, at Pontefract. I spent the day there, two miles down." He shrugged wryly. "I wanted to know."

She reached out and covered his hand with hers. "At least he saw his ambition realized, Peter," she said gently. "Were you ever married?"

He told her briefly of his wife and the circumstances of her death and then, with a quick smile, remarked that the significant episodes in his life did not make for light-hearted conversation. But she shook her head emphatically. She had the peculiar Russian soul that can never savor happiness without putting it into perspective with tragedy and sadness. Such episodes added a depth to character. The death of her own father had heightened her love for her mother, and in a way that loss had added a dimension to her dancing, given her insight into the emotional aspect of her art.

But then they did turn to lighter things. She asked what else, apart from the ballet, occupied his spare time, and he talked of sailing. As he described the sensation of a yacht moving only to the whim of the wind, the sound of a crisp bow wave, and the lapping of water along a hull on a peaceful night, she saw him relax visibly.

"Can we do it?" she asked eagerly, and he smiled and said, "You don't get seasick?"

"I don't know. I never tried."

"Never?"

She shook her head. "Peter, I've been too busy so far in my life!"

"All right. A friend of mine has a Dragon. I'll borrow it for a day."

"Do Dragons swim?" she asked impishly.

He smiled. "A Dragon is a design of a yacht. It's old-fashioned now, but they're good boats for a day out."

"I think you like old-fashioned things."

He thought about that, and said, "Not everything. But we're so busy making progress that we tend to cast away some of our better possessions, and even habits."

He signaled the waiter for the bill and asked Maya, "Are you tired?"

She nodded. "A lot's happened today, and I didn't sleep well down there."

They walked the short distance home. As he was unlocking the front door, she said anxiously, "Peter, there's a car parked on the corner with two people in it."

He ushered her into the house and closed the door.

"Don't worry," he said. "They'll be there all night, and for the next few nights."

"They're your people?"

"They're connected."

He opened a small metal box on the wall just inside the door and showed her the switches.

"This is a burglar alarm. If you go out in the morning for a walk before I'm up, make sure you switch it off."

"I won't go out without you."

He smiled at her. "Maya, you'll be quite safe. People will be keeping an eye on you."

They walked through into the sitting room.

"Would you like some coffee?" he asked.

She shook her head and he sensed her feeling of unease.

"Maya, I generally do a couple of hours' work before I go to bed."

"So late?" she asked.

"Yes, I suppose it's a mental clock. I find I concentrate well around midnight."

There was a silence while they stood in the middle of the sitting room, looking at each other. Then she moved close to him and looked up at his face.

"Peter, thank you—for everything. I promise I won't be a nuisance or get in your way. I just need a little while to adjust."

She reached up and cupped his face in her hands and kissed him very lightly on the lips. A gossamer touch, no more; then she turned and left the room. He stood still for a long moment, looking after her, his face touched with a hint of puzzlement. Finally he shook his head and moved to the drinks table and poured a glass of Cognac. Then he selected a tape and slotted it into the cassette deck, punched a button, and the soft sounds of Grieg's *Peer Gynt Suite* filled the room. He reached up and cleared a row of books from one of the shelves. The gap revealed a steel plate about two feet across and one foot high, with a handle at one side. Next to the steel plate was a six-inch square of what looked like black plastic. It had a small switch above it. Gemmel flicked the switch and laid the palm of his right hand against the black square. There was a low hum and a series of clicks. He turned the steel handle and the plate opened, revealing a deep safe. He took out several thick files bound in green ribbon and, together with his glass of Cognac, carried them to the table.

Upstairs Maya lay in bed. She could faintly hear the music. Her eyes moved around the small bedroom. There were two prints of Turner landscapes on the wall. The curtains covering the small window were dark blue with a faint yellow pattern. The wallpaper was a dark, embossed maroon. All the furniture was old. The bed had mahogany head- and footboards and four small posts at each corner. The side tables and chest of drawers were rosewood.

She decided that she liked the room. That it was warm. She also decided that she wasn't going to sleep in it for very long and that when she moved, a few meters down the corridor, it was not going to be primarily for the sake of Vassili Gordik—or Mother Russia.

## sixteen

THE PRESS CONFERENCE WAS COUNTED A SUCCESS. DURING the first few minutes Maya was very nervous, as flashbulbs lit up the room and the cameramen kept calling her name to get better angles.

But once the questions started she forgot her nervousness. The female interpreter, provided by the Home Office, was a small, humorous woman who helped put her at ease.

"Don't worry," she told her. "I'll only translate those questions you want to answer."

So she gave her reasons for defecting with practiced ease. Complained that she had been unable to contact her mother, and explained that she had not yet decided on a precise course for her ongoing career. The early questions from the national dailies all tried to focus on personal matters, and with the aid of the interpreter she put up a thick but charming smokescreen. She was staying with friends and needed time to adjust to a new environment. She smiled sweetly and asked the reporters please to respect her privacy as it was a very trying time. She agreed that the weather wasn't very good, but Russia could also be cold in summer. She thought London was a wonderful city but, no, she couldn't comment on the men because so far she had met very few!

Finally, the specialized correspondents began to get in their questions about ballet and the reporters for the popular press drifted away. After a further half-hour she ended the conference with a brief statement expressing her gratitude to the British government and people for granting her asylum and showing such generosity. Then the Home Office led her gratefully away and gave her a cup of tea.

Two days later the phone in Peter Gemmel's house rang while they were having dinner, and after a brief conversation, he called to her and held it out with a smile.

"They've reconnected your mother's phone. Our people finally got through and she's on the line. No mention of me, please—or of your stay at Mendley."

Maya took the phone joyfully and talked and cried a little, while the chicken casserole she had cooked went slowly cold.

Half an hour after she had hung up, Gordik, Tudin, and Larissa listened to a tape of the conversation. At one point, Maya's mother asked whether she had enough warm clothes and Maya answered yes, but she missed her fur boots. Gordik looked triumphantly at Lev and Larissa, and made a sign, and Larissa played that part of the tape again. When the tape ended he poured three large Scotches and they drank a toast to their swallow.

In Petworth House, at almost the same time, Mr. Grey and Mr. Bennett listened to a tape of the same conversation, but unlike Gordik, they saw no significance in the fact that Maya was missing her fur boots. In fact they found nothing of significance in the entire conversation. Later, while Mr. Bennett made tea, Mr. Grey phoned Mr. Perryman and reported that fact.

Perryman was entertaining the London CIA station chief and his wife at dinner, and while he was occupied on the telephone, the American quickly spooned most of his lentil soup into his wife's bowl. She had a less discerning palate, as well as being a loyal wife.

After the chicken casserole had been reheated, Maya told Gemmel all about the conversation with her mother. The Russians had acted predictably. She had been questioned at length and they had been very unpleasant, accusing her of encouraging her daughter in non-Socialist ways. Her daughter had been ungrateful for all the benefits she had received from the State and from socialism.

Maya had smiled at Gemmel through a mouthful of chicken and remarked that her mother was tough and had enough contacts of her own to ensure that her life would not be made unbearable. In time perhaps Maya could get her out to the West. What did he think? He was noncommittal: much depended on the future political climate. But in any event, her mother was relatively young and in good health.

For Maya the contact with her mother provided an almost perfect ending to a perfect day. In the early morning she had cooked Gemmel's breakfast, something she now did routinely. He always had eggs and bacon, with two slices of almost-burned toast. Only the eggs varied, from poached to scrambled to boiled. She had looked blank at such descriptions, and he had shown her how and remarked with a smile, "If you want to put an Englishman into a good mood it's essential that his breakfast eggs are cooked exactly right!"

So she quickly learned to make poached eggs with a soft yolk but a firm white; scrambled eggs that were creamy and not too wet; and to boil eggs for precisely three minutes fifty seconds and then crack the shell at one end so the yolk didn't harden too much between the stove and the table.

"Is it so important?" she had asked as she served him that morning, and he told her the story of the two bachelors who had shared an apartment for six months.

One of them was an easygoing, lazy, and untidy man who only had cornflakes for breakfast. The other was studious, precise, and fastidious, and his breakfast preparations were a ritual. He always had boiled eggs, and these were cooked for exactly four minutes—not a second more or less. He even had two egg timers in case one malfunctioned during the critical operation. Each morning as he sliced the top off the first egg he would look up triumphantly and say, "Now that's how a properly boiled egg should look!"

After several months this so got on the nerves of the roommate that he took to sneaking into the kitchen in the dead of night, taking the eggs out of the fridge, and pre-boiling them from one to ten minutes.

Thereafter the life of the egg eater slowly disintegrated. Every morning he would follow his normal procedure and every morning the eggs would come out differently. He tried everything—first checking his egg timers, then constantly changing his egg supplier. Even driving out into the country to buy eggs directly from the farmers. The roommate was a sadist. Once in a while he would leave the eggs alone and the egg eater would enjoy a brief but puzzled respite. But then it would start again: soft one morning, rock-hard the next. The poor man went to pieces. He couldn't concentrate on his job, he fell out with his girl friend, and he started drinking too much. Finally he couldn't sleep at night and thus the drama ended.

"What happened?" Maya asked breathlessly.

Gemmel explained that a noise was heard from the kitchen one night, and on investigating, he caught his roommate in the act.

"What did he do?"

"Beat him to death with a frying pan."

"No!"

"Yes. And he was hauled off for trial at the Old Bailey."

"The Old Bailey?"

"Yes, it's the foremost criminal court in Britain."

Maya looked at him in wide-eyed astonishment. Gemmel kept a very straight face.

"What happened?" she breathed.

"He was acquitted."

"Acquitted?"

"Certainly. The judge had his priorities right. He described it as justifiable homicide!"

Maya looked at him closely and then, seeing the corners of his mouth twitching, hurled a bread roll at him.

Now she finished the last of her chicken and asked with mock seriousness, "Poached, scrambled, or boiled in the morning?"

He smiled at her. "Scrambled—and the chicken was delicious."

She inclined her head in acknowledgment and started clearing the table. He watched her move. Even in such a prosaic action she had a fluidity and grace that gave him pleasure. Over the past four days he had decided quite calmly that she was the most beautiful woman he had ever known or seen. Not just obviously, head-turningly beautiful, but with an extraordinary edge. The movement of a hand, or the tilt of her chin, or the way she sat down, or turned, or stretched and yawned when she was tired. It was a feline beauty, unmarred by sharp edges or abrupt movements.

That morning they had risen early and driven down to a small marina near Hamble. It was a perfect English summer day, one of the rare ones. Hot, yet fresh with a gentle breeze. As he prepared the yacht he remarked that the wind could have been a little stronger, but, seeing it was her first time, it was just as well.

They had sailed slowly down the river to the open sea and stripped down to swimsuits. She wore a small black bikini and he had found difficulty in concentrating on the sails as she moved about, exploring the boat and commenting on everything. At one point a large cabin cruiser had passed them going upriver and several girls lay topless on the foredeck. He had smiled at her astonishment and slight embarrassment and explained that these days it was the rule rather than the exception. She had looked down at her own lightly covered breasts and shaken her head emphatically and smiled shyly at him.

"I'm going to stay old-fashioned," she said, and he couldn't decide whether he was pleased or slightly disappointed.

He had dropped the sails a couple of miles from shore, and as they drifted, she unpacked a picnic lunch and he opened a bottle of wine. They were easy with each other, not finding it necessary to fill in silences with idle words. After lunch she lay sunning herself on the foredeck, while he paid out a fishing line in the unexpectant hope of catching a passing mackerel.

On the way back she took the tiller and he gave her rudimentary instructions in sailing. She had a natural touch and within a few minutes was able to judge the wind and feel the boat, and her animated face illustrated the pleasure it gave her.

On the drive to London they stopped at a small country pub and he introduced her to English beer. She took one sip, and pulled a face, and the locals at the bar laughed. Then someone recognized her from a picture in the newspapers and she had to sign a dozen bar mats. The bartender went into the back and came out with an ice-cold bottle of vodka, and she taught them a Russian toast and how to throw it down in one gulp. She was at once shy and friendly, and as Gemmel translated her remarks for the others, he noted the distinct aura that surrounds a natural personality. When they left, the whole bar came out to the carpark to wave good-bye and call out a last toast.

She came out of the kitchen, carrying a tray with a coffeepot and cups. Gemmel was at the stereo set, putting a record on the turntable. She stopped in surprise as the first sounds came out of the speakers.

"What's that?"

He smiled. "I thought we'd have a change. That's a group called Blue Crystal."

She put the tray on the coffee table and fetched the Cognac and two glasses, her head cocked to the music.

"I like it," she said, "but I didn't think it was your type of music."

"Only recently. I've been discovering broader horizons."

She poured the coffee and Cognac, settled into a chair, and picked up an English phrase book. He opened the morning papers, which because of their early start he hadn't had a chance to read.

Ten minutes went quietly by and then, abruptly, he dropped the paper onto the table, got up, and turned off the music.

She looked up curiously. His face was somber.

"What is it, Peter?"

He made a throwaway gesture. "It's nothing. Look, I think I'll take a walk. I've got a bit of a headache. The fresh air might clear it."

She jumped up. "Shall I come with you?"

"No, Maya. Please stay here. I won't be long."

After he had gone she stood looking at the closed door with a hurt and puzzled expression. Then she looked down at the open newspaper. There was a small item headed by a small photograph. Had she understood English she would have read of the accidental death of a sound engineer called Mick Williams. He had recently bought a new, turbo-charged Porsche, which had left the road at something over a hundred miles an hour and come to an abrupt stop against a brick wall.

It was two hours before she heard the key turning in the lock. He looked around the sitting room door and saw her sitting curled up in a chair, watching him anxiously.

"You should have gone to bed."

"Did I do something to upset you? To make you angry?"

"No, Maya, believe me. I just wanted to take a walk, to think a little."

She uncurled and stood up. "Would you like some coffee?"

"No, thanks. I think I'll do a little work."

She glanced down at her watch. It was almost midnight. On the last two nights she had seen him open the curious safe by placing his hand against the black plate. She guessed it was a new electronic type that was programmed to react only to an individual touch. He had always done it casually and then laid the ribboned files on the table and worked while she read a book or listened to music.

"Do you still have a headache?"

"No, it's gone."

She walked over and put her hand on his forehead.

"Anyway, there's no fever."

They stood for a silent moment, looking at each other. Then he lifted his hand and took hers from his forehead and their fingers twisted together and he was kissing her. It was not like the previous, brief good-night kisses. It was not a gentle "getting to know you" kiss. It was a kiss that resulted from four days of mutual physical and mental attraction and it lasted a long time. His other arm went around her and pulled her close, and she rose on her toes and put a hand on the back of his head and pressed against him. When they drew apart she looked up at him and then laid her head against his neck. He spoke into her hair.

"It's impossible for me to keep my hands off you if you stay here. Either you have to leave, or be with me completely."

Her muted voice came back. "I will not leave."

So he took her hand and led her up to his bedroom and slowly, almost reverently, undressed her and laid her on the bed, and kissed her again and ran his lips over the contours of her face, and his hands over her body.

Her mouth and her skin seemed to vibrate under his touch, and as he moved his hand lower, her body arched in expectation—her center seeking out his hand.

He drew back and looked down at her as he unbuttoned his shirt. Her eyes would not hold his. She kept looking at his face and turning her head away, and looking back again; her face mirrored both desire and uncertainty, and he knew it was not the mere thespian prelude of a woman showing a false ambivalence.

He lay down beside her and caressed her breasts, kissed her erect nipples, and looked at her face again. Her mouth was parted, but her eyes were tightly closed.

"Maya, look at me."

She opened her eyes; her breath was warm on his face.

"You must be sure, Maya. I don't want you out of gratitude."

Slowly she shook her head, her long black hair moving sibilantly on the white pillow.

"No, Peter. Go on, please. Go on."

So he kissed her breasts and moved his hand lower again, and she arched up to meet it again and he cupped her, and felt her heat and moisture and gently eased a finger deep inside her tightness—and then abruptly his head came up and he was looking at her closed eyes, his face a mask of astonishment.

"Maya!"

Her eyes opened. Anxious eyes.

His voice stumbled. "You've never . . . ? This is the first . . . ?"

She nodded silently, and with a gasp he rolled away and onto his back, and lay rigid, looking up at the ceiling.

Minutes passed, and then she raised herself onto an elbow and looked down at his face.

"Are you so surprised? Is it something terrible?"

His breath came out, in a snort. "No, of course it's not terrible. But . . . yes, I am surprised."

"Don't you want me then?"

Slowly he turned his head and saw the tears forming in her eyes. She saw a mixture of bafflement and tenderness.

"Yes, I want you, Maya, but . . ."

"But what?" Her tone became bitter. "I'm not experienced enough for you? You've never known a virgin?"

He smiled ruefully. "Not for a long time. A very long time."

"You make me feel like a freak of some kind—just because I've never thrown my body around, because I've had pride in it. Kept myself until I found a man I could love."

At that word he turned again to look at her, saw the edge of anger building.

"Are you saying you love me?"

"I've loved you for three years." She said it simply and with such utter conviction that he could find no semblance of doubt in his mind.

"Since that first brief meeting?"

"Yes," she said emphatically, and still with the edge of anger. "Are you so stupid and blind that you can't see it?"

"Did that have any bearing on why you defected?"

Now her anger erupted. She sat up on the bed, hair in disarray and black eyes flashing.

"Of course it did!"

"And your art?"

"That too! Can't there be more than one reason? Can't the two reasons be part of each other? Didn't you see me dance? Didn't you see me dance just for you? Didn't you feel it?"

And he smiled at her, and then laughed out loud and reached out and pulled her down to his chest and kissed her and said, "Yes, I saw it, Miss Prima Ballerina, and after I left the theatre I walked home, and by the time I reached this house I knew I loved you. I was unable to work, and I kept thinking of you, and how in a few hours you would board the plane and go away, and I might never see you again."

She grinned down at him, in delight and belief. "You could have defected to Russia!"

He laughed again. "That's true, but they would have sent me away for a lot longer than three days." His voice became stern. "Now! Are we going to talk all night, or do you wish to cease being an anthropological curiosity?"

She didn't answer; just lay back and drew him onto her

and he proceeded with caution and wonderment, kissing her lips and face, and then moving down to her breasts, and lower, and running his hands down her flanks and then gently parting them. She was ready, and she was expectant, but she found it difficult to throw away the years of restraint. He drew her knees up and probed gently into her, but she was finely sensitive and each time he tried to move in deeper, she flinched away, eager but frightened. A hesitant fledgling on the edge of a nest, testing and flexing slender wings but frightened to launch herself into the unknown. He drew back and looked down at her and put a hand against her cheek and said, "Wait a moment."

He climbed off the bed, padded naked down the short flight of stairs to the sitting room, riffled through a stack of records, selected one, and put it on the turntable.

As he appeared again at the bedroom door, she heard the sounds of Minkus' *Paquita* floating into the room. The music that he had first watched her dance to. She smiled and held out her arms and he came to her and all her uncertainty had gone. He pulled a pillow down, lifted her from the waist, and slid it beneath her bottom. This time she didn't flinch away, but thrust up to him, and cried out and kept her eyes open, watching his face, and gripping his shoulders, her fingers digging to the bone and thrusting again and then he was deep inside her and she was crying with relief and pleasure and kissing his face and her back was arching convulsively.

He tried to hold back. To keep her on the sensitive edge for a few more moments, but he couldn't and didn't need to, for her face reflected the final release of her body and she moaned into a shuddering climax as he spurted into her.

The record had long ended before they ultimately drew apart. He stayed inside her, held on to her, whispered endearments and listened to hers. Then he grew hard once more and slowly played on her body as an instrument, and it was as though she was dancing to his music and again she climaxed, but this time with a softer intensity, and longer, as he held her on the edge and drew it out from the core of her body.

He finally withdrew and looked down and saw the blood-stained sheet, and kissed her again and said, smiling, "The maid comes tomorrow, and she won't believe this."

So they got up and together washed the sheet and the underblanket and hung them over a radiator to dry, and sat naked in one of the big leather chairs and drank Cognac, and listened again to Minkus and she wriggled and moved on his lap and maneuvered him, and as the sun lightened the windows they made love again and she whispered in his ear that she intended to do a great deal of catching up!

The Palace Security Council of the kingdom of Saudi Arabia meets every Wednesday morning in Riyadh. The agenda usually includes far-reaching issues of national defense and international relations. The members of the council comprise four princes of the ruling family, and six commoners, who could best be described as technocrats. Its function is to report to and advise the king and the powerful crown prince.

One of the commoners was Mirza Farruki, who headed the Saudi Arabian intelligence service, and on this Wednesday morning he gave a report concerning the security implications of various religious tensions being felt throughout the kingdom.

There had long been trouble in the eastern province, which contained a large Shi'ite minority. There had been serious denominational riots the year before, only put down with much bloodshed. It was feared that in the period approaching the Haj, further riots could be expected. Mirza Farruki was not overconcerned, for such troubles were localized, and largely reflected the tensions that existed throughout the Middle East between Shi'ite and Sunni communities. Local security forces had been reinforced, and he reported to the council that the situation could be controlled.

He then moved on to the phenomenon of the rumors which had spread throughout the kingdom and through every Islamic state concerning the coming of a Mahdi, who would be proclaimed at the Haj.

At first Mirza Farruki had taken these rumors, and their implications, lightly. It was not unusual for word of a Mahdi to be whispered in the bazaars and mosques of the kingdom. But on this occasion, the rumors had persisted and intensified and, more importantly, appeared to have no common source. His inquiries showed that they had started almost simultaneously in such diverse countries as Indonesia to the east and Nigeria to the west. And always the rumor was the same: the Mahdi would appear at the Haj.

So great was the interest and expectation that it was forecast that up to 20 percent more pilgrims would appear in Mecca than had been expected.

The rumors had started three months earlier and had at first traveled by word of mouth. Now, however, two events had occurred which not only gave impetus to the rumors but presented a definite threat.

First, the media throughout Islam had picked up the story and publicized it, thus adding credibility by association.

Second, a man had appeared who, without making any claims, was believed by many to be the object of the rumors.

At this point one of the princes interjected to ask if the man's identity was known, and if so, why he had not been apprehended.

Mirza Farruki answered that indeed the man's identity was known. He was an insignificant, simple-minded man from Medina. He had not been apprehended for he had broken no laws, religious or otherwise. The problem was that although he had built up a rapid following, neither he nor his followers spoke of the coming of a Mahdi, or encouraged others to do so. He simply moved from village to village, town to town, and city to city, praying in the various mosques and giving sermons—all of which contained nothing except direct quotations from the Koran. Mirza Farruki pointed out that he could not arrest a man for quoting from the Koran, nor could he impede his travels, for he had committed no crime at all. One disquieting aspect of the affair was that this man, known as Abu Qadir, was accepted and welcomed by both Sunni and Shi'ite communities, and his followers were drawn from both sects, and others.

Another prince now wished to know how large a following he had. Mirza Farruki explained that this was difficult to quantify. He traveled with only a few dozen, the most important of whom was one Haji Mastan, who had been a wealthy and respected figure in Jeddah before giving away his business to follow Abu Qadir.

However, at each place that Abu Qadir visited, there appeared to be a localized following which quickly spread the word of his coming, and ensured that large crowds were present to listen to his sermons.

On two occasions Abu Qadir had been closely questioned by the religious police. On the last occasion a senior officer of the security service had been present. These interrogations had been extremely difficult and frustrating, for Abu Qadir and, for that matter, Haji Mastan never uttered a single word that was not enshrined in the Koran. They appeared to be word-perfect in all six thousand-odd verses!

Mirza Farruki was then asked what he intended to do about it, and he had to admit that his options were limited simply to watching, waiting, and listening. In the event that Abu Qadir, either by word or deed, even hinted that he pretended to be a Mahdi, he would immediately be arrested and brought to trial for offenses against religious laws, the penalty for which was death by beheading.

It was known that he and many of his followers would be making the Haj to Mecca. It was rumored that they would gather in Taif, seventy kilometers to the southeast, and walk to Mecca across the desert, disdaining to use the six-lane super-highway built by the government to transport in comfort the Islamic heads of state who had attended the last Islamic Conference.

Mirza Farruki assured the council that his service would constantly monitor such an individualized pilgrimage. In the event that nothing spectacular happened during the five days of the Haj, then Abu Qadir's following would quickly melt away, as would the problem.

The council was satisfied with Mirza Farruki's report and moved on to discuss the pending purchase of four squadrons of F-16 fighter planes from the United States.

Alan Boyd was puzzled. He knew that Gemmel was overdue for leave, but found it strange, to say the least, that he should take time off so close to the culmination of months of planning and effort. He arrived in London from Jeddah, where he had been fingering the strings that controlled Haji Mastan. Strings that went up past his own fingers to those out of sight in the gloom.

On arrival at Petworth House he had been told to report not to Gemmel but to Perryman himself. The meeting had done nothing to dissipate his puzzlement. Perryman had merely remarked that Gemmel was tired and needed a break, and that the secret of good management was delegation, and as his lieutenant Boyd should be suitably flattered. He listened to his reports and advised in turn that the Americans were on schedule and that the laser satellite would shortly be transported from Palmdale to Cape Canaveral to be mated with the space shuttle *Atlantis*.

It was only later, in the canteen and in the corridors of Petworth House, that Boyd heard the gossip about the beautiful Russian ballet dancer who had defected directly to Peter Gemmel and was now ensconced in his house. His bafflement increased, for Boyd knew him well, and such an association was completely out of character.

Maya craned her neck to look at the inside of the dome of St. Paul's Cathedral.

"It's beautiful," she remarked to Gemmel, who stood beside her. "But we have many domes in Russia."

He smiled and took her arm and led her out of the cathedral and down the wide flight of steps. It was a late sunny morning and he was showing her around the City, that part of London which contains the financial district and many historic buildings.

"A hotbed of capitalism," he told her, as they walked a few minutes, and came to the imposing facade of the Bank of England. She was intrigued by "The Messenger" who stood at the front entrance, a giant of a man, wearing a cloak and top hat.

They walked again arm in arm back past St. Paul's until they reached Old Bailey Street and the Old Bailey itself, and he pointed out the figure of the blindfolded female statue, holding aloft the scales of justice.

"So this is where the egg eater was acquitted?" She smiled and tugged at his arm. "Can we look inside?"

They walked through the arched corridors, and she kept turning to look at bewigged and begowned barristers and lawyers as they hurried importantly along, clutching files and briefs.

Gemmel explained that there were twenty-three courts in the building, and apart from hearing major criminal cases, they also heard even petty cases that had occurred in the City itself. They stopped at the open door of Court Number 17. A trial was just getting under way, and on impulse he took her arm and they went in and sat at the public benches. She watched with fascination as the clerk of the court ordered everyone to rise, and then an old judge shuffled in with scarlet robes and off-white wig and took his place with great dignity at the bench. The clerk read out the charges and Gemmel whispered a translation in her ear.

It was a minor case concerning fraud by a proprietor of a back-street travel agency. Maya studied the accused in the dock and decided he was definitely guilty. He was dressed in a loud check suit, had greasy hair almost to his shoulders, and eyes that could have spotted a bent penny at a thousand yards. But he also had a quick-witted lawyer who was not at all perturbed by the hectoring manner of the prosecuting counsel. The lawyer had found a legal loophole, which he assiduously enlarged until finally the judge intervened, first berating the prosecutor for bringing a poorly prepared case into his court and thereby wasting his time, and then dismissing the case.

"But he was guilty!" Maya exclaimed as they left the court. "He was obviously guilty!"

Gemmel, feeling a trace embarrassed, guided her into a pub across the road, The Magpie and Stump. He took her to the upstairs bar, explaining that it was known as Court Number 10, since the days when the Old Bailey had only nine courts.

They sat at a corner table, and he fetched her a glass of white wine and a Scotch for himself.

She was in a strange mood, looking about her with a subdued, introspective air. The bar had old poems framed on the wall, and a seedy look. He told her something of its history. In the nineteenth century prisoners condemned to death had often been brought to the room from Newgate Prison for their last meal before execution. There was a tunnel which used to connect the pub with the prison. In those days people would reserve tables and spaces at the windows to watch the hangings that took place outside the prison.

"Was it the same in the courts?" she asked. "I mean, like today, with the judge and lawyers all dressed up."

So he told her a little of British common law, and how it had developed by the process of precedent. He could see that something was bothering her, and assumed it was the case they had just witnessed. He started to defend the system, pointing out that although the man may have been guilty, on some occasions the law was weak and malleable. Then she was shaking her head and she had tears in her eyes, and he was totally confused.

"The policeman," she said, "he couldn't do anything! The judge more or less called him a fool!"

Gemmel kept silent, unable to understand where she was heading, and then she noted his puzzlement and covered his hand with hers, and explained how deeply the episode had affected her. Yes, the man was surely a criminal, and in Russia he would automatically have been sent to prison—clever lawyer or not. That was only because the prosecutor and the judge were part of the same team. A judge in Russia could never criticize a prosecutor or policeman. It would be like stabbing himself in the back. But here she had seen a vivid illustration that the arm of the law and the arbiter of the law were totally separated. It did not matter to her that the petty criminal had gone free. It was beautiful that he had gone free, and beautiful that the old judge had told the policeman not to waste his time.

"It's not the buildings, Peter," she said, "or the old-fashioned clothes, or the old-fashioned language. It's just that if a little criminal like that can go into such a place and walk out free, then everyone must be free."

He thought about what she had said, and saw the logic of it, and how profound an impression such a small vignette must have made on anyone used to a totalitarian system which could never admit a mistake.

They had lunch at a wine bar and then he took her to see the Tower of London, the Houses of Parliament, and Buckingham Palace. He should have felt like a tourist guide, but she was in a curious mood and her questions probed into unlikely corners. How much was a Member of Parliament paid? Was it true that he could have another job on the side? Did the Queen really have no power? How rich was she? And how could she remain impartial when left-wing governments were in power? He answered her comprehensively, surprised but pleased by the drift of her questions and the outlook that had prompted them. Finally they hurried back to the house, for she had booked a call to her mother and they had forgotten the time. As they turned into the mews she remarked that she no longer saw the men who had constantly watched the house.

"No more," he said. "All that is past. You can assume that the Russians have given you up as irretrievably lost."

The phone call was not a success. She spoke to her mother for ten minutes, and when she came back into the sitting room he could see that she was upset.

He probed gently and she told him that her mother was sad, was missing her very much. Her friends had stopped coming around to visit her for fear of upsetting the authorities. She was lonely.

He tried to comfort her, pointing out that such a period would soon pass, that it was quite normal and to be expected. But she was deeply affected and went sadly into the kitchen to prepare dinner, and he could only shrug and put on some music in the hope that the mood would pass.

Once again, in Moscow, Gordik, Tudin, and Larissa listened to a tape of the conversation. When it was finished and Larissa had switched off the machine, Gordik nodded with satisfaction and said, "It's clear enough. She will have understood."

"You don't think you're pushing her too fast?" Tudin asked. "It's only been ten days."

Gordik spread his hands in a helpless gesture. "It's impossible to judge. But I have an instinctive feeling that we don't have much time. Besides, if she's going to learn anything, it's more likely to come in the first flush of the romance—while his defenses are down."

Tudin wasn't convinced, and he also suspected that Gordik was pushing Maya to make her move before Gemmel's influence became too strong.

"Anyway," Gordik continued, "they've pulled the surveillance off his house—at least the visible surveillance. We just have to take the chance."

* * *

In Petworth House, Mr. Bennett switched off the machine, looked up at Mr. Grey, and said emphatically:

"Fur boots!"

Mr. Grey was studying a transcript of the previous conversation. He nodded slowly.

"Yes, I mean surely our summers are notoriously bad, but even a worried mother wouldn't go on quite so much, especially a Russian mother. Play that part again."

Mr. Bennett worked the machine and they heard the mother expressing her concern that Maya must be cold, and had she bought some fur boots yet? Maya said no, she had been very busy, but she would get some soon. Besides, it was quite warm and please not to worry. But her mother pushed the point. She could not relax until she knew Maya had proper clothes, and that included fur boots.

Mr. Bennett again switched off the machine and said, "They're prodding her. Just ten days and they're prodding her."

Mr. Grey was deep in thought. Irritated thought. "If only Perryman would put us fully in the picture," he said eventually. "I mean, it would help if we knew what they were after—what Peter's working on."

"Well, for the KGB to be so impatient, it must be something big."

"Undoubtedly," Mr. Grey said bitterly, "and they appear to know a bloody sight more than we do!"

He picked up the phone and dialed Perryman's number.

She was quiet all during dinner, and only picked at her food. After a while he ceased trying to cheer her up. Instead he put a Beethoven concerto on to fill the silence.

"Are you going to work tonight?" she asked as she cleared away the plates.

He shook his head. "No, you've tired me out trekking all over London." He gestured at the turntable. "When it's finished I'll go to bed."

She carried the tray through to the kitchen, prepared coffee, and poured it into two cups. Then she opened her handbag and took out a powder compact. With a small spoon she scraped up a few grams of the powder and stirred them into one of the cups.

The concerto finished and Gemmel drained the last of his coffee and smiled at her across the low table.

"I'm not too tired to make love to you."

Her returned smile was wan, almost pathetic, and he stood up and pulled her to her feet and kissed her.

"Try not to think about it, Maya. She will be all right. Call her again in a few days. You'll see."

He switched off the stereo and the lights and took her up to bed and started to make love to her. She was strangely unresponsive and he saw that her eyes were wet. Then his own eyes became heavy and he remembered nothing more of the night.

She turned the corner and hurried down the road. It was deserted, except for a drunk on the other side who staggered along, oblivious to everything. But even so she stood at the red phone box, waiting until he had passed out of sight. Then she glanced nervously around her and slipped inside. She knew how to work the telephone. She had practiced on an exact replica in Moscow. She dialed the number and it rang only once before it was answered. She pushed in the coin, spoke only two sentences, hung up, and hurried back to the house.

They arrived twenty minutes later. Three of them. As she let them in they greeted her courteously and deferentially. They were dressed in dark clothes and gloves and looked expectantly around as they moved into the sitting room. She had already cleared away the books and they crowded in front of the safe and she explained.

The stairs were narrow, and they had difficulty carrying him down, just as she earlier had experienced difficulty dressing his unconscious body in pajamas. One of them slipped and almost dropped his head, and Maya swore at him in a vicious whisper. At first they held his left hand against the black plate and nothing happened, but they maneuvered his slack body and positioned his right palm and there came a hum and a series of clicks, and the handle was turned and the safe door swung open.

It took them forty minutes to photograph all the documents, and as she sat in the chair, watching, she wondered why they had brought only a single camera. Gemmel was slumped in the chair opposite, but her eyes avoided him.

One of them held the small, powerful light with a battery pack, while another turned the pages and the third clicked away—three times for each page. He frequently had to change the film and on such an occasion the page turner moved to the drinks table and was about to help himself when Maya's cold voice stopped him.

"Touch nothing! Just do it and go!"

He shrugged and moved back to the others and the camera started clicking again.

She rearranged the books while they carried him back upstairs. When they came down she was standing by the open door. One of them said solemnly:

"Comrade Kashva, I am instructed by Comrade Gordik to inform you that you may, if you wish, accompany us now. You will be back in Moscow by tomorrow night."

They looked at her curiously, at her pale, drawn face. She silently shook her head, and they left.

She went back into the sitting room, switched on the stereo, and put a record on the turntable. Then she poured herself a large Cognac and curled up in a chair and listened to *Paquita*. For a long while her face held no expression, but as the music reached its climax her white cheeks became wet with tears. When it ended she poured more Cognac and played it again and by the time it ended again, she had no tears left.

Her mind had passed through every permutation of her situation. Love of country, love of mother, and, finally, love of Gemmel. She could find no way of reconciling the three. She had easily discarded the choice of returning to Russia. She had decided that she did not wish to live without Gemmel. It was as though she had been pointed at him since her birth. Her melancholy soul told her that if she tried to live without him, existence would have no meaning.

She found a pen and paper and sat at the table and wrote for several minutes. The Cognac had made her slightly drunk and the writing was unsteady. She carried the paper to the turntable and placed it on the black record, then went to the kitchen and filled a glass with warm water. Very slowly she spooned into it all the contents of her powder compact and stood looking straight ahead as she stirred until the water was clear. She carried the glass up to the bedroom and placed it on the bedside table, then she struggled to pull the pajamas from Gemmel's body. Struggled because he was slack and heavy and she was drunk and she had found more tears which half-blinded her. For a long time she sat looking at his naked body, then abruptly she stood and undressed and picked up the glass and, with great deliberation, drained it to the bottom.

She lay down beside him, molded her body to his, and twined her legs in his legs, wrapped her arms around him and buried her face in his neck.

He awoke with a terrible headache. It was almost noon and he was cold to the marrow of his bones. With great difficulty he unwrapped himself from the cold, stiff embrace.

# seventeen

"WHY? WHY? WHY?"

Gordik pounded the table rhythmically, while Tudin, Larissa, and the five men from the Research and Analysis Directorate continued to look blank.

Gordik glared at the bespectacled man on his left.

"Why, Malin—why so easy?"

Malin extracted a handkerchief from his jacket pocket, took off his spectacles, and polished them vigorously.

"Well?" prompted Gordik irritably, and Malin did something totally out of character. Perhaps it was because he was tired. They had been sitting there for two hours and his back ached and he had long suffered from sciatica. Perhaps he decided that at the age of sixty, he might as well retire anyway. In any event, he lost his temper and launched a tirade at the astonished Gordik.

What exactly did the comrade want? he started sarcastically. Was he never satisfied? They had received a crumb of information and from it had built an entire bakery. Two months ago they only had a rumor of a major impending Western intelligence operation. Today the comrade had every last detail of that operation. A great

Soviet artist had risked everything to get it. It had been a breathtakingly brilliant operation that had succeeded beyond anyone's dreams. And yet Comrade Gordik was dissatisfied. His mind was so warped with suspicion that he could not accept the obvious, and must go on looking for mice in every little corner. Well, he, Yuri Malin, was an analyst, not a rodent catcher!

He ended up with his face very close to Gordik's, his eyes glaring and his mouth quivering. The others watched, transfixed. Very slowly Gordik leaned closer until his face was only inches from Malin's nose; out of the corner of his mouth he said, "Lev, please go to the bar and pour Comrade Malin a large Scotch." Then he burst out laughing and clapped Malin on the shoulder. "At last!" he said. "You speak from the heart as well as the head!"

Malin glanced about him nervously. His anger had gone and he wasn't sure whether Gordik was sincere or simply dangling him on a string. But then he saw Larissa smiling and he began to relax.

Gordik called to Tudin at the bar to get them all drinks, leaned back in his chair, and said, "Yes, it was a brilliant operation, and it succeeded beyond our expectations. But, Comrades, I suspect that Gemmel was waiting and ready."

"But it makes no sense," Tudin said, passing out the drinks. "As an exercise in misinformation it serves no purpose."

Malin sipped his Scotch and now, greatly emboldened, spoke again.

"Perhaps there is a purpose. Perhaps they wished to convince us that the Americans have truly controlled the laser divergence problem. I mean, it's no use having a potentially sophisticated weapon if your adversary doesn't know about it. Not if it's meant to be a deterrent."

"It's a good point," Gordik conceded. "Our laser experts consider it's highly improbable that the Americans have overcome the divergence problem; but it they have, it's a breakthrough of staggering importance."

One of the other men shook his head. "If, indeed, the British were expecting her, and I'm not convinced they were, it wouldn't be for that reason. After all, if they, or the Americans, want to inform us of such a major weapons breakthrough they could easily arrange a convincing demonstration. Besides, the information coming out of the Middle East tends to confirm that the operation as described is actually under way and moving toward a climax."

"Another good point," Gordik agreed. His voice took on an admiring tone. "What a concept! Take over Islam! What kind of a mind could think that up? And why risk it, even to pass on misinformation?"

"So maybe they weren't expecting her," Larissa said tentatively.

There was a silence while they all thought about it, and then Gordik shrugged resignedly and said to Larissa, "You could be right. Let us not overestimate the British. I would have been happy had our swallow discovered even the merest whiff of information. Just because she uncovered the full details doesn't have to mean that they were planted."

"So what course of action do we adopt?" Tudin asked.

Gordik took a thoughtful sip of his Scotch and said, "That's something to be decided at a higher level, but there appear to be two options. Either we expose it now or wait and see what happens at Mecca. Wait and see if the Americans actually have controlled the divergence problem."

Malin posed the problem: "And take the risk of having the Mahdi proclaimed? With two and a half million observers it could be difficult to overturn that. No matter what we say or do."

Gordik was about to answer when one of the phones on his desk rang stridently. The blue phone, which connected him directly with his boss, the head of the KGB. He crossed to the desk, picked it up and said, "Gordik."

He listened for two minutes, his face registering increasing astonishment, then he said, "Yes, sir," and put the phone down and stood looking at it for a long moment. Then, without turning, he said, "The meeting is over."

Everyone at the table looked at one another in puzzlement and then the five men from the Research and Analysis Directorate stood up and filed out.

As the door closed Gordik turned to Larissa and Tudin and said somberly, "There's been a direct communication from MI-Six. They inform us that Maya Kashva is dead. That she committed suicide."

Larissa and Tudin's faces could have been carved in stone.

"Furthermore," Gordik said, "I've been personally invited to a meeting in London. A meeting with Perryman."

"What was that figure again?" Hawke asked over his shoulder, and Wisner's voice intoned:

"Fifty-two point seven million."

Hawke looked out the window at the sculptured landscape surrounding the CIA headquarters and muttered, "And all for a piece of ass!"

"It could have been worse," Wisner said.

Hawke turned to look at him and at Falk and Meade, who were grouped around the table.

"I mean, if we'd launched the thing you'd have had to add another hundred and twenty million to the bill."

They all had expressions akin to mourners at a funeral, which in a sense they were, for the purpose of the meeting was to bury Operation Mirage as tidily and quickly as possible. The Director had been angrily explicit.

"Don't leave a goddam trace—not even the whiff of an agent's fart!"

Instructions had already been sent to pull the field team out of Jeddah, and the intelligence service of a U.S. client state had been briefed and paid to eliminate Haji Mastan. They couldn't have a disgruntled mole running around, talking out of turn. He was the only link with the CIA, and so, when the KGB momentarily blew the lid off the whole thing, every American official would plead astounded and dignified ignorance. The British, of course, would have to look after their own problems.

Hawke moved back to his seat, and as he sat down with a sigh, one of the phones on his desk rang. The green one, which linked him to the Director.

It was almost a one-way conversation. Hawke's face mirrored his astonishment as he muttered, "Yes, sir," at frequent intervals. When he hung up, the three at the table were all leaning toward him expectantly. Falk was later to remark that he had never seen Hawke so completely stunned, but then he had not been present the night before, when Hawke had received the news from London.

Now Hawke collected himself with an effort.

"Leo," he said briskly, "first things first. Get on the phone and call off the hit on Haji Mastan. And the field team is to stay put in Jeddah until further notice."

"The operation goes on?" Wisner asked incredulously.

"Let's say it's in abeyance for forty-eight hours. There's been a meeting of the National Security Council and one or two suggestions were thrown up. I'm to leave immediately for London and a meeting with Perryman—and with Vassili Gordik!"

Only Wisner had to ask who Vassili Gordik was, and he did.

Hawke smiled grimly. "He's my opposite number in the KGB."

This time Perryman had chosen Regent's Park. He and Gemmel sauntered along with typical Englishmen's gait—hands clasped behind their backs, torsos bent slightly forward, and frequently turning inward to each other as they conversed.

For half an hour Perryman had been briefing Gemmel on the three meetings that had taken place in the morn-

ing: the first between himself and Gordik, the second
with Hawke, and the third with both together.

"How did you find Gordik?" Gemmel asked.

"Remarkably civilized." Perryman's face showed mild
astonishment. "And I think genuinely upset about the
death of Miss Kashva. Incidentally, he refused my offer
of allowing them access at the postmortem. Said it was
totally unnecessary."

He glanced at Gemmel's troubled face and quickly
changed the subject. "Hawke, on the other hand, was
somewhat difficult."

"I can imagine."

"Yes . . . well, he does have a point. They have ex-
pended a large amount of money and I suppose his job
was definitely on the line."

Gemmel smiled fleetingly. "But you won him over?"

"Oh, yes. But his attitude was one of hurt indignation.
He had already received fairly explicit instructions in
Washington."

Earlier Perryman had explained the background to the
meetings, mentioned that initial contacts had taken place
at the highest level both in Moscow and Washington, and
commented that it was truly amazing how rapidly matters
could be arranged when one dealt with people in a position to make quick decisions, especially when prime national interests were at stake.

The Russians had seen the logic immediately. Operation Mirage was quickly approaching its climax and its
objectives coincided perfectly with the Soviets' own interests. It was simply a matter of a suitable trade-off and
recognizing common ground. "There were acres and acres
of common ground," Perryman had commented. First of
all, Russia would have between fifty and sixty million
Muslims within its own southern and eastern borders by
the end of the century. Concurrently, it would become a
major importer of oil from Islamic states, and runaway
prices would be disastrous for the fragile economies of
the Eastern Bloc. In the short term, they were mired deep

in Afghanistan, and one aspect of the trade-off was that if Operation Mirage succeeded, the United States would allow the Mahdi to use his influence to make life easier for them. In return, he would assist the Americans in re-establishing influence in Iran, and the Russians would keep out of the picture. In fact, zones of influence throughout the Middle East had been demarcated. It was, Perryman had remarked, a replay of history at the time when, in the sixteenth century, the then Pope had arbitrated in the dispute between Spain and Portugal and virtually divided the unconquered world between them.

The Americans had seen the benefits and it had been vividly pointed out that with the Russians as a full partner, there could be little chance of the plot being uncovered. Perryman had, somewhat caustically, asked how long it would have taken the KGB to zero in on Haji Mastan, especially wtih CIA agents practically falling over each other in Jeddah. The Americans had also seen the advantage of giving the Russians a spectacular, first-hand demonstration of their new laser technology. It would make future SALT talks much smoother if the Americans were negotiating from a position of known strength.

So a deal had been struck, and for the first time in history, the CIA and the KGB would become partners.

"A frightening prospect, on the face of it," Perryman had said. "But in this case it's rather tidy."

"And where does it leave us?" Gemmel now asked. "I mean as far as the operation is concerned?"

"Well, obviously, we'll now take a back seat. The Americans will once again run Haji Mastan"—he gave Gemmel a bleak smile—"with a Russian liaison team, of course. It's been decided that they will send a team to the field HQ in Amman, to monitor the final stages. Our position will be that of an honest broker interacting between the two parties."

In spite of his mood of intense depression Gemmel had to smile at Perryman's terminology. Ever since the collapse of the Empire, countless British politicians had tried to cast Britain in the role of the honest broker.

"And my own position?" he asked.

They had reached a junction in the path. One way led to the zoo and the other to a children's playground. Perryman gestured at the playground and they walked in silence, found a bench, and sat down.

"Your own position," Perryman said firmly, "was clearly defined at the third meeting. You will continue in the operation as our senior representative."

"That must have taken some doing?"

Perryman shook his head. "Not really. Gordik was quite amenable."

"And Hawke?"

"Less so. He made the obvious rude remarks about MI-Six and our security. I sensed in his attitude a strong personal motivation. He obviously feels badly let down by a 'friend,' so it's natural that his disillusionment should be all the greater. In fact he was astonished to discover that you had not been summarily dismissed."

"And Gordik wasn't?"

Perryman smiled thinly. "Comrade Gordik is a shrewd man. At our first meeting he hinted that we knew all about the swallow, that we had prepared the nest, so to speak."

"And?"

Perryman smiled complacently. "I gave him a look which was supposed to be enigmatic and all-knowing at the same time. I think I succeeded, because he dropped the matter. He clearly believes that we are basking in our role of the honest broker and that we will use it in an effort to gain influence between the two superpowers—and, of course, to reap concurrent benefits from the result of the operation."

Now Gemmel smiled and asked, "So what's the next step?"

"Another meeting," Perryman replied briskly. "Just the three of you. This evening in Gordik's suite at the

Savoy Hotel. I must say that for a dedicated Communist, Gordik likes to live well." He slid Gemmel a wry look. "But that seems to go for most intelligence agents these days!"

Gemmel hardly seemed to be listening. The playground was deserted but for a man and his two young sons—one about three years old, the other five. The man wore a pinstriped business suit, a head of gray hair, and a harried expression as he dashed back and forth, first pushing one boy on a swing and then catching the other as he arrived at the bottom of the slide.

Apart from the piping voices of the children, there was a silence. Then Perryman asked softly, "Did you love her, Peter?"

Gemmel nodded very slowly, his eyes never leaving the playground and the two young boys.

"I'm truly sorry."

Gemmel turned to look at him, then gazed back at the playground. "Just don't say anything about breaking eggs to make omelets."

Perryman didn't reply to that. After a few moments Gemmel started talking again, in a low monotone, as if to himself. "I know. I know . . . I should have known better. Apart from anything else, she was half my age . . . but I just couldn't help it. Couldn't help it. Couldn't stop myself . . . didn't want to. I knew what she was. I was prepared, but kept holding on to the slim chance that we were mistaken; that the approach would come from a different direction." He shook his head as if to clear it. "It's been so long . . . and she was beautiful . . . in every way. You couldn't believe how beautiful."

"Perhaps I can," Perryman said gently. "About a year after my wife died—oh, it must have been eight years ago now—I found myself in a very depressed state. I suppose realization had at last sunk in, and at the time we were going through a very sticky patch at the office. Matter of fact, I was doing your job at the time. I think you were in Berlin then on the Becker case."

Gemmel nodded. He was a little surprised at the rare, familiar tone that Perryman was using.

"Well, one day," Perryman continued, "I decided to take a break. I talked it over with Henderson and he agreed." He smiled at the memory. "It was late September, and wet and miserable. I walked down Oxford Street and into the first travel agents I saw and told them to book me a holiday somewhere in the sun—anywhere, just as long as it was soon. It turned out to be Greece—Mykonos. Well, the hotel wasn't very good, but it was on a sort of rocky beach. Being late in the season it was half-empty—mostly elderly people, Scandinavians in the main. But there was one young girl, about twenty years old. A Finn. She had arrived the day before me." He glanced at Gemmel, and seeing his obvious interest, he continued. "I had a room with a terrace overlooking the beach, and I spent most of the first week just sitting out there, reading. The girl always sunbathed directly beneath the terrace. She wore only the smallest bikini bottom—no top— and she was quite breathtakingly beautiful. Curiously, none of the local Lotharios bothered her. She had an air of detachment, almost as though she carried a sign reading 'Keep Off'; do you know what I mean?"

"Yes," Gemmel answered. "I know exactly what you mean."

"Well, during that first week," Perryman resumed, "I watched the sun turn her golden brown. She had long flaxen hair, which became even lighter as her skin darkened. After a while I found it impossible to keep my eyes off her. It was sort of embarrassing; I felt a bit like a peeping Tom." He smiled. "There I was, fifty years old and acting like a teen-ager."

"What happened?" Gemmel asked, filled with curiosity.

"Yes, well, on the Saturday night I dressed up—you know, dinner jacket and so on. It's something people rarely do these days, but there was supposed to be a small band playing after dinner and I wasn't sure what people would be wearing." He smiled again as his mind took him back. "I felt a bit foolish when I entered the bar. Everybody else was dressed very casually. The girl was sitting by herself at the bar. She was in slacks and a blouse. I ordered a drink and noticed her looking at me and smiling. I can tell you, I felt very self-conscious. Then she drained her glass and spoke to me. She said, 'Will you please order me another drink? I'll be back soon.' And she got up and left. So I ordered the drink, but she wasn't back soon. In fact everyone else had gone in to dinner and I was beginning to think that she wasn't coming back. Then she walked in. For a moment I didn't recognize her. She was wearing a long black evening gown and a silver necklace. She had put her hair up and she carried a small sequined evening bag. She looked absolutely exquisite. She didn't bother with her drink, just took my arm, and said, 'Shall we go and eat?' We had a very wonderful dinner."

"And then?" Gemmel asked.

"And then we had a very wonderful two weeks. Very wonderful." He took a deep breath and sighed. "The point is, Peter, I was completely overwhelmed. I never tried to understand it. Of course, I remembered my position. Considered all the possibilities. After all, she was Finnish, and I was the number-two man in MI-Six and—at the time—very emotionally vulnerable."

"Did you check?"

"I did not. To be honest, I hardly even considered it." He glanced at the younger man and smiled. "So you see, Peter, there are times when we all let our defenses down."

"Did you ever see her again?"

"No. I assumed it was a passing thing for her and didn't press it. Neither did she." His expression was wry. "So she was no swallow, but believe me, Peter, I do understand just a little of what you are feeling."

He looked down at his watch and stood up. "We'd better go, or you'll be late for your meeting."

* * *

As it turned out; Gemmel was a little late. A traffic jam in Leicester Square slowed him up. But at the Savoy he had no trouble parking. The green-uniformed doorman admired the Lagonda and waved him to one of the few spaces by the entrance. As he rode the elevator to the fourth floor he tried to decide how he would greet Gordik. He was, in any event, determined to keep himself under tight control.

He rang the bell beside the door, and after a few moments it slowly opened. They looked at each other warily. Then Gordik stepped aside and Gemmel walked into the small foyer.

"We hardly need introduce ourselves," Gordik said with a tentative smile. "After all, we must have often studied each other's photographs."

"That is so," Gemmel agreed stiffly. "Has Hawke arrived?"

"Yes, he's having a drink in the sitting room." Gordik started to move toward a closed door, but Gemmel's harsh voice stopped him.

"Before we go in, I'd like to ask you one question."

Gordik turned and there was a tension in the air.

"Ask."

"Did you know she was a virgin?"

"Yes, I knew she was a virgin." Gordik studied Gemmel's face while his answer sank in. He noted the lines of exhaustion around the eyes and could detect the rigid control that Gemmel was exercising.

"Mr. Gemmel," he said, "now, let me tell you something before we go in, and then, although we cannot put the matter from our minds, we need not talk about it again. It was inconceivable to me that Maya Kashva would commit suicide. I cannot say that had such a possibility occurred, I would not have sent her. In our work we both have to perform unpleasant duties. I can say that her death affected me very deeply, and my close associates. I knew her for only a short time, but in that time I developed an affection for her that was greater than I realized. I can also tell you that I promised her that her mother would be allowed to join her if she elected to stay in the West. Believe me or not, but it's a promise I would have kept."

Gemmel drew a deep breath. "So you sent a virgin swallow. I could not imagine you would be so subtle."

Now Gordik smiled. "I had no choice, Mr. Gemmel. I sent her first to our Swallow School and she kicked the chief instructor very hard in his only asset. So hard, in fact, that he is obliged to look for alternative employment."

Gemmel tried to smile, but it would not come. He gestured at the door and Gordik opened it and waved him through.

A bar, complete with three barstools, had been set up, facing the large window. Hawke sat on one of the stools, looking out over the river. He turned as they entered, glanced coolly at Gemmel and then back at the view. Gordik moved behind the bar, saying, "Again, introductions are unnecessary. If our files are correct you drink Scotch and soda, Mr. Gemmel." He picked up a bottle of Chivas Regal and started to pour the drink.

Gemmel eased himself onto a barstool and said, "Hello, Morton."

Hawke continued looking out of the window and, without turning his head said coldly, "Well, 'Pete,' I just hope she was a good fuck."

Gordik was watching Gemmel and he saw the control snap and he started to move, but he was far too late.

Gemmel's right hand traveled in a blur just as Hawke began to turn. He took it on the left side of the jaw and was unconscious before he hit the carpet.

Later, the hotel doctor came out of the bedroom and said to Gordik, "He's all right now, sir. He'll be out in a few minutes."

Gordik showed him to the door, then returned to the

bar and poured Gemmel another drink. He was obviously enjoying himself.

"It makes a change," he said with a grin, "for a Russian to have to keep the peace between Western allies."

"It was very stupid," Gemmel said. "I apologize. It looks like I might now be out of the picture altogether."

"I hope not. I was looking forward to working with you and, incidentally, with Hawke. I see us as a formidable triumvirate. Would it help if I left you two alone for a while?"

"It might," Gemmel replied.

Gordik drained his glass and stood up. "Call me when you're ready," he said. "I'll be down in the bar." He smiled sardonically. "The American bar."

As the door closed behind him Gemmel took a glass, poured three fingers of Canadian Club, added a single cube of ice and a splash of soda. The bedroom door opened and Hawke came out. The left side of his face was badly swollen and beginning to darken into a bruise, but he walked steadily—almost briskly—to the bar and sat on a stool. Gemmel pushed the drink toward him. He picked it up, took a large gulp, and twirled the glass thoughtfully in his fingers. Then he gave Gemmel a long, level look and said:

"I guess that whole episode with the girl affected you more than just a little."

"It did, but I made a terrible mistake and another when I hit you. I apologize."

Hawke took a deep breath. "Okay. I don't apologize for what I said. You had it coming." He stroked his jaw and with difficulty managed a half-smile. "But I should have said it from across the room."

For a moment Gemmel couldn't say anything. He was overcome with a turning, tumbling feeling of gratitude toward the American. Gratitude for his generosity and for the size and scope of his character. He decided to try and explain, at least as far as he was able.

"I'm truly sorry, Morton. Things went blank. I know it's difficult to understand. Perhaps one day you will. But you won't like me any better for it. The fact is I was totally vulnerable. You know me a little and the friendship we've built up means a great deal to me. It's never been easy for me to make friends. You know what this business is like. One becomes obsessed with secrecy; of compartmentalizing one's life; of living in a different world from everyone else; of being just different."

Hawke was listening with total attention, fascinated to be witness to the emotions of a man who lived almost entirely within himself.

"It's a little easier for you," Gemmel went on. "You have a wonderful home life. I've seen it. You can come home from work and put it aside and live like a normal human being. You get mad with your wife because she redecorates your house, but I've seen you together, and after all these years, I guess, you love her as much as the first day. You've raised children, fine sons; you can take pleasure and pride from their futures. I had it once. The same hopes and expectations. The same road going off in a straight line in front of me. When that road ended a large part of my life ended with it. It's like having an operation on part of your brain, cutting out the bits that give contentment. So I was vulnerable. I suddenly found myself again with an emotional future. Again looking down a straight road. All my feelings had been in a sort of cell—a condemned cell. Suddenly there was a reprieve. The door was unlocked. I had been years in that cell, ever since my wife died, mentally sitting on a bench, spending my days looking at a locked door. When the door opened I was shocked—frightened. I saw it open with light outside. After all those years I was frightened to get up and walk out. Frightened to let my emotions face the world again. But, Morton, I had to get up and walk out of that cell—I just had to. Of course I had the girl checked out. Of course I had suspicions, but I pushed them back, tried to ignore them." He glanced up at Hawke and stopped talking, suddenly intensely embarrassed, as only an introverted man can be embarrassed by opening up his mind and his feelings to another person, albeit a friend.

Hawke was moved. He said gently, "You risked everything. The greatest chance an intelligence agent ever had. You put that on the line, Peter. I thought I knew what love meant, but maybe I was wrong. I couldn't see myself doing the same thing."

"I don't suppose you'll ever have to," Gemmel said, and there was a trace of bitterness in his voice. "But, Morton, I thank you for at least trying to understand. The question now is whether you want me to continue in the project. After all, you can call Perryman and tell him I physically attacked you and he'll pull me out."

Hawke shook his head. "Let's say it never happened. But, Peter, the situation has changed now. You talked in Washington of the back seat your people would take if Operation Mirage succeeds. I guess you realize that you're going to have to take that back seat now. With the Russians involved we'll be running it together. I've already sent instructions to our people in Jeddah to take over direct control of Haji Mastan from Boyd. The Russians will assign their own men to work with ours. From now on you'll be only maintaining a watching brief." He glanced down at his watch and his voice became brisk. "Where's that Russian? We'd better get down to details."

Gemmel moved to the phone, saying over his shoulder, "He's having a drink in the American bar."

Five minutes later Gordik re-entered the suite. He looked inquisitively at the two men sitting at the bar and then his face split into a smile.

"I take it we're friends again?" Without waiting for an answer he moved round the bar, poured himself a drink, and topped up their glasses. Then he looked critically at the bruise on Hawke's jaw. "It could be worse," he said.

Hawke managed another smile. "To quote Jack Dempsey, 'I forgot to duck.' Now, can we get down to business?"

They went on to talk technicalities. It was a strange but stimulating discussion, each not wishing to disclose too much too quickly, and yet curiously eager to prove the skills and capabilities of their respective organizations.

Gordik asked about Haji Mastan and the other Arab agents in the field. He assumed that they were all covert Christians, and when this was confirmed, admitted that his own Arab agents were of similar background.

"Of course, you use Arabs of the Greek Orthodox faith. They hate Islam, and you have a rich recruiting ground in the Lebanon, and parts of Iran and Iraq. We are fortunate in having our own Arab Christians in Russia itself."

"How are you placed in Saudi Arabia?" Hawke asked, and Gordik smiled a touch complacently.

"Let's say we are adequately provided for, Mr. Hawke. We shall certainly have a good representation at the Haj, and will be in instant communication."

They went on to discuss various aspects of setting up the base HQ in Jordan. A large, walled villa on the outskirts of Amman had been prepared. Gordik advised that he would be bringing with him Lev Tudin and a secretary, together with half a dozen communications and security personnel. "After all, Jordan is not exactly a client state of ours," he said with a disarming smile.

As the discussion proceeded, Gemmel found himself slowly pushed into the background, and Hawke's words came back to him. He was now obviously merely an adjunct to the mainstream of the operation.

When they had covered all the salient points, Gordik filled the glasses and they drank a toast to cooperation, and then another—to the success of Operation Mirage.

# Book
# *four*

# eighteen

THERE HAD NEVER BEEN SUCH A CROWD AT THE IBN
Tulun Mosque in Cairo. At least, not in living memory.
But for days the word had been passed: Abu Qadir had
crossed the Red Sea from Jeddah and on Friday would attend the evening prayers.

Many had been skeptical, but had still been drawn by
curiosity.

He arrived an hour before sunset with a dozen followers
who cleared a path through the crowd. A hush descended
as with his slow, deliberate step he moved to the open
baths with their splashing fountains, and washed his hands
and feet. He seemed oblivious of the crowd during his
prayers, but afterward he moved among them and many
pressed forward to touch him, or just to be close. When
he finally spoke he was brief and only those nearby could
hear his voice, but the words were quickly passed back
in concentric waves.

"I am only a warner and a bearer of good tidings to
people who believe."

Thus he started with a quotation taken from Sura VII
of the Koran. His message was simple: Change was in the

offing. Soon all would be clear. A sign was due. He, Abu
Qadir, would make his pilgrimage to Mecca and wait for
that sign. He would gather with friends in Taif and he
would cross the desert to Mecca, and during the Haj all
would be made clear.

He stopped speaking, and the crowd parted and he left
the mosque. Many among the crowd were affected by his
simple words, and vowed to make that same journey across
the sea, and then across the desert.

Abu Qadir spent two more days in Cairo, praying and
speaking in many of the city's mosques. Haji Mastan was
always by his side, apart from a two-hour period when he
went to visit his brother. There was a man waiting for him
there, a man who spoke perfect Arabic, but who was not
an Arab. A man who gave him a small steel box just a
little bigger than a cigar box and with a series of switches
and dials down one side.

A huge Air Force C5A Galaxy transport plane touched
down on Runway 13 at the Kennedy Space Center, and
taxied slowly to the mating facility. The space shuttle
*Atlantis* was parked with open cargo-hold beside a giant
crane. The C5A came to a halt on the other side of the
crane and security personnel moved in to ring the entire
facility.

An hour later, Elliot Wisner and a number of his team
watched as the crane deposited the massive, slug-shaped
apparatus gently into the bowels of *Atlantis*. The Ken-
worth trailer was carefully backed in and connected and
then, on its ninety wheels, it trundled off with the shuttle
in tow toward the giant gantries of the launch facility.

Hawke was obviously in charge; in spite of the purplish
bruise on his face he was a dominant, predatory figure,
stalking through the villa, checking on everything from
the thickness of the mattresses on the myriad, makeshift
bunks, to the wiring-up of the telecommunications equipment.

Gordik, on the other hand, epitomized the gate crasher at a party who enjoys himself enormously and is oblivious to the resentful stares of the host and legitimate guests.

They had all arrived in the early afternoon aboard a U.S. Air Force Hercules transport plane, under cover of a U.S. military aid team. Even the Russians had worn U.S. Air Force uniforms, but on arrival at the villa they had all changed into civilian clothes, with the exception of Gordik, who now stood at the makeshift bar resplendent in the uniform of a full colonel, complete with medals and combat ribbons.

The villa was a rambling, three-story structure, which now housed thirty-two people. It had an enormous ground-floor dining and reception area which Hawke called "the recreational facility." Meade had been responsible for the fitting-out of the villa and had made sure that there was a plentiful supply of liquor, Islamic state or not. Just off the recreational facility was the communications center, which housed a battery of sophisticated radio and telex equipment. The Russians had brought some of their own, but this still lay in its packing cases, for they had quickly discovered that the American equipment was compatible with theirs. The communications technicians of the three teams had soon established a working rapport and the villa was now linked, by both voice and print-out, to Moscow, London, Washington, the Kennedy Space Center in Florida, the Johnson Space Center in Houston, and a variety of field stations and even individual agents.

The American team took up the rest of the ground floor and most of the first floor. The Russians were on the second floor and the British had a couple of rooms in what had been the servants' quarters.

They were all gathered now in the recreation facility. Leo Falk was behind the bar, dispensing drinks and flirting with Larissa, who was the only woman on any of the teams. She was dressed in a Lanvin blouse and a Givenchy skirt, and drew covetous glances from most of the men. Gordik and Meade were also at the bar, engaged in deep conversation. Tudin was in a corner, engrossed in a game of chess with another Russian. Gemmel and Boyd were seated in an alcove.

"I just wish I knew what was going on," Boyd said resentfully.

"You will, Alan, in the course of time."

"Well, I don't understand it," Boyd continued. "You send me to Taif with a sealed package and instructions to hand it over to one Maqbul Saddiqi after appropriate password identification. He turns out to be a boy of no more than twelve! I mean really, Peter, what is going on?"

Gemmel made placating noises and was saved from further questioning as Hawke entered the room and clapped his hands loudly. All conversation stopped.

"Just a quick briefing," he said loudly, and then lowered his voice slightly. "Now that we're all settled in I just want to lay down a few ground rules." He gestured at Gordik. "I've already discussed them with Comrade Gordik and we're in agreement. Although this villa is secure and our own people are maintaining a twenty-four-hour external cover, it's still necessary for us to be circumspect. As far as the Jordanian authorities are concerned we're part and parcel of the U.S. military aid mission and several of our number will be working with the Jordanians on a day-by-day basis in order to keep up that cover. Nevertheless, our very numbers make us conspicuous and so it's been decided that nobody will leave the villa until the operation is complete, in six days' time. The only exception to this will be two daily limousine services between the American Embassy and the Russian Embassy." Again he indicated Gordik. "Obviously the Russians want to maintain their own secure contacts with Moscow and we wish to do the same with Washington. The fact that we have a joint team manning our communications system here means, in a sense, that we're reading each other's mail." He smiled sardonically. "Not that we have any secrets from each other."

To Gemmel he said, "Peter, I hope it's all right, if you

don't mind using our Embassy communications. Frankly, the less traffic between the villa and our embassies, the better."

"It's no problem, Morton," Gemmel agreed. "I don't think we'll have much either to send or receive."

"Good." Hawke rubbed his hands together briskly. "Now to more mundane details. There's a bulletin board outside the communications room and mealtimes have been listed on it. Please try to be punctual. We're using U.S. Army cooks and they'll try to vary the food as much as possible and to take into account the tastes of our Russian friends." Another smile twitched at his lips. "I understand Comrade Corporal Brady makes a mean borscht! In general terms I'd be grateful if everyone, apart from communications personnel, retired not later than midnight. It's also been decided that the only liquor to be served or kept in the villa will be here in the recreation room." He paused and asked, "Are there any questions?"

"Just one," Gordik said. "Is the countdown for the launch of the space shuttle proceeding satisfactorily?"

"It is," Hawke replied emphatically. "As you know, these things have become fairly routine and we don't anticipate any problems. In any event I'll keep you fully informed."

"What news from Taif?" Gemmel asked.

"There's already a considerable gathering. Abu Qadir and Haji Mastan arrived yesterday with their usual small following, but our agents report this morning that there are already between two and three thousand pilgrims gathered on the outskirts of the city and that the numbers are expected to rise sharply over the next three days. Incidentally, the annual camel sales are held at the same time and many of the traders will likely join Abu Qadir's personal pilgrimage. Anything more?" His eyes swept the room, but there were no more questions, and with a curt nod he turned back toward the communication center.

"I feel like a bloody schoolboy!" Boyd said, and Gemmel laughed.

"It's just his manner, and if I know the man at all, I'd say he's very excited deep down and he's trying hard to bottle it up. If this thing comes off it's going to put him in a very strong and unique position in Washington."

"That's very nice for Hawke," Boyd said sarcastically. "But we're really being left out of the picture. I get the feeling we're only here on sufferance. It's a bit unfair, Peter, after all—we did most of the early leg work."

"It was inevitable," Gemmel said, and punched him lightly on the shoulder. "Don't worry, Alan, one way or another we'll get some benefits."

"I hope you're right," Boyd said moodily, and glanced at his watch. "Anyway, I'm going to get a few drinks in before dinner." He headed toward the bar.

There were three objects lying on the table, forming a triangle: a Koran, a curved dagger in a silver scabbard, and a revolver. The revolver was a Tokarev and the man sitting at the head of the table had taken it from a KGB agent whom he had assassinated two years before in Damascus. The man was Sami Zahaby and he was the leader of a cell of the Muslim Brotherhood, a secret society formed in 1928 by Hasan al-Bannā' in Egypt, a society dedicated to purging all Islamic governments of any deviation from Koranic law and practice, a society whose members were prepared to assassinate even heads of state if they didn't conform with fundamental Islamic law. The four members of this particular cell were gathered in a large house in Amman's souk, a house belonging to a wealthy merchant who had been a Brother for the past thirty years.

Zahaby was in a sanguine mood, which for him was a rare feeling. For the past three years he had been operating in Syria and had participated in the demonstrations and killings which had almost overthrown the Syrian government. Only the most savage reprisals had put down the uprising. Over one thousand of the Brotherhood had been arrested and incarcerated in Syrian jails. Two hundred and forty of them had been summarily executed. Because of the state of tension existing between Jordan and Syria, the Jordanian government had given active assistance to the Brotherhood and offered sanctuary to its members. Zahaby had narrowly escaped capture and arrived in Jordan for what he expected to be a brief respite. In the meantime he had taken over leadership of this particular cell, and although he hadn't any plans directed at the Jordanian government, he was always on the lookout for any way to harm the Syrians or their mentors, the Russians. In truth, he was a man who hated inactivity and for months now his impatience had been growing. Several times he had driven past the Soviet Embassy in the Jabal district and seen at least two men coming and going whom he knew to be KGB agents. One of them had served for two years in Damascus and had been the chief adviser to the Syrian security organization—an organization which had decimated the ranks of the Brotherhood.

So Zahaby had formulated a scheme: at best to kidnap this officer, or at worst simply to kill him. This man was now working under the name Zhukov, and was nominally assistant military attaché. For the past three weeks Zahaby had mounted a cover watch on the Russian Embassy and he knew which car Zhukov always used. The next time it left the Embassy, Zahaby was going to attack. The meeting was to finalize all arrangements.

He was only in his early thirties, in fact the youngest member of the cell, but the other men around the table deferred both to his intellect and aggressiveness. They listened with respect as he outlined his plan and instructed them in their roles. Other members of the Brotherhood had arranged to steal two cars. These cars would be stationed close to the Embassy, near the third rotary—or third circle, as such road configurations are known in Jordan. As soon as Zhukov's car joined the circle it would be sandwiched between the Brotherhood cars, and Zhukov abducted. There were then four escape routes available. Zhukov would be brought back to this house in the souk and over one hundred Brotherhood sympathizers and activists would seal off the area while he, Zahaby, extracted the answers that he needed. Sympathizers within the Jordanian security service would ensure that the search for the Russian was not pressed home with enthusiasm. In particular Zahaby wanted to know what future plans the Syrians had for containing the Brotherhood in that country. Zhukov would have been instrumental in formulating those plans.

The meeting ended and the four men reached out and placed their hands on the Koran.

"As Allah wills," Zahaby said vehemently.

"As Allah wills," the others echoed in unison.

Five Bedouins sat around an open fire outside a tent. A whole city of tents had sprung up on the outskirts of Taif—some, the traditional dwellings of desert nomads; others, makeshift shelters erected by the city people who had come to join Abu Qadir's personal Haj to Mecca.

The Bedouins had slaughtered and cooked a lamb, and after the meal, as they sipped small cups of sweet black coffee, they told each other stories and jokes.

One of them leaned forward, pushed more dried camel dung onto the fire, and said:

"When A'isha, the daughter of Talha, was given in marriage to Mus'ab, he said, 'By God, this night I shall kill thee with passion.' He took her once and then fell asleep and did not awaken till dawn, when she shook him and said, 'Wake up, killer.' "

They all rocked with laughter and then another offered his contribution.

"A man said to a woman, 'I would like to taste you, to know which has a better flavor, you or my wife.' She answered. 'Ask my husband, he has tasted us both.' "

More laughter, which abruptly stilled as they looked up and saw the figures of Abu Qadir and Haji Mastan, standing in the firelight. They began to scramble to their feet with embarrassed faces but Abu Qadir held out his hand, palm down.

"Be still, my brothers."

He looked at the coffeepot standing on a stone by the fire, and one of them asked hesitantly, "Will you take coffee with us, Rasūl?"

The others watched Abu Qadir's reaction with interest for *rasūl* means "apostle,—one who is sent." Haji Mastan glanced anxiously around, for there were scores of religious police in the encampment. But Abu Qadir smiled and nodded, and they made room around the fire and poured two cups of coffee.

Abu Qadir took a sip from his cup and said, "You make good coffee and you tell good jokes. Now hear this one: A man wrote to his beloved, 'Send me a vision of you in my dreams.' She wrote back, 'Send me ten dinars and I will come in person!' "

The Bedouins erupted in laughter. One of them was emboldened to ask, "Were you ever married, Rasūl?"

Once again Haji Mastan glanced nervously behind him into the shadows, while Abu Qadir shook his head.

"No, brother, but the Haj is upon us, and it is truly a time to think of such matters."

"And to see them!" another said, with a broad grin and in reference to the fact that women who normally wear the veil are forbidden to do so during the Haj, so it is a good time to arrange marriages. It is also a good time to do business, both on a local and international scale, and during the five days many contracts are agreed on in Mecca. The five Bedouins were camel traders and had come first to Taif to its traditional camel market before making the journey on to Mecca.

The oldest of them now asked, "Is it so, Rasūl, that in the morning you will walk to Mecca?"

"It is so."

"You will not journey on the mighty road that the king, in his wisdom, may Allah bless and preserve him, has built to give comfort to some pilgrims?"

There was an expectant hush, for the old Bedouin had spoken with a trace of sarcasm.

Abu Qadir looked away to the lights of Taif. Two billion dollars had been spent to build dozens of palaces for the Islamic heads of state who had lived in them for the three days of the recent Pan-Islamic Conference. Also a magnificent conference center, four hotels, and the superhighway to Mecca.

"I will walk beside the mighty road," Abu Qadir answered simply, and then, as if to answer the unspoken question, he added:

"All the peoples of the world are Allah's children, but in His breast He keeps a special place for Arabs, and He gave us two gifts. Through His Prophet Muhammad, may Allah bless and save him, He gave us the Koran. And He gave us also our land; some were ungrateful, for it was barren and had no tillage, but under the land He gave us that which is the heritage of all Arabs."

The Bedouins were listening intently and so was Haji Mastan, whose expression showed a mixture of fascination and puzzlement.

"Such a heritage," Abu Qadir continued, "should not be used profligately, nor should it be used to glorify mankind. Allah the Merciful and the Compassionate instructs us in the Koran: 'O you who believe! Do not consume your property among you in vanity.' "

This was greeted by a profound silence. The Bedouins looked at each other knowingly and then one asked, "Will you speak so in Mecca, Rasūl?"

Abu Qadir reached out and placed a hand on his shoulder. "After the Feast of the Sacrifice, my brother, I will speak of many things."

He looked at the oldest of the Bedouins. "I came to seek you out, for I am told that you are Ibn Sahl and the possessor of many camels, you and your brothers here."

"It is so," the old man replied. "Would you honor me and ride one of my camels to Mecca?"

"I will walk," Abu Qadir replied, "but there are some among us who are old and some who are sick."

Ibn Sahl leaned forward and said simply, "They are your followers and our brothers and sisters, Rasūl. They will follow you upon our camels, and even though my bones are old, I will walk with you to Mecca!"

"May Allah bless you and keep you, Ibn Sahl. You will walk beside me."

He gathered his robes around him and stood up, and they all stood up and crowded close and touched his clothing, and then he moved off into the darkness with Haji Mastan.

At dawn the tents were struck and a great column of pilgrims moved down the hills and onto the dry desert plain. At the head of the column Abu Qadir strode along with his purposeful walk. On his left was Ibn Sahl, and on his right, Haji Mastan. At the rear of the column were the old and the sickly, borne along by scores of camels. One of the old was a frail woman in her sixties who had been helped up together with a heavy sack containing her possessions. Her twelve-year-old grandson walked along beside the camel.

The column stretched out for over a mile beside the black macadam of the six-lane highway, and many of the Mercedes and Lincolns and Cadillacs slowed down on the way to Mecca so that their air-conditioned passengers could view the spectacle.

Mirza Farruki passed by in a Range Rover of the Saudi security service, and through binoculars he examined the front of the column and the man who had been the cause of his increasing insomnia.

# nineteen

"FIFTY-NINE SECONDS AND COUNTING."

Rufus Cabell, the launch director, didn't leave his console. By now, with an average of one launching a month, the process had become practically routine. So he watched the *Atlantis* only on the monitor.

But he was curious about the payload: first because it had been injected into the rigidly planned mission schedule, and second because there had been an inordinate amount of securtiy surrounding it since its arrival from Palmdale—far more than was normal for an intelligence satellite, which was how the mission had been described. He knew that it was going into a geostatic orbit, somewhere over the Middle East, but he did not know exactly where, because again in a total departure from routine, control of the mission would pass to the Johnson Space Center in Houston immediately after the shuttle separated from its external fuel tank.

In Houston, Elliot Wisner was watching a monitor in the mission control center. He heard the voice intoning "Thirty seconds and counting," and as each second ticked away his excitement mounted—an excitement caused not just by the launch itself. He reflected that few scientists in history could have had the results of their work demonstrated in such a spectacular manner and to such an audience as was now gathering in Mecca.

"Ten seconds and counting."

Without taking his eyes from the screen, Wisner pulled out a handkerchief and wiped his sweating palms and offered up an unconscious prayer that there would be no abort at this late stage.

The prayer was answered. The engines ignited, the external power lines dropped away, and, with its characteristic pause, the shuttle lifted off from the sea of yellow flame.

Wisner watched it curve into the sky, and then allowed himself a contented sigh.

In Amman, Hawke, Gordik and Gemmel stood behind the duty communications officer, watching the teleprinter tap out the sequence. When there finally appeared the words "Separation of ext. fuel tank complete," Gordik pounded Hawke on the back, and the American grinned hugely.

"Sweet as sugar!" he exclaimed. "Twenty tons lobbed up there like a quarterback throwing a TD pass."

"Touchdown. American football," Gemmel explained to the puzzled Russian, and then they all went out into the recreation area and Hawke proudly announced the success of the launch to the assembled teams.

Then he gave them another briefing.

"Our field agents," he said, "and that includes both teams, report that there are now over ten thousand pilgrims following Abu Qadir from Taif to Mecca."

There were murmurs of astonishment and Hawke smiled grimly.

"It's also estimated that within forty-eight hours there will be in excess of three million pilgrims in Mecca."

More murmurs of astonishment, and Falk spoke up.

"That's a twenty-five percent increase over last year. The normal annual inflation is less than ten percent."

"You attribute that purely to Operation Mirage?" Tudin asked.

"Not entirely," conceded Hawke. "This is the beginning of the Islamic fourteenth century and that must have a bearing. However, a lot of those pilgrims have resulted from our operational propaganda." He looked across at Gemmel. "The British did good work on that early on."

"What's the mood in Mecca?" Tudin asked.

"Very expectant," Hawke replied. "But our agents also report that the religious and security police are very much in evidence—and very nervous."

Now Gordik spoke for the first time. "I trust that Abu Qadir will not be indiscreet. If he so much as whispers the word Mahdi the Saudi security forces will leap on him faster than a hungry cat on a fat mouse."

Hawke shook his head. "Don't worry. He won't say a word until sixteen hundred hours on Thursday. He is totally under the influence and control of Haji Mastan."

He turned and went back into the communications center, and conversation started again. Gemmel walked to the bar and accepted a drink from Falk. Gordik and Meade started a conversation, which had something to do with "dead-letter drops."

Larissa watched Gemmel from the corner of her eye, then said in Russian, "I'm glad you hit him."

He turned to her and smiled slightly. "I shouldn't have. It was very unprofessional—and he didn't deserve it."

"Well," she said enigmatically, "there's nothing more boring than a total professional." She drained her glass and slipped off her stool. "Good night, Mr. Gemmel." With a glance at Gordik she left the room, and Falk watched her go, wistfully. Slowly the others started drifting out, leaving only Gordik, Meade, and Gemmel and a half-empty bottle of Scotch on the bar. When Gemmel left, their conversation had turned to "interface cutouts" and the complete uselessness of embassy-based field controllers.

Later that night Hawke lay in bed, mentally tired but unable to sleep. He could picture Abu Qadir leading his followers across the desert to Mecca. Among those followers were his own agents and those of the Russians and the British. Reports were now flowing into the villa in increasing quantities, and up in space, poised and waiting, was the satellite containing the most advanced laser ever built. For a while he allowed himself to conjure with the moral implications and he realized that he was leading an effort to perpetrate one of the greatest acts of deceit ever attempted on mankind. It was as well for his peace of mind that he was not an emotional or a romantic man and that his thoughts were largely occupied with the techniques of his profession. What areas of imagination he did have ranged ahead to the results and the opportunities that would accrue from this act of deceit. He was fundamentally a patriotic man and he believed without question that what he was doing was for the good of his country and its people. He believed that the actions of the oil-rich countries of the Middle East were inherently selfish. He couldn't see that they only acted to preserve their own national identities and their own aspirations. He saw himself and the entire Operation Mirage as striking a blow for what he conceived to be civilization. His nature was practical to the point where he could easily embrace the Jesuitical theory of the ends justifying the means.

Once again he went through the sequence of events which would culminate in the valley of Minā on the coming Thursday, and once again his memory took him back to the jungle of Malaya and the white-haired old spy whose fertile mind had set in motion the chain of events. He mentally ticked off what could go wrong and found comfort in the fact that so far the operation was proceeding like clockwork. He had even come to accept the presence of the Russians. Perryman had been right. There were vast areas of potential collaboration. With the Mahdi installed and controlled jointly by the CIA and the KGB, it would then become merely a matter of horse trading between the two supreme powers. A trading which would result in a stable Middle East, guaranteed long-term oil prices, and the easing of tension in an area which all too frequently had threatened to instigate a major conflict. His own position in the CIA would become paramount. After all, Directors were political appointees and came and went with each change of administration. For the foreseeable future he, Morton Hawke, would be the effective kingpin of the organization. It was an intelligence agent's dream. At that moment a waking dream, but in his peace of mind he rolled over in bed, snuggled his head deeper into the pillow, and turned it into a sleeping dream.

Great events in history can be caused or disrupted by the most insignificant items. In this case it was to be an automatic thermostat. Several hundred million dollars had already been spent on Operation Mirage. The thermostat in question was worth only a few dollars. It was installed in a Volga limousine of the Russian Embassy in Amman, and as the Russian chauffeur drove Lev Tudin the last mile and a half to the Embassy, his eyes constantly flickered to the temperature gauge. The car had been overheating for at least a month, but the bureaucratic wheels of the Soviet Foreign Service turned slowly and still a replacement thermostat had not arrived. They barely made the Embassy compound, and as Tudin went up the steps into the building, the chauffeur had lifted the hood and with the help of a heavy cloth was gingerly uncapping the radiator to a hissing of steam.

Tudin was doing the regular daily shuttle between the villa and the Embassy. He carried signals from Gordik to Moscow Center and would have to wait an hour to check the encoding and to decode any incoming messages. He was something of a puzzle to the Embassy staff, for it was unusual for a Russian to be loose in Amman. Even the Ambassador was unaware of his mission. He had received priority instructions from Moscow, informing him that an operation of vital national importance was being monitored from Amman and that he should give all assistance to Vassili Gordik.

Even the senior KGB operative at the Embassy, Colonel Zhukov, had been told no more than the Ambassador. He had, however, taken steps to inform himself of the whereabouts of Gordik and his team and had been astonished to discover that they were ensconced in a villa together with very senior American and British intelligence operatives. He had used his personal code to communicate with the head of the KGB, informing him of the situation and asking for instructions. The instructions had been short and explicit—in effect: mind your own business.

It happened that Zhukov was leaving the Embassy at the same time as Lev Tudin. He had met Tudin once briefly in Moscow, and as they came down the Embassy steps they exchanged a couple of pleasantries. They bade each other farewell and Zhukov was about to get into his car when he noticed the Embassy chauffeur in deep discussion with Tudin. He got out of the car and walked over.

"It's the thermostat, sir," explained the chauffeur. "I think it's finally stuck completely and I doubt if I can get Comrade Tudin back without the whole thing boiling over."

"It's no problem," Zhukov said expansively. "I'm on my way to the residents' compound and I'll drop Comrade Tudin off first." He noticed Tudin's skeptical expression and smiled to himself complacently.

"Don't worry, Comrade," he said. "I don't know the purpose of your mission but as the station head here, it's quite natural that I know where you're based. It's not far from the residents' compound." He gestured toward his car.

Tudin shrugged and got in the passenger seat and they pulled out and past the guards and onto the main street.

Across the road from the window of a house an Arab lowered his binoculars, raised a small transceiver to his lips, and pressed a button.

"He's coming out now," he said. "He has one passenger."

A quarter of a mile away on one of the approach roads to the third circle, Sami Zahaby acknowledged the message and picked up the UZI submachine gun from the space between the seats of the old Mercedes.

"He's coming out," he said to the Brother who sat behind the driving wheel, and glanced at his watch. "It's six o'clock. He's finished for the day and he's on his way home. He has a passenger." With his left hand he picked up his transceiver, pressed the button, and issued instructions to the four Brothers who were waiting in an old Ford beside another road on the other side of the third circle.

Zhukov was telling Tudin about the rigors of Middle East service. At the same time he was gently probing into what Gordik was up to in the villa. He was totally intrigued, for Gordik was his direct superior and he could not understand how an operation could be mounted from Jordan without his being informed. He found Tudin very uncommunicative and this irritated him, and perhaps it was because of the irritation that he let his guard down and was not his normal observant self.

As they swung into the curve of the rotary he was about to ask how long Tudin expected to remain in Amman when he abruptly realized there was a black Mercedes immediately behind. In his rearview mirror he could see two Arabs in the front seat. Both were wearing traditional robes with their heads covered. An alarm bell began to ring stridently in his head and he was about to hit the accelerator when a dark blue Ford pulled across in front of him from another access road. He braked sharply and his car went into a right-hand skid and sideswiped the Ford. There was a grinding clash of metal and then both cars came to a halt, facing the center of the rotary. He was aware of the four men disgorging themselves from the

Ford and his right hand went under his jacket for his pistol as he screamed a warning to Tudin.

He was too late. The car windows were open because of the sultry heat, and before he could raise his pistol, a submachine gun was thrust in his face. Two other men were at Tudin's window, threatening him in the same way.

The operation was smooth and easy. Both Russians were bundled out of the car and into the Mercedes in the space of twenty seconds. The gray Ford had been damaged beyond driving and its four occupants piled into the back seat of the Mercedes on top of Zhukov and Tudin. A few other cars had stopped at the spectacle, but before anyone could react, the Mercedes sped away.

It took seventeen minutes for Gordik to receive the telephone call from the Embassy, and instantly the atmosphere in the villa became charged with tension and apprehension. The problem for Gordik was that he felt totally helpless. The first thing he did was to inform Hawke and Gemmel and they immediately went into a crisis conference. It took another hour before a picture began to emerge, a picture that put Hawke into a flaming rage. Both he and Gemmel had immediately contacted their own field headquarters in Amman. The astonished heads of the local CIA and MI6 were suddenly confronted with the fact that two of their most senior officers were in the city and furthermore were involved in an operation in collaboration with the KGB. They were informed that two KGB agents had been kidnapped and they were ordered to attempt to find out without delay who the kidnappers were. As their field agents were being contacted, Gordik, Hawke, and Gemmel went through all the permutations. Under normal circumstances they would have suspected one another's intelligence service. This was obviously and quickly discarded, as was the intelligence service of the Jordanian government. There was no love lost between Russia and Jordan, but it was unthinkable that the Jordanians would kidnap an Embassy car in broad daylight.

It was Gemmel who finally offered the correct suggestion and it was John Masterson, the local MI6 resident, who confirmed it.

"The Muslim Brothers," Gemmel said, putting down the telephone. "We've had a little local success at infiltrating them and our agent reports that the kidnapping was carried out by the Brothers." He gave Gordik a long, hard look. "The question is, Vassili, were they after Tudin or the other man in the car? Who is he and why might they want him?"

Gordik sat back in his chair, his mind racing. He already knew that the driver of the car was Zhukov and he knew that Zhukov had been very instrumental in the crackdown on the Brotherhood in Syria. The news was both good and bad. The accidental change of cars probably meant that the Brothers had no knowledge of Tudin or his mission. Their target had to be Zhukov alone and Tudin was merely a bonus.

He decided to come clean. Briefly he explained all the salient facts to Hawke and Gemmel. Hawke pushed back his chair and paced up and down the room, cursing volubly.

"A fucking car breaks down," he said bitterly. "One fucking car and it jeopardizes the whole operation!" He shook his head in frustration. "Of all the people, the fucking Muslim Brotherhood!" He looked at Gordik narrowly. "You know what they are? You know what they represent?"

Gordik nodded glumly. "I know very well. I've directed a lot of activity against them."

"That's great," Hawke snorted. "So you know they have no compunction at all. Now tell me," he said grimly, "how much resistance does Tudin have? What's his field experience—his training?" He looked at the small calendar on his Rolex watch. "We have no more than seventy-two hours. Abu Qadir is entering Mecca just about now. Will Tudin hold out?"

Gordik's expression became even gloomier. "I think

it's not possible. He has very little field experience. He's a thinker, not a man of action." He shrugged eloquently. "As to his resistance, of course he's been through our normal courses, but I doubt that any training can prepare a man for what the Muslim Brothers will do to him."

"Shit!" Hawke spat the expletive and began pacing again. Gemmel reached out a foot and pulled Hawke's chair back to the table.

"Sit down, Morton," he said firmly. "It's time for cold, clear thought. It's a question of hours, not days. We have to get Tudin out, and fast."

Hawke stood looking at him, his face a mixture of frustration and anger, and then he walked back to the table, sat down, and glared at Gordik.

"We have a chance," Gemmel said placatingly. "As I told you, we've had some success in infiltrating the Muslim Brotherhood. That's not surprising. The British first encountered them in the thirties in Egypt, when it was a client state of ours. I can even tell you that we tacitly supported them when they tried to assassinate President Nasser in nineteen fifty-five."

Gordik and Hawke were watching him closely.

"It's true," he continued, "that for the past decade our influence here has declined very considerably, but we've always tried to hold on to our long-term agents. Masterson's a good man. He's been an MI-Six resident here now for over four years and he knows his way around. He'll try to find out where they're holding him and there's not much else we can do except wait. Once we know we can plan a course of action."

It took Masterson one and a half hours to discover where the Muslim Brothers were holding Zhukov and Tudin. He arrived at the villa carrying a large-scale map of Amman and a worried expression. A meeting was immediately convened. It included Gordik, Gemmel, Falk, Masterson, the local head of station of the CIA, and the deputy of the KGB. The American was called Johnson, a bespectacled and serious man in his late forties. The Russian was younger, with a short, beefy figure. He was called Kalinin.

The map was hung on one wall and Masterson began his briefing. He was a tall, erect man, with a military bearing, and in his late fifties. He walked with the aid of a stick, for he had been a tank commander in the Second World War in the desert and had been badly wounded in his right leg. He was a little nervous in front of the high-powered audience, especially as impatience was written vividly across the faces of Hawke and Gordik. He pointed with his stick to a spot on the map.

"This is the house of a merchant named Salah Khalaf. He's a known sympathizer with and a possible member of the Muslim Brotherhood. His house is large and surrounds a courtyard. I'm told that there's a large cellar and I assume that's where they're holding the Russians."

Gordik glanced at his watch, his face immediately relaxing. "Good, excellent work. We have a team standing by at the Embassy. I'll send them in immediately."

Masterson gave a look to Gemmel, who held up a hand. "Wait, Vassili, let him finish."

"It's not that simple, sir," Masterson said to Gordik. He was surprised to hear himself address the Russian as "sir" but somehow the man's appearance and position merited it.

"Let me explain," he went on. "The house is situated almost in the middle of the souk. It's a very densely populated area, the streets are extremely narrow, and, believe me, there'll be scores of Brothers in the house and surrounding it. Your team would have to approach on foot and they wouldn't get nearer than two hundred meters without the alarm being given. The whole area is a rabbit warren and they could move Zhukov and Tudin out and hide them away elsewhere within minutes."

Gordik's face fell. "But we have to risk it," he said. "We can't just sit and do nothing."

Hawke interjected, "What about the Jordanian authorities?"

Gemmel supplied the answer. "Not a chance. They must already know about the kidnap and obviously they're waiting for the Russian Embassy to contact them, but even so, they will do very little." He glanced at Gordik. "You know their antipathy toward the Russians and their current tacit support for the Brotherhood. It would take days to get them to move, and even then any action from that side would be halfhearted at best."

"So what do we do?" Gordik asked impatiently.

"I'm sure Masterson has some ideas," Gemmel said, and they all looked at the nervous figure of the Englishman.

"I can see only one way," he began hesitantly. He pointed with his stick again at the map. "It would only be possible to approach this close at these locations." He indicated three points forming a triangle around the souk. "From that point on it will be necessary for a very small team, disguised as Arabs, to penetrate through the souk to the house and thence effect an entry." His voice became more brisk and took on a military tone as he detailed his plan. "As soon as entry has been effected and the shooting begins, the rest of the team go in fast from the three different directions. They'll have to shoot their way through the souk in what will be a running battle. The men who have already entered the house will then try to keep the Russians alive—and themselves—until the rest of the team arrives. There will then be another running battle to get everybody out." Again his stick pointed to the three locations on the map. "Our transport will be waiting here." He lowered his stick and looked quizzically at Gordik, who sighed deeply.

"It hinges entirely," Gordik said, "on penetrating the defense screen and getting into the house before the real shooting starts."

"Exactly," Masterson agreed.

"What do you think, Morton?" Gordik asked.

Hawke shrugged. "One way or another, it's going to be a bloodbath, but we're going to have to try." He gave Gordik a hard look. "And if the advance team does get in, and if it's going to be difficult to extract Tudin, then they'll have to kill him."

Gordik nodded. "We accept that."

Johnson now spoke for the first time. "Who's going to be the advance team?"

"Who've you got?" Hawke asked.

The man shrugged. He was also nervous at this sudden call to action. "I've got two or three good men, but frankly, Mr. Hawke, this is a suicide mission. I wouldn't like to have to order them in."

"You'll do what you're damn well told," Hawke grunted, and Johnson sat back, abashed.

Now Gordik spoke a few words in Russian to Kalinin, who replied with two abrupt sentences. In English Gordik said, "We also have some good men and it's our responsibility and we have no compunction about ordering them in." Again he looked at his watch. "The sooner the better. We'll need help to arrange the backup teams." He looked at Masterson. "How many do you think we'll need?"

"At least thirty," Masterson replied. "Fully trained and well armed."

Hawke started to say something but Gemmel held up a hand, stood up and walked to the map, and studied it closely for a few moments. Then he turned and looked quizzically at Alan Boyd.

"What would you say to a little activity, Alan?"

"Just you and me?"

Gemmel nodded.

"Why not?" Boyd said with a faint smile.

"Good." Gemmel turned to Gordik. "Now we're going to be sensible. No one's going to wander through that souk and get close to that house without being dressed like an Arab, without walking like an Arab, smelling like an Arab, and talking like an Arab. It happens that there are only two people around here who can do it. Alan Boyd and myself. At least we have a chance, albeit a slim one."

A silence descended on the room while each man considered Gemmel's words.

Eventually Gordik said, "It's our responsibility, not yours. It was our mistake."

"The responsibility is immaterial," Gemmel replied. "Our whole operation is now at risk. We haven't come this far to see it blown away, at least not without making every effort. It so happens that both Boyd and I speak perfect Arabic, we're both dark, and we both have passed as Arabs before. We've also worked together before. There's a better chance with just the two of us than a whole bunch of people blundering around." He looked at Hawke for support, and got it.

"I think you're right, Peter. What we have to do is make damn sure that we get to you in the least possible time." Now he pushed his chair back and stood up and examined the map. He traced a finger from the house to the three locations that Masterson had pointed out. "My guess is three to four minutes. What do you think?" he asked Masterson.

"It's possible," Masterson agreed. "If we have three teams at these locations, at least one of them may get to the house within that time schedule. If it can be arranged I would suggest ten men in each assault squad. We would need at least two waiting with the transports, so, in total, thirty-six men." He thought for a moment. "I can provide no more than six or seven, counting myself."

Again Gordik had a rapid conversation in Russian with the KGB deputy station head.

"We can do up to twenty." He smiled mirthlessly. "Of course, it means blowing every one of our agents to you people."

Hawke laughed. "We probably know half of them anyway, and it'll be a quid pro quo. We'll supply the other fourteen. Now, let's get down to details."

Again Gemmel held up a hand. "It will be dark in an hour and most Arabs will be eating half an hour after that. Now, this has to be planned as a military operation and we have to bear in mind that we'll have Russians, British, and Americans in the team. There has to be a single leader." He gestured with his thumb. "Masterson here speaks Russian and Arabic. He's had military experience and he knows the area better than anyone. I suggest that he formulate the plan and have overall command. I further suggest that you, Vassili, and you, Morton, stay here in the villa."

Both men started to protest, but Gemmel argued forcibly and logically. He pointed out that Operation Mirage was now reaching culmination. They were needed in the villa to continue monitoring it and their agents in the field. Also their presence at the rescue attempt could not help much and might even provide the specter of a split command. He and Boyd were laying their lives on the line and would feel more confident if Masterson alone were in command.

Eventually Hawke and Gordik had to agree, but for the first time Leo Falk spoke up.

"You're forgetting something, Peter," he said, his face very tense. "I also speak Arabic. I'd like to come with you and Alan."

Gemmel shook his head. "Thanks, Leo, but the answer has to be no. Yes, you speak excellent Arabic, but with a strong accent. Also you're fair and you have a ruddy complexion and blue eyes. Anyone getting a close look at you will know you're a foreigner."

"He's right, Leo," Hawke said. "But I add my thanks."

"In that case," Falk answered, "I go in with one of the backup teams."

"That you can do," Hawke said. "If Gordik and I are to stay here they're going to need you."

Masterson looked at his watch. "Right," he said briskly, all his nervousness gone. "If I'm to be in command we have to start now. I suggest that you leave me to work out details with Johnson and Kalinin."

There was a scraping of chairs as everyone stood up.

Lev Tudin had passed through the spectrum of fear and reached the point at which he was able to withdraw from himself and examine it. First of all, the uncomprehending panic of the actual kidnap, and then the physical pain of a savage beating when they had first been bundled out of the car, through the alleys of the souk, and then down into the cellars. He had never known physical violence and his mind could not encompass the agony as he had lain bound hand and foot on the concrete floor with three men kicking his body from all angles. He believed that nothing could compare with the pain, the humiliation and helplessness.

But for the past two hours, he had come to realize emphatically that he was wrong, for he had witnessed the interrogation of Zhukov. The first savage beatings had been merely a softening-up, a prelude of what was to come. Zahaby's immediate interest was, of course, Zhukov, and once the initial beating had stopped, Tudin had been tied to a chair, Zhukov had been stripped naked, and the torture had begun. The cellar consisted of one large room. A heavy wooden door led to a flight of steps which came out in the courtyard. Thick blankets had been nailed around the edges of the door to deaden all sound. It was necessary, for Zhukov suffered with great volubility.

Tudin had once read a quotation from Hemingway indicating that if a man doesn't scream under torture, he's feeling no pain. Zhukov was feeling much pain. Zahaby had rigged a makeshift but effective instrument. From an electrical wall socket wires snaked to a wooden box at Zhukov's feet. The box contained a rheostat. More wires were connected from the box to clamps on the end of Zhukov's penis and on his lower lip. It had taken a long time for Zhukov to crack. For over two hours Zahaby and his two assistants had increased the power until Zhukov could stand no more. Occasionally they had thrown buckets of water over him, both to revive him and to accentuate the electrical contact. Twice Zahaby had rung the changes, taking off the clamps and applying simple brute pressure. The first time burning Zhukov's left arm and left leg to the bone with a blowtorch. The second time cutting off the fingers of his right hand one by one and cauterizing the stumps from a small pot of pitch. Tudin could never believe that a man could be so strong or so stoical, but it was finally the electricity that had broken Zhukov, and for the past five minutes he had been talking.

Zahaby took no pleasure from the torture. He was, like all Muslim Brothers, fighting what he believed to be a holy war, a jihad. The Russians were his enemy. Hundreds of the Brothers had been tortured in Syrian prisons by security personnel who had been trained and advised by this man. If there was no pleasure, there was also no pity, but now there was the gleam of success in his eyes as Zhukov began to mumble names and places. One of the assistants scribbled answers into a notebook. Finally Zahaby looked across at Tudin, and asked Zhukov:

"And this man? Who is he and what does he do?"

There was a silence while Zhukov looked at Tudin through pain-filled eyes. He shook his head.

"I don't know. I was told by the Ambassador to take him to my home for dinner. That's all I know."

Tudin's eyes moved from Zhukov to Zahaby. He felt as though his heart had expanded and its pumping filled his entire body. Slowly Zahaby shook his head, then he reached down to the wooden box and twisted the handle. Zhukov's body arched against the ropes that constrained him and once more screams filled the cellar.

This time Zahaby had miscalculated. The body of the tortured, broken man was beyond such pain and something—his heart or his brain—gave out. Zahaby turned off the current and one of the assistants reached forward and felt Zhukov's pulse and shook his head in exasperation.

"No matter," Zahaby said. "We have enough from him to give the Syrians some of their own medicine." He turned to look at Tudin and said in English, "So, now you will have to tell us yourself."

Tudin had pretended not to speak the language but his fear must have shown in his eyes and Zahaby smiled.

"I doubt that you were just a dinner guest."

One assistant began to cut Zhukov's body from the chair while the other approached Tudin. He cringed into the chair, his whole body quivering, his mind already screaming.

Gemmel and Boyd were seated eighty meters away, drinking small cups of strong, black coffee. The evening had turned cold and they were reasonably able to wear the cowls of the burnouses over their heads as they sat at the table of a small coffee shop in the packed alleyway. On each side of them were street vendors, calling out their wares. Across the alley a silversmith worked at the doorway of a small shop. They had been there for ten minutes, talking to each other in Arabic and noting the apparently casual guards that surrounded the entrance to the house at the end of the alley. There were two more lolling against a wall only ten meters away.

They had made their way to this coffee shop by a circuitous route, stopping once to buy a bolt of cloth from a street vendor. The cloth now lay between them on the small table. Beneath their robes they wore heavy leather belts. Attached to each belt were six concussion grenades, a Colt 1911 revolver, and a Scorpion machine pistol. The Americans had provided the grenades and the Colts and the Russians the Scorpions. They were the ideal weapon for close-quarter combat, being only ten and a half inches long with the butt folded, and firing at a cyclical rate of seven hundred rounds per minute. As they had been kitted out at the villa, and as Gemmel had handled the Scorpion and listened to the Russian explaining its simple functions, he had felt a surge of confidence. If they could break through the protective screen and get into the house itself they would have a chance. There had been another bonus. Just minutes before they had left the villa Masterson had received a phone call from one of his agents, advising that the current password of the Muslim Brothers was "The Dagger on the Koran." He could not confirm that this would be enough to bluff their way through. There could well be other, more pertinent passwords.

Gemmel finished the dregs of his coffee, looked at his watch, and said to Boyd in Arabic, "Two minutes and the other teams will be in place."

"We try and bluff our way past these two?" Boyd asked, with a minuscule nod at the two lolling guards.

"Yes, but if it doesn't work you give them a burst from your Scorpion and I'll head for the door."

The seconds ticked away in both men's heads. Gemmel glanced again at Boyd and felt another surge of confidence. His big, bluff face was impassive, his fingers holding the coffee cup entirely steady. Gemmel could not think of any other man in the world whom he would rather be with at this moment. He even felt a twinge of guilt that Boyd was about to put his life on the line. After all, unlike himself, he didn't know entirely what was at stake. Then he pushed these thoughts from his mind, looked again at his watch, and nodded at Boyd. They stood up and Gemmel picked up the bolt of cotton. Boyd had his hand tucked casually inside his burnous. As they walked up the alley the two guards pushed themselves from the wall and barred their way. Gemmel looked one of them directly in the eye and said, with authority:

"The Dagger on the Koran."

"What is your business?" one man asked.

"We go to see Salah Khalaf," Gemmel answered.

"He's not there."

"Then we'll wait," Gemmel said, his voice rising in pretended impatience.

"You will not wait," the man answered arrogantly.

"You will not pass here. Not without the words which give you access."

Gemmel went cold, realizing that there had to be another password.

"What's your business?" the man repeated, and Gemmel noticed his hand sliding under his burnous.

Boyd didn't wait. From the corner of his eye Gemmel saw him turn slightly and then came the staccato clatter of the Scorpion. Chaos erupted. The two guards were flung back by the arc of bullets, dying as they hit the cobblestones. Screams rang out as street vendors and passersby dived for cover. Gemmel and Boyd sprinted forward, the bolt of cloth flung aside, their Scorpions now out in the open. Boyd was ambidextrous, holding his machine pistol in his left hand and a grenade in his right. As he leapt over the body of one of the guards his two hands came briefly together and the pin clattered to the ground. Ahead five more guards made a screen across the carved wooden door of the house. Guns began to come into open view. Boyd hurled the grenade and he and Gemmel dived to the ground, burying their heads in their arms. Boyd had always been a perfectly coordinated sportsman and the grenade bounced off the top of the door, dropped to the cobblestones among the five guards, bounced once and exploded. Gemmel was up first, running in a crouch and firing a two-second burst from his Scorpion. It downed the one man who was still on his feet and the door unprotected stood in front of them. It had a huge steel lock, and as Gemmel quickly examined it, Boyd took up position, his back toward him, facing the now deserted alley. To the left one of the guards lay clutching his belly and moaning.

"Get back," Gemmel shouted and pushed Boyd away, raised the Scorpion, and fired the last of his magazine into the lock. He reached under his burnous and took out another magazine. He clipped it in, and then took a step forward and his right foot crashed against the door. It sprang open, revealing a wide courtyard and two men running across it. Again a burst from the Scorpion, and Gemmel and Boyd were in the courtyard, eyes darting about. Boyd saw a man on the roof, saw him just in time. He pushed Gemmel violently in the back, sending him sprawling as a burst of submachine-gun fire sent bullets ricocheting across the flagstones. The push saved Gemmel's life. He rolled and twisted, bringing up the Scorpion, and fired a long burst at the parapet. It was answered by a short scream and then silence. Gemmel looked back and saw Boyd lying on his stomach. He crawled toward him.

"Are you hurt, Alan?"

The reply was muffled and painful. "Both legs. They're smashed."

Gemmel started to pull away Boyd's robes to see the damage, but Boyd snarled at him:

"Leave me. I'll watch the entrance. Find Tudin."

He struggled up on to one elbow, then pulled four more grenades from under his stomach and laid them on the flagstones beside him.

"Go on, Peter. I'll watch your back."

Gemmel turned and his eyes swept the courtyard. They alighted on the heavy trapdoor in the corner just as it began to lift. A hand appeared, holding a pistol, and a single shot rang out and Gemmel twisted away, feeling the burn of the bullet across his left shoulder. As he fired back the trapdoor dropped again.

"It's the cellar," Boyd said from behind him. "That's where they'll be. Go, Peter!"

Gemmel unclipped a grenade, pulled the pin, and keeping his thumb clamped on the lever, edged toward the trapdoor. Just as he reached it firing erupted behind him and then the crump of a grenade. He turned to see Boyd pointing his Scorpion at the entrance to the courtyard. Two more bodies now lay in the alley. Gemmel turned back to the trapdoor, grasped the heavy iron rung, pulled it up four inches and slid in the grenade.

In the cellar Zahaby stood facing the blanketed door,

holding his Tokarev pistol. The body of Zhukov had been
tossed into a corner. Tudin sat naked, strapped to the
chair, his face white, the electrical clips connected to his
lower lip and his penis. The two assistants stood behind
him, their faces mirroring fear, their eyes watching
Zahaby. The explosion blew down the door and the Muslim
Brother outside rolled in on top of it, his face and upper
body smashed by the blast.

Zahaby rapped out an order and crouched down, his
pistol pointing at the exposed stairway. The two assistants
moved cautiously from behind the chair and edged toward
the entrance. One of them looked back over his shoulder
and Zahaby hissed a word at him. With a cry of
"*Insh'allah!*" both men dashed for the stairway. Both died
at the foot of it, cut down in a swath of bullets.

By now Tudin was beyond pain and beyond fear. He
had only an all-pervading sense of shame, for two minutes
earlier, just before the first sounds of gunfire, he had told
an incredulous Zahaby about the villa and about Operation Mirage. He had been broken in only ten minutes and
all he could think of was Zhukov lying dead in a corner.
Zhukov, who had held out for two hours. Tudin's twisted
and tortured mind knew that a rescue was being attempted.
He could only think that it was too late for Zhukov.
Zahaby had risen from his corner and started to edge back
so as to put Tudin between himself and the door. Tudin's
mind began to work again. With a violent, pain-racking
effort he twisted in the chair, upending it and crashing into
Zahaby, sending him sprawling. Zahaby cursed and his
gun began to move and Tudin waited for death and then
Gemmel was in the room in a rolling dive and for a second
Zahaby hesitated, his gun between the two of them. In
that second Gemmel fired and Zahaby's body was smashed
across the room by the force of the bullets until it came
to rest alongside the dead, naked figure of Zhukov.

Gemmel drifted in and out of sleep. It had been four
hours since the successful rescue of Lev Tudin. Curiously

enough it had been Leo Falk who had reached the cellar first. He had looked at the four dead men and at Tudin's weeping face and at Gemmel cutting him free, then he glanced at his watch and said, panting but with immense satisfaction:

"Two minutes, fifty seconds. Did he talk?"

Gemmel cut the last rope and helped Tudin to his feet. "Yes, he talked, but it doesn't matter." He gestured at Zahaby and the two other Arabs. "They're dead."

In the courtyard he had found two Russians putting Boyd onto a stretcher. There were armed men all around and from beyond the walls the occasional stutter of automatic fire. Within minutes they began the withdrawal, taking the dead and wounded with them. It took eight minutes to reach the transports. Four of the team had been killed and two wounded on the way in. Another three had been killed on the way out. Casualties were fairly evenly balanced between the Russians and Americans. All the wounded, including Boyd, were taken to the Russian Embassy. Gemmel had tried to go with him but Masterson was very military and decisive and insisted that he should return immediately to the villa to report. He had looked briefly at the flesh wound on his shoulder and pronounced it nothing serious.

At the villa the relief of Hawke and Gordik was much in evidence. They were both generous in their congratulations. Hawke had poured him a stiff drink, while Gordik examined his shoulder and gave Larissa unnecessary instructions about how to treat it. Then Gordik had spoken to the Embassy and told Gemmel that Boyd's condition, although serious, was not critical. Within forty-eight hours he would be flown out with the other wounded direct to Moscow. He would have the best treatment possible before being sent on to London.

Meanwhile, the British, Russian, and American ambassadors were trying to placate the enraged Jordanian authorities.

"That's what ambassadors are for," Gordik said complacently.

Finally, the drink and the aftermath of the action had been too much, and Gemmel had taken himself to bed while Gordik and Hawke had gone back to the communications center.

"It's all happening," Hawke had said, with a grin. "Abu Qadir is in Mecca and the crowds follow him wherever he goes. Nothing else can go wrong. We're going to nail this one down!"

So Gemmel had gone to bed in his small room at the back of the villa, but a relaxed sleep had evaded him.

He heard the tap on the door and the sound of it opening and looked up to see Larissa standing there with a tray.

"You didn't eat," she said. "I thought by now you might be hungry."

He pushed himself up, feeling a twinge of pain from his shoulder. She put the tray beside the bed and rearranged the pillows behind him. There was a big, steaming bowl on the tray.

"Borscht," she said with a smile, "and I supervised Corporal Brady so it's the real thing."

He was suddenly ravenous. She settled the tray on his knees and watched as he ate.

"I wanted to thank you," she said. "Lev Tudin is a favorite of mine. He's not really a man for operations like this. He's a thinker. But he's a good man and I would have missed him. We all would have missed him."

"He had a bad time," Gemmel said. "I hope it won't affect him too much."

She shook her head. "He'll get over it. Inside he's quite strong."

For a while he ate in silence and then she said softly, "And will you—will you get over it?"

He glanced up at her. "I'm not new to this kind of thing."

"I didn't mean that," she said. "I meant Maya."

Another silence. Then he said abruptly, "That too was just another operation. From your point of view a very successful one. As you see, people get hurt in this business."

"Yes," she agreed, standing up, "but that doesn't mean to say we have to obliterate our feelings completely."

He didn't answer and she stood at the door for a moment, looking at him, then said:

"I think I understand now what happened to Maya in London; why she did what she did."

Again he didn't answer and she went out, closing the door quietly behind her.

# twenty

MECCA AND THE SURROUNDING HILLSIDES WERE ENVEL-
oped in a sea of white. More than three million people
from almost every part of the world had discarded their
traditional clothing, performed the ritual bathing, and
garbed themselves in the two simple white sheets of the
Islamic pilgrim. All were now equal in their own eyes, as
well as the eyes of God. Princes and paupers, men and
women, black and white, brown and yellow—all were
brothers and sisters.

A feeling of profound joy permeated the atmosphere.
For three days they followed the traditional ritual of the
Haj. They circled the Kaaba, calling out, *"Labbaik, Alla-
huma, labbaik.* Here I am, O Allah, here I am."

Then they filed into the Kaaba and kissed the black
stone and entered into a state of ritual consecration. In
the evenings there was much feasting and good humor. It
was a great milling sea of nations: illiterate villagers from
the mountains of Pakistan; fishermen from the Pacific
waters off Indonesia; tall, graceful Ibo tribesmen from
Nigeria; a great segment of mankind, joined together in
the most fervent and international religious ceremony on
earth.

But in spite of the tumult and the seeming chaos, the mass had a nucleus ever since Abu Qadir and his followers had entered the city by the Mi'la Gate. The attention of the multitude had been focused.

And so had the attention of Mirza Farruki and his team of security agents, and also the attention of six agents who had nothing to do with Mirza Farruki. Three of those agents carried tiny radio transmitters manufactured in three different countries, but all with signals powerful enough to be picked up by sophisticated receivers in Jeddah and transmitted on to even more sophisticated receivers in the communications center of the villa in Amman.

And so, like very few nonbelievers before them, Hawke, Gordik, and Gemmel were able to follow intimately the progress of the Haj as it approached the day of the Feast of the Sacrifice.

Mirza Farruki had already reported to Riyadh that there was an extraordinary and universal air of expectation. Pilgrims were openly talking of the coming of the Mahdi, and now it was even being rumored that he would be proclaimed on the day of the Feast of the Sacrifice. He had infiltrated several of his agents among the followers of Abu Qadir, and although among his following people were already calling him Rasūl, Abu Qadir himself and those closely around him maintained their attitudes of simple, and modest, devoutness and had done nothing to flout the religious laws or customs.

Mirza Farruki concluded his report by stating that in any event matters would now run their course. If in the Minā valley on the day of the Feast of the Sacrifice the expectations of the pilgrims were not satisfied, and satisfied profoundly, all talk of a Mahdi would cease. It was even possible that their disappointment and anger might be vented on the person of Abu Qadir and his companions.

The day arrived, and all morning the sea of pilgrims poured out of Mecca and into the valley of Minā like a great tidal wave. Some carried lambs, goats, or sheep and others led camels. Most of the smaller animals were already dead, slaughtered in ritual ceremony in front of the Grand Mosque; others were alive and bleating as though possessing foreknowledge of their fate.

In spite of the mass and the crush, Abu Qadir walked in a space, for his followers had formed a tight, moving circle about him. Haji Mastan walked behind him, carrying a dead lamb, and next to him strode Ibn Sahl, leading a young and valuable camel which was to be his own sacrifice, for during the journey from Taif and the subsequent days, the old Bedouin had been deeply affected by the presence and companionship of Abu Qadir.

By the early afternoon the multitude had sifted and settled itself like a gigantic amoeba into the valley and up among the foothills. The pilgrims had performed the ritual ceremony of stoning the devil, and then they all faced the hill of Arafat and offered up prayers. Mirza Farruki had positioned himself close to the circle of followers that surrounded Abu Qadir, Haji Mastan, and Ibn Sahl. He could clearly see all three of them prostrate in their prayers. Other eyes were also watching the trio rather than the dry ground, and mouths were whispering not prayers but commentaries into tiny concealed microphones.

In the villa in Amman, Hawke, Gordik, and Gemmel listened raptly as the reports flowed in. The air was charged with tension as the agents described the scene, their voices quivering with the mounting drama. These reports were interspersed with the quiet tones of the American telex operator as he read out the signals from Houston.

Hawke glanced at the digital clock on the wall and said, "In about three minutes Haji Mastan will slide a finger into a slit in the belly of that lamb and throw a switch on the homing device. The satellite will pick up the signal, and after precisely five minutes, the laser will fire and three million people are going to shit themselves!"

And then the voice of the telex operator was rising in concern and excitement.

"Mr. Hawke, sir! We have a malfunction. We have a malfunction!"

In Houston, Elliot Wisner was literally screaming at the mission director, "You have three minutes, you hear? Three minutes!"

The mission control center was seething with activity as dozens of technicians sitting at rows of computer and telemetry equipment went feverishly through their trouble-shooting procedures.

The mission director was glancing alternately between the giant wall clock and the banks of monitor screens in front of him.

"It's never happened," he muttered to Wisner. "We have a total, I mean total, lack of telemetric contact."

An assistant approached and handed a sheet of telex paper to Wisner. He read it and snarled, "I know! I know! Tell him we're doing everything we can!"

Sixty seconds later Gordik watched the clattering telex machine, snorted in derision, and said, "Everything? Is this the much-vaunted American technology, Mr. Hawke? Or is it a trick?"

Hawke didn't reply. He was listening to the voice reports coming in from the Minā valley.

The prayers had ended and it was the time for the sacrifices, but there was a quiet in the valley as all eyes turned inward to the giant circle and the three men it contained. Ibn Sahl started to lead his camel forward, but Abu Qadir raised a hand to stop him. Haji Mastan lifted the lamb with a hand tucked under its belly and slowly walked out and placed it in the center of the cleared circle. There was an expectant hush and then Ibn Sahl's voice was raised as he spoke loudly to Abu Qadir:

"It is not right, O Rasūl, that you must make such an

insignificant offering." His arm moved, jerking forward the head of his camel. "Honor me, O Rasūl, and offer up this camel which is the pride of my herd."

But Abu Qadir shook his head, and in a clear, carrying voice said:

"My brother, it is not the value of the sacrifice which matters, but the devotion and the humility with which it is offered, for does not Allah see into the hearts of all men and know what is there and pay no heed to vanity?"

His eyes swept around the circle, at the mass of people pressing in against the linked arms of his followers. Then he walked forward and picked up the large lamb and held it up and said in a penetrating voice:

"Even this lamb, which is fat and succulent, is a manifestation of vanity."

Slowly he moved toward a segment of the crowd, his eyes probing and alighting on an old woman and her young grandson, and the scrawny, pitiful carcass of the goat which she had brought as an offering. His followers parted and he laid his lamb at her feet and said gently:

"Mother, accept this with my humbleness and give me in turn your offering that Allah may bless us both."

And he picked up the scrawny goat. Haji Mastan was at his side, his face working in panic, whispering in his ear, and clutching at his arm. But Abu Qadir swept him aside and strode purposefully to the center of the circle and laid down the scrawny goat, and slowly stepped back a dozen paces and raised his eyes to the heavens.

In Amman the voices vividly relayed the scene through the speakers in the communications center and Morton Hawke slumped into a chair. He hardly seemed to hear the telex operator informing him that Houston had still failed to re-establish contact with the laser.

Gordik was looking between Hawke and Gemmel much as a spectator would watch a rally in a tennis match.

"What happens now?" he asked.

Gemmel supplied the answer. "If the laser functions—

and it's a big if—it will do so in about sixty seconds. The beam will home in on the lamb at the old woman's feet, which will then self-destruct in a cloud of green smoke, and probably destruct the old woman as well."

Gordik smiled grimly. "Hardly an act of Allah, the All Merciful and Compassionate."

Abu Qadir slowly raised his arms high above his head and his voice rang out.

"Allah! You have called me through Your angel Gabriel and I am here."

The crowd murmured and pressed still closer and strained against the linked arms. Mirza Farruki started pushing his way determinedly toward the circle, signaling to his agents. At last he could act.

"Let the believers observe your sign!"

Abu Qadir's voice echoed across the valley and the multitude strained forward in mass anticipation.

"Negative," said the telex operator in a shaking voice. "Houston reports negative contact."

Hawke had slumped forward in his chair and buried his face in his hands. Gordik was watching him in fascination, all his instincts telling him that this was no act, and so no trick either.

Gemmel glanced at the wall clock and said softly, "It's past the time, way past. So Allah has spared the old woman; He is compassionate!"

"But not to Abu Qadir," Gordik said grimly. "Thanks to American technology, or lack of it, and incompetent agents, the crowd will shortly tear your Mahdi to pieces."

There comes a moment when quivering expectation demands satisfaction, and that demand now flowed in a foaming wave from three million souls and flooded into the circle and onto the rigid man and the sacrificial goat.

Slowly Abu Qadir sank to his knees, once again raised his arms, looked imploringly into the sky, and called:

"A sign, Allah! Give Your Mahdi a sign!"

Three million pairs of eyes looked up into the clear blue evening sky and at that moment saw a perfect column of shimmering green light which bathed the valley and centered on the scrawny goat and held it illuminated for two heartbeats. Then the goat disintegrated in a cloud of expanding, green smoke which rolled slowly over the rigid figure of Abu Qadir.

Nothing moved in the valley—not a grain of sand; not a rock; not a stunted shrub; nor a single muscle among the three million pilgrims.

Mirza Farruki had reached the circle of followers but now he was a frozen statue and so were his agents, and the other agents in the petrified multitude.

Haji Mastan, in his panic, had pushed his way out of the circle, fighting his way through the packed crowd, but had seen the faces in front of him and had turned and was now also transfixed, his head twisted behind him, his arms outstretched against those in front.

Abu Qadir was the first to move. The green smoke had dissipated, leaving a shallow black cavity in the desert sand. He placed his hands flat down in front of him, and slowly pushed them forward until he was prostrate.

Like a wind blowing across a vast field of corn the pilgrims followed his example until the valley of Minā was carpeted in white bodies, all facing inward.

A low moaning word reverberated down to the circled figure:

"Mahdi!"

# Epilogue

A MALAY SERVANT MOVED OUT OF THE SHADOWS WITH A second bottle of Château Margauz and refilled the three glasses.

"It's amazing how well it travels," Perryman remarked, savoring the bouquet.

"It travels in the climate-controlled cargo hold of a jumbo jet," Pritchard said gruffly. "One of the few benefits of modern technology." He turned to his other tuxedo-clad guest. "Tell me again, Peter. I do wish I'd been there to see the faces of Gordik and Hawke."

Gemmel leaned back in his chair and with a wry look at Perryman said, "It was mayhem. Total mayhem. There were yards of telex messages all over the floor and Hawke kept muttering 'How in hell . . .?' and Gordik was on the radio to Moscow."

Pritchard's eyes were half-closed as he visualized the scene. "And when Haji Mastan turned up in Jeddah with the homing device?"

Gemmel smiled. "More mayhem. Especially when he told them he'd converted to Islam. That the Mahdi had forgiven him for his duplicity and offered him redemption and a chance of Paradise."

"And Gordik? How did he take it?"

Gemmel shrugged. "He had his own team in Jeddah. They questioned Haji Mastan at length, were convinced he was sincere. They also examined the homing device together with the Americans. Confirmed that it was the sole and genuine article."

Pritchard sighed in satisfaction and Perryman said, "Of course the satellite and laser self-destructed. The shuttle was still in orbit and made a pass twenty minutes after the event and found no sign of it."

"So there's total confusion." Pritchard smiled.

"There is," agreed Perryman. "But it won't take long for the Americans to discover that the design of the telemetric circuits allowed for a cutout-and-override situation. They'll link that to Rance and his death, and then they'll conclude that as he also designed the homing device, he could have designed another and they'll smell the biggest rat ever."

"But they can prove nothing," Pritchard said complacently. "And they can do nothing, and neither can the Russians, without implicating themselves." He took a sip of wine and said contentedly, "The perfect operation. Consider the results. In one step we've put Britain back among the superpower league. Certainly the Americans will find out how we did it and so too will the Russians, but they can't overturn the situation. Already the Mahdi is proclaimed and acknowledged throughout the Islamic world, and particularly in the Gulf area—the crucible of world power. He is our man—lock, stock, and barrel. The Russians and Americans will have to come to us, cap in hand. Of course they will want to depress the price of oil, but now they will find that it will rapidly go up, at least until our own stocks are depleted, when just as rapidly it will come down. By then, using her oil revenues, Britain will once again have become a major industrial power. Neither the Russians nor the Americans will dare to assassinate the Mahdi. Imagine the turmoil it would cause. They're stuck with the situation. We shall give them handouts as we see fit, depending on our own interests. Once again we shall sit at the head of the table in world councils. Before the Second World War we were the only major power in the Gulf and for thirty years that has been eroded until we became nothing. Now, once again, we pull the strings and they can do nothing about it."

He surveyed his two guests contentedly. "From the beginning, planting Abu Qadir fifteen years ago, until the culmination now, it has been a copybook operation. The greatest ever. Meticulous planning and unending patience. The result is perfect—simply perfect."

"There were casualties," Gemmel said, and the other two looked up at the tone of his voice.

"Peter, there are always casualties," Perryman remarked gently.

"Naturally," agreed Pritchard. "But in this operation they were minimal. One telemetrics expert and a sound engineer. By the by, that first little miracle must have been something to see!"

"It was," Gemmel said. "Abu Qadir should have got an Oscar; but there were other casualties."

"Ah, yes, you mean the ballet dancer," Pritchard said. "A pity, of course, that it happened. But it was essential that the Russians become involved; become party to it, so that they were implicated and finally recognized our coup and its results. You know how they are, Peter. It was vital that they believed they were forcing their way in and not being invited. They're so suspicious of invitations." He looked at Gemmel narrowly. "Did you grow a little fond of her?"

Gemmel didn't answer, but his face was somber.

"An intelligence agent," Pritchard said primly, "cannot allow such feelings to divert him. For such a goal all personal emotions must be subjugated."

Gemmel sighed. "Obviously, Pritchard, you must be the perfect example. After all, you have not seen Abu

Qadir these past fifteen years and you can surely never see him again."

"That's true," Pritchard agreed solemnly, "but I have given him the greatest gift any father could give a son: the total devotion of a billion people."

He turned and gestured at the shadows behind him.

A few moments later, from across the dark river, rolled the opening bars of Wagner's *Götterdämmerung*.

## ABOUT THE AUTHOR

A. J. Quinnell is the pseudonym of a writer who wishes to remain anonymous because his future books will detail intrigues between nations and cultures and will move freely over international boundaries. He desires the same freedom for himself.